Footsteps in the Night

Beat Back the Tide

Two Novels by
Dolores Hitchens

Introduction by Nicholas Litchfield

Stark House Press • Eureka California

FOOTSTEPS IN THE NIGHT / BEAT BACK THE TIDE

Published by Stark House Press
1315 H Street
Eureka, CA 95501, USA
griffinskye3@sbcglobal.net
www.starkhousepress.com

FOOTSTEPS IN THE NIGHT
Originally published by Doubleday & Company, Inc., New York, and
copyright © 1961 by Dolores B. Hitchens. Condensed version appeared in
Cosmopolitan, February 1961. Reprinted in paperback by Permabooks,
New York, 1962.

BEAT BACK THE TIDE
Originally published by Doubleday and Company, Inc., New York, and
copyright © 1954 by Dolores B. Hitchens. Reprinted in an abridged digest
edition as *The Fatal Flirt* by Mercury Publications Inc., New York, 1954.

"Sins, Sorrows, and Skeletons in the Closet"
copyright © 2020 by Nicholas Litchfield

ISBN-13: 978-1-944520-93-9

Book design by Mark Shepard, shepgraphics.com
Cover painting by Tony Patrick
Proofreading by Bill Kelly

First Stark House Press Edition: July 2020

Sins, Sorrows, and Skeletons in the Closet

Nicholas Litchfield

The critically and commercially successful American author Dolores Hitchens (1907-1973), who was most prolific throughout the 1950s and '60s, consistently drew praise for her masterful atmospheric writing and tightly woven plots, as well as her realistic dialogue and authentically drawn characters. Justifiably ranked as one of the nation's leading mystery writers, she was able to imbue her male protagonists with masculine toughness and bring realism and complexity to her female characters. The fact that she was a female mystery writer in a male-dominated field didn't escape the notice of eminent mainstream book reviewers like Anthony Boucher, who held her work in high regard, appreciating the prevalent "male toughness of attitude" resonating within novels like *Beat Back the Tide*. Here was an "unusually readable," brooding chiller—Hitchens's best yet, in Boucher's opinion—exploring hard-edged characters and gritty situations, with a proficient storyteller capable of utilizing the "properties and devices of the female suspense novel."

Prominent journalist Nora De Toledano, writing for *The Knoxville Journal*, was equally complimentary of the author's reliably credible, deftly handled approach to popular crime fiction. In the congested 1950's marketplace, where so many works came across as derivatives of Dashiell Hammett or Raymond Chandler, Dolores Hitchens was "among the few" writers adept at presenting tense, believable psychological mysteries with "vividly plausible" male characters and "outstanding" characterizations of women, especially "lonely women and women deprived of their men."

Beat Back the Tide, a Crime Club selection from Doubleday that was first published in 1954 and is included in this double-novel collection from Stark House, is a nicely paced, moody mystery that is considered to be one of Hitchens's best works. Like many of the author's novels, it is set in Southern California and features hardy, ambiguous characters that may or may not have committed past crimes, and a remote, eerie backdrop. This time, the setting is a lavish house on a cliff with a hazardous makeshift path to a private beach where a murder and a fatal accident have taken place.

The central character, Glazer, is a wealthy building contractor who has just hired former-schoolteacher-turned-nurse Francesca Warne, a widower in her late twenties, as governess to his invalid, seven-year-old son, Jamie. Alas, there is "an aura, a miasma, of disaster" about Francesca, and soon after her arrival, a series of alarming events lead Glazer to question her sanity. Her peculiar, "sly and elusive" behavior and irresponsible guardianship of his "small and frail" boy make him keen to terminate her employment, but romantic aspirations keep him from doing so. Although "plain and unappealing," his craving for companionship leads to an infatuation with her and allows him to be persuaded to investigate the murder of her sleazy, alcoholic husband two years earlier. His sleuthing piques the interest of snoop Billy Holt, the local newspaper editor, the abhorrent martinet policeman Byronson, as well as a whole host of dubious people with a connection to the victim and skeletons in their closet. Ultimately, Glazer's probing into the past opens old wounds, puts his own life in jeopardy, and leads to violence, betrayal, and fresh murder.

Hitchens's unnerving tale has a wonderfully dark, ominous tone, and the many shifting viewpoints and criss-cross motives help shape it into a thoroughly riveting, intricate page-turner. Her ability to delve beneath the surface of her characters, exploring their flaws and motivations, gives her protagonists depth and authenticity. Under the "smooth exterior, the businesslike politeness" of the successful, self-made contractor, Glazer, lurks an uncouth viciousness. Born into poverty, he was a hoodlum in his youth, and although marriage and parenthood have tamed him, when threatened by a man wielding a knife, he finds "the promise of violence" invigorating and embraces the opportunity to confront a new foe.

Francesca, on the other hand, is a psychologically damaged victim of violence who is seemingly "eaten up by some perverse yearning for punishment." In Glazer's mind, she should be thankful she has escaped a bad marriage, and yet she is possessed by a strange urge to unravel the mystery surrounding her husband's death. Unattractive, unsafe, and unnatural to him, "like an illness," he is nevertheless intrigued and besotted by her to the extent that his infatuation isn't tempered by the possibility that she may, in fact, be a murderess.

When it first came out, *Beat Back the Tide* garnered many favorable reviews from newspapers like *The New York Times*, the *Los Angeles Times*, the *Brattleboro Reformer*, the *Pasadena Independent*, and the *Daily Oklahoman*. It's "swift pace," and "abundant suspense," and meticulous focus on characterization and atmosphere made it stand out as an exceptionally thrilling whodunit that had "all the spice expected of a Crime Club selection."

The other story included here, *Footsteps in the Night*, another Crime Club selection, this time from 1961, is a chilling yarn about the murder of a kind, respectable fourteen-year-old schoolgirl whose family recently moved into a new upscale suburban housing development in Southern California. The story is structured around the lives of the residents—a fascinating, motley bunch that consists of a sex fiend with a conniving, sadistic wife; a bothersome, goofy old grandfather; a middle-aged spinster with a young gigolo for a lover; a sour, short-tempered developer; and a reclusive investment banker and his melancholic, crippled teenage son, both of whom are reviled in the community because of their unsightly, pink stucco house that dominates the scenery. The sharp, calm and collected Lieutenant Ferguson, a careful listener with the patience of a saint, helps the narrative shift between the various households, discovering the interesting occupants' sins and sorrows, as well as exposing the skeletons in their closets.

Scrupulously plotted and never less than utterly compelling, *Footsteps in the Night* is a stimulating, suspenseful drama with some neat little surprises and a satisfying conclusion. As with *Beat Back the Tide*, Hitchens peels back the curtains sufficiently to give readers a greater sense of the tastes and opinions of her numerous characters. You find that the gossipy, guarded, suspicious, scheming people in her communities question themselves as much as they question others. In the town of Dellwood, situated in the pretty little cuplike land in the hills above Pomona, while the residents spy on each other, prying into each other's personal business, they dwell on their own inadequacies and worry about public perceptions and whether or not they fit in appropriately in the neighborhood. You understand their pain, their petty grievances, and their desire to deflect suspicion, and indeed, you become fully engrossed in the unhappy plight of the members of these four disparate families.

Footsteps in the Night received the same sort of critical praise that was bestowed on *Beat Back the Tide,* although the *Star Tribune* remarked that "the atmosphere of suspense and creeping terror is excellent but, like some of the other Hitchens stories, most of the characters are so repulsive they give a disagreeable flavor to an otherwise well-written, well-plotted mystery." Others, such as Elmer Davis of the *Tucson Citizen* and Anthony Boucher of the *New York Times* deemed the writing "assured and sympathetic" and noted the "shrewdly and compassionately observed" characters.

Personally, I admire Hitchens' dexterity in vividly conjuring up an abundant community of interesting if tarnished principal characters and, in the case of both these brooding, chilling tales, marvel at the way she craftily weaves a convincing, absorbing story that ably connects the various, dissimilar inhabitants to criminal activity and gruesome murder. These exceptionally well-written "skeletons in the closet" mysteries showcase the author at her very finest.

—March 2020
Rochester, NY

Nicholas Litchfield is the founding editor of the literary magazine *Lowestoft Chronicle,* author of the suspense novel *Swampjack Virus,* and editor of nine literary anthologies. He has worked in various countries as a journalist, librarian, and media researcher and resides in western New York. Formerly, a book reviewer for the *Lancashire Evening Post* and syndicated to twenty-five newspapers across the UK, he now writes for *Publishers Weekly* and Colorado State University's literary journal *Colorado Review.*

Footsteps in the Night

Dolores Hitchens

One

When the horrifying murder occurred at Dellwood, the newspapers made much of the fact that the first of the houses had only been finished in August, and that the victim had lived at Dellwood for less than a month. The place had scarcely been started before the murder smeared it.

The history of Dellwood went back further than that, of course. The pretty, cuplike bit of land in the hills above Pomona—it was in oranges— had been owned for years by a family named Dronk, who lived there in the middle of the grove in seclusion. The subdivider bought the land from Dronk in the early spring. For a while nothing much happened. Then surveyors came, the trees were bulldozed out of the ground, streets were pegged out, lots were leveled. There would be forty-three homes here eventually, all very modem and ranchy and sprawling, with Western touches like wagon-wheel gates and barn-gables over the garages. By May most of the streets were paved, sewers were in, and some foundations had been poured.

There remained at the upper edge of the tract, in a half-acre reserved by Dronk, the home of the original owner. It was a gawky two-story pink stucco with a red tile roof, straight out of 1926, the year it had been built.

At about the time the first homes were being completed, the subdivider, a man named Cooper, drove around looking it all over. He was a big man, freckled, with an outdoor air. When he looked at the pink stucco, his nose wrinkled as if at a bad smell. It was too bad, he thought, that that man Dronk had insisted on staying here. My God, his old house didn't belong! It looked goofy! He should have bought one of the ranch-type moderns with part of his profits—sensible, actually, from the tax standpoint—or else moved away altogether. Come to think of it, he wasn't going to fit in any better than the house. At any rate, he should have let the pink relic fall to the wreckers. That half-acre would have made a nice little park and barbecue area. Dronk Park, since he would have donated the land. Pretty soon everybody would have forgotten and called it Dellwood Park, and would have been proud of the fact that it was exclusive, that you had to live up here to enjoy it.

The subdivider had made much of the possibilities for privacy. There was just one street leading into the pocket-like valley from the Pomona suburbs, and there were already a couple of stone pillars and a gate-house. Probably the people who bought up here wouldn't want the expense of a full time gate man, but there would be a sign, Private Thoroughfare, with added warning to keep out strangers and peddlers and other undesirables. A big selling point. Made them feel they were millionaires in their thirty-three-thousand-dollar houses.

Mr. Cooper gave a final squint, from the car window, at the disgusting pink relic and then drove down to his office behind the gatehouse, where people would be waiting for him. Miss Silvester was almost always there, with more yap about how the paint must match what she had picked out for carpeting and drapes. And perhaps that young couple, the Ranalds, would be palpitating with plans for some stupid thing like a flower-arranging nook in the service porch. And almost certainly Mrs. Forrest Holden would greet him, iron-jawed, with another demand to be allowed to move in at once. It had something to do with her husband's asthma. And with the plaster on the walls still wet, yet!

Finding the land was fun—a challenge these days, actually—and the designing and building were fun, but Cooper thought gratefully of the day now when the last of the homes would be turned over to their new owners and he could take his handsome profits and go look for new orange groves to conquer.

On the twenty-first of August, a clear hot day, the first three of the completed homes were officially opened for occupancy. They sat proud and spanking new at the end of Palomino Lane. Around them the thin new grass filmed the raw ground. The dwarf evergreens seemed to have a startled look, from the shock of transplanting. The ivy was just a sprig here and there. But the homes were complete, they worked right down to the last hinge and faucet, and their owners were happy.

Mr. Cooper made a little ceremony out of handing each new owner his key. Miss Silvester examined hers as if there must be something the matter with it. Mrs. Forrest Holden received hers coldly, reminding Cooper, without saying anything about it, how much later it was than the promised date. And the Arthurs, the family with the grandfather, seemed merely eager and grateful. The grandfather had already asked Cooper if he'd mind if he played at gate man, and Cooper, foreseeing possible complications, had suggested that old man Arthur wait until more people had moved in, and then sort of put it to a vote.

Palomino Lane was at the upper end of the tract, where building had first begun. Further down, the rest of the houses were in varying stages of construction, those in the vicinity of the gatehouse still little more than framing. Mr. Cooper had been hampered by the shortage of good workmen, and also by a sense of caution which caused him to build as he sold, though selling was really no problem in southern California. All you did was throw up the walls, put out a sign, and step back to keep from being trampled.

The moving vans came in the afternoon. Everything Miss Silvester put into her house was brand new, and everything Mrs. Forrest Holden brought was old and waxed and shining. The Arthurs, with two little kids and the grandfather, had a great collection, mostly junk. But the Arthur house was the only one where anyone was singing.

In the pink stucco house, Mr. William Dronk patted his lips with his napkin, rose from lunch, and limped to the windows to watch the activity below.

The dining room of the pink stucco was six-sided, a funny little turret of a room, jutting out on the west end of the house. Mr. Dronk peered through the pane, studied what the movers were doing, then glanced behind him. Kim was still at the table, bent over the dish of pudding, and in the kitchen beyond, Mrs. Campbell mopped invisible crumbs on the sink, in her half-blind way. Mr. Dronk said, "Well, they've finally come. We have neighbors now, Kim. You'll have other teen-agers to run around with."

Kim was sixteen, a pale, fair boy with a bony face and big hands. He lifted his eyes briefly, in the perplexed, tentative way he had. "Ummm hmmm," he said.

"Try to be friendly and hearty and outgoing," said Mr. Dronk, as if he were outlining a political campaign, "but don't let them impose, don't let them get away with anything. Be sure they understand who you are."

Kim hunched lower, stirring the pudding, not looking up again.

"You can invite them here to the house. Play records, have a game of checkers or ping-pong in the basement. Show them your stamps and your ship models."

"Yes, Father," Kim said. He seemed withdrawn, unlistening. He made a hole in the chocolate gob and poured in more cream.

"I've lived here more than twelve years," Mr. Dronk said, "and at first it was a relief, I was glad to be alone, but now ..." He coughed behind his hand.

Kim knew when they had moved here, though he could barely remember it. They had come when the doctors had wanted to operate on his foot, and when his mother had run off with the man who trained race horses, and when Mrs. Campbell's eyes had begun to go bad. All of these things had happened at about the same time and in Kim's mind they were inextricably woven like the opening, arrested shot of characters in a television play. It had been like *that*, and then his life had begun— what he remembered of it.

"I want you to have friends," his father went on. "Unlike my father. He protected me too much. You'll meet these children when they take the school bus, all together in the morning, and you can choose among them, the ones you think you'll like."

"You won't be the lone one at the bus stop now," Mrs. Campbell reminded.

"I don't give a damn," Kim said with explosive loudness.

"Now, Kimmy ... Kim—"

"They'll imitate the way I walk."

Mrs. Campbell turned around so that she faced the sink; she mopped all the corners with her wet sponge. At the windows, his father stood helpless. A vast, hot shame flooded up into Kim, the way he always felt when he reminded them. They wanted to pretend, even his father with his crazy limp wanted to pretend, and Kim rebelled. "You ever have anybody hobble along beside you, grinning?" he demanded of his father. "You ever have them groan and grunt, their foot turned in, and have to act like you didn't care? Did you?"

William Dronk licked his lips. He felt chilled, defeated. Behind him the vast bulk of a moving van turned and backed in Palomino Lane, and its white side and red lettering moved in miniature from pane to pane like the progress of some lumbering animal. "Kim, listen to me. The one thing which can destroy you, can twist your life—"

"It's already twisted." Kim got up from the table and paused by the chair, his gaze on the door across the kitchen. There was always this moment of preparation, of girding himself so that he should walk as normally as possible. Then, with a stiff, set look to him, he went out.

Mrs. Campbell began to talk to herself. "You're right, boy. Keep your distance. They're just trash. You remember those two boys you brought home from school last year? Well, these won't be any different."

"Mrs. Campbell."

"Yes, Mr. Dronk."

"It doesn't depend on them. It depends on Kim's attitude, his approach, his not being thin-skinned and touchy."

She made a noise deep in her throat, half growl and half laughter. Mr. Dronk waited, but she didn't turn around, she went on mopping at the sink counter with her head bent. She was like Kim, somehow, in that she could defeat him this way, by withdrawing into scorn. Mr. Dronk looked at his watch, a defensive tactic. "Well, I've got to get back to the office. And by the way, we've got to start thinking about school clothes for Kim. It won't be long—the middle of next month."

"I'll check through his things with him," she flung over her shoulder.

"Fine. Well, I'll see you tonight."

Mr. Dronk worked in an investment house, a small one, in Pomona. He was very glad these days that he had such a thorough business background, since selling the land to Cooper had put him in possession of so much money. He enjoyed the selection and purchase of stocks and bonds for his own portfolio, something he hoped to leave, much increased in value, to Kim; he also savored the respectful envy of his associates. Until now his income had been modest, the salary from the job combined with what he got off the oranges once a year, and he still found himself with the ingrained habits—such as now, looking speculatively at that Miss Silvester. Cooper had told him that she was an old maid and must have money. She had paid cash for the house; it was the only one sold so far in the tract that didn't have a big mortgage on it. For a moment Mr. Dronk wondered how he might approach her with a suggestion about some good common stocks.

At her house, Miss Silvester was oblivious of Mr. Dronk getting in his car across the street. She regarded the pink monstrosity, and those in it, as scarcely belonging in Dellwood, anyway. It was a leftover, a nuisance; she knew that Mr. Cooper had hoped it might be torn down and the grounds made into a kind of park.

She stood on the flagstone porch, neat in a straight blue cotton frock and black patent pumps, and instructed the movers. There were three of them with the truck, two dull and heavy-set middle aged men and one dark and young and handsome one. Miss Silvester kept a calm and casual manner, glancing impersonally at each as he came up the walk carrying some item of furniture, and telling him where it went inside the house, but every time the dark young man went by and answered her glance with a bold stare, a kind of electric tingle touched her nerves. She noted that he had on old blue jeans and a T-shirt, not clean, and soiled tennis shoes, the shabbiest kind of clothes. But his skin was bronze and his muscles bulged and rippled under the thin knitted fabric, and something about the shape of his mouth made her think of eating grapes.

Presently when things had to go into the rear bedroom she went back there to supervise. He followed, carrying a pink chair, and in the closeness of the hall she caught an odor from him, a man-sweat kind of smell, with tobacco in it, and hair oil, and she fought a desire to swallow nervously, almost choking over some congestion in her throat.

She stood in the middle of the room. The brown rug had been laid. It seemed awfully quiet; he was standing there looking at her. She said, "This isn't going to be an ordinary bedroom, it has to look somewhat like a den or an office. I'm going to do my work here."

He set down the chair. It looked foolish and fragile, there next to his big legs. "What do you do, ma'am?"

"I'm an income-tax consultant."

"Oh, is that so?" He lifted his arms to stretch himself, a motion absolutely animal, with a ripple of flesh across his torso. In the depths of his eyes was an expression, a mixture of amusement and interest, that Miss Silvester found almost unbearable. He shouldn't be looking at me like that, she thought; my goodness, I'm old enough to be his mother. "Is it like bookkeeping?" he asked.

"Yes, in a way."

"This is a nice house you've got," he said admiringly.

"I think so,"

"What about your husband? Is he an income-tax ... whatchacallit ... too?"

She had a strange urge to say, Yes, my husband is an income-tax whatchacallit and he will come home at six o'clock, and I hope he remembers to bring the steak. There was some obscure point of pride involved. But then she heard her own voice saying, "I don't have a husband. I'm going to live here all by myself."

He grinned, his teeth big and white in his tanned face, and said lazily, "I figured."

Of course he had figured, she realized in confusion; he could see that what was being brought in was all woman-stuff. Even though the boxes of personal gear were almost lost in the magnificence of the new furniture, a husband, were he even a mouse of a man, would have had an ash-stand or two, some fishing equipment, tools, things like that. She stood there blushing, and hating herself for feeling so self-conscious. "Well, I will need the blond desk over against the wall, close to the windows, and that floor lamp with the parchment shade beside it."

He didn't even glance over where she wanted the desk; he fished a pack of cigarettes out of a pocket of the jeans, a book of matches, and lit himself a smoke. She could hear the other men in the hall, bringing the last of the stuff for the front bedrooms. She felt a sudden surge of nervous warmth and weakness, and perspiration came out on her temples. She moved her hands awkwardly, not knowing what to do with them.

She wished all at once that she could see herself in a mirror.

Well, not a mirror, exactly. She wished she could see herself from outside, the way he saw her. Surely he hadn't missed that she was in her forties ... forty-two. (Forty-seven, her conscience whispered.) And then there were those fine lines around her lips and on her forehead, and a faint dusting of white all through her fair hair, like a breath of snow. Surely those bold, seeking eyes of his hadn't missed that.

She met his gaze timidly. "Are you tired?"

He laughed, and she saw what a ridiculous question it was; you didn't get tired when you were as big and as young and as strong as he was.

"I just craved me a smoke," he said. He blew cigarette smoke into the air, and she wondered hungrily if the smell might linger, if on some quiet night months from now she might catch a hint of it; might turn from the desk to find the memory of him there, big and vital, against the shadows.

Because, of course, when he walked out of here and got into that truck with the others and drove away, she would never see him again.

One of the others dropped something with a thud in another room, and cursed about it, and Miss Silvester didn't even hear. She was wrapped in an aching moment, looking at a pair of dark eyes across an impassable chasm.

At this moment in the Arthur house, Billy Arthur picked up a soup ladle and cracked his little sister, Nancy, over the head, and Nancy screamed. Mrs. Arthur got down off the stool—she'd been hanging kitchen curtains—and smacked Billy's bottom. Then she looked around for the old man. He was queer and crotchety, and she had a simmering temper all the time because he had to live with them. She found him slipping out the side door to the garage. "Just remember, Father," she told him, loudly, because he was somewhat deaf. "Just remember to keep away from that gatehouse. We won't have you pestering people and making us ridiculous."

He nodded and stood still on the garage floor. The door was up. He looked skinny, almost cadaverous, against the light. "Sure. Sure, I understand."

From the look of guilt, she knew that the gatehouse was the place where he'd been headed.

Two

At about four that afternoon, Mr. Cooper was talking to the carpenter foreman outside his office when he heard his phone ring. He went in and lifted the receiver, and a man's voice said, "Hello, is this the Dellwood office? May I talk to somebody there about buying a house?"

"Cooper speaking."

"You're the builder?"

"Yes, sir."

"My name's Bartlett. My family and I were driving around last weekend and we happened up there and we liked what we saw, and we were wondering if any of the homes were still for sale—"

"If you'd like to come up—"

"—By that, I mean something pretty well completed," Bartlett went on, ignoring the interruption, "since we have to move soon. We're in Pasadena at present, and the place we've rented for six years has been sold and it's put us on a spot."

Cooper's mind was working like an adding machine. For some reason he couldn't define, Mr. Bartlett sounded like money. "I'll tell you what ... everything that's completed or even near it is sold, but it's possible we'll have a cancellation or a resale. Why don't you give me your phone—"

"We'll be up to see you around five-thirty," Bartlett told him, in a tone that commanded Cooper to wait. "We'll see if we can't work out a deal."

Cooper was already sifting through the people he'd sold to, weighing them as to gullibility and ruggedness; he settled almost at once on the Ranalds. Not only were they young and totally ignorant of their rights as purchasers under his contract, they still had a lot of wild ideas about what they might want put into their house. He knew, with a sudden burst of relief, how easy it would be to get them to accept a place still in the framing stage, where they could indulge in further changes. "All right, sir," he said to Bartlett. "I'll meet you here at the office. It's just inside the gate, to the right."

"Fine. By the way, we noticed the little gatehouse. My wife liked it. Five-thirty, then." Mr. Bartlett hung up.

Mr. Cooper went out to finish talking to the foreman, and he noticed someone across the street lingering at the gatehouse, and he frowned. The gatehouse had been meant as more of an ornament than anything; it was scarcely more than six feet square, a Snow-White-and-Seven-Dwarfs kind of thing, gray shingles and tiny lead-paned windows and a cobblestone step, nothing in it now but some defective wiring that had to go back. Old Mr. Arthur had gone up on the step and was peering in through the little pane in the door, and Cooper felt a surge of anger.

There was a possibility of unpleasantness, the old man making an obnoxious nuisance of himself. Cooper had already made it plain that no gateman was needed at present, wouldn't be unless the buyers all got together and decided on it, but no doubt the old man was bored and wanted something to do.

But having a hired gatekeeper was exclusive and upper-class and having somebody's goofy old grandfather was something else.

Somehow his anger at the old man was a raveled edge of his anger at his wife. Cooper and his wife were separating with a great deal of bitterness. She claimed, perhaps justly, that he paid no attention to her, that he was wrapped up in his work. On Cooper's part, he felt betrayed. He *had* worked hard. He had done so from a dedicated opinion that a successful business career was the most desirable thing on earth. Now this sudden switch, her scorn of him and her desertion, had left him with a short temper that he found hard to control at times.

Walking toward old man Arthur, his nerves were sizzling.

"Mr. Arthur?"

With deliberate cruelty, satisfying his irritation at the old man, Cooper had waited until he was directly behind him. Old man Arthur jumped in fright. He must be rather deaf, and Cooper had startled him. He turned around in a scared way. He wasn't a handsome old man, Cooper thought, he was skinny and there were big brown age-spots on his skin and his hands trembled. Nobody was going to like seeing him squatting there in the little house, keeping track of everyone who came and went, maybe even—God forbid!—taking it on himself to act like a real gateman and ask names and who they meant to see, and like that! Mr. Cooper felt his gorge rise.

"I was just … just walking by," the old man said in a quavery voice. "Got this far, thought I'd rest a minute. I'll be going right back, I won't stop but a minute." He said this with such an air of guilt that Cooper wondered if he hadn't heard something on the subject from his daughter-in-law.

"I wanted to remind you," Cooper said, controlling his anger, "that we aren't opening the gatehouse yet, there isn't any call for a watchman. When the time comes—"

"Yes, I understand," The old man stepped quickly off the little porch and retreated to the curb. He had a cane, a big knobby stick that shone from years of rubbing, and by its aid he let himself down on the curb and let out a sigh. "Just a minute, then I'll be going along home."

"Don't get too tired," Cooper said automatically. He went back to the foreman. As he walked, he considered some of the angles … providing this man Bartlett was as sold as he sounded on the phone. There were additional profits in a resale; he could claim a commission on the sale, if nothing else, but Bartlett might even be anxious to pay a little more, say thirty-four five.

When he thought of the old man, and glanced that way again, the Arthur grandfather was gone. Well, all it took was a little firmness. Mr. Cooper went into his office to await the Bartletts.

They drove in almost on the dot, five-thirty, and Cooper stayed in the office, sizing them up while they got out of the car. It was a new Buick. Backing out of the driver's seat, Mr. Bartlett looked like a sleek executive type. Thirty-five, a hundred and seventy, with big shoulders and a slim middle. Brooks Brothers and Florsheims and a good gym; and then he turned around to face the office and Cooper was surprised. He wore black-rimmed heavy glasses and a funny little mustache, and Cooper wondered with almost a touch of indignation why he wanted to ruin that first impression that way.

The woman had on a dark coat and gray gloves, and as she came up the walk she twitched at herself and muttered something to her husband, and Cooper decided in disgust that she was the fussy, nagging type and his expectation of unloading the house quickly began to dim.

The girl following them was a teen-ager. Thirteen or fourteen, and Cooper gave her a glance and then his eyes riveted. She was in first bloom, and she was a beauty. Loose, dark curling hair and a face like a pale cameo, and a neat little walk like a queen's! By God, Cooper thought, girls were surely developing early these days! It must be the climate, or vitamins or something. Here was this little kid ... she must still be in junior high, couldn't be over fifteen at the most ... and she'd turn the head of any male under ninety! With a sense of marveling at nature's wonders, Cooper got out of his chair and went to the door and extended his hand in greeting.

Bartlett's handshake went with the glasses and the goofy mustache; it was limp as a fish.

Cooper arranged the chairs. The woman said, "My husband's quite taken with your houses, Mr. Cooper," letting him know that the liking was all in one direction and that he was going to have to work to sell her. The little girl stood back by the door, rather shy, and then Bartlett said, "This is our daughter, Pammy."

"Pamela," said the girl in a soft voice.

"Pleased to meet you, Pamela," Cooper said, surprised that she sounded just like a little kid. He took the big cardboard sheet from the desk drawer and spread it on the desk; it was the plot of the subdivision. He put his finger on the Ranalds' lot. "This is the place I had in mind. I believe I might be able to get it for you. I don't believe this young couple's really ready to move in, yet."

Mrs. Bartlett inched closer and frowned. "Palomino Lane? That's where the houses are finished, isn't it? And isn't it near that old place, that pink stucco?"

He knew now what the objection was going to be. "The pink stucco belongs to Mr. Dronk. He owned all this valley, had it in oranges. I believe he inherited the property from his father. A very old family. Very important hereabouts."

"That pink house doesn't seem to go with the rest of it," said Bartlett mildly, looking at his wife as if for approval. Cooper felt his temper rising. What was the matter with the man? He'd sounded firm and full of confidence, eager to buy, on the telephone. Now here he was, wishy-washy as hell, letting the woman make objections.

Cooper decided suddenly on a drastic course. He picked up the big sheet, opened the drawer and slid it in. "I'm afraid that's all we have to offer. Providing you want what you said you wanted, a place where you can move in right away."

A couple of pink spots came into Mrs. Bartlett's cheeks. "We have a few weeks yet, Mr. Cooper. We just don't want to be rushed into the first thing you offer us. We'd like to have a little choice. Don't you have something a block or so from there, nearer the gate, that might be finished in ... say, a month?"

Cooper shook his head firmly. "Everything I have that's anywhere near finished is sold. As a matter of fact, I'm not even sure *that* house is available. I was going to do a bit of persuading to get it for you."

"Oh, I see." She and Bartlett looked at each other.

"Tell you what," Cooper said, "I'll take you around to those that are still for sale, and then you can have a better idea of what you want."

He took them in his car, and showed them what was left, mostly raw foundations and framing, and then to finish it off he took them into the Ranalds' place, and he marked the covetous look on Mrs. Bartlett. She stood by a window that gave a view of Dronk's hideous pink stucco, and then turned firmly away. "I guess we'll take it. Providing of course you can get it for us."

Even so, there was a bad moment when they went outside. Dronk's boy was out in the yard, doing something to a flower bed under the direction of the housekeeper—pulling out some spent annuals, Cooper thought—and one of the Arthur kids down the block, the kid named Billy, rode out of the garage on a tricycle and hollered, "Dronk ... *drunk*. Dronk ... *drunk*," and Cooper almost swallowed his cigar. The two in the big yard across the street, the kneeling boy and the old woman, pretended not to hear, and when the kid on the tricycle got tired of it he quit.

They were at the car, when Pammy Bartlett said, "His mother ought to wash his mouth out with soap."

"Now, Pammy," said Mrs. Bartlett, cautioning, "they'll be our neighbors, so watch what you say!"

"Little brat!" said Pammy, and she smiled at Cooper as if knowing that he shared her opinion.

Across the street, Kim rose awkwardly, bracing himself with the spading fork. He saw the group at the car, he noticed the girl and how pretty she was. Mrs. Campbell was stripping seeds from the spent zinnias, muttering under her breath. "That's something new," Kim said. "Drunk."

"Trash," said Mrs. Campbell through her false teeth.

"He's just a little kid, too."

"There's big and little trash, never you fear. Size has nothing to do with it."

Kim looked at the old lady seriously. "Are you glad that Dad sold off the land and got these people up here?"

"I am not. And he's beginning not to be."

"If I'm not happy I'm not going to let him know," Kim said firmly. "I'm not going to act like a baby anymore, the way I did at the table today. It's not his fault I'm crippled, too. This bad foot runs in the family. It's just something I've got to live with."

Mrs. Campbell seemed to bite back something she was about to say.

"Look, some people are born blind. Some are born so horribly crippled they never walk at all. And some have polio, and end up living in an iron lung. I'm luckier than any of them. I can get around. When I try hard, I can even almost not limp."

"Yes, I know you can," she nodded. She went on stripping the dried zinnia heads, working by feel, mostly, since her sight was so poor. In the late sunlight, the thick lenses over her eyes gave her a weird, dreary expression.

"If I was a show-off, a real operator, I'd walk over and meet that new girl," Kim said. "She's a real cool chick."

Mrs. Campbell turned her half-blind stare toward the street. "What're they doing?"

"Mr. Cooper's showing them the Ranald house."

"That's odd."

Mrs. Forrest Holden turned from the front windows. Her husband had just come into the room. He was a meek, gray, tired, skinny man about two inches shorter than his wife. He had on a dark business suit and carried a brief case. "Cooper is showing the Ranald house to some new people," she said with an attitude of suspicion. "I wonder what he thinks he's doing?"

"Perhaps he's using it as a finished model." Holden put his hat tentatively on a table and then picked it up quickly.

"The Ranalds are crazy about that house," she went on. "I must have run into them a dozen times in the past week, they were in and out, in and out, and they always had a big collection of sketches and magazine articles, things they wanted added to the house."

He made a soft-footed tour of the room, looking at the furniture. "You have made it all look very cozy, Mae. It fits well. I like it better here than in the San Diego house."

She threw him a provoked look. "We didn't go to all this trouble just to have the furniture fit!"

"I thought ..." He stopped there, as if the bald malice behind what she had said had just penetrated. He fiddled nervously with the hat and the brief case, swallowed a couple of times, and then said, "I'll put my things away." She followed him toward the hall, something stalking in the way she walked. "I decided that all of your things had better go into the rear bedroom. It's the quiet side of the house. You won't be bothered by noise from the children, or anything like that."

He had stopped just inside the hall. "Mae—"

"And you can depend on me, I'll keep them out of your way." She pursed her mouth, watching his stooped back, and then added, "Of course the Arthur children are quite small. They're scarcely more than babies."

"Yes, I noticed,"

"You did?"

"How could I help?" he said with a sudden flare of exasperation. "The boy was on the sidewalk screaming insults at those people across the street, the housekeeper and that crippled kid. He was making fun of the name.... Drunk, he was yelling it."

A faint smile twitched the edges of her lips.

"Well, I'm going to put my things away and change my clothes."

He went off down the hall. She remained standing. She had the air of having pulled off some subtle skirmish, of testing and finding some point of weakness, some raw sore. She waited until he had gone into his room and closed the door, and then she returned to the windows. Cooper and the three Bartletts were out at the car, now, with the girl standing free of the others with the sunlight in her face. Mrs. Holden's face twisted and she caught at the gray velvet drapes.

After a moment of staring, she whispered, "Sell it to them! Sell it to them!" Her breath made a faint fog on the pane.

In his room, Holden sat on the edge of the bed with his eyes shut. He too was whispering to himself. "What am I? What in hell am I?" He felt the choking tide of asthmatic congestion rising in his throat; he opened his mouth to wheeze. A tear glittered in the corner of his eye. "I'm not what she says I am. No matter how much she insists. The thing that happened in the garage in San Diego was an accident. She just happened to come in at the wrong moment. The child suffered no harm." He took out his handkerchief and mopped away the tear.

After a short while of vacant staring at the opposite wall he stooped and began to take off his shoes.

He hung his coat in the closet. His three suits were there, huddled at one end of the rod as if the space were begrudged, along with his brown overcoat and the jacket he wore to work in the garden. The deer rifle in its leather case stood in a corner in shadow, and his swimming eyes passed over it and returned.

There was a creaking sound in the hall, as if she might have come to the door to listen. He slid the panel shut and turned to the dresser, picked up a brush and touched it to his thinning hair, his face tense and watchful.

Three

Miss Silvester went into the kitchen and experimented with the light switch. Under the overhead glow the place was clean and sparkling. Beyond the windows with their crisp new curtains, night had fallen, the first night she would spend in her new home. There was an air of unfamiliarity about it, a hint of adventure, not unpleasant. She examined the immaculate new range, built into a tiled recess, with its adjacent oven sunk into the bricked wall. Then she opened the refrigerator.

She had gone to market in Pomona late in the day, and now there were a lot of citrus, lettuce, wheat germ, fresh tomatoes, lamb chops and liver, and a quart of yogurt, along with other foods that Miss Silvester considered healthful. In the cupboards were cans of soy beans, whole-wheat wafers, and prunes. After examining her stores she decided upon an orange-and-yogurt salad with plenty of lettuce, a lamb chop, and a pot of tea.

She was just pouring boiling water into the tea pot when there was a soft rap at the back door.

It surprised her. She put the pan of water down quickly, walked past the breakfast nook, and looked out through the pane. He was out there against the dark, dressed just as he had been that afternoon, shabby T-shirt and jeans, nothing to warm him except a sweat shirt tied carelessly by its sleeves over his shoulders. He was looking in at her with the wise, lazy look she had remembered all day, smiling a little, and in his fingers he was holding up a spoon, one of hers.

She fumbled with the unfamiliar door latch, a sudden sweat coming out all over her body, and angry at herself for the rush of confusion and her awkwardness over the door. It would amuse him.

When she had the door open he held the spoon in to her. "I found this in my hip pocket when I got home. It must have dropped out of a box and I stuck it in my jeans and forgot it." Under the mockery at himself and the story was a faint thread of wistfulness, hoping she would believe him, that struck Miss Silvester like a sudden blow.

But all she could say—stupidly—was, "Come in before the chop burns."

Heat rushed to her head as she stepped back, as he went past her. What was the matter with her? Here he was, tall and beautiful, perfect, the person she'd thought of all afternoon, the thought of him like an ache, and all she could say to him was, Come in before the chop burns. What kind of greeting was that? She was a ninny, a fool. She stood, holding the silver spoon that was warm from being next to his body, brushing dazedly at her hair with her free hand, while he walked past, while he looked into the skillet where the chop sizzled. "Looks good," he said. "Smells good." He began to fish for cigarettes. He turned to face her.

Across the line of his cheek bones she could see where he'd shaved, she could see the fine downy growth above and the smooth skin below, a little shiny yet from soap, and she thought, he shaved tonight before he came here. He shaved to get ready to come to see me. There was a hot, beating sensation in her breast; she tried to say something gay and bantering but no words came. She looked at him mutely.

He lit the cigarette. "One chop. That's kind of lonesome."

"Let me …" She licked her lips. "Let me put in another one, for you. You stay for dinner! Oh, would you?" *No, no, no*, her thoughts intruded, you're gushing. You'll overwhelm him. She laid the spoon on the sink, then moved it to the window sill. She'd want to keep that spoon separate from the rest, a souvenir. *Dear God, let it turn out to be* … Her thoughts veered; there was nothing at all that this could turn out to be. She was too old for it ever to be anything. She got a grip on herself and turned to him with a smile. "How about it? You'll want more than one chop, though. I'll bet you have a good appetite."

He nodded almost shyly. "Make it a couple, then." He leaned his hip against the tiled edge of the sink. His hair had been wet when he had run the comb through it. It shone darkly under the light.

She took the packed meat from the refrigerator. "Where did you go from here? Did you make other deliveries?"

"We went back into L. A., the warehouse, for some stuff." His tone dismissed what he had done; he blew smoke into the air, a breath like a sigh. "Where did you live before you came here?" he asked abruptly.

The meat slipped through her fingers, the grease spattered and popped. She bit back a cry of pain. "In … in town," she said. "An apartment. I decided to try a change. You know how it is … the place was getting trafficky and stuffy." She tried to keep her tone light, not to betray the grim truth about those other surroundings. She glanced at him swiftly. But he was gazing incuriously at the dark window above the sink.

His profile was as perfect as an outline on a coin.

"This is a real nice place. Lots of room. Modern. You picked up a lot of good stuff to go in it." He turned his head, looking directly at her; she tried to meet his gaze and couldn't; it made her heart pound. "What do they soak you for one like this?"

The conversation had shifted subtly; this was almost like prying on his part. She said unevenly, "Not too much, considering. Thirty thousand ... around thirty thousand."

"It's nice." There seemed nothing in his tone of avarice or envy, though she listened for it, dreading it, and hating her own suspicions. "It's nice when everything is new."

Her thoughts echoed: *new ... young.* It's wonderful when everything is fresh with youth, the world and the sky, and even the wind that blows.... She bent unsteadily to adjust the gas flame under the skillet and when she rose he was right beside her. He reached for the hand with which she had adjusted the flame, held it, turned it palm upward. "You burned yourself."

He was so close that his bulk seemed to shut her in. The beating sensation filled her body like the surge of wings. "No, it's nothing at all," she whispered, trying to pull the hand free, trying not to look at his mouth that was bending toward her.

He held her palm opened and put his mouth on it and kissed it, and Miss Silvester almost fainted.

He stood holding her, waiting, and she wouldn't look at him.

"Well," he said after a moment, "I guess I'd better go."

She jerked convulsively. "But I've started your dinner!"

"No, I'd better go." Now she was looking at him, and it was his turn to avoid her. He still held her hand, his other arm was at her waist, but there was the feeling that he would withdraw at any minute. "I guess it wasn't such a hot idea, my coming here," he said. "I guess I didn't have much of an appetite. I didn't really come for dinner."

"Why did you?" In her confusion she yanked her hand free and grabbed the front of the T-shirt. The material was thin and wash-worn. She was struck again by his youth, by how careless he was with himself, unknowing, almost crude. He'd shaved to make a good impression, but hadn't known enough to wear a shirt. Under the thin material she touched his flesh, warm and firm. "Why did you come back tonight?"

His voice was husky. "I guess I had a crazy idea you kind of liked me."

It was up to her now. The next move must come from her. Miss Silvester tried to think of any precedent, of any experience in the past that might give a hint of proper action now. She shivered with tension, though her head was hot.

He let her hand go, gently.

There was nothing in the past to guide her. She had the sensation of looking back over a desert without landmarks, over a barren arc of gray days during which she had progressed mouselike and almost invisibly from ordinary bookkeeper to forms, invoices, tax receipts and bank statements. A she-being attached to an adding machine. A human cipher with a lunch in a paper bag. So it was as a pioneer that Miss Silvester lifted her arms and put them around the strong young neck and abandoned herself to love. "I do," she whispered. "I like you terribly. What's your name?"

He stirred and sat up in the bed, and she was instantly awake, full of alarm. "What is it?"

"I've got to go." He moved over to the edge of the bed and she heard him fumbling with his clothes.

"What time is it?"

"Your clock over there says a quarter to three."

She hadn't foreseen this time of departure, of parting; there was an odd awkward sense of loss. He had carried her in here like a whirlwind, and now in this funny dark cold middle of the night he was taking himself away.

"Are you ..." She wanted to ask, are you coming back, but shyness tied her tongue. Instead she substituted, "Do you have a car outside?"

"I left it down by the gatehouse. Out of sight. I hiked the rest of the way." Suddenly he stopped dressing and leaned across the bed, putting his weight on her, and his hands searched for her hair. "I can't come back tonight," he said, as if knowing the question she had wanted to ask. "You going to have a phone put in? I'll call you."

"They promised ... the phone company promised ... right away."

"You're home during the day?"

"Yes. Yes." In a flash of insight, Miss Silvester tasted the dry loneliness of waiting, of trying to work at the desk with the phone there by her elbow, hoping that he would call.

"I'll see you in a couple of days." He kissed her on the mouth, a hard strange kind of kiss. Nothing like eating grapes, Miss Silvester thought. More like a promise of violence. She touched his cheek gently with her hand, and then he drew away and resumed dressing.

She knew his name, Ross Havilland. He was twenty-six and he had worked as a mover's helper for a little more than a year.

The mystery of the rest of him, of where he lived and with whom, of what had brought him into her life and of what had caused her to behave as she had, benumbed her senses and scorched her flesh. She lay with her eyes squeezed shut while he finished putting on his clothes and left the room. Then she got out of bed, turned on the lamp, put on a nightgown and leaned toward the dresser mirror, studying herself.

She had read a lot of fiction in which the heroines changed greatly after a thing like this. This experience was supposed to ripen a woman, to bring out a sensuous bloom. She plucked up the lace neck of the gown to cover her collarbone.

There didn't seem to be much difference. Perhaps age had something to do with it. Perhaps it had to happen first when you were younger.

She looked mostly gray and tired, she decided.

Just gray and tired. That was all.

Mrs. Forrest Holden rose on one elbow, listening to the steps that went past in the dark outside. There had been an instant of savage hope, in the first instant of awakening, but then she had known that the steps couldn't possibly be those of her husband. There wasn't even enough resemblance to make an accusation logical. She listened, deciding that this was someone much younger and heavier. Then she had padded from the bed to the window. The only thing to be seen was a light on in the bedroom down the block, the house belonging to that spinster. For a long moment Mrs. Holden studied the light; she wondered if Miss Silvester could have been sick and called the doctor.

Mrs. Holden went back to bed. The steps had receded into silence. She waited, half expecting some sound from Holden's room, but he was apparently sleeping soundly.

As long as she was awake, she could do some planning for the day ahead. She could figure out something to make him squirm again. It didn't have to be anything big or significant; he was like a raw worm, he wriggled at the merest touch. Even a look, the right kind of look, could bring on his asthma. What she had better do—she laughed to herself at the sudden inspiration—was to tell those people, the Arthurs, that Mr. Holden wasn't an entirely well man and that small children irritated him beyond all reason. Then she could put on all sorts of little acts, getting the children out of his way, making a fuss over any chance contact between him and them, and the parents would merely think him an irritable old idiot, while Forrest himself would be ready to drop with fright and shame!

Lying in bed, she hugged herself.

It would be better, oh how much better, if that lovely young girl would move nearby! The most dazzling prospects of intrigue and mischief soared through her head. I'll bet I could drive him into a nervous breakdown inside a month, she thought gleefully. I'd have the child in for cookies ... or whatever teen-agers like. I'd throw her at him like a bomb! With me watching, what could he do but shiver and shake like the blob of unmanly fear that he is?

With deep scorn and disgust she pictured his wretched sniffling, his choked attempts to breathe. She was convinced that he could bring on the asthma at will, like a child being sick when it expected to be punished, an effort to escape its just deserts.

Then her mind turned back for a brief cold memory of the thing that had happened in San Diego.

I could have turned him over to the police. Then and there. The child would have backed me up. I know she would.

For a moment she pictured her husband's white, twitching face, the little girl's bent shining head, the kind of tableau they made there in the sudden light when she had opened the side door of the garage. Her husband had jumped with fright. With guilt, too, of course, though he persisted in that ridiculous yarn—the little girl had said that a bug or something had crawled into her clothes. A likely yarn.

A man's face doesn't shine and sweat and twitch like that, over a flea-hunt!

She remembered her mother, an old woman with a white pompadour and chicken-claw fingers, and how her mother had warned her all those years past, that she would be sorry if she married Forrest. And now she was, of course. Mixed up in the regret was something secret and shameful, her inadequacy as a wife—she licked her lips, turned her thoughts from this channel back to Forrest. Yes, she was dreadfully sorry that she was married to this ... *fiend* was such a silly word to apply to anything like Forrest, and yet that's just what he was. A fiend.

Hating him was so much fun, though, it was sometimes hard to keep the righteous regret to the forefront.

Across the street in the second floor of the big pink monstrosity, Kim Dronk got out of bed to go to the bathroom. He paused in the middle of the dark room, listening to the echo of footsteps on paving. It seemed awfully funny for people to be up here in the valley, walking around in the quiet of nights that had never been disturbed.

He went over to the window and looked out. From this second-floor window, with the added elevation of the rise of ground, he could see the whole expanse of the little valley, all the way down to the night light at the gate. Near at hand, the completed roofs made him think of some jointed thing laid out, or of a fallen row of giant dominoes. Lower down, against the glow cast by the lights, were spider-like skeletons. He looked to see who might be out walking, but saw no one. The sound of the steps had gone. There was a light on in one of the houses; he thought it might be the one occupied by the slender woman with the pale hair, the one his father had called Miss Silvester.

Kim stood looking, frowning with thought.

Soon there would be a lot of strangers up here, people he had never seen before, people who had never seen him. Whenever Kim met somebody new he looked into their eyes, seeing the word form there, *cripple*. And that's how it would be now, until all the houses were filled, and until everyone up here took him and his funny walk for granted, like a part of the landscape.

He remembered the girl across the street, the pretty girl that Mr. Cooper had brought with her parents that afternoon. When that little Arthur kid had been making such an ass of himself, hollering *Dronk ... drunk*, she had seemed to resent it.

Maybe she would be his friend, if she moved in.

He stood at the window for a minute or so longer, looking at the houses. They represented a complication in his life that he was uncertain about coping with; he had a sudden, aching desire for the valley to revert to what it had been, empty and peaceful.

Down near the gates, a black car crept out into the street with its lights off, moved into the highway leading to Pomona. Kim watched it go, uncomprehending. Then he yawned and closed the shade.

Four

For more than a week, Cooper had trouble with the young Ranalds, until he almost despaired of prying them loose from the house. It seemed that Mrs. Ranald had been reading the fine print in the contract, and knew her rights. Then Cooper had an inspiration; he had them come up and see some sample tile he had in. It was expensive stuff and he hadn't really been considering buying any of it, but with the profits of a resale to the Bartletts in view he could be generous. Mrs. Ranald had fits over the tile, as well she might; it was handmade a little at a time by a ceramist in Pasadena and even enough for a sink panel cost outrageously. Then Cooper, in another burst of inspiration, told them about the burnt Mexican brick he intended to use for a few of the fireplaces and chimneys—it hadn't been available for the first homes, might not come in in time except for the very last few, and with this as bait the Ranalds turned happily to one of the places being framed down near the gate.

Cooper then called Bartlett and told him the sale was as good as made.

Mrs. Bartlett came out right away and had the wall between the kitchen and the game room knocked out and a snack counter put in, and a window seat built in the girl's room, but even while the sawing and painting went on, they moved in. Mrs. Forrest Holden sized up their stuff behind the draperies in her living room, and decided that they were worth cultivating. Even aside from the girl; whenever Mrs. Holden looked at Pamela, in a slim serge skirt and a pink sweater, she had to stifle fits of laughter.

School started six days later, and on the first morning Pamela was at the bus stop, waiting, when Kim got there. She shifted her notebook and purse and held out her hand. "Hello. I'm Pamela Bartlett."

Kim wanted desperately to be adult and casual, but he was dazzled. He had trouble getting the notebook out of the way, shaking her hand— her hand felt like a little warm live animal inside his own—and then moving to the bench without stumbling over his crippled foot. "I saw you move in," he told her as she sat down by him. Stupid remark, she'd think he spied on them like that woman next door, that Mrs. Holden who peeked out through the curtains all the time. "Well, I kind of couldn't help it, I'm right across the street."

"I know. Your house looks interesting," Pamela said. She was much shorter than Kim, her black curly head came about to his shoulder, but under the fluffy bangs her face was almost that of a woman. There was some mischief, a touch of teasing, in the way she looked at him, a look that made a Kim tingle. "Have you lived in it a long time?"

"We came here when I was just a little kid," Kim said. "The house belonged to my grandfather, he came up here in the early twenties and planted oranges and built the house. He turned it all over to my father and went to live in Florida." That was the time, Kim recalled, when his mother had deserted them; his grandfather had agreed with the doctors who had wanted to operate on his foot, and when his father refused to have the operation, and when his mother had left, the grandfather had sort of washed his hands of them all.

"Sometimes older homes have more style than the newer ones," Pamela told him. "They look like they have a history, or something."

While she talked to Kim, he was watching Mr. Cooper, down near the gatehouse. Cooper was talking to the building foreman, but he seemed to be aware of the two teen-agers on the corner. He kept looking over the other man's shoulder toward them, and Kim had the impression that it was Pamela he stared at.

"Our house isn't old enough to be interesting," Kim said. "You'd have to have a house built around 1890. Then you'd have cupolas and gingerbread and maybe a widow's walk."

Before he was through explaining about a widow's walk, the school bus came.

The last thing he noted, looking back as they passed the turn below the gatehouse, was Mr. Cooper with his stare riveted on the back of the bus.

It made Kim uneasy. He wondered if there had seemed anything wrong, his sitting there talking to Pamela. He hadn't sat too close, there had been no move from either of them to touch the other, except when she put a hand briefly on his arm to call his attention to the bus coming, and that hadn't amounted to anything. Not anything, that is, that Cooper could see. Under Pamela's touch, Kim had turned warm all over.

Miss Silvester jumped when the phone rang.

"Hello."

"This is Ross."

"Oh." Her heart had begun to pound suffocatingly. She brushed at her hair, tugged at the neck of her frock, as if he might be able to see her there at the desk. "How are you?"

"I'm low. Real low." He sounded dragged-out, discouraged, not at all the tone to go with his muscular good looks, and Miss Silvester choked with a premonitory panic. "I was hoping I'd have a chance to come up there to see you tonight...." He paused as if thinking over the visit and what it had promised. "... but I'm going to have to work overtime instead. I'm going to have to work overtime a lot in the next few weeks. Every night, if I can swing it. I need an extra hundred bucks like crazy."

She was at a loss, not knowing how to answer. Something spangly and magic, a silver fairy-dust, seemed to be dying in the air. The thought of not seeing him in the near future made her throat ache, made her hands tremble. She said weakly, "Can't you come tonight ... just for a little while?"

"I guess not." The tone was flat, withdrawn, as if he were already considering the job ahead.

The room seemed definitely darker. Miss Silvester looked in fright at the windows behind her, realizing that there must be some momentary cloudiness, some haze, interfering with the sunlight. The room took on the gloomy vapors of a dungeon. Tears stung her eyes and she felt terribly alone, and until that instant she had not seen that the hope of his phoning her had had so much warmth and excitement in it. She reached unsteadily for the lamp, snapped it on. But in its glow the white phone looked dead and waxy.

"Ross, are you still there?"

"Yeah, I'm here, but I've got to get back. Lunch is over." He made it sound ironic.

"Wait. If you ... if you need a hundred right away, why couldn't I lend it to you?"

"Oh ... No, I don't want you to do that." His voice seemed to stiffen with male pride.

"Yes." She grew firmer, warmer again too, by the moment. "Yes, I insist. A hundred doesn't amount to anything. I'll have it here for you this evening."

"I don't want to borrow money from *you*."

The tone set her apart, made her something special as far as he was concerned, someone whose good opinion he valued, someone too cherished and too intimately desired to be used as a lender. Miss Silvester quaked with happiness.

"Just this once, though, Ross. Let me be your friend!"

"I wouldn't feel right about it somehow."

"Yes, you will. That's just silly."

"I'd have to work like hell then to pay you back."

"I don't care *when* it's paid back!"

Over the wire she sensed his uncertainty, his hesitation. She was undermining his stiff-necked pride. He was wonderfully big and strong, and so of course it was hard for him to accept a favor from a woman, but he was beginning to weaken! "Anyway," she urged breathlessly, "don't start working overtime just yet. Not tonight. Come up and talk it over. Promise you'll at least do that!"

"Well ..." His voice dropped to a whisper. "I do want to see you. Man! Do I!"

"Come, then!"

"About eight o'clock?"

"Just after dark. We'll have dinner, the way we did before."

"We'll have dinner afterward," he corrected, his tone suddenly lazy and assured. "Bye for now."

She put the phone on its cradle and leaned back in the chair. The ledgers and papers spread out on the desk swam in a mist of tears. She was weak, shivering with relief. Suppose he hadn't agreed? Suppose she hadn't had the inspiration about lending him the money? Suppose the warmth and the expectation and the excitement had died, day by day, in the backwash of silence? She leaned on the desk and shut her eyes and the papery smell of the ledgers and the other paraphernalia rose to fill her nostrils.

She lifted her head and looked at it, looked at the patient labor that had taken all her days, taken the years of her youth, and had finally, along with the small inheritance from her uncle, given her this new house and the new furniture and the adventure with Ross.

When she had first realized that her uncle had left her the money, and when she had added the total to what she had in the bank and thought of getting out of the gray-dishwater apartment and the gray-dishwater life she led, it had seemed that fate could provide no richer change than this. She hadn't dreamed of anything further, any kind of romance. But now the feeling of security and the pride in the new house was nothing. The man filled the horizon of her life. She couldn't imagine existence without the thought of him—and she'd only had him here twice!

I love him. She said the awkward alien words softly to herself, staring at the work all laid out on the desk.

What does money matter when you love someone?

I can give him the hundred out of the inheritance. It's just sitting in the bank, drawing a little interest.

She began to plan the trip to Pasadena. She would have to make it before the bank closed.

In the late afternoon, Pamela and Kim walked up from the bus stop and paused to talk for a moment on a corner near their homes.

Mrs. Holden was out in the yard, inspecting the sprigs of new-planted ivy. When Kim and Pamela parted, Pamela looking back to waggle slim fingers in farewell, Mrs. Holden edged nearer the sidewalk.

"How was school?" she asked, when Pamela came even with her.

"Oh ... like all first days. A gasp," Pamela said, preparing to step past.

"Are you in the same classes with ..." Mrs. Holden nodded toward Kim, who had crossed the street and was walking slowly up the walk to his front steps. He was making a great effort to control the limp, and it was obvious even at a distance. "... with the crippled boy?"

"With Kim? Oh no, he's a year ahead of me."

"I was sort of hoping he'd walk this way with you," Mrs. Holden said, something rapid and uneven about the way she said it. "There's a big box in the garage, too heavy for me to lift alone, and I wanted to ask him to help."

"I could call him," Pamela said, coming to a full stop.

"Well, it's ..." Mrs. Holden let her voice trail off. She was pink in the face; the unaccustomed flush made her look as if she had a fever. "Perhaps I can do it alone, after all. I hate to bother people."

"Maybe I can help."

Mrs. Holden appeared to think about it. Perhaps she was considering the ridiculous aspects of it, a woman as big as she was accepting help from an undersized teen-ager; or perhaps there were other angles, more obscure. After a moment she said, "Would you mind coming over about five o'clock? We can try it then."

She didn't explain why the box couldn't be moved now but might be moved at five, and Pamela wondered. There was an oddness about her, a funny sense of something underhanded and tricky; Pamela sensed it and was repelled. She had only the vaguest impression of Mr. Holden, though for some reason she tried to remember now what he was like. He seemed a wraith compared to the big, vital, and somewhat belligerent Mrs. Holden.

Pamela went home and changed her clothes, putting on capri pants and a blue cotton shirt. She brushed her hair. Then she went into the kitchen and munched an apple. Her mother was there, sitting at a little counter where there was a telephone and order pads and a collection of cookbooks. She was working perplexedly at something to do with the budget.

"Pammy, do you have to *crunch* that way?"

"Please call me Pamela," said the girl, dropping the apple core into the sink. "Mother, don't you think Mrs. Holden is kind of off, some way?"

"Now what do you mean by that?"

"There's something funny about her."

"I hadn't noticed." Mrs. Bartlett's fingers twitched above the row of figures.

"She wants me to help her lift a box."

"Well, be careful, you don't want to strain your vital organs," her mother said primly, her tone hinting at the delicacy of the subject.

"And you know something? That old grandfather, the Arthurs' grandfather, he's always sneaking down there to creep around that little gatehouse. Isn't it weird?"

"He's so old, he's probably growing eccentric," Mrs. Bartlett decided. She was only following Pamela's remarks with half a mind; her real attention was on this hideously misbalanced budget.

"And that Mr. Cooper's always staring."

Mrs. Bartlett glanced at her. "Staring at *you?*" she examined her child's appearance. "Those pants are too tight. And you outgrew that shirt a year ago. Pammy, you're conspicuous!"

Pamela brightened instantly. "Where?"

"Just ..." Mrs. Bartlett made a futile motion with the hand holding the pencil. "Just conspicuous, that's all. You know what I mean. I've got to buy you some new things, as soon as I get these bills straightened out. The charge accounts have to be paid or they'll start calling your father at the office. Oh, I'm so tired of wrestling with checkbooks and accounts! I wish your father would take over."

"Poor daddy, we'd really be in a fog. Do you suppose we look as funny to these other people as they do to us?"

"I haven't seen anyone looking funny," Mrs. Bartlett said. "It's just your imagination."

"She wants me back at five," said Pamela, going to the door.

Mrs. Bartlett nodded. She didn't even ask Pamela who wanted her at five. She made a neat entry into the budget of thirty-seven dollars, and bit her lip at the sum which emerged.

There was an area between the Holden house and the wall of the garage, floored with brick and sheltered by a redwood lattice. Mrs. Holden was waiting here when Pamela came up the walk. She made Pamela think of a spider, there in the shadows. "It's very nice of you to come back," she said. "I thought you might forget. Would you like a cookie and a glass of milk first?"

"No, thank you."

"The box is in the garage, on the floor in the corner." Mrs. Holden had stepped aside. "I have to see about something in the kitchen." She smiled, her teeth shining in the dimmed light. Pamela glanced at the open side door of the garage, at the thick gloom within.

"Isn't there a light?"

"Yes. I have to find a bulb for it. I'll be right out again." Mrs. Holden had gone to the steps that led to the kitchen; she went up the steps to the narrow porch and then turned as if to see whether Pamela had gone into the garage. She smiled again, the teeth glassy and repelling. "There's nothing in there to hurt you!"

For no reason, except a sense that there was something haywire about this big woman and her dark garage, Pamela felt gooseflesh rise on her skin. She glanced out through the opening in the trellis, half hoping Kim might come into view. She should have gone first to his place, brought him with her. A perfectly natural thing to do. Why hadn't she? The sunlight was long and slanting out there, the last rays dying among the orange trees left standing above his house, along the flank of the hill. It had a promise of twilight in it, something ghostly and forlorn, and she shivered. She looked at Mrs. Holden. "I really can't stay long."

"I'll be right out again," Mrs. Holden repeated, and stepped through into the kitchen. There was a moment of silence, and Pamela knew without looking that Mrs. Holden was watching her through the pane, waiting for her to go into the garage.

It must be some kind of game. But what?

Pamela took a last look at the street and then went over to the open side door of the garage. Well, it wasn't too dark, once you got used to it. She went inside. There were a lot of cases and packing boxes and barrels, and one over in the corner as Mrs. Holden had said, a cardboard box, but it was huge. Pamela went and tested it, trying to shift one corner. It was strange that Mrs. Holden had thought the two of them could hoist it to the shelves overhead. It was quite heavy; it must be full of tools.

From somewhere quite close, Pamela heard the sound of a car's tires on paving, heard a motor purr and die, a door slam. Then there were footsteps.

Someone came into the bricked passageway and paused there. Pamela, suddenly uneasy, moved away from the heavy box. In the next moment a figure darkened the open doorway. A man's voice said, "Mae? Are you in here? I'll get that box up where you want it."

Pamela wanted to say something but her tongue seemed stuck to the roof of her mouth. She made some sort of noise, though, and the man bent forward peering, and said, "Mae?" again, in a hoarse treble.

This must be Mr. Holden. There was no reason at all to be scared.

Pamela collected her wits, and began: "Mr. Holden, your wife asked me to come in here and...." All the while, he was walking forward with his head thrust out in that peering way, a shaky and uneven way of putting his feet down, as if he were treading the path of an old nightmare.

"You're not—"

"No, I said—"

The light went on over the inside of the door, blindingly bright.

Mrs. Holden stood there, fussing with the button on the little panel. "Well, there was a bulb here after all." She kept her eyes on her husband. He seemed caught there between them, facing Pamela, stopped now but still bent forward in that agonized, funny way. To Pamela he seemed absolutely green, sick with fright; his appearance made her heart jump. What was the matter with him?

Mrs. Holden said, "I guess that will be all, Pamela. You had better go home."

It was as if she had somehow put Pamela and Mr. Holden at fault, as if she had caught them doing something ... *dirty*. Pamela's face flushed. She felt inside as scared and shaky as Mr. Holden looked. What was the matter with these people?

In the kitchen at home, Mrs. Bartlett was worrying over the cost of the new draperies. When Pamela came in, her mother gave her a glance, then frowned. "What on earth happened to you?"

Pamela blinked the tears down. "Mr. Holden. He scared me to death. In their garage."

"What?"

"Oh, it wasn't anything really." Pamela went back to her bedroom to dry her eyes.

Five

It was half-past six.

In the Arthur kitchen, young Mrs. Arthur turned from the pile of dishes in the sink. She had to yell to make herself heard above the TV hubbub in the living room. "Bill! Bill! Where's your father?"

A mumble answered, "Oh, he's around somewhere."

On the TV screen, the hero had lost his gun and was starting a rockslide on the villains below. The noise was house-shaking.

"Turn that damned thing down and find your father!" Mrs. Arthur screamed.

"Oh, hell. What's with you and Dad? You're always ragging him."

"I am not. I want him to behave himself. Mr. Cooper is sore, and we're going to be made fools of, the old man playing gatekeeper. The other people up here won't like it."

"He might keep out a few tramps."

"He's sneaky and nosy. He's making an ass of himself, and there'll be complaints. Go find him right now."

"Oh, for Pete's sake," muttered Mr. Arthur, who liked to settle down after dinner with the paper and a can of beer.

Billy Arthur turned from the TV set and saw what his sister Nancy was doing, taking the clothes off her doll, and he grabbed the doll, tearing its hair, and now to the rumble of the rockslide was added the human and immediate screams of a little girl. Mrs. Arthur ran in and paddled Billy with her hands wet, leaving wet marks on his seat. In the middle of all the rumpus Mr. Arthur got up and left, taking his beer, and went outdoors and looked around. His father was not out there, and Mr. Arthur thought briefly of walking down to the gatehouse, and then decided against it. Cooper was probably gone by now, and the old man could be gateman undisturbed; actually to Arthur it seemed the most harmless kind of fun for an old man and he couldn't understand his wife's and Cooper's attitude.

Musing in the dusk, Mr. Arthur decided that it might be a good idea if he pointed out to his dad that the *night* gateman was the important one. Burglars and such. Probably in the dark nobody would notice him there anyway. He'd have to slip in the house without any noise, of course, when he decided his tour of duty was over. Have to make that plain.

Mr. Arthur finished the beer and poised the can to toss it, then remembered where he was, the new house and the new neighborhood, a bunch of snobs if he ever saw one; he took the can inside and put it into the plastic bin.

It was half-past six, and Miss Silvester sat under the glow in her dining nook, a cup of tea on the maple table, her hands clenched on the polished surface. Outside the day was dying and it would soon be dark, and Ross would come. It was the maddest madness of all, sitting here with her heart pounding over a man almost twenty years younger than she was ... (*twenty-one*, the trickling whisper echoed) ... and all tied in a knot because she couldn't figure out how to give him the money.

Couldn't meet him at the door with it. That would seem awful. It would seem as if she were paying him for coining in, for ... For a moment, before the blank eyes of her mind, she glimpsed exactly what it would seem she was paying him for, and the pounding died and there was a cold stony stillness, like the beginning of a retch; and then she forced herself to drink some of the tea, and was warm again.

It would have to be done lightly, lovingly, even if possible teasingly, and she knew her own heavy-handed ineptness when it came to anything like that. She had grown up in an austere, outspoken home where feelings hadn't been spared, where subtleties in regard to others were disdained.

She couldn't ... she didn't dare ... be clumsy and blunt with Ross.

She tried to think of words, gay and charming words. She knew that there were people in the world who could treat money like a toy, could no doubt make anyone else feel he was doing them a favor by taking it, but she sensed that such people had not lived a life of slow saving, of adding to a bank account bit by bit like an ant adding to its store of provisions.

There was a soft rap at the door and she started. But it was only the crippled boy from across the street, the Dronk boy. He had a paper bag filled to the top with oranges. He held them out to her. "We thought ... in case you like orange juice for breakfast—"

She was touched. He was a handsome boy, she thought, outside of his handicap. "Oh, thank you. Will you come in?"

"Thanks, I guess not."

He was already retreating, trying to walk in such a way, she saw, that the crippled foot would come down straight and firm. "I love orange juice for breakfast," she called after him, not knowing what else to say. He looked back at her and smiled. The thought occurred to her, his father or the housekeeper might have sent him, wanting to be neighborly.

She put the oranges in the refrigerator bin. She was frowning. It hadn't occurred to her before this that the change of surroundings, leaving the impersonal apartment and living in a house involved neighbors, callers, people who expected to visit and be visited, or even casual drop-ins who merely wanted to gossip a bit over a cup of tea. The thought of someone barging in here while she had Ross in the house left her dry-mouthed with fright. What would we do?

The thought of throwing on clothes while she summarily disposed of Ross in a closet brought a touch of shamed color to her cheeks. It made her think of some old ribald book, Rabelais or somebody, she had glanced into once by accident in a library. The people in that book were always being surprised in bed, and having to leap into chests or crannies, utterly vulgar—the thought that such antics were to be considered funny was even yet beyond her comprehension.

She hurried to the front of the house, dismayed now, expecting someone to be hurrying up the walk; but the street was empty.

If anybody comes ... ever ... she told herself, I'll just be very short and abrupt. After all, I work at home. That's a valid excuse. I can simply tell the caller that I have a set of books to get out. Maybe I might even put a small sign in the front window, Accountant and Tax Consultant. No, she corrected, that wouldn't look right in this neighborhood. I'll just have to tell them.

She stood chewing her lips. It was growing quite dark by now, and there were lights in the Dronk house. What a shame, she thought for the hundredth time, that that pink monstrosity has to sit there dominating the scenery. Mr. Cooper had hoped we might have a little park. I don't want them spying on me, she thought, and it would be easy, the house sits on the slope. They can look right down into my windows.

She yanked the cord that drew the cream-colored draperies shut across the big panes.

There was a cheerful rap at the back door, *tap te tap tap*, so utterly unlike what she had expected, that she stood rooted. She knew instantly that it was Ross, and his mood communicated itself to her through that carefree *tap te tap tap* as if she could see him grinning through the door. She had thought ... what had she thought? That he would come slinking and cringing, ashamed to be needing to borrow money? That he would be embarrassed and morose?

She went unsteadily through the house to the kitchen, again, and opened to let him in. The sight of him had the impact, as always, of an unexpected blow. Big and virile and young ... and she was aware that she had no right to expect him at her door, that it was she who should be grateful and cringing. She moved back before him, and he walked in, the light glinting in his hair, and he said, "My what big eyes we have! Did I scare you?"

"Oh, no." Beyond that, she was mute.

He came close and put his arms around her, sought her mouth with his. She let him kiss her passively at first, and then caught fire and clung.

"Well, that's better."

She lay against him, against the solid bulk and the heart-pound away inside, and tried to bring her breathing back to normal.

"Have you got it for me?"

His tone was casual, even offhand, and it was a moment before she realized that he was talking about the money.

"I should have told you, I guess," he went on, "that I need two hundred. This hundred tonight is for a debt I've got to pay right away. But there are a couple of other things—"

"I could give you a check."

"No. But if you get around to it—"

"I can have the cash for you tomorrow night."

"No, I don't need it that soon."

He grabbed her off her feet then, lifting her as if she weighed nothing, and strode off down the hall. She clung with her hot face pressed against the T-shirt; his flesh was hard and young under her digging fingers and the knitted fabric slid over the hardness like a loose skin. She knew that there were things she ought to be thinking about, this surprising cheerful casualness of his about the money, for one thing, so different from the way he had sounded over the phone, and his wanting the extra hundred but not intending to come back the very next night for it, and how she ought to talk sensibly to him about his finances and find out what was really happening—all of these things needed thinking about, but right now there wasn't time.

Mr. Holden got up off his bed. The room was dark. He went into the adjoining bathroom, switched on the light, opened the medicine cabinet, took out the bottle of pills. It wasn't time yet for another one, but this was one of the worst attacks he'd ever had.

He was practically choking to death, his throat raw, and his heart felt like a big laboring steam engine all ready to burst. When he had washed the pill down, he stood gripping the edge of the washbowl, wheezing, his mouth open like a fish's. His reflected image swam beyond the unwilling tears, a man trying to breathe through the throttling agonies of asthma.

And every time he thought of the young girl there in the dark garage, his own stumbling progress through those boxes, fumbling ... God, he might actually have touched her in another moment! ... and then the light, Mae at the door—every time he remembered all of this, the choking sensation tightened until it seemed his eyes must pop from his skull!

I ought to call a doctor, he thought weakly.

Doctors got curious though. Some of them seemed to have the idea lately that asthma wasn't a case of ragweed or dust, of being choked by something blown on the wind. Some of them wanted to know all about the family situations, your relationship with your wife, how you were doing on your job, who or what was getting under your skin and stuff like that. And when you mumbled around, trying to avoid the questions, they either looked wise and smiled or else pounced like a cat.

No. No doctor, then. The Tedral should do its work pretty soon.

He went back into the dark bedroom, stood in the silence listening. Mae must be in the living room, watching television; he could hear the faint echo of music and voices. She liked schmaltzy polkas and waltzes, and Westerns. He left the bedroom and crept down the hall, thinking to slip out the rear door and have a breath of air.

She turned from the television. She was on the couch, a lamp behind her outlining her head, making it bigger, making the jaw heavier in silhouette. She watched his progress toward the kitchen. "Are you going back to the garage?" she asked.

He stopped. He put up a hand as if to wring the congestion from his throat by force. "Mae. You've got it all wrong. There just wasn't anything to it."

She smiled. She smoothed the black silk skirt. She had pretty good legs for a woman her age; now she stretched out her ankles in a motion that was somehow feline.

"I can't understand," he complained, "what the child was doing in there anyway."

"Don't you?"

"I'd just driven up," he said in his desperate wheezing voice, "and hadn't any more than stepped from the car. Do you think I'd had time to entice her in there?"

She gave him a level ironic glance. "How long does it take?"

He stood there defeated, gasping. The iron woman on the couch across the room swam giant-size through his tears, a great goddess on whose lap his manhood must be laid. After a moment he went out through the lighted kitchen to the patio space between the house and the garage, where he sucked in the night air.

There were lights in the Dronk place across the street. The old-fashioned windows, glowing now, made it seem taller by night than by day, a regular tower of a house, a museum piece, and in his misery Mr. Holden was aware of a flash of anger. Why couldn't that crippled man and his crippled son have had the decency to move on, to let the place be wrecked and hauled off the way Cooper had wanted, leaving the remnants of the grove and space for a little park? Why did the thing have to remain, spoiling the view, an anachronism, a regular Charles Addams kind of old house?

Well, not that. Not slatternly and with cupolas full of bats. But bad enough. Mr. Holden choked with indignation.

He walked on, into the rear yard. Under the night sky there was the smell of new-turned earth where plantings had been made, and from below, the new houses being built, the odor of raw lumber.

If he stayed out long in the dark, she would be coming to look, thinking God knew what. Thinking he had a raped child under one of the bushes. He turned, still wheezing, to go back inside. He thought in that moment that he saw someone, some indistinct figure leave Miss Silvester's rear door and slip off down through the unfinished houses. He couldn't be sure. A plane was droning overhead in the dark, drowning any sound of steps. And there was no light above her door.

He paused, wondering if he ought to go and check. But no. He thought, I'm imagining things. That old maid! Mustn't make a fool of myself.

It must have been a stray dog, or something.

Nevertheless, he listened for an instant for sounds of alarm before he went back indoors, where Mae permitted him to sit on the opposite end of the couch and look at her choice of programs.

Kim carried the paper sack of oranges to the back door and knocked. He could see into the lighted kitchen, could see Pamela in the breakfast nook with a stack of books, doing her first day's homework. When she heard his knock, she looked up. In that moment Kim was aware of a deep pang. She was such a pretty girl, she'd have lots of guys after her before long, and he wouldn't stand a chance. Not the way he was, not cr— She was rising, now, coming to open the door.

"Oh, hi!"

"Thought you might like some oranges. They make your hair curly, they tell me."

"Come in. Dad and Mom are having a budget conference in the den. I'm lonesome."

He set the sack of oranges on the drainboard. "I guess you're busy."

"Just desperate for something to do. Wait. Let me get a sweater. I'm tired of putzing around in the house. Let's go for a walk!"

A walk wasn't Kim's idea of amusement; it was in sitting still that he felt almost equal to his contemporaries. But he saw the truth, that she thought so little of his limp that a walk in the night air seemed perfectly natural. He was abashed, grateful, at the same time.

She had on green capri pants and a pale blue shirt, a white woolly sweater thrown over her shoulder. Kim thought that she was the most beautiful thing he had ever seen. When they stepped outdoors, the light from the kitchen shone on her blowing hair; she brushed it back. "Where'll we go?"

"Around the block?" He was dreading the uneven sound of his steps on the paving.

"How about up above your place?" she said. "Up through the trees. Did you know I've been up there already?"

"Yes, I saw you," he admitted. "Day before yesterday."

"There's a little canyon, all bare and rocky, that leads up into the hills."

"I always called it Bobcat Creek," Kim said. "Not that there's ever much water there. Only when it rains a lot, then there's a kind of trickle. But I did see a bobcat."

"Oh, did you? But dreamy! What was he doing?"

"Running from me."

"Was he big?"

"Not very."

They crunched across the cultivated acre or so above Kim's house, breaking a path through the orange trees, and then on the night air was the old free smell of the open country, the bare hills, the stony heights, where the parched grasses of last year, feathered thin, lay in the ashy dust.

"The stars look so close," she breathed, touching Kim's arm.

"It's pretty dark," Kim said, wondering if he should take her back.

"Let's find a place to sit. And we can talk."

They talked for more than an hour, an enchanted hour in Kim's life, but when they reached Pamela's house again, her mother met them, angry and excited because Pam had left without telling her. She told Kim not to take her daughter out again.

Six

Two nights later, shortly after nine o'clock, Kim was in his room reading when he heard some sounds from downstairs, his father's voice and others, and something in the exchange, some muffled anger answered by his father's patience, drew him into the upper hall to see. In the entry below were Pamela's mother and father; Mrs. Bartlett had on a long black coat and her hair was wind-tossed; Mr. Bartlett wore a heavy sweater.

"We came here because just the other night your son took her up into the hills, some forsaken spot, and kept her until all hours. I spoke sharply to him about it." Mrs. Bartlett's voice had a different edge to it now, Kim noted; there was a shade of terror in it that shocked him. He went down to the landing and stood there.

His father turned to look at him. "Kim, do you know where Pamela Bartlett is?"

"No, I don't."

Mr. Bartlett came to the bottom of the stairs and put a hand on the newel post. Behind the heavy horn-rims his eyes sparkled with anger. "Did you talk to her after school?"

"On the bus, yes. We sat together."

"And when you got home?"

"I said good-bye to her on the corner."

"Didn't you make a date to meet later?"

"No, sir."

Mr. Bartlett's lips twitched, twitching the funny little mustache like a black brush under his nose. "You didn't ... uh ... signal with the window shade or by clicking your lights, or anything like that?"

"I'm sorry, sir, but I don't know what you mean."

"He thinks that you and Pamela might have had a signaling system of some sort," his father put in.

"We didn't." Kim stood on the landing as on a point of vantage and had no desire to come lower. He had the feeling that if he came down Mr. Bartlett was going to grab him, that already some kind of label had been pinned on him, a mark of guilt and shame. "I don't know where she is, honest," he said to Mrs. Bartlett.

She looked frightened and perplexed. "There isn't any logical place she could go. It's so isolated up here. So empty of people. In town it might have been the soda shop, or a girl friend's house—but here there's nothing but the ... the dark."

"Something drew her out of the house," Mr. Bartlett said angrily. "That's the mystery. When and why she went. We thought that she was in her room, doing her homework. I don't know if you understand how the house is laid out, but she could have gone by the hall to the rear door and we wouldn't have seen her. But what took her out? It's as my wife says ... there's no place up here for her to spend an idle moment."

"There's just that vacant wilderness back there ... where she went before, with your son," Mrs. Bartlett insisted.

"She and your son are the only teen-agers up here," said Mr. Bartlett with a close look at Kim.

Kim's father limped to the phone on its little table near the living-room door, stood there tentatively as if he might call someone. "Would the Arthurs have asked her to baby-sit with the children while they went out?"

"She'd have told us about it!" Mrs. Bartlett cried.

"We don't permit her to do baby-sitting anyway," Mr. Bartlett put in harshly. "Why should we? She doesn't need spending money."

"It was just an idea," Kim's father said, taking his hand off the phone.

"A much better idea—question your son," said Mr. Bartlett.

Kim's father looked up at him, still standing there on the stairs. He frowned. "Come down here, Kim."

Kim came, trying to walk evenly. He faced the Bartletts. He saw that Mrs. Bartlett had been crying, and the breath of fear touched him again the way it had when he'd first heard her voice tonight. But behind the glasses, Mr. Bartlett's gaze was savage. "Just tell me, youngster. Just tell me everything that happened since you left school today."

Kim tried to think of something to say. "It was ... just like any other day. I came home and fooled around. Did my homework, listened to a few records, replaced some tubes in my radio ..." His voice died because Mr. Bartlett wasn't really listening, or at least not listening to what he was saying. Trying to hear something in his tone, maybe; the sound of lying. A cold rage emanated from the man, as tangible as the breath off an iceberg.

The glasses winked as Bartlett bent his head. "Pammy's been awfully nice to you."

"Yes, she has."

"She's that kind of girl. She goes out of her way to be friendly and helpful. She's the sort who rescues birds with broken wings and lost dogs and stray cats, anything hurt or crippled."

Kim's eyes didn't waver. Behind him, his father made a harsh broken noise, a pained noise.

"And so ... because she's been decent to you, we're asking you now where she is. Tell us where you went tonight."

Kim's father said, with an obvious effort at supporting Kim, "I don't see why you insist that he knows where she is. Kimmy wasn't with her. He's told you so."

Mrs. Bartlett suddenly cupped her face with her hands and screamed, "She's gone and we can't find her! Oh, my God, we can't find her anywhere!" She rocked back against the banister and one of her heels turned and she almost fell. Mr. Bartlett grabbed her. She screamed again. "We've got to call the police!"

"Dorothy!" Mr. Bartlett's tone was whip-sharp. "We missed her less than forty minutes ago. We can't lose our heads now. We agreed when we started out, we'd ask everyone up here first, we'd be calm. There's some reason behind all this and it may be perfectly innocent and logical. From Pammy's point of view, that is." He propped Mrs. Bartlett against the edge of the stairs and turned to Kim's father. His face was hard and white and hating. "We want information, Mr. Dronk. Your son took our daughter out two nights ago, walked her off God knows where, kept her out in the dark for quite a while. When she got home her shoes were full of dirt and her sox ragged with stickers. They'd been up in the hills. Pammy thought it had been quite a lark. Now I think that your son had better admit—"

"I didn't see Pamela tonight," Kim said, looking Mr. Bartlett straight in the eyes.

"You deny that you know where she is now?"

"Yes, sir."

Bartlett stood looking at the phone, his jaw working; perhaps he was thinking of what Mrs. Bartlett had screamed about calling the police. Kim waited. He was beginning to be scared, now, really deep-down afraid, because Mr. Bartlett seemed so determined that he must know where Pamela was. There was a terrific pressure of anger and blame directed toward him from these two people. And besides this, there was the strangeness of Pamela's disappearance. Where could she be?

Kim's father spoke reasonably. "Just where have you looked for her, so far?"

It was hard for Bartlett to answer in an even tone. "We went up through your trees to the hillside. We thought of course she must be there again, with your son. I had the flashlight, and I flashed it about, and we called. There wasn't any answer. Then we went home and got the car and toured the streets where they're finishing the houses. There wasn't any sign of her. And so we came here."

Mrs. Bartlett had taken her hands from her eyes. Her jaw was shaking. "It's late," she whispered. "It's so terribly late."

Kim's father nodded. "Have you asked any of the other neighbors?"

"Since you won't help us, we'll have to," Bartlett said.

"May we go with you?"

"Why should you?" Bartlett had grabbed his wife and turned toward the door. "What's it to you?"

"We're your neighbors," said Kim's father.

Bartlett gave him a close-lidded look. "I think that's where the trouble lies," he said.

They went out, the door thudding, and there was a crackling moment of silence, and then Kim's father said, "Kim—"

Kim gave him an unbelieving stare, put a hand on the banister.

"No, I'm not doubting you," said his father, as if coming to the decision in that moment. "But where do you suppose the child could be?"

"I don't know. But I'm going for a jacket, and I'm going out to look."

His father stood silent as if thinking, and then said, "I'm going with you."

"You don't have to."

His father's voice took on a cautious tone. "It's this way, Kim. Hard to understand, perhaps. If there is really something wrong, if—" He wasn't looking right at him, Kim saw, but over his shoulder, as if the careful words must be summoned out of space. "—if she's been ... uh ... hurt, it would be better if you didn't find her alone."

Kim tried to figure out what his father meant, and all the while, it seemed that a cold current had drifted down the stairs to envelop him. "Hurt?" he asked.

"She's a very attractive little girl, and sometimes ..." His father stopped to cough, and then he didn't finish the sentence. "These people are all strangers. Wait for me, Kim."

The Bartletts went up to the front door of Miss Silvester's house. There were lights inside. The draperies were drawn. Mr. Bartlett put a thumb on the button by the door.

She opened the door and peeked out at them, tousle-haired, her eyes bright under sleepy lids. When she saw who it was, a kind of shock showed in her face. "Oh ... yes?"

"Miss Silvester, could we see you for a minute?"

She opened the door and stood back. She wore a pink robe. Even in the midst of her terrible fear about Pammy, Mrs. Bartlett noticed how unlike her usual self Miss Silvester seemed. She was ordinarily such a mousy, spinsterish kind of woman, only now there was something lushly disheveled, moist-lipped, and breasty about her. She'd been in bed, though it was early for it; she wore a thin pink gown under the pink robe. In one corner of the room a hi-fi was playing softly, an indication that being in bed had been temporary. She said, "What is it?" and brushed the pale hair off her face, and must have noticed Mrs. Bartlett's fixed, attentive stare. She tightened the neck of the robe.

Mr. Bartlett was looking at her in a superior kind of way, as if her mild befuddlement displeased him. "Our daughter isn't at home. She's stepped out without telling us—to see someone, to do something ... We've no idea who or what. Do you know where she is, Miss Silvester?"

Miss Silvester seemed to have trouble getting her wits together, to take it in. Her mind seemed on some other plane entirely. "You mean, that little schoolgirl? The pretty one?"

"She's the only teen-age girl up here," he said tautly.

"Yes. Yes, I've seen her, I mean I've noticed her." Miss Silvester seemed to be thinking around the problem, perhaps including it in some larger scheme of which they were unaware. "Not tonight, though. I have no idea where your daughter might be now."

"Do you remember seeing her after she got home from school?" Mrs. Bartlett put in, in her quivery voice.

"Home from school?" It was a blank echo.

"Yes. She gets here about three-forty-five or so. Sometimes almost as late as four." Mrs. Bartlett suddenly wanted to scream. The woman looked so ... so *immoral* ... in her pink, fluffy gown and robe, tousled as she was ... and so uncaring. Not even comprehending. "Don't you understand? Our little girl is missing!" Her voice rose into a scream and she had the satisfaction of seeing Miss Silvester snap out of her dreamy mood.

"Oh, surely not! Heavens ... not that," Miss Silvester muttered.

Now it was Mr. Bartlett who seemed suddenly unnerved. He stammered brokenly, "Miss Silvester, have you had anyone in here tonight?"

Miss Silvester forgot about the neck of her robe; her eyes seemed to bug at him. "What ... what did you say?"

"I mean ... company. Anyone who might have seen Pammy—" He made a shattered motion with one hand, then covered his eyes with it.

Miss Silvester licked her lips. "There hasn't been anyone. No one at all." And the cracked, scared tone told both the Bartletts she was lying.

Mrs. Bartlett pounced. "Who was it? Who's been here?"

Miss Silvester moved backward and they followed, as if to pin her on the wall, pin her with the point of her own lie. "Get out," Miss Silvester said nervously. "Get out of my house!"

"Tell us the truth or—"

The doorbell rang.

The Bartletts turned. Miss Silvester scampered past, threw open the door as if for a deliverer. But it was only Kim and his father, and as soon as they looked past her and saw the Bartletts, they nodded and began to withdraw. "Wait a minute!" Miss Silvester screeched. "Get these people out of here! I won't have them threa—trying to make me say what isn't true!" All the sleepy look had vanished, all the softness; she looked hagridden, scared to death. Mr. Dronk paused on the step.

"We're going," Bartlett said. He took his wife by the arm and marched her to the door, out past Kim and his dad. "We'll see the Holdens," he flung at Dronk from the dark sidewalk. "Don't bother to follow us."

Miss Silvester closed her door and leaned panting against it, shutting out the soft autumn night and its incomprehensible terrors.

The events of the past few hours tore through her thoughts like a fast-running reel of film.

"Whatever it is," she said to the room at large, "it has nothing to do with *him*." She stood taut and listening; the only sound was that of the music from the hi-fi. She ran to the machine, lifted the lid, clicked it off. Sudden silence filled the room. Still bent there, she whispered, "Besides, he must have gone long ago. An hour or more. He wouldn't have waited around. And he couldn't have.... Not after—" She clapped her hand over her mouth as if even the thought must be stifled.

Mrs. Holden's pouter-pigeon bosom strained the buttons of the blue quilted housecoat. She held a magazine, the room was brightly lit. She admitted the Bartletts at once, moving inward with an effect almost of eagerness, her eyes fixed on their haggard faces.

"Pammy's missing." Mrs. Bartlett no longer tried to control her crying. "She's gone and we can't find her. And it's getting late!"

"She's disappeared?" said Mrs. Holden. "At this hour?"

"Have you seen her? Have you noticed her today at all?" Mr. Bartlett asked harshly.

"I believe she went past about four o'clock this afternoon. It was my impression she must have come on the school bus." Behind Mrs. Holden's iron visage was no hint of the vigil, the spying, the whirl of conspiracies which had filled her mind, thoughts as black as a flock of crows.

"Is your husband home?" cried Mrs. Bartlett.

There was an odd, abrupt moment of silence during which Mrs. Holden's eyes grew murky. "Yes, he's here. Do you want me to ask if he's seen her?"

"Please!"

Mr. Bartlett's manner held a sudden touch of suspicion. "May I ask him?"

She gazed at him with regret, as if he had taken away some sort of anticipated pleasure. "Of course. Down the hall, the last door on your right. I believe he's reading in bed."

When Bartlett got halfway down the hall, he could hear the wheezy agonized breathing. He rapped on the door. The wheezing stopped as if choked off with fright. Then Bartlett came to the door, skinny and undersized in an old flannel robe.

"Have you seen my daughter?" Bartlett asked without preamble.

He thought that Holden was going to faint in his tracks, right there facing him, holding the door. A gray, shriveled look passed over the man and the wheezy breathing rose to a screech. "I ... I don't believe ... I don't know what you mean," he managed to stammer.

"My little girl is missing. Have you seen her tonight?"

"No. Not at all."

Bartlett had the strangest feeling, as if Holden were a cotton doll he could knock over with the flick of a finger. The arm holding the door swung waveringly upward. Holden seemed to be trying to reach his mouth. When his fingers touched his face, he dabbled at the perspiration on his upper lip. "I'm having a very bad attack. Asthma," he muttered.

"I can see that. Do you have any idea where Pammy might be?"

"No. No."

Bartlett swung around and went back to the living room. There was something smug and monstrous about the big woman in the blue housecoat, something satisfied, catlike. Bartlett didn't speak to her. He caught his wife's hand. "It's time we called the police."

"Shouldn't we ... the Arthurs?" Her face shook as she tried to quench back the tears.

"No. This is as far as we should go."

In the street, hurrying along the sidewalk on the way home, he told her how he felt.

"They're just not telling us the truth. None of them."

"I f-felt that. What does it mean?" In her fright, she stumbled, clung to him.

"I don't know. Let the police handle them."

Seven

The first to come was a sheriff's patrol car with a couple of uniformed officers. They parked in front of the Bartlett house after circling the block once. They listened to what the Bartletts had to say. One of them left them to knock on neighboring doors. The second man—he gave Mrs. Bartlett his name but her numbed senses didn't hang onto it for more than a moment—asked to see the girl's room.

Both officers seemed to be skimming the thing, getting certain routines out of the way, and to trembling Mrs. Bartlett their attitude was callous. She herself had entered a phase of nightmare. Somewhere inside, the core of her being seemed to be coiling and squeezing itself smaller and smaller, far down and away from the horror to come, while at the same time her senses stretched outward, agonizingly seeking the chop of fate. She stumbled down the hall, leading the officer to Pammy's room, his heavy step behind her like something she could never outrun. Like the thing, whatever it was, that came closer at each passing moment.

"Dear God," she whispered, "let Pammy be safe. Somewhere."

The lights were on as Pammy must have left them.

The officer looked around. He went to the dresser and examined all the knickknacks, the miniature perfumes and the toy dogs and the musical powder boxes Pammy had collected, and then he stepped to the closet and moved the sliding doors a little, and looked at Mrs. Bartlett. "Is anything missing?"

She couldn't even see him for the blur of tears. "I don't know."

"Will you look, please, ma'am?"

Mr. Bartlett was standing in the doorway. "I checked, officer, before we started out to look for her. I don't think that a thing is gone. She went out in what she had on."

"And what was that?"

"Slacks—"

"Capri pants," Mrs. Bartlett corrected desperately.

"Pants and a blouse and a pullover sweater. Flat-heeled shoes."

The officer nodded. He came away from the closet. He looked over Mr. and Mrs. Bartlett as if weighing them against some values of his own; how they were apt to wear during the next few hours, perhaps. "Has she ever done this before? Has she ever run away from home?"

"No, never," said Mr. Bartlett, as if the officer were stupid for asking.

"Sometimes kids get funny ideas," the Sheriff's man offered. He seemed to be trying to buck them up.

"Pammy never had a f— funny idea in her life," wept Mrs. Bartlett. "She's a very sensible child. Very consid— Very—" She broke down into sobbing.

"Now, ma'am," said the officer with a touch of sharpness, "crying won't help. We'll do everything we can, and I can assure you we'll find your girl, if she's to be found."

No comfort there. Mrs. Bartlett cried, "What do you mean?"

"We'll find her," the officer corrected, more firmly. He went back down the hall, outside to the car. In the silence, the Bartletts could hear the mutter of the police radio as he opened the car door.

"They'll get reinforcements," Mr. Bartlett said. He leaned above his wife, touching her shoulders. "Try to be calm. Try not to cry anymore."

She had a handkerchief in her hands; she began tearing it savagely into ribbons. "I'm sorry we ever moved up here. I'm sorry we chose this house, made Cooper get it for us, made those other people give it up. I wish I'd never seen this place. Nor that pink stucco.... *Hoodoo!*" She screamed the last word at him and then buried her face against his chest.

They stood in the dark, halfway up the rise behind the house, in the midst of the few remaining orange trees. "What do you think, Kim?"

"The Bartletts went up there. He had a light."

"Still, there's quite a bit of brush in the canyon," said his father. "And they may have mostly just called, expecting her to answer." He clicked on the big flashlight for a moment, then snapped it off. There was a sort of shadowy glow reflected from the sky, enough to make out the shapes of the trees and the aisle between them. "We ought to take a good look, go up in the canyon a way, make sure."

"All right."

His father hesitated. "There isn't anything that you … you didn't tell me, is there, Kim?"

"No, there's not."

"You're going to be asked that, Kim, until she is found."

"I guess so."

Kim started to walk up the slope. His father came more slowly. Kim tried not to imitate his father's shuffle, though to do so would have made it easier. He tried to pick up his feet and put them down in a straight, ordinary line, the way other people did, and it meant a wrench in the crippled leg all the way to the hip socket.

"Yes, Dad."

"Is she a moody sort of girl?"

"No, not a bit."

"She didn't drop any hint, any indication—"

"No. I knew her folks were sore about the other night. I didn't offer to see her after school, since then. I thought maybe they'd cool down. She thought they would. We didn't do anything wrong, but they didn't understand that. They thought because we'd been out in the dark—" He paused, breathless from the effort to walk normally up the steepening rise. "Well, anyway, what Mr. Bartlett said about Pammy … Pamela … is the truth. She's nice to everybody."

"I can't understand why she should disappear like this."

"I don't either," Kim said, beginning to walk again.

The canyon was a dark wedge in the face of the hills. Mr. Dronk put on the light. Scrubby sage and dwarf manzanita came to life under the beam, looking strangely stark against the dun-colored earth. Mr. Dronk flashed the light up the canyon, and in the diminishing perspective the twiggy branches seemed to creep and crowd. Kim shivered. In spite of his father's presence, he felt terribly alone. This was not at all the same place that he and Pamela had come two nights ago, when the stars had been big and soft overhead and the night wind full of desert smells.

"There's nothing like a path," said his father uneasily.

"No, you just have to walk in the bottom where the water's run."

His father hesitated, obviously half baffled by the rough footing ahead. Then he began to pick his way through the rutted wash. He kept the light on. He turned it under each bit of wild shrubbery as he came to it, no matter how small. Then Kim said behind him, "She's not here, Dad."

His father stopped and half turned. "How do you know?"

"Well, I just know."

His father turned the light on him. "No, Kim. How *do* you know?"

Kim put up a hand, sheltering his eyes from the strong beam. "It's just a feeling. But look. If you want evidence ... the bottom of the wash. The sand hasn't any tracks in it. We didn't come up this far two nights ago. And nobody's been here since, either."

Mr. Dronk swung the light and examined the bed of the narrow track where winter's brief rains had run. There were a few light marks, those of birds or of desert mice perhaps, but nothing like a human footprint. "You're right. But suppose ... suppose she didn't walk down here. Suppose she walked higher. Up there." He turned the light upon the sandy rise and flicked it from side to side. "She's a young, agile girl."

"She isn't here," Kim said stubbornly. "We're just wasting our time."

"Didn't you mention something, she'd been up here before, alone?"

"Daytime," Kim answered.

His father's voice took on a hoarse, patient note. "Kim, is there really nothing, nothing at all that you know—"

"I've told you. If you don't believe me, who's going to?"

"I wish you hadn't brought her up here, at night, like that."

"So do I."

"Where do you think she is, Kim?"

At least, Kim thought, his father had quit calling him by the little-boy nickname, Kimmy. "I don't know."

"Now you tell me she isn't moody, but didn't she have a mood to come up here in the dark?"

"It was just walking, just somewhere to walk while we talked."

"Well, what did you talk about?"

"We ..." Kim hurdled the brief, aching moment of reluctance. "We talked about what we hope to do ... someday. She wants to be a nurse or a science teacher."

"And what did you tell her you wanted to be, Kim?" said his father.

Kim couldn't see his father's face behind the dazzle of the light. "I just said I'd like ... that I wanted my foot operated on. That I wanted to be like other people."

The wind stirred in the canyon, stirred the night-smell of empty places and of dust.

After a moment his father said, "I guess we'd better go back."

When they reached the house they saw the Sheriff's cruiser across the street. One of the Sheriff's men was at the door of the Arthur house.

Young Mr. Arthur came to the door in his socks, with a can of beer in his hand, whiskery, kind of tired. Behind him the room held the glow from the TV set. Mrs. Arthur was looking toward the door from the couch. The Sheriff's deputy said, "We're looking for Pamela Bartlett. Do you know her?"

Mr. Arthur put the can of beer on a table by the door. "Isn't she that teen-age kid, a couple of houses down? Sure, we've seen her." He squinted against the porch light. "What's wrong?"

"We're just inquiring," said the officer. "Have you seen her this evening?"

The husband looked at his wife. "Did you see her?"

"I'm trying to think."

The TV set flashed a commercial, the sound jumped, and there was the image of an upset stomach full of what looked like lightning bugs on a rampage. Mrs. Arthur jumped off the couch and switched off the machine, came to the door and stood just behind her husband. "What's happened?"

"We'd like to know if anyone here has seen Pamela since she got home from school tonight," said the officer, no change in his voice or expression.

"You mean she's *missing?*"

The officer glanced past them. "Do you have anyone else living here? Uh ... children she might have talked to today?"

"Our kids aren't much more than babies," said Mrs. Arthur. "They've both been indoors since about five this afternoon, getting bathed and fed and put to bed. I don't think they'd know anything that would help. And as for—" She stopped short and glanced at her husband.

After an unwilling moment Mr. Arthur took it up. "My father lives with us, but he's just an old fellow."

"And where is he?"

"Uh ... lying down, I guess. Dell, go look in his room. Tell him the officer wants to ask some questions."

She had stepped back a little, putting a definite space between them. She brushed at a strand of hair that had clung to her cheek from lying on it on the couch. "You go tell him."

Mr. Arthur hesitated. He seemed disconcerted, at a loss; he appealed to the Sheriff's man. "He might be taking a nap, he might be asleep right now. Sometimes he does take a nap after dinner." He looked at the impassive officer, then half turned, then stopped again. "If he isn't in his room he might be outside. Sometimes he goes for a little stroll ... you know ... just to get out of the house."

"Maybe you'd better see," said the officer.

"Sure. I'll be right back."

Mr. Arthur went down the hall to the door of his father's room and put his ear to the panel. He heard a noise from inside, lifted his head with an air of relief, rapped lightly. "Dad."

There was a rough cough, or grunt, in answer. Frowning, Mr. Arthur opened the door. His father was seated on the edge of the bed, facing the door. The bedside lamp was lit. His father's posture was hunched; he seemed to be bent there examining his clenched hands. Mr. Arthur stepped close, then made a muffled exclamation of surprise and alarm. Across the deep-veined flesh of the right hand was a long bleeding scratch, or shallow cut. When his father lifted his face, Arthur saw the bruised swelling below one eye. "Hey, what happened?" He sat down beside the old man. He reached as if to touch the injured hand and the other snatched it away. "Wait a minute. How in hell did you get that?"

The father's eyes squeezed shut tightly and two glittering tears crept out upon the furrowed cheeks.

His son licked his lips; his expression was one of astonished dismay. "Where've you been? Outside? Look, there's a cop at the door right now. He wants to ask some questions about the Bartlett girl. You know, that little teen-ager. He hasn't admitted it, but she must be missing."

The old man twitched his head around, turning to face the lamp. With the light on his profile other marks showed up, a swelling on the bridge of his nose, a puffiness on the lips.

"Hey, somebody really swatted you!" cried the son.

The old chin rose stiffly, the dewlaps beneath almost transparent against the light, the throat working.

His son stood up suddenly. "My God, have you really got us into something? It doesn't seem possible.... And yet Dell said you were going to." He waited, color flooding his face, his fists clenched.

His father threw him a single look.

"Why won't you tell me what happened?"

In reply, tears welled again in the pale old eyes.

His son looked over the shabby coat and pants by the light of the lamp. "You've fallen or crawled somewhere. Mud on your knees. Grass or ivy stains. Wet spots. By God ..." Arthur lunged around as if expecting the cop to be at the door, looking in. He swung back to the old man. "Where's your cane?"

The pale lips moved, but no words came.

His son looked around for the big knobby stick, but it was not to be seen. "What've you been up to? Have you done anything to that kid? My God, would you do something awful like that?" He stared fixedly into his father's face, and then as if in rage he leaned forward and tried to yank the old man up, get him on his feet, but it was like trying to get a sack of bones erect. The old man seemed to rattle inside himself, a skeleton in skin and clothes. "You goddamned old fool!" Arthur flung him savagely back upon the bed.

He stood there then, listening, his fists working and his face full of fear.

The old man got himself sitting up again, got his feet planted on the rug. There was a look of shock, of pallor, a shattered expression, uncomprehending and dazed.

The younger man seemed to pull himself together by an act of will. He sat down again on the bed, not so close to the old man, not making any effort to touch him. "Now, we're going to use some sense in this thing. We're going to use our noodles. No matter where you went nor what happened, you're going to keep your goddamned mouth shut. Do you hear me?"

The old man bent his gray head.

"Where in the hell's your hat?"

The old man pointed to the floor at the foot of the bed.

The hat had been stepped on; it was damp and dirty. Arthur beat it fiercely against his pants-leg to remove the bits of dirt. Then he took it to the dresser and used the old man's clothes brush on it. Then he threw it into the top shelf of the closet.

He sat down again. He was breathing heavily. He stabbed a frantic hand through his hair. "Oh, God. To think, here we were, all set with a new home, a really nice place, a new neighborhood where we might have made some friends, all those cranks who were sore at you left behind. We thought." He drew his mouth into a grimace of mockery.

The old man tucked his clenched hands between his knees and rocked forward as if in pain.

"I'm glad you didn't tell me anything. I don't want to know. What I don't know won't—" The old man interrupted; he had begun to cry with a sucking noise through the phlegm in his throat. "Well, then, cry, goddamn you! Cry your goddamned eyes out. Cry till you're blind! I've got to go and tell a lie to the cop."

But a few minutes later, at the door, young Mr. Arthur seemed calm enough. He looked at the officer and smiled faintly and said, "My old man's asleep, lying down, he hasn't been out. He hasn't seen anything of the little girl."

The officer nodded and turned and walked away into the dark.

Dell was staring at her husband; he couldn't meet her eyes. Dell knew. She was practically psychic, that way. She went down the hall like a whirlwind.

Eight

The younger of the two deputies was named Rossi; he was twenty-eight, had been married two years and had one child, and represented—with his husky physique and several years of college and excellent military record—exactly what the Sheriff's office was looking for in recruits. He stood by the patrol car and looked in at the older man, who was using the radio phone. When Sorensen turned to get out, Rossi said, "Well, what do you think?"

Sorensen stepped out and hitched up his uniform pants over the beginnings of a belly, touched the gun in its heavy holster, frowned. "Hunnnh. Hard to say." The front door of the Bartlett house was open just in front of him, and light streamed out to illumine this part of the street. "In ninety-nine cases out of a hundred it's a runaway. The kid's had a fight with the parents, or there's a boy friend they don't like, or the allowance's been cut, or something like that. The kid skips out. But in that one case out of a hundred ..." He drew a deep breath.

"How would a girl clear out of a place like this?" Rossi asked. "It's not on a bus line. If she'd had a car ... No, she's too young to drive, anyway."

"If the car was gone they'd have told us."

"All those unfinished houses—"

Sorensen nodded. "Guess we'd better take a look."

Within five minutes they were joined by two more officers in a second patrol car. The four men picked different directions and took off on foot, carrying powerful flashlights.

Rossi, carrying his light, crossed the street to the big pink stucco. He had roused the housekeeper a few minutes before, learned that Kim and his father were out.

Now, rounding the house by way of the narrow cement walk leading to the rear, he met them unexpectedly face to face. In the brief moment of sizing them up as they came forward, slowing and momentarily dazzled, Rossi was aware of a sharp touch of distaste. They were both crippled. The older man walked with a distorted side-to-side swing; the boy seemed to make an effort to minimize it, though a trace remained, enough to make his movement a sort of echo of the other's. Rossi was an intelligent and educated man and he had an excellent grasp of the impartiality expected of a police officer. He quickly repressed the feeling of hostility, or of prejudice, or whatever it was, almost before it had time to form. "Mr. Dronk?"

"Yes. And this is my son, Kimmy. You're from the Sheriff's office?"

"Right."

"And you haven't yet found—"

"No, sir."

Dronk had come to a full stop in the midst of the light, Kim right behind him. From force of habit, Rossi took a couple of steps to the side so that the light fully shone on Kim as well. Mr. Dronk glanced back at his son and frowned. "We went up through the trees to the hills. There's a canyon, wild country. We didn't find any footprints or any other sign she might have gone there."

"What made you think she might have gone that way?" Rossi asked.

Dronk sheltered his eyes. "Look, can't we step around to the porch light? This isn't very comfortable."

Rossi obligingly turned the flashlight so it illuminated the path back to the front of the house. The housekeeper had put on the porch light during her talk with Rossi, and it still burned. Dronk went up the steps with his heavy, swinging walk and Kim and Rossi followed. "Do you want to come in, officer?"

Rossi shook his head. "What gave you the idea she might have wandered up to the hills?" he asked again.

"She did that one day, one afternoon ... My son saw her go past our house. The Bartletts were new here and she was just exploring, curious, the way a youngster would be. Then ... two nights ago"—Dronk fished out a pipe, not to light it; he just fumbled with it while Rossi watched him—"two nights ago she and Kimmy went for a stroll, a perfectly innocent kind of thing, and they went up that way and talked—"

"This was after dark?" Rossi put in.

"Yes. It was after dinner. You see, Pamela and Kimmy go to school together. There were things, I guess that had happened at school, that they wanted to talk over—"

Rossi was listening closely. He was keenly aware of Dronk's worry and discomfort, of the apologetic way Dronk was talking; he knew suddenly that there was more to this than what Dronk was telling him.

Dronk said, "Though this was a perfectly innocent excursion, just a walk after dark, the Bartletts made a fuss over it. They thought that Pamela should have told them she was going. Asked permission, maybe."

"In other words," Rossi said slowly, "from their point of view, she disappeared just two nights ago, the way she has now."

"Well … no. Kimmy was with her. If anyone had come asking, if there had been any kind of inquiry, I'd have noticed at once that Kimmy was gone too and I'd have suggested that they must be together."

"Did they come and inquire?"

"No. Kim—"

Kim said, "When we got to her house, her mother was having a fit. Mr. Bartlett was mad, too. I guess Pamela and I just didn't think, we hadn't let them know and that was the wrong thing to do."

"How long had you been gone, all told?"

Kim said, "I guess … about an hour. Maybe a little more."

Rossi said slowly, "Well, that's about the same length of time she's been missing now, I believe." Rossi thought to himself that he understood Dronk's discomfort and apologetic manner. Dronk had hated to imply that the Bartletts were excitable, overly protective parents to their daughter. "Perhaps I'll just have a look through those trees," he offered, moving to the steps.

"We'll leave the porch light on," Dronk said. "It may help a little."

"Yes, it might. Thanks."

Rossi went up through the cultivated ground, flashed the light around under the orange trees. He came to the edge of the hilly rise, where the cultivation ended, where the dried wild grasses and manzanita took over. He turned the light up the flanks of the hills. "Hell," he thought, "this is wild country. No one would go up here at night. Not a young girl, alone, anyway."

He returned by way of the Dronk house to the street below.

Mr. Bartlett came out upon his porch and when he saw Rossi he walked quickly out to the Sheriff's cruiser. "What's happened?"

"Nothing, sir."

"Where is the other man? Why don't you have more officers? Why aren't there at least a dozen looking for my daughter?"

Rossi said patiently, "Mr. Bartlett, is it true that your daughter did just about this same thing, walked out at night without telling you, just a couple of nights ago?"

"That Dronk boy coaxed her out. But she came home again." Bartlett suddenly caught what Rossi was getting at; he made an angry sound. "Now wait a minute. We lectured Pammy, we made her promise she wouldn't do it again. And she wouldn't have. Not unless that Dronk boy came sneaking with some plausible lie!"

Rossi wondered if Bartlett understood how close he was coming to making an open accusation. "But you didn't hear or see the Dronk boy tonight?"

"No. But we didn't see or hear him that other time, either. She just left with him." Bartlett was quite angry; he was staring at the house across the street, where behind the screen of shrubs and trees the light shone in the high porch.

"That thing should have been torn down," he added vindictively.

Rossi's partner came up from the other direction. He clicked off his light as he came close. "I found a half-dozen or so houses down this block, look ready to be moved into. But they're all locked up tight."

"Pammy wouldn't go into a vacant house!" Bartlett said in scorn.

His wife came to the door. She had on the black coat again; this time she'd tied a scarf over her head. "I can't just sit and wait," she called to her husband in an exhausted, scratchy voice. "Where did you put the flashlight?"

Sorensen said quietly to Bartlett, "It might be best if you just kept her quietly at home."

Bartlett turned and went to the house. He walked hunched, his hands jammed into his pockets.

"Any luck at all?" Sorensen asked Rossi. "Any hunches?"

"I found out one thing. She slipped out of the house just two nights ago, went up to the hills with the kid across the street, Dronk's crippled son. The Bartletts were steamed up over it. Now, they didn't mention this at all when we first talked to them, and you'd think they would."

"Ah, they're all alike," Sorensen said. "It can't ever be what it was before, this time it's got to be serious, something like kidnaping with all the trimmings." Nevertheless, by the light reflected from the Bartlett house, he looked uneasy.

"Well, we'd better go see what they've found in those stacks of lumber and supplies," Rossi suggested.

"Yeah, let's go. Maybe they'd like some help."

The smells of raw graded earth, cut wood, asphalt and tar, and others undefined greeted them as they walked down the paved grade to the lower levels. The row of unfinished framing stood etched against the dim sky; it made Rossi think of a game he'd played as a kid, with matchsticks. They parted at the third corner, having seen neither of the other officers. Rossi crossed from the paving to an unfinished porch and shone his light in upon the planks of a sub-floor. The roof was up on this one, making it darker inside, and the windows were in, shining glassily under the torch, though the walls still lacked siding. Rossi crossed the sub-flooring. There was an echo from beneath, and he wondered about the amount of space down there. Have to be searched, if they didn't find her elsewhere; but the search had better be done by daylight.

At the other side of the house, his light shone out upon the yard, picked out stacks of siding and shingles. The earth had been heavily trampled, ground into littered dust, and here and there were heaps of broken cement and cut ends of wood. Rossi crossed the yard. He was beginning to wonder how they were going to keep track of the areas which had been searched. All of this partially finished stuff looked alike.

He examined seven or eight of the framed places, and then entered a block where there were only foundations. He could see the gatehouse across lots and below—though not very distinctly—by means of the ornamental gaslight on its post just inside the gate. He stopped in his search, looking at the little building which sat alone, wondering if anyone else had had a look inside.

He went on, crossing several yards and using his flashlight, but every now and then he lifted his eyes to the flickering glow beside the entry gate. Finally, some hunch driving him, he went out to the paving and walked down. The place looked smaller than ever when he got closer, and he wondered what it had been built for. Vines had been trained to grow over its shingles, there were a couple of window boxes already trailing geraniums, and he realized that it had been here longer than any of the houses. It must be meant as some permanent part of the landscape, in contrast to the contractor's obviously portable office and sheds right across the street. Rossi went up the short but meandering walk, stood on the cobblestone step and shone his light in through the small pane in the door.

There seemed nothing on the floor but a tumble of clothing of some sort; and then the light picked out the spread and shining sheaf of hair, the tucked-up feet and one arm dropped like a broken doll's.

"Oh, my God," Rossi said without knowing he said it. He yanked on the door so hard the knob almost came off in his hand.

He knelt by her, touched the arm gently. He felt for a pulse, though he knew it was useless; she was already much too cold to be alive. The brilliant light of the flash, propped so that it shone above her and reflected off the wall, seemed to shut him in with her in the core of a nightmare dazzle. The little house seemed to ring with the sound of his own breathing.

Rossi was careful with the door in going out, belatedly thinking of fingerprints. He found Sorensen a block away by means of the winking flashlight. Sorensen listened calmly to what Rossi had to say. He glanced at his watch, noting the time. "You'd better go back and wait there. I'll call in." He turned the beam of his light skyward, clicked it on and off for the space of half a minute. "Keep an eye out for Randy and Mason. Maybe they'll see that and come along."

Rossi went back to the gatehouse. He stood on the curb and sized up the surroundings. There were no houses very close. All the area around the little gatehouse had been planted to ivy and shrubs, and behind it along the fence a few of the original orange trees remained. The nearest buildings were the office and a couple of supply sheds across the street on the opposite side of the gate, all in deep shadow now. The gaslight didn't show much, the flame wavered and flickered. There was no mantle in the lantern, just the tip of gas fire. It gave the whole scene a look of darksome unreality. Rossi shivered. What was in there was real enough, though. It seemed to Rossi he could still feel the unnatural coolness, the papery stiffness, of the girl's skin.

He walked around, using the flashlight on the ground. The ivy was undisturbed on either side of the walk. There was no sign of a struggle.

Up the street a short distance in a place where a couple of remaining orange trees made a deep shadow, a car had stood. Rossi found some fresh oil spots on the paving, the smudged and dusty marks of old ones. He made a mental note to call them to Homicide's attention. He searched under the trees with the light but there were no footprints in the fresh earth. He looked for any other traces about the place where the car had stood, thinking perhaps of blood, but there was nothing. The paving was almost new and the oil spots, both fresh and faded, showed up quite plainly. Anything like a bloodstain would have been perfectly obvious.

Rossi decided that the car which had dropped the oil had stood here more than once, that it probably belonged to the contractor or one of his subordinates.

He flicked the light across the street, where the foundations sat in the midst of settled dust, plumbing connections sticking up from the fresh cement in a pattern without rhyme or reason. It occurred to Rossi that the place must be pretty busy in the daytime, with all the work going on. Tomorrow the Homicide men were going to have to talk to everyone up here—carpenters, painters, electricians, bricklayers, roofers, plumbers—and try to find out if anyone had hung around after hours. A hell of a job.

Tonight they'd concentrate on the people living here, the Bartletts' neighbors.

The man in charge of the investigation was a lieutenant of detectives named Ferguson. By midnight he had certain facts lined up.

Pamela Bartlett had suffered at least three blows on her head from a heavy, blunt, rounded weapon.

She had been manually strangled.

Her clothes had been disarranged but there was as yet no definite evidence that she had been sexually attacked. (This lack of such evidence would not prevent the newspapers from calling it a sex crime.)

There was dirt and what looked like gravel scratches on one side of her face, leading to the presumption that the original attack had been made outdoors, that she had fallen and struggled briefly on open ground.

Her shoes were missing.

In one hand had been clutched a metal button of the type commonly used on men's denim work clothes, and an attached shred of material. This was by far the most significant item found, and was completely suppressed in any conversations with the press.

By midnight also, the gatehouse and its environs were illuminated by portable floodlights, roped off, guarded by uniformed cops, among them Rossi. Cars were parked up and down all the adjoining streets. There were Coroner's and D.A.'s men there, as well as Sheriff's deputies and reporters. Cooper had been called from his home, and was being interviewed in his office.

Lights burned in all the occupied homes on Palomino Lane.

No one could be deaf to the turmoil going on down by the gatehouse.

Nine

Miss Silvester went into her bedroom and hastily stripped off the pale pink robe and the pink chiffon nightie. They were still so new that they smelled of the store rather than of her body. She hung them in the closet, at the end out of sight. Then from the dresser she took fresh pants and white cotton bra, a white slip, and put them on quickly. From the closet rack she chose a brown cotton dress she'd worn for two summers; it was rather faded. She slipped on hose and brown sensible-type shoes. They would be coming back and she would be ready for them.

Something was happening down there by the gate, with all those lights and motors racing and the dim echo of men calling to each other. It was possible that something very bad had happened. She turned resolutely from that line of conjecture to her own problems.

The Bartletts had been dreadful. Threatening, really. And even in the eyes of that officer—Sorensen?—she'd read a sharp curiosity and the beginnings of disapproval—just because she was wearing that robe and gown. What did they think she was? Some crone of eighty?

She stood before the dresser mirror to brush and pin her hair. It was a time to take stock, look around; and in the mirror she saw the ash tray on the bedside stand, full of cigarette butts and a crushed empty pack, as Ross had left them. As soon as her hair was fixed in its usual smooth style, she went through the house, gathering all the evidence of his having been there. She dumped it all down the garbage disposal, washed it away with a grinding of metal teeth. She mopped out the ash trays with a damp paper towel and disposed of it.

There was one more thing, though it was securely tucked away in the closet. That morning she had gone shopping, she had bought Ross a silk robe, heavy navy silk piped in red, luxurious and yet masculine; and it hung in the closet along with her own clothes.

"I'll tell them it was my father's ... if they find it," she said to herself, looking around the kitchen where she and Ross had cooked and into the dining nook where they'd eaten.

Why should it be their business, anyway? she thought.

But it would be.

She wondered if there was any way she could get hold of Ross. He had never told her where he lived, nor whether he lived with his family or in some rented place alone. On a feverish hunch, she took the phone book from its drawer in the kitchen cabinet and looked for his name; but it wasn't listed locally. The best she could do, she decided, would be to try to get him at work early in the morning.

And meanwhile, sit tight.

He had already been gone quite a while, and she'd even had time to doze off, when the Bartletts had barged in demanding to know if she had seen their daughter. So of course, no matter what the police had found, there was no connection between his visit and anything that had happened, and she would just keep still.

Even though, dozing, she'd heard that noise from outside—or thought she'd heard it—it was still not her business to speak up.

Mrs. Forrest Holden went down the hall to her husband's door and rapped, then opened it. He lay in there on the bed, propped up with pillows. He rolled his head to look at her. His eyes had a blind, bulging, half-pleading look that made her want to laugh. "Forrest, I think you had better go and see what's going on."

"What do you mean?"

"Why, you must have heard it even in here, all that rumpus they're making down by the gate. I can see the lights from the kitchen step. There must be cars by the score. And men yelling."

"Mae, I feel terrible. I don't know when"—he stopped, choking and wheezing—"don't know when I've had an attack as bad as this."

She put on a puzzled expression. "What could have brought it on? What were you doing when I was shopping tonight? Let's see, I must have been gone at least an hour. Did you overexert? Did you go out in the night air?"

"No, no, I just read the paper and waited for you to get back."

"You didn't eat much dinner, afterward," she recalled, stroking her chin with a forefinger. Her figure in the blue quilted robe filled the doorway. His eyes wavered and dropped before her thoughtful stare. "Night air is bad for you. The doctors said so."

"I wasn't out in it. All I did was to read the paper and wait for you to come home with the stuff for dinner." He seemed to be begging her to believe it.

"Well, even though you aren't feeling too good, I think you should go out long enough to see what the police are doing."

He straightened on the pillows, pulling the gray robe taut over his skinny knees. "If I go down there they'll ... notice me."

"Oh, I don't think so," she answered, pretending not to understand what distressed him. "Everybody's got a certain amount of curiosity. We can't be expected to just sit here, and not wonder. Not with all that racket."

"Mae—"

"Pretending we *don't* notice it might seem stranger yet," she added, now giving him a significant glance, as if they shared some unmentionable secret.

He sat up quickly and swung his legs over, sat there hunched and shaking. Acting the part of the helpful wife, she brought him his pants and shoes, laid his coat at the foot of the bed. "You'd better wear a scarf." She took one of red plaid out of the dresser.

"Not that. It's so conspicuous."

"It's warm," she insisted. "Do you think they won't pay any attention to you if you wear the black scarf? Don't be silly."

He began to dress slowly. "What do you suppose they've found?"

"Must be the little Bartlett girl," she said, bending to straighten a fold of bedding, not looking at him, the bent posture indefinably sly and watchful.

"If she was out at night, if something's happened," he said, "it could be anything. A hit-and-run accident. Or even a heart attack. Even young people have them. It could look suspicious and yet not be—"

"Well, you'd better find out. I don't like not knowing."

He put on coat and scarf, got his hat, plodded down the hall to the front room. He paused at the door. "Maybe they don't want outsiders down there right now."

"Maybe they don't and if so they can tell you," she answered matter-of-factly. "Just tell them you heard the racket, and ask what they're doing."

He went out and walked east to the corner, then down the slight grade where the houses were in the process of finishing. He saw the lights and heard the cars. He knew that he was doing something he shouldn't, that Mae had pushed him into danger. Every nerve in his body screamed to return to the safety of the house.

Pretty soon, beside one of the parked cars, he met a couple of men who were just standing there talking. They broke off at his approach, and the nearest said, "Hey, there. Where'd you come from?"

Mr. Holden choked back a desire to cough. "We live on Palomino Lane. My name's Holden."

"You mean you're one of the neighbors?" By means of the reflected glow, they exchanged a glance. "What's the name again?"

There was something obviously unofficial about this pair, and even to Holden's inexperienced eyes they weren't detectives or anything like that, and yet he felt too unsure of himself to refuse to answer. "Holden. Forrest Holden. I live with my wife—"

"How long since you moved in?"

"You know this kid, this Bartlett girl?"

"She lived next door, maybe?"

"When did you see her last?"

They were closing in on him, shooting questions as they came. Holden backed against the car, tried to edge round the headlights to the street, but the more agile of the two cut him off.

"What was the name again?"

"Forrest Holden."

"You live next door to the Bartletts?"

"No, not exactly. You see the street curves a little, and there're two other houses that—"

"How well did you know the kid? Has she been in your house?"

"I don't know. My wife might—"

"What kind of a kid was she? Friendly? Fresh? How about the phone? She ever tie up the party line?"

"Who was her boy friend?"

"Hey, how about other teen-agers up here?"

Mr. Holden's throat congealed; he breathed through a narrow, whistling gap; he had the sensation of hands gripping him and he pulled at the scarf.

"You having trouble, bud?" asked one of the men in a curiously easy manner. "Trouble breathing, maybe?"

"She was choked to death, you know," the other added.

"Oh, God," said Mr. Holden.

"You came down to see the body?"

"Oh no, no...." The nearest had a hand on the hood of the car, was leaning into Mr. Holden's face. Mr. Holden wanted to lift a hand, put it in the middle of the gray-coated chest, and push. But of course he couldn't. "I had no idea. My wife was curious. We couldn't help noticing—"

"You mean, you didn't even know your neighbor's teen-age daughter had been murdered?" cried the leaner, closer yet.

"Terrible—"

"What'd you come down here for, anyway?"

"You wanted to see the body?"

It was an echo, beating its way round inside his head. "No. No."

"She's not pretty ... anymore," said the furthest. His hat brim threw a shadow into his face, through which his eyes gleamed, to Holden exactly like a tiger's. "You know what choking does to them?"

"Yes. I mean, no. It's this asthma—"

"You're really in a flap, aren't you?"

"How long did you know the kid? You friends with her folks?"

"No. Why, we've hardly—"

"Now look, Mr. Holden. Just give us some direct answers. We're not trying to rattle you. I guess you saw the lights and heard the racket and got curious. Is that it? Now, how about a little information about the neighbors, how the girl got along with everybody and if she had a boy friend up here and—"

"Now who's this?" said a voice; and it was official.

"Oh, hell," said the reporter, taking his face away from Holden's.

The man was a cop; he was in uniform, a pistol on his hip, boots. Must be a motorcycle cop, Holden thought numbly; must be up here to direct traffic.

"He's a neighbor of the kid's," said the reporter with the tiger eyes.

The cop took Mr. Holden's arm. "Come along with me. You can talk to the lieutenant."

Holden went. He had the feeling that, at not this step but at the next, he was going to fall flat on his face. He couldn't breathe but he was afraid to make any move to tug at the scarf.

They came to the lighted area, and it was like stepping into an arena. Holden felt that a hundred pair of eyes fixed on him as the cop led him forward; fixed on him and condemned him and hanged him, right there. He lifted a hand to shield his eyes, but it was shaking so badly he let it drop. Better to go blind than to let them see how he was trembling.

They came to a stop. They were in front of Cooper's office building and a tall man had just come down the two wooden-plank steps.

"Lieutenant Ferguson, we found this man hanging around up there."

"That right? Who are you, sir?"

"My name's Holden. My wife saw the lights, and heard the noise—"
He kept expecting Ferguson to cut him off the way the reporters had,
but Ferguson waited patiently and in silence. "She wanted me to find
out what had happened. You see, we knew earlier ... the little girl was
missing."

Still Ferguson waited, saying nothing. All he did was to draw Holden
a little to one side, so that they would be out of earshot of Cooper in the
office, and some reporters near the steps.

"My wife came into my room a few minutes ago. I was lying down. I'd
been inside all afternoon, all evening. I suffer so from asthma." He
paused to wheeze for breath, and still the detective was calm and interested, in no hurry to interrupt. "I tried to explain to Mae that you
might not want any outsiders. Curiosity seekers. But she was so determined." He knew that he sounded weak and foolish. He was sweating, too, and the wool scarf was itchy on his sweating throat. "Do you
have any clues?" he blurted, wishing in desperation that the other man
would say something.

"Clues? Well, Mr. Holden, we're just beginning our investigation."

"Oh, sure, I understand that."

"Have you talked to any of the newspaper people?" Ferguson asked,
glancing over Holden's head.

"They said she'd been choked to death!"

Ferguson's long plain face expressed mild disappointment. "That's sort
of jumping the gun. We haven't had time for the coroner's report."

"But that's what it looked like?"

Ferguson's nod was so brief and noncommittal that Holden couldn't
decide whether it was agreement or dismissal. Ferguson took his arm
gently. "Come this way for a moment, Mr. Holden." He led Holden past
the gatehouse and the lights, off up the street to where a signal flare
burned on the pavement. "Have you ever seen a car parked here late
in the day?"

Holden was so surprised at the unexpected question that he merely
goggled around at the shadowy trees and the wall beyond. "There are
a lot of workmen here during the day. Even when I come home there
are some still—"

He paused, expecting Ferguson to say something, but Ferguson merely
waited. Come to think of it, the builders usually parked along the
streets near the houses where they were working. This spot was kind
of off by itself, behind the gatehouse.

"Or it might be Mr. Cooper's car."

Ferguson shook his head, and Holden remembered that Cooper had
a little bare space, not quite the size of a lot, on the other side of his of-

fice. He parked there and usually any callers—prospective buyers and others who must be supply salesmen—stopped at the curb directly in front. He and Mae, when they had come looking, had parked right before the wooden steps. Holden licked his dry lips.

"I guess I don't know who it could be," he admitted.

"Well, that's too bad," Ferguson said mildly.

"Is there ... anything else you want to know?"

"Later tonight I want to talk to you and your wife, and all the other neighbors up here," Ferguson said. "Suppose you go home now and take something for that asthma, and wait."

"Yes. Thank you." Holden felt like a rabbit when the trap opens. The rush of freedom was almost something he could taste. He started off quickly.

"Mr. Holden."

"Oh, uh, yes, sir?"

"You can tell your wife what you've heard, since she's so curious," Ferguson said, "but just sort of leave the neighbors to us, hmmmh?"

"Yes, sir."

Mae was waiting by the front door. In the brightness of the room her majestic bulk loomed larger than life. She had put on a touch of lipstick in his absence, perfume too. "Well, Forrest."

He ripped the damp clinging scarf from his neck. "She's dead. They didn't say, but it must have happened in that little gatehouse. Choked to death." He fell into a chair, shuddering.

She stood there as if examining him in dismay. "Did you act upset while you were down there? Were you perspiring the way you are now? Really, Forrest, you look dreadful."

"I'm sick!"

"Did you explain to the police that it's the asthma?"

He lifted his dazed stare to her face. "*What's* the asthma?"

"Why, the way you're acting, this shaking and strangling. You're almost having a fit. If they saw you like this, they must have wondered." With a sudden shift of emphasis that caught him off balance, she said, "Just who did you talk to?"

"Well, first, a couple of reporters. They told me the little girl was dead."

"What did you say to them then?"

"I don't remember. They didn't let me talk, not complete sentences anyway. They kept cutting in." He sank his gray face into his hands.

She went to the couch and sat down. She took a handkerchief out of the robe pocket and blew her nose. In a conspirator's voice she said, "Forrest, I'm going to stand by you."

He jerked his head up. "What?"

"I'll stand by you." She nodded at him across the room, her bright eyes full of meaning. "I'll stand by you the way a wife should, the way I did before."

The room seemed to move, to drop away, all of its color fading to shadows, the familiar shape of the furniture dissolving into twisting smoke. Only Mae was real, was unchanging; she sat there like a rock in the midst of his nightmare. And he was terribly afraid.

There was something familiar about it, too. A loss of footing, as if he'd suddenly stepped into a mess of shifting sand, and this feeling was old, old—all during the years of his marriage to Mae he had somehow been off balance, on the defensive, trying to convince her that what she was thinking about him wasn't the truth.

He tried to say, "You're wrong. I haven't done anything bad." But no words came out.

Ten

Mr. Bartlett bore up better than might have been expected. The police had come for him and had taken him down to the gatehouse, where he had identified the body of his child, standing stiffly in the little space that was achingly bright with light. Ferguson didn't keep him. Ferguson thought that Bartlett looked not so much bereaved and lost, as braced for the hell to come; perhaps the best attitude under the circumstances.

When Bartlett got home, and met his quivering wife, and told her that yes, it was Pammy and she was dead, she'd been murdered, he needed all of his strength and composure. Mrs. Bartlett flew into screaming hysterics, literally a mad woman, and two cops had to help Bartlett hold her there and keep her from tearing off down to the gatehouse.

They got a doctor. The doctor tried to sedate Mrs. Bartlett enough to get her to bed, but it was impossible. In the end they called an ambulance, the ambulance men wrapped her carefully in a sheet-blanket to keep her from tearing at her clothes and hair, and took her out in a wheeled stretcher. At the last moment, waiting on the sidewalk, the cop's flashlight discreetly turned to the pavement nearby, she had a lucid interval. She looked up into the cop's face and said, "Will you tell whoever's in charge ... get that Dronk boy."

The cop misunderstood, though he caught the note of reasoning sanity. He thought Mrs. Bartlett said, *Get that drunk boy*, and made a mental note to pass it on to Ferguson.

The ambulance moved away with a low wail of its siren. Mr. Bartlett went into the house and shut the door. The doctor had asked pointedly that he not go to the hospital, not try to see his wife for a few hours. He walked across the big silent room to a leather chair, sat down, took cigarettes from his coat pocket, then just sat there with the pack and the matches in his hands, looking at nothing.

Perhaps he was listening, perhaps he was engrossed in echoes out of the past, out of the years of Pammy's life, the baby gurgles and the three-year-old babble, the magic piping of five, the serious wonderings of ten, the grownupness of thirteen. If unheard voices beat about his ears, he gave no sign. He sat like a man who must fight off phantoms and hang onto reality, must hang onto it with bodily strength, with every reserve he had.

When Ferguson finally arrived and rang the bell, Bartlett called, "Come in." He was still seated; he had a cigarette going. He seemed pale but composed.

Ferguson came in, crossed the room, sat down on the end of a couch. He sized up the place swiftly. It was a well-furnished room, nicely arranged and yet without any individuality to speak of; the stuff had cost money but there was no over-all impression of any plan or color scheme. Ferguson thought that the wife must have picked it all out, guided by some composite picture from the home magazines. He said to Bartlett, "I hate to intrude at a time like this, but every minute counts. We want to get on this thing."

Bartlett nodded stiffly, tapping ashes into a tray on the table.

"I'm going to have to ask some rather obnoxious questions."

"I'll answer as best I can."

Ferguson hitched up a knee, crossing his legs. "Was your daughter ever in any trouble? Was she, for example, ever reported as a runaway? Ever suspended from school? Caught shoplifting? I mention these things, not because I think she may have done them, but because they are the commonest type of mischief we find."

Bartlett looked through him. "Pamela was never in any trouble of any sort."

"Was she an impulsive girl? Did she make friends easily, and was she easily influenced by such friends?"

"I see that you just want to know what sort of girl she was," said Bartlett, "and so I'll save time by telling you. Pammy was compassionate. She was very tender-hearted toward anything or anyone she figured to be an underdog." He put a cigarette into the ash tray; his fingers had started to shake. He folded his hands together. "She would do anything for someone who had troubles, or was handicapped, or who in any way appealed to her sympathy."

Ferguson already knew about Kim Dronk. Mrs. Bartlett's parting remark had been passed on to him and he had correctly understood what she had been trying to say. "She would be drawn to anyone crippled, for instance?"

"She was, yes," said Bartlett, obviously waiting for Ferguson to ask who.

But Ferguson didn't ask. "What happened today? Can you tell me, exactly, hour by hour, what your daughter did up until the time she disappeared?"

"It was like any other day."

"Can't you tell me?"

Bartlett seemed withdrawn, almost sulky, as if Ferguson had disappointed him. "We had breakfast at seven, as usual. Pammy ate in her robe and slippers and then went off to dress for school. I went to my own room to get ready for work, and my wife stayed in the kitchen to clear the dishes. I left at eight. Pammy was here in the living room with her books, about ready to leave for the school bus, and I kissed her good-bye." He decided to light a new cigarette. "Mr. Ferguson, why did you ask whether my daughter was ever in trouble? What on earth could being a runaway, or shoplifting, have to do with what happened here tonight?" The match flame danced and shook.

"Perhaps nothing," Ferguson admitted.

"Wouldn't it have been much more to the point to have asked if she had disappeared briefly, any time in the near past?"

"Had she?"

"Two nights ago," Bartlett began, with an air of arriving at a desired objective, "this Dronk boy coaxed her out, took her up into the hills, some wild canyon, and kept her for more than an hour. We were terribly upset. It was a kind of ... *preview* ... of what's been done tonight."

"Do you believe that Kim Dronk murdered your daughter?" Ferguson asked.

"I know these facts," Bartlett answered. "She had a great pity and liking for the boy. She felt sorry for him. I think that if he had made up some excuse, some lie, that she would have slipped out to be with him again, in spite of the promise she had made to her mother and me."

"Was she in the habit of breaking promises?"

Bartlett hesitated, then shook his head. "No, I can't say so."

Ferguson said, "What about tonight, after you came home? How much did you see of her?"

"After dinner she and I did the dishes. We often did. Then I joined my wife here and we watched TV. We thought Pammy was studying in her room until about eight-thirty. That's when we discovered she was gone."

"I'd like to see her room now," said Ferguson, as if this represented the obvious next step in some plan he had made.

Bartlett nodded and rose, led the way down the hall. At Pammy's door he stood aside and Ferguson stepped in.

This room expressed a personality where the rest of the place did not, Ferguson thought. It was a room that belonged to someone young and carefree. Plenty of clothes in the closet, but they'd been hung up casually; Pamela hadn't been too clothes-conscious. The cosmetics were sparse, just a half-dozen lipsticks and an eyebrow pencil. Ferguson opened the cap of the latter; it had never been used.

He went back to the door. "Do you think your daughter was happy here?"

"She was very happy," Bartlett replied. He was facing the other end of the hall, not looking into Pamela's room. "She seemed to have everything she wanted. My opinion—" He shut his eyes briefly, then opened them with an air of tiredness, of needing to go somewhere to sleep. "—my own opinion is that someone played on her sympathy and inexperience. That's the only way it could have happened."

They went back to the living room; Ferguson crossed to the door. "That's very important," he said. "I'll keep it in mind."

"She wasn't a wild girl, nor disobedient, nor looking for trouble," Bartlett insisted. "She was kind and tenderhearted...." He suddenly turned his back and bent his head, on the verge of breaking down.

"You'd better get some rest." Ferguson let himself out. There was a uniformed officer at the curb, holding a light. Ferguson spoke in passing. "I'm going to see Dronk and his son."

"I guess we'll be up here all night, Lieutenant."

"You can bet on it."

Dronk opened the door promptly. "Come in, Lieutenant. Mrs. Campbell and my son are in the living room. This way." He led Ferguson through an arched entry.

It was all very neat, but an anachronism nevertheless. It had all been here for a long time. The high-backed sofa was covered in mohair and there were tassels hanging from the chair arms. The fireplace was imitation, a stucco mantle above a gas log, the kind of thing they did in the twenties. The ceiling was high and coved, the plastering ornately scrolled. Between throw rugs, the hardwood floor had darkened from years of waxing. For a brief moment Ferguson wondered why Dronk hadn't given up the old house, taken one of the new ones.

He greeted the woman and the boy. He had met Kim out on the sidewalk in the dark, with the father, but now he sized him up in the bright light. He thought that the boy's composure covered up some nervousness and fear.

Dronk had seated himself. "Mrs. Campbell has something to tell you."

Ferguson looked at her; at the eyes behind cataracts, the seamed face, the patient overweight figure. "Yes, ma'am?"

She said, "My eyes are about gone but there's nothing wrong with my ears. About eight-thirty tonight—I was in my room, the radio was on, it was just before the half-hour newscast—just at that time, I heard someone running."

Ferguson, as was his habit, made no reply but to wait.

"I didn't have the radio on very loud. I don't care for this rock-and-roll, this jumping kind of music. I was going to turn the volume up when the news came on. That's why I heard this ... from outside. It sounded like a—like a stampede."

"You mean, more than one person."

She shook her head. "Just one."

"What about direction?"

"Away from here. Downhill. I know he was running downhill without knowing why I know—if you can understand that."

"How about length of stride?"

"Oh, it was a man. A woman makes a tip-tapping sort of noise. These were ... almost jumps."

"Suppose we go to your room and you can show me where you were sitting in relation to the window, and so forth."

"That's a fine idea." She rose and went without hesitation to the arched doorway, so Ferguson figured she could see dark from light, or else knew the house from years of living in it. They went upstairs. Kim and his father waited below. Mrs. Campbell's room surprised Ferguson; he realized he'd had some expectation of servant's quarters. But this was one of the main bedrooms, second floor, at the front of the house. A big three-windowed bay faced the street. The blinds were not drawn and two of the windows, those on either side, were raised a couple of inches.

He took a quick glance around, seeing the plain white bed and the neat uncluttered dresser, the chairs in the bay and the little table there with its portable radio.

"You were sitting here?" He sat down in the rocker and glanced at the window. The opened space at the bottom was little more than a couple of feet from his elbow. It was quite possible that had she been sitting here, she would have heard anyone running in the block across the street. "Could he have been up above here, in the hills for instance, and run past?"

She seemed to think it over, and Ferguson wondered if she suspected him of wanting to trap her. Of course the story was a perfect alibi for Kim and his father, and that was the reason Ferguson distrusted it. It was so pat it sounded like a lie. "I don't think so," she said finally. "I don't think he was on this side of the street at all. It was as if he'd ... come from someplace else." She frowned and Ferguson wondered if she knew how weak it sounded. Where could a runner, such as she described, have come from? Thin air?

He waited.

"When I was a girl," she said, "I lived with my folks on a farm near San Bernardino, and there were lots of jack rabbits. Sometimes when you walked in the fields, or even down the country road, a rabbit would jump right out at your feet and go leaping away."

"That's how this sounded tonight?"

"Yes, it did to me. I might have it all wrong, not noticing at first, and he could have been in what's left of the grove and run down without my hearing him—but I don't think so. He just seemed to jump up and get going ... over there." She nodded at the dark panes.

She was seated on the side of the bed. She didn't show any nervousness or evasion; she seemed honestly to be trying to pin down her impressions of what she had heard. But in Ferguson's mind disbelief was growing.

He glanced around at the room. "You've lived here quite a while?"

"We moved here when Kim was a baby."

"How long have you been with the Dronks?"

"Since Kim was born. I was his nurse. He was a very sickly baby and with the club foot and all, they had to have someone for him. Then his mother ran away with another man, and I just stayed. I love him very much. He's like my own son, exactly."

Ferguson thought, not unkindly, *And you're doing what any good mother would do. I wish I could believe you.*

"If you think I'm making this all up to help Kim, though, you're wrong," she said with surprising abruptness. "I'm not a liar. I'm not saying, either, that this running man had anything to do with what happened to the little Bartlett girl, but if he did, and I kept still, it would be worse than a lie."

Ferguson rose. She was no fool and she had known exactly what he had been thinking. "We'll look for footprints in the morning."

Back in the living room, Ferguson resumed his seat. Dronk was looking at him curiously, so he said, repeating, "We'll see what we can find in the morning."

"Someone else should have heard this, too."

Ferguson nodded. "We'll find that out." He glanced at the boy and said without preamble. "Suppose you tell me about this walk you and Pamela took two nights ago."

Kim flushed. "We didn't do anything wrong. We just talked."

His father broke in: "Don't be on the defensive, Kimmy. Just go through what happened, all you can remember, the details."

Kim seemed to brace himself, rather than to recollect. Ferguson guessed that the details were plain enough in his memory, and that he simply resented going over them. And still, there might be something in it he had to hide. "Dad and I had picked some of the oranges and Dad thought we ought to share with the new neighbors, so I've been taking them around. Two nights ago I took a sack to the Bartlett back door. Pamela was in the kitchen nook with her books. She said her folks had been working in the den, something about the budget, and that she was tired of being indoors and wanted to go for a walk. I thought she meant around the block, but she said no, she had already been up to the canyon and that's where she wanted to go, again."

Analyzing it as he listened, Ferguson decided that the girl had been subtly implying that Kim should avoid being aware of his handicap. She had picked out quite a rough walk for the two of them.

"That's where we went," Kim said, "and we sat on a couple of rocks up there in the dark, and we talked." He stumbled here and Ferguson's quick ear caught it and he wondered what the conversation had been about. "Then I took her back home."

"What did her folks say?"

"They were sore."

Ferguson thought it over for a moment, and then asked, "Why do you suppose Pamela might have left her home tonight?"

Kim said tightly, "I've said and *said* it.... I don't know."

"Would she have gone for a walk if she'd been feeling restless, the way she did two nights ago?"

"I don't think she would have gone without telling her mother and father."

Ferguson couldn't find anything behind the serious gaze with which Kim met his regard. Kim seemed honestly convinced that Pamela Bartlett would not have gone out without a word to her parents. "It's a most important point," he added. "Why she went out without telling them."

"Maybe she ..."

"Yes?"

"Maybe she called to them. Maybe she thought they heard her."

Ferguson scratched a kneecap through his pants. "She knew they were watching TV in the living room. It would have been as short a way to the rear door, if she'd gone through there to speak to them."

"I don't know, then. I don't know how it could have happened."

Eleven

They were outside, close to the house. Miss Silvester heard the stirring in the new-planted shrubbery, and when she had gone to the back door, ostensibly to check the night latch, she had seen them on the slopes below. They had big lights close to the ground, throwing the surface into sharp relief. They were going to find Ross's footprints.

She couldn't wait any longer. She had to get hold of him, to warn him. She went back into the living room and sat down and dialed for information, got the number of the movers. There might be someone there at night, even at this hour; lots of places worked round the clock when work was heavy.

She got the distant exchange, and then the phone rang. It went on ringing, and the echo of voices from outdoors seemed louder than the thump of her own heart. Nobody was going to answer. She'd have to wait until morning, after all.

Suddenly there was a click, and a voice said, "Yeah? Who is it?"

For a moment she couldn't get the words out; they were tangled in her mind and her throat worked voicelessly. Then she said, "I have to get hold of one of your men, one of your workmen. It's very important."

"Heh?" She knew by the single syllable that he was old and deaf, a night watchman, that he hadn't answered at first because he'd been sleeping. "What's that?"

"I have to get hold of a friend," she cried desperately, willing him to alert understanding. "I don't have his home telephone number, all I know is that he works for you. For the moving company. It's terribly important that I reach him right away!"

"Look, lady, it's the middle of the night! There's nobody here now."

"I know. I know he isn't at work! But aren't there records, aren't there files or something in the office that give home addresses and phone numbers?"

"Office is way upstairs, ma'am." He yawned and she knew he was ready to hang up.

"Please! If you only knew...." She sought frantically for something to jolt him. "There's been a *death!*"

"Oh, yeah?" At least he had shown a touch of interest.

"There's been a death. A horrible accident. He has to know, right away."

"Well ..." He was teetering, not quite decided.

"Please! Please!" she begged.

"What's his name?"

She told him, and he went away, and the line hummed.

Someone rang the doorbell. It startled her so, she almost dropped the receiver. She covered the mouthpiece. "Who's there?"

She waited, aching with fright, and there was no answer. It was the police, of course. They'd found the footprints where Ross had walked from the house and now they wanted to ask questions. She could go to the door and ask them to wait, then hurry back to the phone. But they wouldn't wait, and they'd wonder why the telephone call was so important. And then they might even ask questions about that. She decided to sit tight for another couple of minutes.

How far was the upstairs office? And how slow was the watchman? And how long, once he got there, would it take him to go through the files and find the number she wanted?

The doorbell rang again.

She wanted to scream with rage, with fright. She was sweating, though the room was cool. The skin of her scalp prickled and there was a spot between her shoulder blades which felt as though a giant screw were being turned in the flesh. "Please ... please hurry!" she whispered into the empty line.

Time ticked by, and she was like a fiddle string being stretched tighter and tighter.

There was a sudden heavy pounding on the door, and she jumped in terror and screamed, "Can't you wait a minute? I'm coming!"

A muttered voice said something out there, so he must have heard her.

A second loud click sounded on the line and for a lurching moment she thought that the watchman had hung up on her, and then she heard his voice and realized that he must have picked up an extension phone in the office. "Well, here it is. Got a pencil?"

"Yes. Yes."

"Audrey five-seven-four-three-five. Got that?"

She was scribbling it across the pad. "Yes. Oh, thank you so much!"

He grumbled something in reply and the line went dead.

She tore off the sheet of paper, folded it, slid it under the base of the phone. Then she rushed out into the entry and flung open the door. She felt wild and overheated, almost choking with exertion. A tall man in plain clothes looked in at her with a calm, shrewd expression that instantly chilled her. "Miss Silvester?"

"Yes."

"My name is Ferguson." He held out an open leather folder and she saw the badge and the I.D. card in its plastic case. "May I talk to you for a minute or so?"

"Come in." She led the way, wondering how she looked, wondering if she seemed flushed and disorganized. She sat down and indicated a chair for him just inside the door—a hint.

He asked without preamble, "Have you talked to anyone about what's happened here tonight?"

"I inquired of a uniformed officer who was out in front—this must have been an hour ago. He told me that the little girl's body had been found in the gatehouse."

"Had you known that she was missing?"

"Oh yes. Her parents had been here earlier."

She didn't like the examining way he was sizing things up, the room and herself. She clenched her hands on her lap. Get it over with, she thought, commanding him to hurry so that she could rush back to the phone. She brushed at the sweat on her temples. "I don't know any of the details, of course."

He nodded, seeming at ease in spite of her naked urgency. "Did you hear anyone running, outside, tonight around eight-thirty?"

The question caught her off-guard. Her eyes flew wide with shock. She made an ineffectual gesture, as if warding off a blow. Ferguson sat a little straighter. "No."

He waited, as if she must be about to change her answer.

"I didn't hear a thing," she got out, the words tumbling, her throat constricting so that she went off into a spasm of coughing.

"Miss Silvester, this is a pretty important point."

"I didn't hear anything! Not a sound!"

He slumped a little. She was shaking inside, quivering, not where he could see it—thank God!

"I'm not involved in this thing at all," she got out, trying to sound firm and assured.

Ferguson rubbed one eye with a forefinger as if to rub away the sting of sleep. "I guess everybody up here is involved, in one way or another," he said mildly.

"I'm afraid not, no, Mr. Ferguson. I can't help you at all."

He was silent, thinking, and then said, "After the girl's parents came, and left—what did you do?"

"Do?" She was grasping at her scattered wits. "Why, I got dressed, of course!"

"You were in bed?"

He was trespassing here, he had no business asking what she had done with her evening; she stared across at him with unconcealed loathing.

"It's pretty quiet up here, evenings," he said as if musing.

"It's very quiet." *Go, go, go!*

He nodded and moved his feet and she thought he was about to rise. Then he said, "Did anyone leave your house by the back door?"

What should she say? She knew that all color had drained from her face, that the shaking had come into the open, that even her hands were trembling. Why couldn't she lie and dissemble? What was wrong with her? What made her feel so *guilty?* "I don't know," she stammered, knowing as she said them that the words were stupid.

"You don't know if anyone left by your back door?" he prodded, not at all surprised nor annoyed, just searching.

"Well ... the ... the boy from across the street—" *Now where,* her thoughts flamed in triumph, *had this idea come from?* "—the Dronk boy was here with some oranges. Or, was it last night?" She sat hunched, frowning. But she had covered for that moment of stupidity.

"Do you think he was down here tonight?" Ferguson asked.

"It's hard to remember. It seems every time I turn around, there he is. Night or day." A lie, an inspired lie; build on it. "I don't suppose—" She licked her lips, forcing herself to show something like dismay. "—he had anything to do with this...."

"We haven't a definite suspect as yet, Miss Silvester; we're just making inquiries."

"He was friendly with Pamela Bartlett. I've seen them together."

"Tonight?"

She shook her head. A lie could get too big, too involved, and then it boomeranged.

"But you didn't hear anyone running?"

She drew a deep breath. "If it were the Dronk boy—he couldn't run, could he?"

"That's right." Ferguson was looking across at her alertly as if her opinion mattered; and she had to crush back the shame that made her want to cry. What had made her say such an awful thing? Her thoughts seemed to whirl on themselves like a funnel of dust and trash, dirt, and she wondered with self-loathing why she hadn't just said, yes, she had heard somebody running but she didn't know who.... And then the freezing jolt shook her, they'll find out about Ross somehow, sometime, and then they'll say—

Ferguson had actually risen to his feet, had turned to the door.

"By the way, could I trouble you for a drink of water?"

"Uh ... certainly." She rose, dazed, her feelings in conflict. She went into the kitchen; for a moment it all looked unfamiliar under the bright light and she had to stop and think in which cupboard she had put the glassware. She ran water into the glass; with too much force, it boiled over upon her hands and she had to dry them.

When she got back into the living room, she saw that Ferguson had crossed as if to meet her, and was standing by the table with the phone. It even seemed, for an instant, as though his hand were moving from the instrument, as if the motion with which he extended his arm had begun beside the scratch pad.

When he had drunk the water and left, she sat down and swiftly dialed the number she had written.

The phone rang and rang at the other end of the wire, but no one answered.

It was the grayest dawn young Mrs. Arthur had even seen. The dreariest, the dullest; and as soon as she opened her eyes on the familiar bedroom, a great jolt of fear shot through her and she felt like screaming.

She jerked her head to look at her husband, but he was still asleep. The house was silent. She crept out of bed, over to the window, peeped from behind the blind. By the gray light she saw the empty street—no, not quite; a police car sat at the curb down there. She let the blind drop. She stood looking at her sleeping husband.

This is the day we've got to do something about the old man.

The frantic planning, the harsh decisions of last night bubbled in her thoughts. Today they must sneak the old man out of the house in such a way that no one noticed his going. Pack a few clothes, something to eat, and take him into the city and rent a room in a skid-row hotel, the shabbiest, the most crowded, somewhere in the deep midst of that last refuge for nameless and homeless and faceless old men. And leave him. And forget him.

There wasn't anything else to do.

If the police wanted afterward to make something out of the old man's taking off, let them. And let them try to find him.

It had been Bill's decision. She actually hadn't known enough to suggest it.

She went to the closet, took a cotton robe off a hook, put it on, slid her feet into sandals. In the hall someone had dropped a toy; she stooped and caught it up in passing. It was a little wooden car, a part of Billy's freight train. She was opposite the old man's door by then, and she paused for a moment to listen, half dreading any signs of grief or distress, the little car in her hand.

She bit her lips, looking down at the toy. "The babies have to have their chance," she whispered, as if explaining it to the sleeping old man. "We can't have them disgraced. It isn't fair."

She stopped at another door, pushed it inward. Nancy lay in her little white bed, pink and angelic, fair hair escaped from her pony-tail and spread on the pillow. A very faded brown teddy bear shared the covers. Young Mrs. Arthur brushed the sleeping head with a light kiss. In the next room she found Billy curled in his crib. One glance and she knew that he was all right. Funny that she felt this need to check on them, as if some horrid danger threatened. She went on down the hall, turned left and entered the big kitchen.

She opened a storage cupboard. She would have to plan and pack what the old man would need, enough food for a week if possible, a week in which he could stay alone in the hotel room and not have to venture out. For a brief moment the image of what his life would be, and his help-lessness in it, shocked her. Then she cast the thought aside.

No use making more than a few sandwiches; they wouldn't keep past a day or so. Canned goods would be best; mustn't forget to include an opener. She reached for pork and beans, tuna fish, Vienna sausages, corned beef hash. She lined the cans on the sink and did mental arith-metic. The old man was so stubborn and confused; how could they im-press the necessity of a schedule on him, make him understand that he must ration what they gave him? The best way, she thought, would be to put each day's food in a small separate sack, and then the whole works in a bigger sack. Then, just before leaving, Bill could sit down with his father and explain. Drum it in.

She put a flame under last night's coffee, sat in the breakfast nook to drink a cup.

She would have to pack the old man's clothes. Bill would have to sac-rifice his suitcase. The money was going to be a problem; they had so little to give the old man and yet he couldn't be cast adrift entirely des-titute. He had, after all, made most of the down payment on the house with his savings.

Bill could pay a month's rent for him. But no, no one must see Bill there, there must be no chance of discovery that Bill had taken him away. They would simply have to trust to luck that the old man would manage his money and the stock of food until it was safe for him to get out and find something to do.

She comforted herself, there were always jobs for old men. Gardeners and handymen and such.

The main thing, the old man would have to keep out of sight while Bill drove the car down through those gates and past the gatehouse.

Make him lie in the back, cover him with a blanket.

A nudge of fear shook her. Suppose the cops were looking everyone over this morning when they left? Asking questions and glancing into the cars? What would Bill do then?

She left the kitchen, uneasy now, and started for the hall to ask Bill about this possible danger.

The doorbell rang.

She stopped at the hall door. In the silence she felt her own heart pounding, she felt the rushing pulse in her brain. She put a hand out to the wall to steady herself.

How can they expect anyone to be up at this hour? I can just ignore it. No, I can't. They'll never go away.

She crossed the front room slowly. The uncarpeted floor was cold, the furniture looked skimpy and battered. The house had been much too ambitious a move for them, all wrong, and now this horror ...

She opened the front door.

"I'm sorry to bother you, Mrs. Arthur, but we've just found this. Does it belong to your husband's father, by any chance?"

The detective held out the big knobby cane, worn smooth by years of use. She wanted to shake her head, No, she wanted to say, certainly not, and she wanted to slam the door. Slam it and lock it and never open it again. But Ferguson's gaze warned her. The old cane had already been tagged as the old man's.

There were stains on the wood, and thick dust.

She opened the door and stepped back, and Ferguson walked in.

Twelve

They had waited impatiently for first light.

Ferguson had tried to relax in the back seat of his car, his legs stretched out, chain-smoking, adding up what he had done and what was left to do. He had already stationed a uniformed man at the gate, to thoroughly inspect all cars going and coming; Sorensen's bulk was visible in the dimness out there now. He had called headquarters and asked for a check on the phone number he had found gouged into the top sheets of Miss Silvester's scratch pad. On departing at midnight, Cooper had told him that several new families were due to move in today, and Ferguson had instructed him to call and ask them to postpone the move. Later today he intended to ask that a juvenile officer visit the school in Pomona, talk to teachers and friends of Pamela Bartlett. And of Kim Dronk. Also, another nudge, a half-formed hunch, told him to inquire in the neighborhoods from which the Holdens, the Arthurs, and Miss Silvester had moved.

When the skies began to get gray, Ferguson got out of the car and shook himself, went to Rossi's cruiser and looked in. "Let's start. I think we'll find it. Keep an eye out for her shoes."

But instead, Rossi had found the cane, a block and a half directly above the gatehouse, between two unfinished houses. He had yelled for Ferguson, his voice hollow in the morning quiet. Ferguson came running. The stains on the wood, clotted with dirt, were obvious enough but it was impossible to tell whether this was really the spot where the girl had been attacked. The ground around all of the new construction was a welter of footprints. Dust had been pounded fine. The only place where there had been any recognizable prints at all had been up there at Miss Silvester's, where the ground between the ivy sprigs had been raked and sprinkled.

Ferguson had squatted above the cane.

"Must have fingerprints on it," Rossi said. He was immensely pleased at having found the cane.

Ferguson grunted. He took out a handkerchief and lifted the cane gingerly by its lower part, turned it this way and that and blew gently on the dust. "They might get something off it." He stood up. "Right now I'm going to try something." He led the way back to Cooper's office, where a light still burned; he laid the cane on Cooper's desk and lifted the phone.

When Cooper answered, he sounded like an old man, exhausted. "What's that?"

"I asked who uses a cane up here."

It took Cooper a long while to get his wits working. "Wait a minute. What's this all about?"

"These people up here ... Who uses a cane? Mr. Dronk for instance?"

"I've never ... Oh, I get it. No, you want the old man, the Arthur grandfather."

"Anyone else?"

"Not that I know of."

Ferguson hung up and looked at Rossi. "Did you or Sorensen talk to an elderly man in the Arthur house?"

Rossi remembered. "They said he'd been lying down, sleeping."

"Come on." Ferguson picked the cane up gingerly, touching it as little as possible; there was going to be a beef anyhow; he was supposed to let it lie until the experts looked it over. He and Rossi got into the cruiser and drove up to the Arthur place. Since it was far down the street from the Bartletts, Ferguson hadn't gone there last night, had planned to drop in this morning. Now as they pulled up, he sized up the house. It was as new, as fresh and shining as the others but there were touches that indicated the presence of children. A path had been beaten over the shortest route through the new ivy, toys and tricycles littered the breezeway between house and garage, there was a heap of dirt as from a toy pail on the cement drive.

When Mrs. Arthur answered the door, he knew that she had something worrying her, and when he held out the cane and asked if it belonged to the old man, the look of fear and shock told him all he needed to know. He was aware of a moment of satisfaction, followed by distaste for what must come. He wondered with a touch of weariness why they had tried to lie.

He asked Rossi to wait, and went inside, with the woman moving ahead of him as if he carried some contamination.

She stood there shaking inside the robe. "I'll get my husband."

"Call your father-in-law, too, please."

"Will you talk to Bill first?"

Ferguson shrugged, wondering what she hoped to gain by the delay. The old man had as much chance of sneaking out of this valley as he had of flying to the moon.

Bill Arthur came quickly, tying a robe over pajamas. He had the same look of shocked fright as his wife. "Yes, sir."

Ferguson displayed his I.D. with his free hand. Then he directed Arthur's attention to the cane. Arthur made no attempt to come close or to handle it. A sullen expression settled in his eyes. "That's Dad's all right. He lost it somewhere."

"When?"

When Arthur hesitated, Ferguson added, "I'm going to have to talk to him about this."

"Look, officer, Dad is old. He's easy to rattle. He loses control. No telling what he'll say."

"I'll still have to hear him say it."

Bill Arthur went for his father. To Ferguson's surprise, the old man appeared fully dressed even to his hat, and Ferguson thought instantly: *They had him all ready to go*, and he knew what the young people had planned as surely as if he had heard them scheming it.

Ferguson showed the cane to old Mr. Arthur, who had sunk into a chair. The old man nodded slowly when Ferguson asked if the cane belonged to him. Ferguson then asked for a sheet of newspaper, laid the cane on it on the floor and turned to the old man.

"When did you last have this, Mr. Arthur?"

His face seemed paper-white, a maze of furrowed lines; the lips moved stiffly and Ferguson thought for a moment of a turtle he had seen closely once, in a zoo. "Last night. I had my cane last night. I went down to the gatehouse."

Bill Arthur put in, "Dad has this thing, this kind of hobby or whatever, about playing he's the gateman."

"I see." Ferguson looked at the old man more measuringly. "You stay down at the gatehouse quite a bit?"

"Only evenings," the old man quavered. "It's something to do. Nice down there, quiet and nice, and you see people going and coming. Not so many now but in the days to come—"

"Tell me about losing the cane. I see you had a fight with someone," Ferguson said. The marks on the old man's face and hands were quite plain. "Who hit you?"

Young Mr. Arthur's hands tightened in fists, waiting for the answer. He'd like to hit the old man himself, Ferguson thought; right now he hates his father for the mess he's gotten them into.

"I don't know," the old man said at last.

A child's voice woke in a howl in some other part of the house and Mrs. Arthur flew distractedly from the room.

"Somebody parks a car down there sometimes," old Mr. Arthur went on slowly. "Out of sight, right around there where the trees were left, the orange trees, must be a dozen or so of them still standing there alongside the gatehouse."

"You've seen the car?"

"Seen the car. Never could see who got in and drove it away."

"And last night?"

"Had a hunch. Had a hunch I might meet the feller if I took a walk up through those houses ain't finished."

"And did you?"

The old eyes searched Ferguson's face, looking for some sign of belief. "Yes, I did."

Ferguson waited.

"He went by. Big feller, young, in a hurry. I spoke to him but he didn't speak back. I turned around and started up here. It was dark. And he sneaked up behind me and hit me. I fell down. I couldn't see nor speak. I tried to holler."

Ferguson's manner hadn't changed by an iota, but the son couldn't hide his disappointment and rejection. It was implausible, the weak talk made up by an old man at the end of his wits, a cover-up for unmentionable violence.

Ferguson waited a moment and when the old man didn't continue, he prodded him. "You say he hit you. What with?"

"I don't know. It's kind of mixed up. His hands, maybe."

Young Arthur growled in despair.

"Did he run away afterward?"

"There's that," the old man said slowly. "When he ran away, he ... he limped."

The words seemed to hang in the silence, scrawled there in air, the incomprehensible addition to the tale.

"This is pretty important, Mr. Arthur."

"Well, I know that. What I figured must have happened ... I fell against him and he turned his foot. He hit me a couple of extra licks for it. He hurt himself and then he had to limp away." The old man seemed to be trying to sit straighter, to show dignity, to invite belief. The pale old eyes were steady.

"He went back down to the car?"

"I don't know."

There were so many holes in the story, such a scrappy lack of detail, and yet it could be just the sort of thing he would remember if it had happened as he had told it. Ferguson asked, "Just where were you when he attacked you? On a street? Curbing? Or in among unfinished homes?"

The old man looked confused. "I remember seeing a light."

"Shining in your face? A flashlight?"

"No, no. Someone's window light."

"A big pane like a patio or den door?"

"No."

"Did you go toward it?"

"I tried to. Tried to holler for help, too."

"Mr. Arthur, why are you so sure that the man who attacked you is the same man you passed going down toward the gatehouse?"

Young Arthur let out a faint sound like a sigh, and Ferguson thought that he repressed the grim beginnings of a smile. But the old man seemed perfectly blank, as if he scarcely comprehended Ferguson's question.

"Isn't this the truth," Ferguson suggested, "that you passed a young man in a hurry and that shortly afterward you were struck from behind by someone who ran away limping? Someone you didn't see?"

The old man's gaze fluttered about the room as if seeking the answer Ferguson wanted.

Young Arthur couldn't control his impatience any longer. "For God's sake speak up, Dad. Everything depends on this!"

"It does?"

"Don't you *see*—" the son began, his tone breaking savagely; but then Ferguson shook his head in warning.

Old man Arthur looked at Ferguson almost pleadingly. "What is it you want me to say?"

"Well, let's go at it this way. How fast did the man run away?"

"Fast as he could limp."

"And you were ... where?"

"Trying to get up. Trying to holler for help. That's when I saw the window light."

"Do you think anyone might have heard you?"

"I don't know."

"You didn't hear an answer?"

"I don't remember any. I got home somehow, got indoors without her hearing me." A jerk of the head indicated the unseen presence of young Mrs. Arthur. The child had quieted and Ferguson suspected that she had come into the hall to listen. He wondered in that moment if the scheme to spirit the old man away might have been her inspiration.

"Mr. Arthur, did you at any time see or hear anything of the young Bartlett girl, Pamela Bartlett?"

The moment of waiting while the old man decided, must have been hard on the son. Young Arthur's jaw moved as if he might be grinding his teeth. But finally the old man said mildly, "No. Why would I?"

"Didn't your son tell you that she was missing? That when we found her she was dead?"

A look of deep hurt, the memory of a shameful injury, pinched the old man's face. "Yes, he said something."

"And do you understand now, we think she was murdered with your cane?"

There didn't seem to be much impact in this information. Ferguson tried to study out the old man's point of view. He could simply be covering up, of course, afraid to show fear or anything else. But if he really was innocent in all of this, the lack of interest could mean that he was still in a kind of shock from his own experiences—plus the verbal hustling he must have had from his son and his son's wife.

"I lost the cane somewhere," old man Arthur said finally.

"You dropped it when he hit you?"

There was a space of silence while the old man searched his memory, and then he said, "I'll bet he turned his foot on that." His gaze settled on the cane. "That's how he hurt himself. That's why he limped."

His son could no longer keep quiet. "Dad, Dad, shut up! Don't you even know what you're saying? *He limped. Limped!* Can't you get it through your head? You're talking about the Dronk boy!"

The old man blinked, and Ferguson turned on the son in angry warning. But young Arthur was past stopping now.

"Come on out and say it—the Dronk kid knocked you down and beat you up because he thought you'd seen something to connect him with the murder! My God, can it be any plainer than that?"

The silence crackled, and then Ferguson said quietly, "Had you thought of the Dronk boy before this, Mr. Arthur?"

"No, I hadn't. Mostly because it wasn't that kind of a limp."

"What do you mean?"

Young Arthur got up and went out to the kitchen and Ferguson heard the rattle of the percolator under the water tap.

"He hurt his foot," the old man said finally.

"Now, why do you think that?"

The old eyes squinted, sighting down Ferguson's steady gaze as down the sights of a gun. "You know ... when you hurt yourself, you go hopping. You hop two, three times on one foot before you touch down on t' other. And you cuss. That Dronk boy don't go that way. He limps. But he limps on every other step. Do you get what I'm trying to tell you?"

"I understand."

Ferguson wondered how much he should discount the old man's story. It would seem that he had concocted someone who limped, and then when the son had brought in the name of Kim Dronk, his courage had failed him, or he hadn't wanted to identify definitely. Or again, it could be imagination, or perhaps even the truth.

"You heard him cursing?"

"Seems like I did, now I come to think."

In the kitchen, Bill Arthur put the percolator on the tiled counter and plugged it in; and then because he could no longer endure the old man's meanderings, he went out into the rear yard. There was a bricked area here, scattered with toy wagons and trikes and blocks and forgotten dolls, and beyond was a new swing-and-teeter-totter apparatus. The ivy was sickly because it was badly trampled. They'd need a fence, of course, but hadn't had the money to put one up at once. Across the way he saw someone looking at him. Holden, the little gray guy. He looked shrunken and sick, Arthur noticed. He had on an overcoat over pajamas.

Arthur walked toward him, taking cigarettes from the robe pocket. He was boiling within, full of anger at the stupid old man and the sly cop. He called to Holden, "Hello, there. I guess we'll be in for it today."

Holden took a few tentative steps in his direction, huddling down into the coat. "What do you mean?"

"The cops. They'll swarm us. Of course it's the Dronk kid, they know that. But they'll have to put on a show."

"They know—?"

"It's in the bag. My dad was knocked down by the murderer, heard him run away limping afterward. What's that sound like to you?"

Holden didn't say anything. Arthur thought that he looked funny. He must have asthma or something; he breathed with a wheeze. The wheezing didn't improve, but a look of great relief spread on his face.

He seemed to come out of a kind of daze.

"That's wonderful!" he said, and Arthur went on watching him curiously.

Thirteen

"I mean," Mr. Holden corrected after a moment, "that it's good to know that we aren't all under suspicion. I've been awake most of the night, trying to figure out how I could prove I was at home, in the house, when it happened. My wife had gone shopping. We have just the one car, and she goes into town in the evening and gets the groceries for the week—" He was talking too much, chattering, and sweat was coming out on his face, and he couldn't stop. The young man's eyes had been curious and now were growing hostile. "It's terrible for the boy, of course. What was it ... one of those sudden sex attacks?"

Bill Arthur was aware that he had done something stupid and reckless. "Just keep it under your hat," he growled. "I shouldn't have said anything. What my dad heard is evidence and they'll want to keep it secret."

"Yes, of course." Holden cocked his head toward his own house, though Arthur hadn't heard anything, "I believe my wife's up. I'd better be going."

The tails of the overcoat flapped on his skinny calves. Arthur turned away in disgust. What a mouse of a guy! And that old dame, that pouter pigeon with the big jaw, looked like an ex-madam, she'd be a terror to live with. Now much subdued because of his own error, Bill Arthur went back inside to check on the coffee.

In the front room, the detective was trying to straighten out the time with the old man, but the grandfather didn't carry a watch and had no idea just when he had been attacked last night.

In the Holden house, Mae Holden stood in the bedroom door tying the sash of her robe. Holden had dressed, then gone into the bathroom to take a pill.

She listened to the gurgle of water. When he came out into the hall and met her standing there, he smiled placatingly. But she asked at once, "What have you been doing?"

"I just went out for a breath of air ... calm my nerves. That young Mr. Arthur was in his yard and he came over and said it's known now, the boy did it."

She plumped the bow of the sash between her fingers. A tiny smile twitched the corner of her mouth. "Well, that's quite a stroke of luck.

Quite remarkable."

"If he is guilty, it's better to know it at once. The rest of us can quit worrying."

She nodded and turned to lead the way into the other part of the house. "We can plan something while we have breakfast."

"Plan something?"

"You can't afford for them to doubt, even for a moment."

He trotted at her heels, his eyes full of fear. "We can't meddle with this thing, Mae. We mustn't."

"We won't be meddling. As you say, the boy did it and they'll be looking for evidence. If they had it, they'd have gone up there and arrested him, and so far they haven't done it. That means they're waiting for something more. And maybe we can provide." She went into the big kitchen and opened a cupboard and took out a small skillet and put it on the counter. Holden had retreated to the nook. She threw him a sharp, examining glance. "Straighten up. You mustn't go around cowed and shaking like that. They'll notice it."

"Mae ... Mae, for God's sake—"

"That's exactly what I mean. That quavering, gnawing your nails, sitting hunched like that."

"Don't. Don't make me—"

Her movements were measured and precise; she took out a pan and put water to heat, got out the teapot and slipped a tea bag into it, set down the cream pitcher and went to the refrigerator for the milk. "I'm not making you do a thing," she said. "I'm just pointing out what might be wise." She put the skillet over a flame, added a chunk of butter, dropped in three eggs, and stirred them with a fork to scramble them. "Fix the toast," she commanded.

He crept to the bread box, went back to the table in the nook where the toaster sat gleaming in the early sunlight. "I can't make up some lie and put it over, I wouldn't even know how to begin—"

"A scream," she said suddenly, decisively.

"What?" He almost dropped the slice of bread he'd been putting in the toaster.

"There's always a scream. You might have heard it."

"I didn't!"

"From up there in those orange trees, that bit of a grove they kept above the house." She poured boiling water into the teapot.

"I wasn't outside, not once. How could I have heard a scream?"

"You just thought you heard it," she corrected. "And that's perfectly natural. All of us *think* we hear things, when we really don't. And then we aren't quite sure. But in a case like this, it's always best to mention what we think we've heard, even if it might be a mistake,"

He wrung his hands distractedly. "What are you trying to make me say? It's just gibberish."

"You aren't telling a lie. You think that you might have heard a scream, and you're mentioning it, now that the truth's begun to come out about the Dronk boy."

He made a fluttering motion like a moth's under an inexorable pin. "How could I say such a thing, adding a lie to whatever they've got against him already?"

"You're just going to help the police."

"I can't do it!"

She put the scrambled eggs on two small plates and turned to the table. He was crouched behind the toaster as if behind a bulwark. "A scream," she said. "Don't think you're the only one. That Miss Silvester isn't telling them about the man she had there. I'd swear to that."

"Miss Sil—"

"She has a man there every other night or so. And furthermore, I know who he is. He's one of the movers, one of the men who brought her furniture. He parks down by the gate and slips up to see her, and after he's there for a couple of minutes the lights go off in her bedroom."

"But how on earth do you—"

"And then he goes. He never stays long. I've got something figured out. He's not crazy about her. How could he be? So it's something else."

Reflected in the side of the chrome toaster, she was an outsize monolith patterned in pink cotton, pinheaded, remote, the kind of figure— in Holden's asthmatic sight—in front of which babies used to be sacrificed. His hands were sticky and trembling; his throat had shut. "You *know* this?"

"Of course I know it. Do you think I'm stupid? She's an old maid at the silly age and he's got her over a barrel. She's paying him."

Holden cried squeakily, "But if there's this strange man—that's evidence! Why not go to the police with *that?*"

"I might in time. Right now there's this scream."

He peered at her through the tears brought up by the struggle to breathe. "They won't believe me."

She brought the peach jam to the table and sat down. "You had better assure their interest in the Dronk boy," she said between chompings. "Suppose they got the notion to check backgrounds, went back to the old neighborhoods, and talked to people? Suppose they asked our old neighbors about us? About *you?*"

"But there couldn't have been any gossip! I didn't actually—"

"Do you think they were blind?"

He sat there looking at the congealing eggs, his expression scared and sick, his breathing labored.

His wife passed him the jar of jam. "Eat something. You'd better see the police right after breakfast. And then go on to the office as usual. As if there was *nothing at all* on your mind."

A few minutes later in his bedroom, reaching for his pants on a hanger, he saw the hunting rifle in its corner like a hidden genie, promising the last final relief and revenge in a puff of smoke like that from Aladdin's lamp.

He licked his lips, and began to dress.

Ferguson sat in his downtown office, adding up the facts. The night without sleep had left him grainy-eyed, oversmoked, hollow. His clothes felt as if he had worn them a week, sleeping under culverts. His feet hurt, he was aware of his bunions. He had read the morning papers and noted that, true to his inner prediction, the reporters were calling it a sex crime.

He had made notes for the coming conference with his captain.

Pamela Bartlett had died of manual strangulation.

At some short time following death, she had been beaten with a blunt object, almost certainly old man Arthur's cane.

She had not been ravished, though her clothes had been disarranged.

The button found clutched in her fingers came off a widely sold brand of workmen's denim overalls and jeans.

The time of death as placed by the coroner was somewhere between eight and eight-forty of the previous night. At that hour in this season of the year it was dark, though it had not been dark for long.

Added to these known facts were certain things, answers to questions, which Ferguson believed without being able to prove.

Why had she left her house? Ferguson thought she had gone out in answer to the cries of the old man. Pamela's bedroom was at the rear of the house, she had had her windows open, she had heard something of the scuffle and the yells for help, and she had left through the kitchen without telling her parents. The fact that she hadn't spoken to them indicated that she had been more puzzled than alarmed. Ferguson knew that his belief ran counter to that of her father, who was sure that Kim Dronk had somehow signaled her to come out to him.

She had been choked to keep her quiet for purposes of sexual attack, the fact of death perhaps not being recognized at once by the murderer.

The use of the old man's cane as a weapon had been an opportunistic cover-up. Ferguson was suspicious of that button, too.

Why had she been put into the gatehouse? Obviously to get her out of sight. But why not among the unfinished foundations, the stacks of lumber in the blocks above? Even to an outsider, the gatehouse would seem the obvious place to look if a young girl were missing.

He was frowning over that part of the puzzle when the phone rang at his elbow. He put down the pen, shuffled his notes together, picked up the receiver; it was Rossi in Cooper's office.

"A Mr. Holden, one of the people who live up here, came by with a story, he'd heard a scream last night. Thought it came from above the Dronk house. Somehow I discounted it, it sounded like something he'd thought up afterward. But then I got to thinking, and I went up there and looked around, and I found Pamela Bartlett's shoes."

"Where?"

"Tossed in under one of the orange trees, not more than fifty feet from the back of the Dronk place. Her father identified."

"Keep them out of there," Ferguson said. "I'll be up there right away."

Rossi was standing guard at the orange tree when Ferguson got there. It was a brilliantly sunny morning by now, and everything looked fresh and bright and alive, and Ferguson, trudging through the plowed earth, thought of the young life snuffed out last night in evil and darkness, and his jaw took a grim tilt. The shoes were scuffed and had dirt in them. She'd worn them, struggling for her life.

When he and Rossi had examined all the surrounding ground without finding any identifiable footprints, or any other significant object, Ferguson slid his first two fingers into the toes of the shoes and went down to the Dronk house. He knocked, and the housekeeper came, looking at him uncertainly through the film of blindness. "I want to see Kim and his father."

"Yes, sir. I'll call them."

Dronk's walk across the expanse of the kitchen was that of a man too tired to pretend he could step straight, and his face was haggard. He looked at the shoes without comment.

"Have you seen these before?"

"I presume they're Pamela Bartlett's shoes. No. I've never seen them."

"One of your neighbors heard a scream last night." (Rossi should have taken Holden with him, made him pinpoint that scream.) "When we investigated, we found these, a very short space from your back door, Mr. Dronk."

"I can't help where you found them," Dronk said, standing crookedly, favoring his crippled foot. "And there wasn't any scream. That part's a lie." He must have noted Ferguson's expression of interest, for he added, "It's a lie because if there had been a scream one of us would have heard it. And the only sound heard here last night that might apply was the sound made by a running man. That's an item I would think would bear investigation, Mr. Ferguson."

"I'd like to talk to Kim."

"He's dressing for school. Mrs. Campbell—"

"I'll call him," she said. Her half-blind stare, directed toward Ferguson, made him think of a blind cat's.

Kim looked brushed and clean, a tall pale fair boy with the awkwardness of adolescence not quite outgrown, and when Ferguson looked at him he felt a certain amount of misgiving at the impression of innocence. Every time he tried to get away from Kim in this thing, something came along to yank him back to him. Ferguson held out the shoes.

Kim reached for them, then withdrew his hand when Ferguson shook his head. "Are they Pamela's?"

"Have you seen them before?"

"I guess so. They look like the ones she wore a lot, around home, after she got home from school."

"Can you think of a reason for Pamela to have been near your house last night?"

"No, sir."

Well, that was old territory. Defenses long since built, if they'd been needed. "Do you think you would have heard a scream ... say, fifty feet from your house, there among the trees?"

Kim glanced at his father, but Dronk's morose stare was fixed on the scraped and dusty shoes. "I guess so."

"And did you hear a scream?"

"No, sir."

He wasn't going to break this thing with easy questions like this, Ferguson thought grimly. He was going to have to chew a bit.

"Were you in your kitchen during the evening? Eight o'clock or so? Getting a drink of water, for instance?"

"I have a drinking glass in my bathroom upstairs," Kim explained, "and if I wanted a drink of water after dinner, that's where I'd go."

"Kim wasn't downstairs," said Mrs. Campbell, speaking harshly, "and there wasn't a scream. If anyone says there was, they're lying, and you ought to concentrate on *why* ... why they need to lie. And why they're so determined to make out it must have happened up here."

Ferguson went back down the rear steps to the walk. "Would you mind staying home from school today, Kim, in case we need to ask you further questions?"

Kim hesitated, but his father spoke at once. "I would mind very much. Until you really have some basis for suspicion, I think Kim had better keep his usual routine." Dronk had straightened, and his voice was defiant.

They'd called his bluff and Ferguson had nothing further to play, no hidden trumps or aces, nothing to back up what he had done—just this new idea, to make Holden pin down time and direction, and exactly what had happened in regard to this scream he had heard.

He went down to Mrs. Holden's front door and rang the bell. She came at once. "When does your husband get home, Mrs. Holden?"

"Around five o'clock."

"When he comes, tell him not to go out again, that we want to see him."

A flushed, alert look had come into her face. "I can call him right now." The shape of her filled the door, and Ferguson noted that she had no waistline at all, she had a large bust and below that she was barrel-like. He wondered for a brief instant if she ever tried to diet.

"It's not necessary, I'll see him at five."

"It wouldn't be a bit of trouble to telephone him right away."

Ferguson shook his head. He thought to himself, puzzled by it, that the woman seemed pleased. She was anxious to make the call. He wondered, touching his hat as he turned away, if a woman that big could be so little and mean inside that she took pleasure in the discomfort of others. Her husband, for instance.

Fourteen

The phone rang and Miss Silvester stumbled from her chair, raced to it, picked up the receiver with a jerk. "Yes?"

His voice shocked her, mean and hard as a clenched fist. "What the hell are you trying to pull off? You trying to get me in trouble, or something? The night watchman says you made him give you my home phone number, and now you've been bothering the boss. What's with you? You're nuts or something?"

It left her gasping; she stuttered, "I've got to see you ... must talk to you. Oh Ross, it's desperate!"

"What's it about? That murder business in the papers? You think I'm coming up there *now?*"

"Where are you?"

"I'm home."

"But you said ... the boss told you. And I've been calling—"

"The boss dropped by. And I haven't been answering the phone because I didn't feel like it."

"Please, Ross! If we don't talk, if we don't get our stories straight, anything could happen!"

The silence was ominous. Then he said, "You've been talking to the cops about me?"

"No ... no. But they found your footprints, and they're going to keep hounding me until I tell them *something*."

Silence again. She leaned on the little table, and it creaked under her weight. The sunlight in the kitchen, through the open door beyond, had a nightmarish brightness.

"Maybe you'd better drive down into town."

"Yes."

"I'll tell you what to do. There's a bar on Brookmill, Wally's. Look up the number in the phone book. I'll meet you there in about ..." He must have paused to look at a clock. "... about forty minutes."

"I'll be there, Ross!"

"Wait a minute. You think a cop might tail you?"

"I don't think so. Not yet."

"Okay. See you there."

She dressed hurriedly. She went to the garage, backed the car, looked for official observers. She didn't see a policeman until she reached the gate. A uniformed officer was standing there talking to Mr. Cooper. Cooper waved her to a stop; she braked reluctantly and waited behind the wheel. Cooper must have been up all night, she thought; he looked sagging and unshaved, with hangdog eyes. He looked in at her, bracing himself with a hand on the car. "Miss Silvester, this is a terrible thing ... I hope you aren't too upset, that they aren't causing you too much trouble."

"The police? Oh, no...." Involuntarily she raced the motor, wanting to go.

"Were you able to give them any help?"

"I'm afraid not, no." She felt the curious gaze of the uniformed man across Cooper's shoulder; her heart thudded. In another moment he might walk out into the street and ask why she was leaving. Or could he do that?

"This officer, Mr. Rossi, says they believe someone's been coming up here evenings, parking here by the gate, perhaps visiting somebody." He leaned closer, his eyes on a level with hers, and she saw how bloodshot they were, and caught the whiff of whisky. Without volition, without planning it at all, her foot trod on the gas pedal and the automatic transmission meshed and the car spurted away. Cooper stepped back with an exclamation of surprise and the rearview mirror showed him in the middle of the road, watching. She sailed off through the gate, into the straight drop of the highway beyond, and through a blur of fear she saw the city below.

It took a hall-hour of befuddled driving before she found Wally's Bar. It was a ramshackle wooden affair between a machine shop and a trucking depot. She parked the car and got out, straightened the beige skirt of her new suit. Wally's door opened into a twilight gloom where a jukebox wailed. She stepped in and looked around. To the left was a bar, a kind of nicked and chewed wooden counter with ratty crepe-paper decorations on the wall and ceiling, as of some celebration long since over. To the right across an open space were some booths. They needed paint and the floor needed scouring, and as Miss Silvester stood there in the beige suit and white gloves, new handbag, and little brown hat, she knew that in Wally's Bar she looked a freak.

The bartender, drying beer mugs, flashed a glance at the rear booth, and Ross raised himself from behind the wooden divider, and beckoned.

She went back there, her heels tapping. Ross and the bartender were the only ones here. She slid into the booth across from Ross. He looked her over and grinned cruelly. "What are you all dressed up for?"

"I didn't think it would be a place like this."

"What's wrong with a place like this? Hey, Mac, a beer for the lady."

When Mac put the beer in front of her, it slopped over a little. The smell made her a little sick. "Ross, we have to talk."

"Okay, we talk. What have you told the cops?"

"Nothing."

"And if you go on keeping your mouth shut, what's to worry about?"

"They aren't going to quit until they know everything." She was gripping the edge of the table, the beer was dampening the white gloves. "They know now that I had a visitor, a man, they've found where the car was parked down by the gates, and somehow ... somehow—"

He was drinking the last of his own beer, boredly. He had on the usual T-shirt, a faded sweater over his shoulders, the sleeves tied at his neck. He looked big in the small space of the booth; his bare arms were full of rippling muscle, his hair gleamed from a wet comb. But Miss Silvester felt as if she were looking at him through some spectral glass, or from an immense distance, and there was nothing whatever to remind her of the hot yearnings of their meetings at her home. He was alien. She had no way of reaching him.

The bartender went on watching her while he wiped the counter across the room. She tucked her toes together. "We can't get rattled. We have to tell them the same story or they won't believe either of us."

He rubbed a hand across his mouth. "I'll tell you what I'm going to say ... if they do run me down, if they do ask me."

Just then the jukebox changed records and a pounding bass filled the low-ceilinged room. Ross looked at the box and frowned. "Just a minute.

I'm going to turn that damned thing down." He got out of the booth and went to the jukebox and fiddled with some adjustment in the back. His familiarity with the machine, and the bartender's tolerant attitude, betrayed that Ross was a familiar of the place.

She watched him across the room again. She tried to meet his eyes, tried to ignore the bartender's smirk, "What's the matter with your foot?"

"Nothing's the matter with my foot. Nothing at all." He sat down and met her gaze levelly, and now he was not only alien, but hostile. The sudden memory of what they had done together brought a flush to her face as if at the thought of a vulgarity committed by a stranger. "As I was saying—hey, what's the matter with you?"

"I'm all right."

"Well, if the damned cops ask me anything, tell them sure, I was up there, you had some shelves you wanted built and some furniture moved around,"

Her mouth felt pinched and stiff. "They won't believe you."

He waved a hand at the bartender. "Mac, I came in here because I'm thirsty." To Miss Silvester, grinning, "I guess you don't know much about cops. Sure they won't believe me. What do I care? Cops are like this, as long as you admit what they want you to admit, they're okay. So I admit I was up there, in your house, and I left at such-and-such a time, and I got home at a certain hour and all that crap. You think they're going to lean on me, try to make me say what we were doing?"

"They'll know."

"Hell, yes, they'll know. They'd think it even if we'd been sitting in the front room every minute singing hymns."

"Maybe they'll ... maybe because I'm older—"

He laughed. The bartender brought the beer. He looked closely at Miss Silvester as he sat the glass down. He said to Ross, "Something's funny?"

"Our private joke," Ross told him, and winked.

"She ain't laughing," the bartender said, glancing at Miss Silvester.

"She hasn't caught the point of the joke yet."

Miss Silvester sat pinched and still; under the clean lines of the nice suit she was beginning to feel indescribably dirty.

"So maybe she hasn't got a sense of humor?" the bartender wondered.

"Who needs a sense of humor in a dame?"

They were baiting her. She clenched her gloved hands in her lap. Her eyes were stinging.

"She's dressed up, anyway," the bartender said, sucking his teeth and growing bolder. "Better'n anything else you ever dragged in here. Hell, I didn't think you even knew a woman that wore a hat. And gloves, yet."

"You underrate me, Mac."

Miss Silvester slid sidewise in the crowded booth, stood up. She felt lightheaded with fury, trembling, her ankles wobbling on the new needle-heeled pumps. She knew the cords in her neck showed, that tears had streaked the careful make-up. She said to Ross, spitting out the words: "You're nothing but a … a *thing*."

She turned and strode for the door.

She heard him coming after her, and tried to run, but the slatternly door seemed a million miles away. He grabbed her arm and tried to swing her around to face him. "Hell, can't you take a joke? We were just giving you a line. What's got into you?"

She lifted the handbag and aimed it at his head, and he tried to duck, too late, and the bag skidded into his temple and then across his hair. She yanked free and sped to the door.

Outside in the bright sun a couple of truckers beside a big semitrailer at the ramp next door turned to stare. She faltered toward her car with Ross pounding behind her. He was saying things, rough things, that she was afraid to hear. He was like an animal, a terribly big ugly animal, that wouldn't let go.

She reached the car, fumbled the door open. He grabbed it, his hand big and square, and held it so that she couldn't quite slide in. "You listen to me, babe," he said.

"You humiliated me," she stammered, trying not to cry. "You made me feel cheap. A fool. This wasn't any sort of place to meet and try to plan what we should tell the police. It's been a mistake. All of it's been a mistake, all of it!" She tried to push him away.

"Maybe so. Maybe it was a mistake," Ross said, speaking quietly in spite of the way his breath was coming. He was mad, she could see that. "But it wasn't mine. I didn't start it. That first day, when I moved in your stuff with those other two jokers—you think I didn't take a hell of a lot of jazz afterward? They couldn't miss it, you standing there like a she-dog staring at a steak. I tried to overlook it and then I thought hell, maybe I'll be doing the dame a favor, she looks anxious."

The heat of the sun seemed to shrivel her, pinned there against the hot steel door of the car; she felt as if clothes and skin and even flesh had melted away, that she stood naked to the bone. "But I didn't mean …"

"Sure you did. You weren't wigwagging for a taffy pull. There's just one name for what you wanted." He leaned closer, baring his teeth, and told her the unfamiliar word. Something written on a fence, half-remembered, a word you'd wondered about when you were little, a word—" And now you're scared and you want to quit. You want to go back to being an old maid in a white nightie. You want to get the nasty man out of your hair. You want to go back to—" He told her what she was going back to, practices she'd never heard of.

She jerked forward with a dry retch. "Don't...."

He stood there, not moving. Across the street, in the haze of light, two other truckers had joined the first pair, and all four were highly interested in what was happening at the car.

"Why don't we just take a drive?" Ross said.

"I won't sit in there with you!"

"Get in the back seat. Give me the keys."

She tried to keep her purse from his hands, but he took it anyway. He found the keys. He opened the door for her, and when she hesitated he shoved her in. As the car pulled away, she shot a single glance at the truckers, and they were grinning. She put her head down on her knees and sat shuddering.

They drove, and Ross turned corners—faster than she did—and the sounds of traffic thinned. "I guess I lost my temper back there," he said finally.

"It doesn't matter," she said, muffled against the skirt.

"Sure it does. I shouldn't have said those things."

She felt helpless, utterly lost. He had the wheel of her car and he was driving it, and she was a prisoner in the back seat. And there was something else, something she had almost forgotten, a frightening thing she didn't understand.... When Ross walked, even when he pounded after her in anger, he *limped*.

Meekly, half whispering, she asked, "Ross, what happened to your foot?"

"Goddammit, will you please shut up about my foot? I turned my ankle. That's it, that's all!"

"Where did it happen?"

"Up there, leaving your place."

"Did you see anything of that little girl, the Bartlett girl, who was killed?"

"For God's sake, what kind of a question is that? Of course I didn't see her. You think I'm a murderer? Is that what you think?"

His tone promised ugly things to come if she thought it, and she cringed, rubbing her cheek against the fabric of her suit.

"I left your place and I went home," he added, and she sensed that he listened then for any sign of her disbelief.

"You didn't answer your phone in the middle of the night."

"I always put a pillow over the phone. I don't have to explain to you ... but I've got friends who get drunk and who think it's funny to get you out of bed at 2 A.M. So I don't answer."

"And you didn't go to work today."

"Because I'd turned my ankle."

There was silence then, just the sound of the car, and suddenly she heard a meadowlark's call, clear and high pitched. She jerked her head up. They were out in the country, low hills covered with orange groves, a narrow two-lane road between irrigation ditches, the empty sky.

"Where are we going?"

"To find a place to talk," he said.

A sign said County Picnic Area, and the side road angled down through live oaks and across a stream bed, dry and rocky, to a long plateau where tables and benches and stone fireplaces had been arranged under the tall old eucalyptus. She looked hopefully for other cars, but there were none. The car slid to a stop; he set the hand brake. The silence seemed to settle over them like a backwash of surf. He turned around in the seat. She tried to read his face, tried to find in it some awareness of herself, some hint that meant he was seeing her as a person, as another human being who shared with him the needs and the desires and the dreams of life. But the brightness of his eyes held no recognizable expression, and though his smile seemed humble it roused nothing in her. "I'm really sorry," he insisted, "and I want to say again ... I lost my head back there in town. I guess I thought for a minute we were splitting up."

She felt dismal and remote.

"I've got a bad temper. So what? But when I'm sorry I'm not ashamed to say so." He rose in the seat, put a leg over; his bulk filled the ceiling of the car, and then he dropped down beside her. "We can talk now."

With shaking hands she tugged at the hem of her skirt.

He laughed under his breath and he gripped her arms, dragging her closer. She resisted and he braced himself, and then winced with a suck-in of breath. She knew that he had put pressure on the injured ankle and that there had been a stab of pain.

She wanted to ask him again about his foot, force him to tell her what had really happened last night, what he had seen and done. But she was afraid. He was so big and so strong, and now she knew that there was something unpredictable about him, something violent, just under the surface.

And the place was lonely.

Fifteen

Kim was gathering his books in his room when Mrs. Campbell rapped and stuck her head in. "Don't go yet, Kim. I'm going to talk to your father."

She came back in about five minutes. "Your father has decided that you'd best stay home today, after all."

"All right."

He knew that the decision had been hers, and was puzzled by it. Why shouldn't he go to school?

He went downstairs and found the morning paper, not in its usual place but tucked, folded small, behind the bread-box. Mrs. Campbell could read after a fashion by holding a page about four inches from her eyes. Kim had a hunch that she had read the paper and put it where it was. He took it into the six-sided turret room and sat down and spread it on the table. In just a couple of minutes his father walked in.

"Kim? Oh, for the love of ..." He started to reach for the paper and then drew his hand back.

Kim looked up. "I don't understand all of this, Dad."

"Well ... don't try to."

"Some of it isn't even written the way it happened."

Mr. Dronk sat down across the table. "Look, Kim, let me explain something. Newspapers are in business to make money. Even a conservative family paper like the one we take is going to play up a story like this murder. It has ... elements ... that make for sensationalism."

Kim was frowning. "What do they mean, 'recluse'?"

"They mean me, Kim."

"Is that what you are?"

"Of course it isn't. A real recluse lives completely shut away from the world. You must know something of the meaning of the word."

"I thought it meant a kind of hermit."

"Yes, and hermits don't go into town to an office every working day, and talk to people about investments."

Kim glanced at him doubtfully.

"As I explained, even a staid newspaper like ours is going to sensationalize somewhat in a thing like this. The best way to make it more interesting is to create a few odd characters. Suspects. So I've become a recluse. That makes me sound dangerous."

"They call Mrs. Campbell 'a reticent servant.'"

"That makes it seem that she's hiding something."

"And what's 'enigmatic juvenile'?"

"You."

"I didn't do anything."

"That makes you enigmatic, puzzling, perhaps threatening. I imagine that similar descriptions are being used by the other papers. Some will use stronger words and protect themselves by injecting 'allegedly' into it somewhere."

"Why concentrate on us?"

"Well, they already have a line on us, so to speak. There was some publicity when I divorced your mother. These other people are newcomers. If the case drags out, their turn will come." He rose and came around the table and put a hand on Kim's shoulder. "I'd better be going. You'll be all right here today. Do whatever Mrs. Campbell tells you. Stay in the house. If the detective comes back, call me at the office."

Kim thought that his father made it sound like a sort of siege.

As soon as Mr. Dronk had gone, Mrs. Campbell came in with a dust mop which she gave to Kim. "You're going to be home, you can help me," she said. "Go over all the floors upstairs. Under the beds, too. Shake the small rugs on the back steps. Then I'll let you wash some windows."

Kim understood that she meant to keep him busy all day.

He went upstairs, gathered up the rugs and piled them in the hall, then began to dust the floors with the soft mop. But in his own room he suddenly leaned it against the bed and went to the windows. The patch of grove remaining lay spread to the foot of the brown hills. The pane was up and he could smell the warm spicy odor of the orange trees.

He stood thinking. If Pamela had been murdered up there where her shoes had been found, wouldn't he have heard?

Sure I would, Kim thought. I was in here reading. An enigmatic juvenile with a book. She must have fought for her life. I'd have heard something.

All the fine clods had been pounded to dust around the trees where they had found her shoes, and a kind of path led down toward the house. The police had been over and over the ground, of course, looking for some trace of the murderer.

Well, it had to be that someone had put the shoes up there to draw attention away from something else. Kim wondered if the police understood this as well as he did.

It was strange, too, to realize that while he'd been reading up here, totally ignorant of what was going on, that someone had been down there that close to the house, creeping through the dark with Pamela's shoes in his hand. The thought made Kim feel kind of sick.

And then the memory of Pamela came back very strongly, and Kim's eyes filled with tears.

He turned from the window, took up the mop again, and worked on the floor with hard, quick strokes. When the floors were done he carried the heap of small rugs down to the back steps. Mrs. Campbell was in the front part of the house. Kim left the rugs on the steps, walked off into the grove. He paused by the tree where the earth was trampled, but there was nothing to see. He walked on through the trees, the ground rising a little, until he came out at the foot of the bare brown hills.

In the sunny stillness there was not even a wind-rustle, not even a bird chirping. Kim thought to himself, this was the way it used to be. Quiet, and alone. No one close, no one to spy and question, no one to think you a freak, or worse. He felt a sudden bitter longing for what was gone, the isolation, the freedom. He went up the little canyon a way, and found a boulder washed bare by the winter streams, and sat down.

The silence closed down around him. He drew a deep breath.

He watched some ants in a small hill near his feet, searched out a few cracker crumbs from a pocket, dropped them and watched the ants get all excited. He drew some designs in the sandy wash with a stick. He took a handful of pebbles and tried to toss them all into a fist-sized hole on the other side of the wash. These were things out of the past, things he had done here alone for years; and their familiarity was comforting, and he could almost forget what had happened to the rest of the valley.

He couldn't stay away too long, though. Mrs. Campbell would be worried.

He went back the way he had come.

At the back steps he paused and stooped, turning the cuffs of his pants and dusting out any foxtails and sand. And stooping there he could see into the hole in the latticework under the edge of the steps. There was something in there, blue cloth, smudged and stained. Kim frowned. His father had laid down the law years ago, absolutely nothing must ever be put into the space under the rear of the house, it would cause the worst fire hazard possible. Kim stepped to the hole in the lattice, made sometime in the past to give access to pipes or something, and stooped and reached for the spotted cloth. It fell loose, lengthening as he pulled it forth, and turned out to be a pair of old overalls. Kim lifted it, and then saw other stains besides those of grease and paint, and felt his whole body go cold and shaking.

He thought first of calling Mrs. Campbell, and then decided against it. He folded the overalls into a small bundle and walked around the house to the street. He looked for the police cruiser, but it wasn't in sight. Kim crossed the street, went to the corner, heading downhill toward the gate. As he walked, he noted that there was much less noise of building today, just desultory hammering now and then in the distance. Probably under orders of the police, Cooper had kept everyone out except men doing the most necessary jobs.

The police cruiser and Cooper's car sat beside the office building. Kim went up the steps and rapped at the frame of the open door. Inside, Cooper and a uniformed man were at the desk and seemed to be studying a plot of the building project. Cooper glanced up; then the officer too, and in that moment Kim thought of something, and it jarred him. He knew in that instant that the stained garment was supposed to be found, that it was a part of the pattern, like Pamela's shoes under the orange tree. He held it out speechlessly to the officer.

"What's this?" The man—Kim remembered who he was, Rossi—took the garment and shook it out, and must have seen the stains. His face changed. "Where'd you find this?"

"Under our back steps."

"When?"

"A few minutes ago."

Cooper was leaning across the desk. "What the devil is it? Some kind of old clothes? Looks like it was used to wipe up paint stains."

Rossi nodded; he had folded the overalls into a tight roll. "I'll go with you," he said to Kim, "and you can show me,"

They got into the police car and Rossi drove back to Kim's home. At the back steps Kim showed him the hole in the latticework that closed in the underpinnings of the house. "How long has this hole been here?" Rossi asked, getting down close to look under the house.

"A long time."

He heard footsteps and looked back. Cooper had followed them. Rossi straightened up, sitting there on his heels, and said, "Mr. Cooper, I'd appreciate it if you'd go back and keep an eye on the entrance, keep out any strangers or curiosity seekers."

"Sure. I just came up here in case I could help."

Rossi got back on his knees and went on peering at the dimness. He said, "There isn't another damned thing under here."

"No, sir. My father wouldn't even let us keep gardening tools under there."

Rossi rose, dusting the knees of his uniform. He had put the wadded bundle of blue denim on the steps; now he picked it up again. He let it fall free and studied the front, and Kim noticed now where one of the metal buttons had been torn loose from the fabric.

"Does this belong to you or your father?"

"No, sir. I've never seen it before."

"Couldn't have had it around, maybe, used it to wipe up, and just forgot about it?"

"I don't think so, no, sir."

"Your father ever wear anything like this to putter around in?"

"No, sir. He has some old shirts and a couple of old pairs of pants, regular suit pants, that he uses for odd jobs."

Rossi nodded. "I'd like to use your phone."

Kim showed him the phone and then went to look for Mrs. Campbell. She was upstairs in one of the bathrooms, hanging up towels. When Kim told her what he had found, and where, her half-blind eyes turned on him in a stare of unbelief. "You took it to the police?"

"Yes. What else should I have done? There were blood stains on it. It must have something to do with Pamela's murder."

"You should have burned it in the incinerator," she said bitterly.

"But isn't it evidence, maybe?"

"They'll never believe that you just found it, they'll say you hid it there," she told him. Her normally placid face had turned hard. "The detective didn't believe me, that I'd heard somebody running. Now I know what's on their minds, I'll keep my information to myself. A fool could see that the murderer was running away after he'd ditched those shoes and this pair of overalls, but the cops won't."

"But I took it down to the officer."

"They'll say you did it just to make yourself look good."

Kim went back downstairs. Rossi had just put down the phone. He covered a yawn. "I've got to get home for some sleep." He shook his head as if to shake away drowsiness. "Sit down for a minute, will you? Let's go over this thing."

Kim sat down on one of the hall settees. Rossi leaned on the hall table. The rolled overalls lay beside him. "What made you look under the steps?"

"Well, I'd been walking in the hills. I was dusting my pants to get rid of any foxtails or dirt in the cuffs, when I happened to look over there."

"You reached in and got the overalls right away?"

"Sure, I couldn't figure what such a thing was doing there. Dad's always talked about never having anything under the house because of the danger of fire."

"Did you think about phoning your father?"

"No, I didn't. I thought for a minute of calling Mrs. Campbell but then I decided, since it had blood stains on it, I'd better take it right to the police."

Rossi covered another yawn. Kim got the impression that Rossi was passing time, and he asked suddenly, "Is Mr. Ferguson coming up here?"

Rossi's mouth snapped shut and he gave Kim a sharp glance. "Yes, he is. Do you have something you're saving for him?"

"No, I don't."

"I thought you might have something important you wanted to tell him."

Kim felt impatience well in him. Rossi seemed almost to be urging him to admit to keeping a secret. "I've told you everything I know."

"You never saw these overalls before?"

"No."

"You ever walk around down there where they're working on those houses?"

"Not much. My father told me at the beginning, when they first started to build, not to go getting in anybody's way."

"These look like they might have been used to wipe up paint and grease. Maybe the painters, or plumbers, used them. Old clothes, they'd taken them for rags."

"Yes, I guess so," Kim agreed.

"What were you doing in the hills?"

"Just ... just being alone."

When Ferguson arrived Kim had to go back over much of the same ground. Ferguson went out and looked in under the house. "Who would know about this hole, except you and your father and the housekeeper?"

Kim was puzzled. "I don't know."

"It's not a very big hole in the lattice. You'd almost have to be right at the steps to see it," Ferguson pointed out. "And yet somebody is supposed to have run up here in the dark and stuffed those overalls in there. Seems he'd have to know what he was doing."

Kim saw where Ferguson's remarks were leading. He didn't know how to answer, how to defend himself against this line of reasoning.

"Throwing the shoes in under the tree, that wouldn't have been too hard, there's almost always enough reflected light from the sky to make out the shape of a tree," Ferguson went on with the air of using a probe. "But this business, now—it kind of brings it right to your door, doesn't it?"

Kim knew that you were never supposed to lose your temper with the police. It was what they wanted, really; it was the way they got you rattled. But he couldn't help the anger that stung him as Ferguson sat there on his heels, staring upward. "I don't care how it looks to you," Kim said, trying to control his voice. "I know how it happened. I found the overalls there, and I'd never seen them before."

Ferguson didn't believe it; but he was making an obvious attempt to take it on a kind of tentative trust. He rose and brushed at his pants.

He looked terribly tired. "Who's been up here at your back door? Any of the neighbors? Old man Arthur, the Arthur grandfather, for instance?"

"Mr. Arthur didn't come up this way. He hung around down by the gatehouse,"

"Oh," Ferguson's eyes glinted for an instant. "You noticed that, did you?"

"Yes, sir." Because of Ferguson's sudden attention, Kim was alerted. What was Ferguson thinking? Then Kim understood. They thought he had put Pamela's body in the gatehouse because that was where the old man spent a lot of time, and it would make it seem that the old man might have killed her. But then it would have to be some kind of crazy game, his putting Pamela there and then hiding the bloodstained overalls under his own back porch. It didn't make sense.

Ferguson said suddenly and brusquely, "I'll want to talk to you again later, Kim. Just stay home, will you?"

"Yes, sir."

They took the overalls away, but before they got into their cars they held a sidewalk conference, and from the front windows Kim saw them looking at the place in the overalls where the button had been torn away.

Sixteen

Young Mr. Arthur stood in the bedroom doorway. "Look, Dad, this is the silliest thing yet. We don't want you to go. There's no need for it. Last night, that was just a panicky inspiration, we were all tired out and couldn't think straight. She's said she was sorry, that she didn't mean all those things. So settle down, hunh?"

The old man had a battered suitcase open on the bed and he went on laying clothes in it, darned underwear and faded socks, and shirts that he folded with trembling hands and wrinkled in the process, and an old bathrobe. "I'm gettin' out."

"Then there's this other thing, the police might not ever let you go. You're a witness. Maybe even a suspect. Suppose they tell you that you've got to stay here until the case finished?"

"I'm going to talk to that Ferguson feller," said old man Arthur. "Might get around him some, if I explain what I mean to do, I'm not running away, just going to get a room in town. I'll even rent a room the same block's the police station, if they'll let me leave this place."

"My God, you're carrying a grudge," the son said in anger. "Just because we thought of getting you out of sight for a few days, a perfectly natural idea the way you looked last night."

"You didn't have time to hear me," said the father. "You just went ahead with what you thought, you made out I was guilty of killing that little girl, you didn't ask why I was hurt—"

"You wouldn't talk, dammit!"

"I *couldn't* talk. My wits was addled. You ever been set on in the dark and knocked down?"

"Well, but it's over, Dad. Let's not hold a grudge. Look, she's putting a nice lunch on the table, hot biscuits and honey the way you like them. The kids are down for their nap. We can eat and have some peace and quiet and be friends."

"No friends for me in this house. Not even you." The old man slammed the suitcase shut. It was of battered cowhide, the straps frayed, buckles broken. He sat beside it on the bed and leaned close and tried to work the frayed straps through the slots in the buckles. "One thing I'm fixing to do. I'm going to set that Ferguson feller straight. He's got some cockeyed idea I met one man going down to the gatehouse, and then some other feller sneaked up behind me and conked me one. I guess I know what happened there better'n he does, and it was the same feller. He came back and gave me a walloping and he turned his foot."

Young Mr. Arthur came into the room to stand above the old man. "You're going to mess this thing up. You're going to keep harping and jawing on the subject, and you're going to screw us all, we'll all be suspects. Can't you get it through your head, the one who hit you was the Dronk boy? He thought you'd recognized him."

The old man shook his head stubbornly. His son reached down and grabbed the front of the old frayed coat. His father examined the fist right under his nose with disdainful scorn. "You got you a temper, son."

"You make me so damned mad," his son said, removing the hand. "But, look, arguing isn't getting us anywhere. Don't run off down there and pester Ferguson and give him wacky theories. Just come in and sit down to your lunch."

"Never again at your table," said old man Arthur. He threaded the buckles and yanked on the straps. He lifted the suitcase and headed for the door.

His son watched until he got as far as the hall, almost out of sight, then hurried after. "Dad. Dad, wait."

He caught up with the old man in the living room. Old man Arthur had put down the suitcase to open the front door. "Just this one favor, Dad, Just don't tell Ferguson that crazy opinion of yours."

"Why not?" The old man gave the room a stare in leaving; under the scraggly brows the pale old eyes burned with a bitter memory. "It's the truth."

"The Bartlett girl was killed by Mr. Dronk's son. Rossi and Ferguson have been across the street, talking to the kid. They've found some sort of new evidence, a bundle of clothes or something, and it must link the kid even stronger to the crime. Why won't you accept facts? The two kids were together a lot, they were having some kind of teen-age affair—God knows how far that had gone—and the kid's crippled. He limps, and the man who hit you and took the cane, he limped. My God, how much more do you want?"

His father looked him over closely. "You sound like an old woman. You should have gone to work today, 'stead of sneaking around spying on the Dronk house."

"Now, see here—"

"The trouble with you," old man Arthur began, and then checked himself. Young Mrs. Arthur had opened the oven and there was a drifting odor of hot biscuits. The old man opened the door and stepped out into the sunlight. "Isn't enough time to go into it," he finished, and slammed the door in his son's face.

Mrs. Holden turned from the window draperies. "They found something else up there," she said half-aloud to the empty room. "They took it away, overalls or something." She walked restlessly across the room, then back to the windows. "Now they've gone, they didn't come back, and they didn't arrest that Dronk boy." She stood frowning and chewing her lip. She was wearing a brown cotton dress, cut across the hips in a way that was supposed to make her look slimmer, a yoke set into the skirt and flaring pleats below. She smoothed the skirt, sat down, then stood up and went back to the windows. "Why on earth did I send him off to work? There was excuse enough to keep him home.... That young Mr. Arthur's still over there."

With sudden energy, she went to the phone and rang Holden's office and asked for him.

"I think you had better come home."

"Mae, we're so busy. Mr. Crosson's been on everybody's neck, an order he expected didn't come through and he's—"

"I don't care. I want you here. I'm all alone and certain things are going on that look very ominous. I need someone to go out and find out what's happening."

"But I couldn't do that, even if I were home!" His voice grew high and trembling. "I can't be underfoot every time those cops turn around! They'll ... they'll think I did something."

He couldn't see the grin that split her mouth; the teeth that shone into the phone were like a shark's. "You'll just have to risk it. You can't wander along in the dark, can you? I'd think that you ... even more than I ... would be wondering what they're up to. They found some clothes," she tossed in.

"What?"

Deliberately, she ignored the yelp. "Also, that Mr. Ferguson was here. I guess he wants to ask you some questions. I stalled him off. He doesn't expect you until five."

"Then I'd better wait until five."

"No .. o .. o. Come home right away." She slapped the receiver into its holder and stepped away. Her eyes were bright with anticipation.

In his office, Mr. Holden replaced the phone slowly. He rose from his chair. He had to cough then; he went to the window and choked there with the fresh breeze on his face. He got his hat out of the closet. For a moment he thought of going into Crosson's office to explain that he had to leave, but there was now such a pain in his chest, such a pounding in his head, that he decided to let it go. He passed the receptionist in the outer office, muttering, "I've got to go out for a little while." Let her call Crosson if she wanted to, let Crosson raise the roof or even can him, he didn't care.

He got into the car. Putting the key into the switch, pressing the accelerator with his foot, putting the car into reverse, seemed vast endeavors almost beyond the ability of his shaking body. Once out in the street, the traffic was a gadfly maze in which he wandered stricken. When he turned into the highway that led to the outskirts of the city and then rose toward home, he had to pull over to the curb and wait for a few minutes, sucking in air and squinting and blinking his eyes to clear them of tears.

What on earth was in Mae's mind, that she wanted him up there spying on what the cops were doing? What did she think he could do?

He tried to ignore what his own common sense told him, but it wasn't possible; her motives were too blatant. She wanted him to get into trouble. She wanted the police to notice him, suspect him. She was going to keep on scheming, poking, prodding, suggesting, and dictating until the cops got up enough interest in him to go back to their old neighborhood and ask questions. And he knew in that moment, with a cold sinking of despair, a dying of old hopes, that Mae had spread some kind of word there among the neighbors. Nothing bald, open; but enough. They'd have some suspicions to repeat to the police.

Though his inner thoughts cringed at it, he forced himself to think back, recreating the scene in which Mae claimed to have caught him molesting the child.

It hadn't amounted to anything. There had been nothing evil or dirty in his intentions.

A second scene flashed before his mind, the interior of the garage at the new house and the young Bartlett girl turning startled to meet him, the dim dark and the sudden confusion and fear and then the brightness as Mae had clicked on the light.

Suppose the cops somehow got hold of *that?*

Well, it hadn't been what it seemed, he'd had no idea the girl was in there. He hadn't touched her.

And when he came to examine the scene, there was a certain staginess to it, it had the smell of planning, and a swift suspicion darted into his mind.

Too monstrous, of course. Mae wouldn't have plotted a thing like that. It was just that little accidents played into her hands. Like this murder.

He leaned on the wheel, clutching it, staring into the sunlight, and tried to bring order into his thoughts. He felt lightheaded and sick. There was no use wandering off into a territory of utter nightmare. Mae was his wife. She was married to him for better or for worse. She wouldn't be willfully planning his destruction.

But she was. She was.

Even as the conviction of truth roared through him, shattering his last hope of safety, he was reaching to release the hand brake, to head up the road for home, doing her bidding. He drove, and the road wobbled, familiar scenes crept past on either side. He came to a stretch of old orange groves, the trees dead, some of them uprooted, and then there was an outlying shopping area, and tract houses. He had the feeling that he should abandon the car and run off somewhere to hide. But he couldn't imagine where. There was really no place to go, finally, except home to Mae.

At the gate he slowed, looking around. Cooper was beside his car, on the curb at the right, just standing there morosely; he didn't even look up. Behind him on the steps of the little office sat old man Arthur; he was straight, something angry in his attitude, as if he might be waiting to report something. Holden stepped on the gas.

A new idea drifted in from nowhere. He could go to the police. He could tell them his fears of being involved, he could explain what had happened in the old neighborhood and how Mae had misunderstood and how she held it over him—the scene was complete in his mind at the moment, even to his own jerkings and snivelings, and Ferguson's silent patience. He could throw himself on the mercy of the police department.

It wasn't what Mae would want him to do, though. He was sure of this. Once he had abandoned himself to the very worst, once he had quieted all the dragons of worry and suspense, there wouldn't be very much for Mae to do. At that moment, Holden almost slammed on the brakes to go back to Cooper and ask if Ferguson was about.

It would be such a relief.

What was that old sign, supposed to be painted over a door somewhere: *Abandon hope, all ye who enter here?*

Why, Holden said to himself, surprised at his own sudden insight, I'll bet some of those people who enter are just as happy as can be. They've worried, they've lain awake nights, they've shook at the slightest footstep, they've pictured their own destruction, and now it's all over and they can give up. Sure, they're giving up hope. Hand in hand with hope went things like terror and apprehension. *Good-bye.* Holden waved a hand at the empty street. *Glad to see you go.*

He drove into the paved space before the garage and got out, slamming the car door. He looked up and down the street. If Ferguson's car had been in sight, Holden would have walked directly to it.

He went to the front door and opened it and looked in.

Mae entered the room from the hallway to the kitchen. She had a cup of something steaming, coffee perhaps, in one hand, a fresh piece of toast in the other. She stood there, watching Holden come in, and put the piece of toast in her mouth and bit off one corner with a huge chomp of her white teeth.

"Mae—"

"I've been thinking," she said, swallowing the toast. "Didn't you have an old pair of painting overalls in the garage? You used them that time you painted the porch at our other house. And then you wiped up some grease."

She had caught him off guard, no preparation, nothing certain but that ahead lay some kind of disaster. "No. Wait a minute. What do you—"

"I've been looking for them, and they're gone. I'm sure they were in the garage up until a couple of days ago. Or even yesterday. You used to paint in them, and then you just took them for rags. The police have them now."

"I don't remember any overalls at all."

"They were all faded. Worn through at the knees." She stood sipping and chewing and watching. "Green paint, wasn't it? Well, I'm not sure of the color. But you had them."

"Mae, sit down. Put down the cup of coffee. Tell me what this is all about."

She shook her head. She took another bite of toast. Holden noticed almost absently how she chewed, how the whole side of her cheek moved, a slab of fat that extended down into her neck. "My goodness, you ought to remember if I do. You're going to have to go to the police and explain what happened. Tell them the truth ... or something ... before they come here."

A seeping coldness entered Holden's being; his nerves seemed frost-bitten down to the tips of his tingling fingers and his spine felt stiff and glasslike, liable to break like an icicle at any moment. "I've never owned any painting overalls. Or any other kind."

"The police came and found them," she said.

"Then they were planted. It's a fraud, a fake."

"Then that's what you'd better go and tell the police."

It was like trying to blow a hole in a ton of feathers. Holden walked to a chair and started to sit in it, still stiff and straight because of the fragile icicle spine, and then he changed his mind. He went to the hall and back to his own bedroom. There, carefully, gently, he bent himself toward the corner of the closet where the hunting rifle stood propped behind the coats. He had had the gun for years. A friend had given it to him. The friend had been a great hunter and then he had shot himself through the foot in an accident, and he had parceled out the hunting equipment helter-skelter, with no regard to whether it was wanted. Holden had never fired a gun in his life.

He took out the gun and hefted it experimentally. He tried to open the breech, but didn't know how. He couldn't remember whether the friend had told him it was loaded or not; but it seemed that he recalled some sort of warning, and the friend had been impetuous about getting rid of his guns. Probably the thing did have bullets in it.

Mr. Holden went back down the hall to the living room. Mae had taken her cup back to the kitchen, and returned; she was at the front windows, wiping her mouth on her handkerchief. When she heard his footsteps she turned around. "Now what on earth have you got that for?" she asked.

Holden lifted the rifle. He was awkward. He wasn't sure just where the gun butt fitted in your shoulder, or perhaps even above it; but he remembered from somewhere that the sights were supposed to line up. He pointed the barrel at Mae and inched his head down and squinted with his right eye.

She just stood there. There was a puzzled look on her face.

He got the sights lined up, but the barrel no longer pointed to Mae but into the window beyond her. He lifted, leveled and aimed it, and then he was confronted by another problem. There was so much of her. He scarcely knew just what to aim at. It was like aiming at the side of a mountain.

Then he found her eye in the sights, bright, round, and fixed.

She screamed and he pulled the trigger.

The room rocked with noise, there was a suffocating smell of gunpowder, the rifle rocketed out of his grasp from the recoil, and Mae went down. She went down like two tons of horse meat.

Seventeen

Mr. Holden stumbled over the gun. The haze of smoke and the acrid smell set him to choking. He found his way out to the kitchen, ran water into a glass, drank it. The house seemed very quiet.

There were certain procedures to be followed at a time like this. He had read about them in the paper. You walked into a police station, or you telephoned, and you said, "Please come quickly. I've killed my wife." It happened all the time, a regular routine.

He drew another glass of water and went to the rear door and looked out. The ivy wasn't doing too well, he noticed. Needed watering, or more manure, or something. Next door, the Arthur place, the ivy sprigs were beaten flat, worn out by the kids on their trikes. He didn't see a soul out there, no one peering, no one coming to ask questions. He thought that somebody must have heard the shot, and then it occurred to him that if it had been heard, it had been taken for a backfire. That was always happening, too. Someone heard the murder shot and later told the police, "I didn't go to look because I thought it was a car backfiring." Mr. Holden sipped the water and marveled at all the routine doings that had grown up about the act of shooting another person, like barnacles on a boat.

The silence was restful.

I must be a monster, he thought, marveling. *It's so peaceful now I could go to my room and lie down for a nap.*

That wouldn't be following the pattern. Or would it? Hadn't there been something in the paper, some weeks past, about a man who had killed his wife and had then rolled into bed and slept through the night, and hadn't made the usual appearance at the police station until the middle of the next morning?

Mr. Holden, to his own astonishment, yawned.

He put the glass on the sinkboard and listened to the stillness.

There was something luxurious about the quiet, something padded and upholstered, deep-carpeted, heavy-draped, scented, and it made Mr. Holden think of a castle somewhere, rich and remote, with him there in the midst of it as safe as if he were in God's pocket.

He yawned again, this time with a jaw-stretching crack. He noticed suddenly that he wasn't wheezing at all, there was no sense of swelling, no struggle to breathe.

He went to the bedrooms by way of the rear hall, avoiding the living room. He took off his shoes and stretched out on his bed. There was the faintest hint of gun smoke in the air, but it wasn't unpleasant.

He let his eyes drift closed. His breast rose and fell lightly, his body gradually relaxed, his pulse quieted.

It was wonderful.

He heard a noise then, a kind of stumbling rattledy-bump, footsteps that thudded, the clatter of something overturned. He sat up slowly, the peacefulness not quite dissipated, and watched the door. His wife appeared in the doorway, her face covered with blood-blotches from the crease in her scalp. She stood there wavering. She put up a hand and touched the wetness and then stared at her fingers.

"You tried to kill me, you miserable little toad!"

"I thought I had," said Mr. Holden, regretfully swinging his feet over the side of the bed. "Now I shall have to do it all over again. Too bad."

She fled screeching, and before he reached the living room he heard the front door slam.

He sat down on the couch and waited, while the screams diminished in the distance. The gun lay on the floor, looking out of place, and after a little while Mr. Holden got up and took it back to the closet. Then he resumed his seat. The police would be here right away, of course. Probably they'd figure he had killed the Bartlett child, too.

But time passed and nothing happened.

It occurred to Mr. Holden that the cops might not be on hand right now, that they could have gone into town with some kind of evidence—that clothing Mae had mentioned, perhaps. Maybe Mae hadn't found anyone to tell except the neighbors, or Mr. Cooper. And they, being circumspect, were keeping their distance.

He had better plan what he should say when the police finally got here.

Instead, he found himself thinking about the murder of the Bartlett girl. She had been a very pretty youngster. No doubt there was a sex angle in it somewhere, though this morning the newscasters had been saying she had not been attacked. Perhaps the attacker had been frightened off at the last minute, or had had a prod from his conscience. Or it could be that at the time the attack was to be made, the man realized he had a corpse.

Mr. Holden felt a wrench of bitter distaste, examining these theories.

Still, he had a hunch about that last idea, that the murderer hadn't really intended to kill, that the killing was incidental to the other ugly business. *When Mr. Ferguson gets here I'll offer him the idea*, Holden thought. When he's putting on the handcuffs, for example. Maybe he hasn't thought of it.

A little time ticked by, and Mr. Holden glanced at his watch.

He wondered to himself what was going on outside. By now Mae must have found someone to listen to her tale of panic. The neighbors would be gathering, curious, scared, thinking that the murderer had been exposed by this attempt at a second crime. The police must be on their way—from somewhere.

He smiled grimly, thinking all at once of Miss Silvester. An old maid. She'd be looking under the bed at bedtime for the next twenty-five years. Mae said she'd been entertaining a man, but that was nonsense. Women who looked like Miss Silvester didn't carry on affairs.

The Arthurs would be quite wrought up. Young Mrs. Arthur would have the kids in the house, as if hiding them from some wild beast. Young Mr. Arthur would be at the front door with some appropriate weapon at hand, say a broom handle, and the grandfather.... Mr. Holden suddenly recalled the scene by the gate as he had come home. Now that he remembered, the old man had had a suitcase with him.

Mr. Holden wondered irritably what had happened to the old man.

There was a sudden distinct knock at the door. The door opened before Mr. Holden could even stand up, and Ferguson came in. He looked all around—looking for the gun, Mr. Holden decided—and then nodded at Holden and said in a normal voice, "Heard you had a little trouble here."

Holden had risen. "Do you want me to make a statement, or something? I admit, I thought I had killed her. I was lying down when she revived."

"So I understand."

"Is she in any danger of dying?"

Ferguson shook his head. "I don't think so."

He walked a little closer, not fast, and though he didn't seem to be staring very hard, Holden sensed that some kind of scrutiny was going on. "Do you want to put handcuffs on me?"

"Perhaps not just yet. Do you want to sit down for a minute?"

Holden resumed his seat.

Ferguson perched on the edge of a chair. It was a fine old piece of maple; Mae had inherited it from an aunt. "Suppose you tell me about Pamela Bartlett. Start at the beginning," Ferguson said.

Holden was surprised at Ferguson's foreknowledge of what he had meant to say. "Well, actually there isn't a beginning. It's kind of vague. Just a few thoughts, a few ideas. And they might not be new."

"Why did you put the stuff up around Dronk's place?"

"What?"

"The shoes, under the tree. The overalls under the steps."

"I don't seem to understand what you're talking about," Mr. Holden said puzzledly. "I've been sitting here thinking, and a few ideas have occurred to me, like for instance the murder might not have been intentional. He was meaning to attack her, but he was too rough and she died."

"Is that what you intend to say?" Ferguson asked, with an expression of sick disgust.

"It's just a theory. Now, this other thing. Mae thinks that Miss Silvester has been entertaining a man during the evenings lately. But she's a tax adviser, isn't she? Works at home? Why couldn't he be coming there on business?"

Ferguson seemed to have withdrawn in some indefinable way, as if Mr. Holden required some bitter thinking-about.

"I really don't quite believe that Mr. Dronk's son did it," Mr. Holden went on seriously. "Although young Mr. Arthur told me out there this morning you were all so sure about it."

Ferguson's attitude was delicate, as if he were picking a pearl out of a mud pie. "Let's talk about that scream you heard, the one you told Rossi about this morning, the one you forgot to mention previously."

"Oh, there wasn't any scream," Mr. Holden said. "That was a lie that Mae made up. She wanted me to keep hanging around and pestering you people until you got suspicious of me."

"Nevertheless," Ferguson answered, "when we went to examine things about the scream, we found the dead girl's shoes. And later a pair of old overalls which we think were used to muffle her face, and also to deaden the sound of the blows which were afterward rained on her." He waited with an air of catlike patience. "Does any of this make sense to you now, Mr. Holden?"

"Not at all," said Holden in relief.

"You deny being the murderer of Pamela Bartlett?"

"I certainly do. All I wanted was to kill my wife."

His glance was steady. He hadn't wheezed once. This was the exact opposite of the scene he had imagined earlier: him trembling and gasping and Ferguson looking at him in pity while he writhed in wretchedness. No, this was quite different, and much better. He straightened the crease in his pants-leg and shuttered a yawn behind his hand.

Ferguson rose. "Well … there's this charge, attempted murder, of course."

Mr. Holden also rose and held out his hands peacefully. "What do you think I'll get? Ten years? Twenty?"

Ferguson merely shook his head. To himself he was prophesying: Holden would plead guilty, the judge would take a look at the old battle-ax of a wife, listen to her yowls and study Holden's meek resignation, and hand down a suspended sentence.

"Aren't you going to put on handcuffs?"

"I don't believe they're necessary. Would you like to pack a few things?"

Mr. Holden packed a bag and then they went down to the gate in Ferguson's police car. Ferguson didn't use the siren, though Holden had thought he might. At Cooper's office, Ferguson parked the car. "I'm going to call someone to come get you. I need more time up here. Uh … do you want to say good-bye to your wife?"

"What?" Holden's breath stuttered, his throat constricting, and then he said, "Certainly not. That woman makes me sick."

While Mr. Holden waited in front of the office, not even being guarded, Miss Silvester drove in through the gate. To Mr. Holden there was something erratic and half-blind in the way she handled the car. He noticed that Ferguson had come quickly to the door and was looking up the street after her.

Miss Silvester went into the living room and dropped on the couch.

She felt drained and dirty. There were spots on the rumpled suit, dust marks on her hose and shoes. She had left hat and gloves in the car. Her hair was tumbled.

The silence of the house closed around her.

It was a lovely house, she thought. Much better than she deserved.

She took a handkerchief from her purse and began to cry.

Something had gone wrong, disastrously awry, and she couldn't understand how it had happened. She had been so pleased over the small inheritance, thrilled to know that she could afford to move away from the drabness into this beautiful place, a home of her own. And it had seemed, in those first exciting days, as if a kind of magic surrounded her, bringing all good things. Bringing Ross, for instance. Of course she had known that he couldn't really be in love with her the way he might have been with a young girl, but still she had thought that there was affection. Under the surface. A gentle feeling. A kind of tenderness with a touch of the maternal.

Now she knew better.

Sitting there hunched, crying into the handkerchief, she shuddered. He had been brutal in the car. She had tried to run and he had caught her. Snatches of memory flashed in her thoughts, and she thought that she would be sick.

"I'm glad I never married," she wailed to herself. "I might have got someone like *him!*"

There was a heavy knock at the front door. She lifted her head. It seemed impossibly bad luck that anyone should come now. She brushed at her hair mechanically, wondering if she dared just stay here still and quiet until they went away, and then a sixth sense told her no. It would be that detective.

She went to the door and was not at all surprised to find Ferguson.

He came in, taking a good look at her, and said, "I'm awfully sorry to disturb you just now, Miss Silvester." He sounded as if he meant it.

"Please sit down and get it over with," she said.

"We've been checking on your friend."

She tightened, quivering all over, and suddenly all the stains and smudges seemed to crackle like lightning, all afire under his stare. There was nothing she could say. She gave him a mute look.

"Ross has quite a record for someone as young as he is," Ferguson said, sitting down slowly. "I guess you knew that."

"No." It was a gasp, a whisper. She was still stunned by Ferguson's matter-of-fact announcement that he'd been checking on Ross—as if he knew all about her connection with him.

"His employers didn't seem to know it either. But Ross first got into trouble in junior high school. A group of about five of his friends got to playing around one night, a twelve-year-old girl, and afterward Ross blackmailed them for their lunch money. He had quite a good thing going. Then one of the kids couldn't take it any longer and told the school principal. You can imagine the mess that followed."

She was staring at him through a haze of horror.

"Ross has always had a bad temper, too," Ferguson went on. "He clobbered a kid in high school, caught him in the school parking lot and knocked him out with a bumper jack, just about split his skull, and after that the kid was blind in one eye and Ross served a term with the CYA."

She thought that her heart had quit beating. There was nothing inside her except a hollow emptiness, no tick-tock of life, no blood, no breath.

"At the CYA honor farm," Ferguson said, "Ross got it in for one of the counselors. He concocted a rather fiendish revenge. He made a snare-trap out of piano wire, and when the counselor went out on his rounds at night, and got caught in it, he was hamstrung. It cut the tendons of his right foot. He was crippled after that. And Ross was transferred to a tougher institution."

A thought occurred, a half-hope. "You must be talking about another person."

"No." Ferguson shook his head. "This is the man you've been seeing, the one who came with the moving van, your new furniture. We haven't been able to locate him but we talked to the other two who were here that day, and we talked to his landlady, and various police departments who've had dealings with him. He really isn't the kind of man you should know, Miss Silvester."

She licked her dry lips. The room, the beautiful furnishings, had taken on a fiendish unfamiliarity, as though she might have just wakened in a padded cell, or in jail, or in hell. "Has he some kind of hold over you? Has he been demanding money?"

She thought for a moment that she could tell him about Ross and how Ross had needed a loan and how she had given it willingly, lovingly, but the words would not come.

"Well," Ferguson said, "let's get down to what you know about Pamela's murder. Ross was up here. We know that. He has a very bad temper. If something went wrong, if he chose to attack the girl and she resisted, for instance, he might be perfectly capable of killing her."

She licked her mouth again, and managed a whisper. "He hurt his foot."

"What was that?"

"He hurt his foot. He limps now."

Ferguson nodded with satisfaction. "He's the one who beat up old man Arthur, then. And that puts him right on the spot. He must have been up here when Pamela Bartlett was killed."

Eighteen

Mrs. Bartlett stirred on the hospital bed, moaned, opened her eyes, blinked several times, lifted a hand. Her husband reached quickly to touch her fingers. At the touch she turned her head, looked at him. For a moment there was a blank, uncomprehending silence.

Her lips moved as if she were whispering to herself. She turned her head again, examining the room. "I had a bad dream," she said, half whispering. "I dreamed that something terrible had happened."

He had been commanded not to say anything to upset her. At a loss, he stroked her fingers and avoided her eyes.

"You look awfully tired," she said. "Have you been up all night? What time is it?" She pulled on his hand, trying to make him look at her. "Have I been sick? I wish they hadn't given me drugs. I've had such a horrible dream and I know the drugs must have caused it."

With his free hand he shifted the heavy horn-rimmed glasses on his nose. "You need to rest, dear."

"But I am rested. Very rested. Except that in the back of my mind there are the ... the dregs of this awful business, this dream about Pamela." She lay there staring at the ceiling and then tried suddenly to sit up. "Was it a dream? Was it?"

"I'm going to call the nurse," he said. "She went out for a cup of coffee. I said I'd stay with you. But you need her now."

"No. Wait a minute. Answer the question I asked you."

"Not now, please."

"But it had to be a dream!" Her voice was a cry, like a child's cry, lost in the dark, searching. "A nightmare! She was dead, and they'd found her body. Murdered!"

He tried to keep her in the bed, he tried to soothe her with words, with pattings.

"Why? *Why?*" She began to scream the word, louder and louder, her body twisting and thrashing, the covers winding about her whipping legs and the pillow pushed over onto the floor.

He tried to stay calm. "I don't know why. I don't know why someone as good and as sweet as our child had to die." His voice broke and he relaxed his grip on her wrists and she snapped free. She sprang to the end of the bed and sat there kneeling, her wild eyes on the door.

The nurse came in, all starchy and white. She wore a Johns Hopkins cap and her smile was tight and professional. "Now, now, Mrs. Bartlett, we can't have all this!" She glanced at Mr. Bartlett. "You know you were supposed to keep her quiet!"

"I don't know," Mr. Bartlett said in an exhausted voice, "what I was supposed to do, but I think she might as well get it over with. Let her scream while the knowledge comes back, and then she'll be quiet. She'll know it's not going to change, it's been done, and she'll stop screaming."

The nurse saw he wasn't going to be any help so she turned to the wife. "Let's lie down again now, shall we? I'll fix your bed for you. Can't have covers on the floor!"

Mrs. Bartlett tried to fight her off, screaming and choking all the while. Mr. Bartlett wanted to run out of the room, but some sense of loyalty made him stay. He couldn't help, but he might put over some vague kind of moral support. Silently, he told his wife, *Scream, scream! I wish I could.*

The nurse finally decided she couldn't cope. She held Mrs. Bartlett with one hand while she punched a button on the wall. In a moment an orderly stuck his head in, took in the situation with a glance. The nurse nodded some voiceless command. He was gone less than a minute, and when he came back there was a second orderly with him, carrying a canvas contraption. The nurse and the two orderlies put Mrs. Bartlett into it, tying her helpless to the bed.

They couldn't stop the screams, but presently the doctor came and gave orders, and the nurse prepared a hypodermic.

Mr. Bartlett braced the doctor in the hall. "She'll just wake up confused, all over again, and have to realize what's happened. How many times do you want to repeat this business?"

The doctor looked almost as tired as Mr. Bartlett. "We have to consider other people here," he said. "If it weren't for that, I'd let her remain conscious. By the way, have they caught the murderer?"

"I don't know. It doesn't seem important right now."

"No, I suppose not." The doctor gave him a quick, sympathetic glance and walked off down the hall.

Mr. Bartlett went to the waiting room at the end of the corridor.

Ross Havilland came into the small office and looked around with an arrogant grin and said, "What the hell did you bring me up here for?"

Ferguson sat behind Cooper's desk. Charts and building plots had been put away. He said to Ross, "Take a chair. I had them bring you here because this is where I am. I'm investigating a murder. The murder happened here."

Ross fished out cigarettes and matches before he sat down. "So?"

"Tell me about your visit here last night," Ferguson said.

Ross flipped the spent match into Cooper's wastebasket, drew on the cigarette, gave Ferguson a level look. "I came up about seven-thirty. Stayed about an hour, more or less. Went home. That cover it?"

"You know we want more than that."

"Like what?"

Ferguson swung in the chair and the bearings squeaked. "Tell me about your meeting with old man Arthur."

"I don't know any old man Arthur."

In spite of the fact that Ross had the cigarette and kept his gaze perfectly centered on Ferguson, lounging in the chair with his head to one side, it was Ferguson who seemed more at ease, was less conscious of having to do something with his hands and his eyes. "Well, let's just say then, the old man you clobbered last night on your way to the gate."

"You're kidding!" He rubbed the back of his neck with his free hand. The muscles rippled under the thin fabric of the knitted shirt.

"We can get tough, Havilland."

"Big, bad cops!"

Ferguson nodded as if Havilland had made some valid point in the conversation. "These people you work with ... they know about your record?"

For a moment Ross almost flinched. "My God," he said, "is that what you've always got to fall back on? My record? The mistakes I made as a kid?"

"Two years ago you were twenty-four," Ferguson reminded.

"I wasn't convicted, either."

"The reason you weren't convicted was that the girl's parents refused at the last minute to press charges. They pulled up stakes and moved out," Ferguson said.

Ross grimaced, shrugged. "You want to know how that really happened? The truth about it? I went up to this house in the evening, see. I thought a buddy of mine had moved there a couple of weeks before. I knocked and this chick came to the door, a real knockout. She was sixteen but I took her for twenty, she was stacked that good. I asked if my buddy was there and she said she'd have to find out from her mother. They had a couple of new boarders and she wasn't sure of the names, and why didn't I come in and wait while she hunted up the old lady. So I went in."

"Save it," Ferguson said.

"Sure. So don't listen. Don't bother to find out the chick was already known all over the neighborhood. A real hot article. Went with anybody. The old folks didn't even run a boarding house. Just had her and her little brother, and for two bits the little brother always ran off to the movies. The old man spent his time in the beer joint down at the corner and the old woman went to prayer meetings."

The uniformed cop was outside the open doorway and Ferguson raised his voice a little and said, "We're going to have to take this downtown. Take it away."

"You can't book me!" Ross jumped from the chair, forgetting himself, and took a limping step and flinched.

"You beat old man Arthur up and you tripped over his cane," said Ferguson, "and he can identify you."

Ross stood there chewing his lip. "That's what you're going to charge me on?"

"It'll do for a start. We've got a murder on tap too, when the time comes."

Ross sat down, rubbed his injured ankle, wincing. "Oh, hell, I'll tell you about the old man. It doesn't amount to a damn. I'd just left a house up here ... you know which house? ..." He waited for Ferguson to answer his smug look, and Ferguson gave him an eye as cold as a fish. "... well, I was coming down here fast between those places where they're still building, and I passed this old coot and he said something. I didn't catch on at first, but then almost at the car I had a second thought. He'd spoken to me and what he had said wasn't funny. So I went back."

"What had he said?"

"He called me a hog."

Ferguson couldn't keep the twitch of surprise out of his face. He watched Ross for a moment and then said, "What were his exact words?"

"I don't remember. I caught the word hog, and when I thought it over I went back and found him. I gave him a couple of whacks, that's all, and then I tripped over his damned cane and just about broke my leg."

"Who else was there?"

"Nobody."

"Miss Silvester didn't come out to investigate?"

"We weren't anywhere near her place."

"Did you hear the old man holler?"

Ross shrugged again. "Oh, he let out a couple of yells but they weren't very loud. As far as I know he just got up and went on."

"You took the cane with you?"

For a moment there was a trace of hesitation in Ross's manner. He put his foot on the floor, testing the injured ankle, working the heel up and down; his face seemed full of thought.

Ferguson repeated the question.

"I threw the damned thing," Ross admitted. "At first I tried to break it over my knee. I was just about crazy with pain. When it wouldn't break I threw it. I heard it hit something, the side of a house or something, and bounce off. By then I was on my way back to the car."

Ferguson nodded. "And when you reached the car?"

"I took off. What else?"

"Did you see anyone around the gatehouse?"

Ross took in a deep breath as if to issue a strong denial, and then a half-puzzled look swept over him. He grinned slightly, as if to himself. "Funny. I just remembered it. There was a car parked the other side of this office, in the dark. My headlights picked up a reflection, the end of the rear bumper."

Ferguson waited for Ross to continue, but Ross seemed caught up in the recollection, musing over it.

"You didn't happen to recall this until right now?"

"Yeah." Ross squinted into the distance. "Weird, isn't it?"

"It kind of gets you off the hook," Ferguson suggested.

"I hadn't thought of it that way."

"Well, think of it. Are you sure you weren't looking at a reflection of a tin can? Or some metal wiring, a piece of electrical equipment, tile or other building materials?"

"It was a car's bumper," Ross said, but not quite as assuredly.

"Then there must have been a fender, too. What color?"

Ross shook his head. "I don't remember."

"The taillight would have given a red reflection when your lights hit it."

"I didn't see a red reflection. I wasn't directly behind the car, anyway. In fact I wasn't even close, I was on the other side of the gate, turning through the gate, going out."

"But you think that a car was in here."

"Yeah. That I'm sure of."

Ferguson motioned toward a straight chair over in the corner. It was piled with building plans and other papers. "Clear that chair off and sit in it and keep your mouth shut," Ferguson told Ross. To the uniformed officer he called, "I want to see Mr. Arthur."

The old man must have been waiting close by, for he came in almost at once. He gave Ross a sharp glance, then turned to Ferguson. Ferguson indicated the chair facing him, the one Ross had occupied. "Sit down, Mr. Arthur, I have a few questions."

"You let me say my piece first," old man Arthur began, in a strong hoarse voice. "I'm leaving home, haven't got all the time in the world. My point—the man I passed in the dark and the one that whopped me was the same feller. Nobody, not even my son, is going to make me say the second time it was Dronk's crippled boy. Didn't limp the same. Like I said, he hopped away on his hurt foot, cussing a blue streak. Dronk's boy don't travel that way. Couldn't."

"We know that the man who passed you went back to beat you up," Ferguson said flatly. "We're not arguing that point."

Old man Arthur took a second look at Ross. "That him?"

"Can you identify him?"

"No."

"You can't say for sure that this is the man you passed, the one you spoke to?"

"It was too doggone dark," the old man admitted.

"When I first talked to you about it, you said that the man who passed you was big and young. Now, didn't you see him clearly?"

The pale old eyes seemed troubled.

Ferguson said gently, "When did you decide that he must be big and young? When he came back and clobbered you?"

"I ... I guess so."

"What did you say to him when you met him?"

"Just ... just something. I don't know."

"Didn't you make some insulting remark? Didn't you call him a hog?"

The old man scratched the side of his cheek, frowning. He looked at Ross again. "He said that?"

"Why did you use the word hog, Mr. Arthur?"

"Didn't *call* him a hog," Mr. Arthur said, as if remembering. "I might have said something about *hogging it all*."

"That's an odd remark. Hogging what?"

"All the ... all the fun. Trying to keep folks cooped up. Making out like I might cause trouble, down there at the gatehouse. Getting that daughter-in-law of mine all worked up so she's chewing on me, too."

"Wait a minute. You said to this young man here, when you passed him—and you'd never seen him before—you said to him that he was making trouble for you?"

The old man nodded drearily.

Ferguson seemed to be groping among invisible feathers. "Didn't you tell me, just this morning, that you had gone looking for this man because you knew there had been a mysterious visitor to one of the homes? That you'd seen the car near the gatehouse? That you wanted a look at the stranger?"

"Well ... that was ... that was *afterward*," the old man said.

"After what?" When old man Arthur didn't reply at once, but just sat there as if searching for a way to say it, Ferguson added, "Where had you been, just before the encounter with this stranger?"

The old man hated to admit it; he looked from Ross to Ferguson as if defying them to pin him down. "I hadn't done anything wrong."

Ferguson said suddenly, "You'd been to the gatehouse, hadn't you?"

Old man Arthur nodded grudgingly.

"You saw this man's car hidden near the trees, the other side of the gate?"

"Sure did."

"And what else?"

The old mouth closed like a trap.

"You saw a car, a second car, beside this office, didn't you? And when you met the stranger in the dark, you were full of fright and defiance. You thought Cooper had caught up with you. And you flung out at him all your resentment because he was trying to prevent you from having a little innocent fun. Isn't that the truth? You thought for the first moment or so that the man coming toward you in the dark was Cooper?"

The old man sighed heavily. "Yes, that's right. I thought it was Cooper because Cooper's car was here."

Nineteen

Ferguson was alone now in the office.

Rossi had brought Cooper from his home in town. Cooper stepped in to the office and looked around as though it were utterly strange and he had never seen it before.

"Sit down please, Mr. Cooper."

Cooper had his hat in his hands. He dropped it on the floor beside the chair, sat down, leaned back as if he might relax, then jerked forward. "What's come up? Something new? You've found new evidence about the little girl's murder?"

Ferguson folded his hands on the desk. He met Cooper's eyes levelly and Cooper fumbled with cigarettes and matches, getting a smoke going. "Tell me," Ferguson said, "about your trip up here last night."

"You mean, about the murder? Well, you know, the officers called me and wanted the office opened up so that—"

"No, not that. Earlier. You came up here and parked in the dark because you wanted to catch old man Arthur playing at gatekeeper. You had a hunch he was hanging around the gatehouse during the evenings and you were going to put a stop to it. Wasn't that kind of a silly determination on your part? Was he really being a nuisance?"

Cooper's face was gray and the freckles on it stood out in muddy patches. "I wasn't up here. There's been some kind of mistake."

Ferguson was not perturbed by the denial. "Just why did Mr. Arthur's wanting to be the gateman annoy you so much?"

"The old nut." Cooper looked up as if catching himself. "I'm not admitting I was here. I'm just saying he got under my skin, hanging around down here where people couldn't help seeing him. Everyone who came, people looking for houses ... real estate agents...."

"Isn't this what happened, Mr. Cooper? You came up here last night and tried to waylay the old man?"

"No."

"He had some idea you were after him. He took off. You tried to circle around, cut him off. You saw his encounter with another man, you saw the old man get beat up, and you decided that should hold him for a while. You were pretty pleased by it."

"You're making a hell of a mistake," Cooper said. "I don't have to sit here and listen to this.... There's nothing to it, and I've got a certain standing in this town, I know some pretty important people."

"Pamela Bartlett was pretty important," Ferguson said quietly. "At least she was important to people like her parents and her friends."

"Well ... that's ... that's ..." Cooper seemed unable to find the proper answer. He had picked up the hat and was wringing it between his hands.

"You were amused by old Mr. Arthur's bad luck. You found his cane, where it bounced off a house, and you listened to his cries, and when he had gone you were puzzled because now someone else was coming. Someone had come out of one of the houses to see what was happening."

Cooper shut his eyes and put a hand over them, rubbing the lids with the ball of his thumb; his mouth was shaking, he didn't try to answer Ferguson.

"What made you decide to attack Pamela Bartlett?" Ferguson asked quietly.

Cooper said nothing; he made a choked sound and leaned forward, putting his elbow on his knee, sheltering his face behind his palm.

"I don't have to be a damned bit clairvoyant to know what happened *after* the murder," Ferguson said. "It's perfectly obvious. You didn't panic. You made careful plans to throw suspicion on other people. You had choked and strangled the girl, wrapping her head in a pair of discarded overalls in some empty house to smother her cries. You beat her skull in with the old man's cane and put the body in the gatehouse—this was to make everyone think old man Arthur had done it."

Cooper tried to shake his head in negation but his wrist wobbled.

"But then you thought about it some more, and it occurred to you that the old man might have an alibi of sorts by now. He might be up there telling his son about the attack made on him by that other man, and the son might do some checking. So it wouldn't hurt to involve a second person, and you thought of the Dronk boy."

Ferguson waited. The silence was complete. Cooper didn't move nor lift his head.

"It had to be you, Cooper. Who else would know about that hole under Dronk's back steps, except you? You went all over the place when you started to build up here. If it wasn't Kim or his dad, it was you, Cooper. No one else would have hidden those overalls in just that place."

Cooper flung up his head. There was mottled color in his face, a hard ragged look in his eyes. "You haven't got a thing!"

"Your car," Ferguson reminded. "Old man Arthur identified your car, and you denied that it was up here. Do you want to start changing your story now? Or wouldn't it be easier just to tell the truth?"

It was obvious that Cooper teetered on the verge of decision. He stared out through the open doorway at the ranks of half-built houses, at the faraway trees and greenery on Palomino Lane. He licked his lips.

His features hardened, and Ferguson was bracing himself for another denial, when suddenly a look of anguish, almost shocking in its nakedness, settled on Cooper's features. He shook with a noise like a sob.

"I wouldn't have hurt her for anything," he said in a dry, squeezed voice, "if I'd been myself. But lately, since I've had this trouble with my wife—my temper's uncertain. I can't control it. It's a feeling that everything is going wrong and I can't stop it. And so when she struggled and when I knew she was going to scream, I just went … berserk."

Ferguson nodded. He opened a desk drawer and took out a pad of writing paper. "Move your chair closer, Mr. Cooper. Use the corner of the desk there and write it out."

"Did you ever go through anything like this?" Cooper asked, his eyes begging. "Did you ever find that you couldn't predict your own behavior? That when you got into a bind you acted like somebody else?"

"I never killed anybody," Ferguson said dryly.

Cooper crouched on the chair, trying to control a tearing anguish; but when Ferguson got up and firmly shoved the chair closer, and put a pen in his hand, he started to write.

They were emerging from the office when Dronk drove in through the gates. Dronk spotted Cooper and turned in to the curb, braked the car and got out quickly. He came limping toward them. Cooper tried to turn away, avoid the meeting, but Dronk seemed oblivious to the man's broken condition.

"Mr. Cooper, I've come to a decision. I've got to tell you right away. I want you to take the land for a park." He waited as if expecting Cooper to respond, say something in reply. "Don't you understand? I'm offering you the land my house sits on, the last of the grove. It can be improved into something quite attractive. If you don't tear the old place down, it might be used as a clubhouse … a young people's center, something like that. We could dedicate it to the memory of this little girl who died here."

"You do that, Mr. Dronk," said Ferguson, pushing Cooper ahead of him toward the police car.

"Is something the matter with Mr. Cooper?" Dronk asked worriedly.

"Just excuse us now, please," Ferguson said.

Dronk stood watching while the officers put Cooper into the police cruiser. He was frowning and uncertain. "It isn't possible … it wasn't Mr. Cooper that—"

Ferguson gave him an absolutely blank stare.

In a stunned way Dronk got into his car and drove on to Palomino Lane. He pulled into the drive. The old pink house looked terribly out of place, he thought. It didn't belong with the low ranchy types down below. Those new people must resent it. Of course they'd want it torn down. Perhaps something new could be built, a community building, named for Pamela Bartlett.

Kim came to the front door. "Dad? You're home early."

His father went to the bottom of the steps, paused there. "They've taken Mr. Cooper away."

"What for?"

"He murdered Pamela Bartlett."

A look of shock spread in Kim's face, and he turned abruptly and disappeared into the gloom within. His father called after him, "Kim! Come back, Kim. I want to tell you something."

Kim didn't come back. Mr. Dronk climbed the steps slowly. He felt tired and lost, a dragging letdown from the long night and day of anxiety. There seemed something hideous and incredible about the crime, as if it should never have happened here where his people had lived for so long. He went into the hall. It suddenly looked gloomy, the ceiling too high, very old-fashioned.

Kim was in the parlor at the windows, looking out. His father went into the room but Kim didn't turn.

Mr. Dronk went close and put his arm across Kim's shoulders. "Will you forgive me, Kim?"

Kim glanced at him over his shoulder. "Why, Dad? Because you sold the land and all these people came here and then this bad thing happened? You can't be blamed for something Mr. Cooper did."

"No, not because of that. But because I kept you here all these years, until you were nearly grown, and I let you do without the chance you wanted. I was afraid to let you take it. I never told you this before Kim, but when you were a baby the doctors estimated that an operation on your foot would have about fifty per cent chance of perfect success, and I was too cowardly to risk it, So I tried to tell myself that I wanted you to be like me, that it would build character to overcome a defect. All lies, Kim. All cowardly lies."

"Don't worry yourself over it now," Kim said uneasily.

"We're going to move away from here," Mr. Dronk said, "and you're going to have the operation, finally. Probably the techniques are a lot more skillful now and the odds are better, but even if they aren't you're going to have the chance you want."

Kim turned around. "Do you mean it?"

"Yes, I mean it."

There was sudden light in Kim's eyes and he grinned. "You know what? Do you realize, Dad ... I'll be able to run!"

"Yes, you'll run, Kim."

"I can't believe it."

They could hear Mrs. Campbell in the back of the house, singing a morose, tuneless song as she got out pots and pans for dinner. Other than that, the old house was very quiet. Kim suddenly put his arms around his father's neck, and clung tightly, and Mr. Dronk remembered the days of years past when Kim had been small; he could place just when it had been, the last time Kim had done this. He felt tears come stinging into his eyes.

"Thank you, Dad. Thank you!"

Kim stepped back, and now he was shaking his father's hand. A very grown-up gesture. His father looked at him wistfully. Probably this had been the last time he would hug his father around the neck like a little boy.

"Let's go tell Mrs. Campbell," said Mr. Dronk. He turned quietly so that Kim wouldn't see the expression on his face or the moisture in his eyes.

THE END

Beat Back the Tide

Dolores Hitchens

Try not to beat back the current,
yet be not drowned in its waters ...
—JOHN HAY

One

It was late twilight, fading to night, and he had gone into the garden, the west end that faced the sea, and had lit his after-dinner pipe, when he became aware that someone had approached the fence and was looking in at him. Through the steel mesh he caught an impression of a slim woman in a black coat, her hair tied in a dark scarf. The last of the western glow shone palely in her face. She had very large eyes; he thought they were blue.

He turned between the banks of roses and went over to the fence. "How do you do? May I help you?"

"Are you Mr. Glazer?"

"Yes."

"I am Francesca Warne."

He felt an immediate surprise and a kind of impatience; she had made him seem rude, though it was no fault of his. "You should have telephoned and let me come after you." He saw that she had set down two small bags. "I hope you didn't walk with your baggage all the way from town."

"I caught a ride," she answered. There was something in her voice that was rough and yet soft, a husky tiredness that struck the ear, not unpleasing; he thought he had never heard a voice quite like it. "It wasn't a far walk down from the highway. And a lovely view." She motioned toward the darkening sea.

He looked at her closely for a moment, hoping she didn't mind his scrutiny. After all, he had taken Emily Graham's word for her, for her tact, her kindness, and her ability. She didn't look much like a nurse to him; she was slight of build, and Glazer was used to thinking of nurses as husky women, able to toss bedridden folk about.

As Emily had explained, however, Mrs. Warne had not long done nursing. She was not a graduate, merely a practical nurse; and previously she had taught the primary grades and still held a teacher's credential. She had seemed from Emily's description to be the ideal person to take charge of a seven-year-old who had been ill and so had lost out on a great deal of school.

Glazer said formally, "I hope you find it pleasant here with us, Mrs. Warne. The view is even better by daylight. My friends who have traveled tell me that the Riviera has nothing on it. Come along to the gate; it's down this way." Then he thought, with anger at himself, that he should have offered to go all the way around and take the bags for her.

But it was too late; she had picked them up lightly.

She came in at the gate, put down a bag, and held out her gloved hand. "I hope I am able to please *you*, Mr. Glazer."

"After all, I'm not the final authority." He smiled to let her see that he was not being too serious about it. "There's Jamie. He's the real boss. I'm very anxious for him to grow stronger and to make up his schoolwork. Most of all, to be happy doing it."

"Jamie. Your little boy." Her eyes moved past him, and there seemed a sudden reserve, withdrawal, in her face. The sea wind lifted the edge of the scarf, and in the indistinct light he had a brief glimpse of black curling hair. A touch of dislike moved him, and he tried to crush it down; it wasn't being fair. Just because the woman was so plain ... After all, she had come to help Jamie, and beauty was no necessary recommendation. "I should like to meet Jamie," she said.

They walked side by side toward the house, he carrying the small bags and Mrs. Warne keeping step. Ahead were the lighted windows of the kitchen wing and the sounds of Mrs. Concannon loading the dishwashing machine and her chatter with Bess, who came out from town to help clean three days a week. "I want you to meet the housekeeper first," Glazer said with a touch of curiosity as to what the women would think of each other. He paused by the front entry to set down a bag, to knock out his pipe into the shrubbery in the flagstone planter. Then, lifting the bag again and noting its light weight, he asked, "You have other baggage coming, of course?"

"Yes, a trunk. The express company will send it out tomorrow."

He opened the door and ushered Mrs. Warne into his house.

From the short hall they came into the living room. It was a room that always drew exclamations from women, and he waited for Mrs. Warne's reaction. But she did an odd thing. Without speaking she turned toward the great windows that looked out over the sea, quickly, as if somehow she knew they'd be there, and she studied the sweep of the horizon and the last smudge of greenish light which was all that remained of that summer day.

"You're very private here," she said at last.

"For everybody except someone on a ship at sea with a spyglass." He put down her bags. "Would you like to meet Mrs. Concannon now?"

She hesitated, and he wondered what the difficulty was, and then with an air of apology she said, "I need to freshen up a bit before meeting people."

"Of course. Stupid of me." He kept his face immobile, turned toward the hall that led to the bedroom wing of the house, became aware that she had started in unison with him. "This way." The words were superfluous. She was a queer one, he decided; sensitive to her surroundings, quick to see where things lay. And quick to know what I am, too, he added: the self-made man who wasn't raised with manners.

When he opened the bedroom door, he got the first reaction from her. She drew a shallow breath quickly; her hand reached out as if to stroke the room's soft beauty. "You have had a marvelous decorator, Mr. Glazer."

"My wife did this before her death."

"It's worthy of the best professional."

"She was a professional." He put her bags in the room, nodded to her, went out and back to the living room. The greenish light on the horizon had faded to a penciling of gray. Bess came in, carrying clean ash trays.

"Mrs. Concannon and I thought we heard you talking to someone." Bess was frank in her curiosity, and he liked it and liked the fact that she had none of the airs of a servant. "Or did we imagine it?"

"I was talking to Mrs. Warne. She just arrived. She's a former schoolteacher, now a nurse, and she's going to help with Jamie for a while."

Bess nodded. "That'll be fine for Jamie. How'd she get here? I don't remember hearing a car."

"She caught a ride."

"On the highway? That's not a very safe thing to do." Bess plopped the ash trays down here and there on tables and chair arms. "You remember that young girl last year, the one they found in the canyon all beat up and raped and robbed? I always wait for the bus, no matter how many fellows honk or slow down to speak; I won't take a chance." Bess's broad pink face wore a smug look, as if she'd outwitted scores of attackers.

"She may have gotten a ride with someone she knew. She used to live here," Glazer answered. He went over to the windows and stood looking out. The bony spine of the headland had been excavated and terraced, then recovered with a lot of very expensive topsoil; Glazer never looked at his remarkable garden without recalling the surprising bill he had paid for the stuff in which the flowers grew. Roses and poppies predominated, tumbling in a golden flood to the brink of the cliff. Glazer thought the color appropriate: golden blooms should grow from a golden soil. Now in the last traces of twilight, it looked ghostly and quiet, framed by the dark waters of the Pacific.

Bess went back to the kitchen. Then he heard steps from the hall and turned to see Mrs. Warne re-enter. Without the black coat and the scarf she was unexpectedly younger and, in an odd way, not exactly pretty, but—"interesting" was a word that occurred to him. The soft black hair took away the harsh lines of cheek and jaw which the tight scarf had exposed. She wore a blue linen frock, and in it her figure looked soft and womanly. He told himself, with pride in his own insight, that now she fitted that strange husky, breathless voice that had so caught his ear.

"I heard a dog barking," she said.

"Jamie has a mutt named Jericho. Part terrier. Part—something else. He's a lot of company, though he does bark too much."

At this moment Mrs. Concannon came in from the kitchen, a little self-consciously, like an actress entering on cue. Glazer noted the curiosity she showed toward Mrs. Warne. He made the introductions. Mrs. Concannon was a large-sized Irishwoman who wore pink uniforms which not only made her look fatter but annoyed Glazer, who would have preferred her to wear ordinary house dresses. She shook hands with Mrs. Warne and studied her face. "How do you do?"

Mrs. Warne smiled at her and at Bess, who had slipped through the door. "I'm very pleased to meet you both."

Bess, reaching for Mrs. Warne's hand, said suddenly, "Why, I've seen you before!"

"I used to live here several years ago," Mrs. Warne answered.

"I guess that's it." Bess withdrew, a little uneasily, Glazer thought, and returned to the kitchen.

Mrs. Concannon seemed to have run out of remarks, and Mrs. Warne just stood, pleasant but speechless. Glazer took a hand and suggested that he and Mrs. Warne now visit Jamie.

The boy's room was at the end of the house. When Glazer had bought the place he had enlarged this room by enclosing a porch with glass, knocking out the wall between and replacing it with an arch, so that the boy's bedroom opened into the large sunny playroom where he could be warm and yet have plenty of space and light. The bedroom furniture was heavy ranch-style stuff, and on the walls were large framed pictures of western scenes, cowboys, cattle, and stagecoaches, two antique pistols in a rack, crossed branding irons, old Spanish spurs, and a small plasticine model of a mountain lion on a rock, snarling down at some prospective prey. It was a very manly room. And the boy in the bed was very small and frail. He was trying to build something with a pile of colored blocks.

Glazer frowned slightly at the blocks. He went over to the bed, and his son looked up at him. The dog stood beside the bed, his paws on the counterpane, and tried to chew Glazer's hand. "Jamie, have you forgotten your manners?"

Jamie hopped out of bed and stood very stiffly in his robe and pajamas.

"Mrs. Warne, this is Jamie."

"I'm pleased to meet you," Jamie said quickly.

"How do you do, Jamie?" She walked over and extended her hand, and after a moment of hesitation Jamie put his into it. "I'm going to be your teacher and your nurse, too, sort of. Get back into bed now."

He obeyed promptly. There was in the child's attitude a great desire to please. He put his hand on his dog's head. "This is Jericho. He likes bananas. Did you ever know a dog liked bananas before?"

"I don't believe I have," she replied seriously.

They talked for a few minutes about dogs, and Glazer listened without adding to the conversation or interrupting. He liked the way Mrs. Warne had approached Jamie; there was no nonsense about her and no sentimentality, a quality he had feared since so many people pitied the child who had been ill so long and showed their pity in a silly excess of affection. Glazer felt that the emotion so roused was bad for the boy, and fundamentally insincere to boot. He heard Jamie ask a question, "Will we do lessons in here?"

"Part of the time," she answered. "On very warm sunny days we can work outside."

"And when school starts in September I'll be all caught up?"

Glazer felt his face stiffen; he turned slightly and looked into the other room. There was a large table with an electric train, a bookcase full of books, a child's desk, a drawing easel, a tank full of tropical fish in which air bubbled softly. On one wall a basketball net hung in its ring. Glazer saw all of these things with an inner as well as an outer eye; he saw each object as it represented some suitable facet of his son's life, a planned activity, a form of mental or physical development. The stiffness spread from his face down into his shoulders and arms, and his hands trembled a little. In anger at himself he forced his attention back to the child and Mrs. Warne.

Jamie was telling Mrs. Warne about the things he had seen in the shallow waters that overlay the shelf of rock at the foot of their cliff. "There are lots of little holes, round ones, where the waves have washed over for years and years, and you can see tiny things in them when the tide is gone. Little tiny crabs, and worms, and sea urchins—" He ran on in a rush, trying to share it all with the quiet attentive woman who had sat down now on the edge of his bed. "We have our own beach, our very own. You go down the side of the bluff—"

Glazer interrupted. "In the morning I'll show Mrs. Warne the way down, Jamie." He turned to her. "You see, there are *two* ways, and I wouldn't want you to try the old one. It's dangerous. When I bought this house, none of the landscaping had been developed. The original owners had left the headland untouched and went down to the water by a sort of natural cow path. When I put in the gardens, I had the men build a path with a stone balustrade and steps built in the steepest places.”

She was looking up at him, the lamplight on her face, and he got an odd impression that her eyes were green. They were quite still, fixed on him, and he wondered what it might have been that he had said which had so gained her attention. Her quiet, intent regard was a trifle disconcerting. It made her suddenly seem so much more a stranger, a woman about whom he knew little, who had come to live in his home.

Jamie spoke, breaking the moment of silence. “I went down once—that old path—when we first moved here. Dad was gone to the job, and Mrs. Concannon forgot to watch, and I got away.” He snickered shyly.

“Jamie’s too old for that sort of thing now,” Glazer said, smiling at the boy. “He won’t do that again.”

“Some stones fell,” Jamie remembered, “and if I’d been standing there, I’d have fallen with them. Only I’d just sneaked past. And all the time up above Jericho was howling. That made Mrs. Concannon look for me and spoiled it all.”

“Saved your life, you rascal.” Glazer rubbed the child’s head roughly. The soft blond hair stood in peaks.

“We will be very careful,” said Mrs. Warne, as if Jamie’s story had frightened her.

Before leaving Jamie’s room, Glazer showed Mrs. Warne the supply of schoolbooks and work materials which he had had sent from Los Angeles; there were many tablets, pencils, and notebooks in the desk. The texts occupied an entire shelf of the bookcase. “These are first-year primers,” he explained, “since Jamie has forgotten almost all that he learned. You’ll have to start at the beginning. Be firm with him. He won’t mind. We’ve talked it over. He knows he will have to work hard.”

Jamie was watching from the bedroom. He had begun to stack the blocks into a pyramid.

In the living room Glazer added to what he had said. “I know that I don’t have to tell you your business, teaching. But the principal of the school here made a suggestion I’d like to pass on. She said that Jamie needs to experience success in his work. He’s been sick; he’s developed an attitude of failure, of expecting defeat. He’ll have to have easy tasks at first.”

“Of course, I understand,” Mrs. Warne agreed.

“At the same time, there must be a sense of accomplishment. He must be given harder work as soon as he is ready for it.” He pulled a chair out for Mrs. Warne so that they could sit facing the great windows on the seaward side. “Someday Jamie has to take over my business, and the job of building contractor isn’t one for a lazy-brain or a weakling.”

"No, it isn't." She was looking out at the view. The sea and the sky were almost the same color now, smoke-dark, obliterating the horizon. A few stars shone and there were boats' lights from the small yacht harbor. "What do you build? What sort of thing? Homes?"

"Recently, yes."

She said hesitantly, "And can you see places from here that you have built?"

"A few." He pointed out the homes, identifying their lights; there were three within view down the coast. "I'm starting a new one for a doctor named Barton. If you look there"—he pointed with the stem of the pipe—"that pale spot, you can just make it out—it's the excavation. It's going to be quite a house when it's done."

"They're all big places, aren't they?"

"Pretty good sized," he agreed.

"I have often wondered," she said after a moment, "how people get enough money to afford homes like that."

"Most of the people who build big houses here on the coast are retired," he answered. "There isn't any industry, no trade except trinkets for the tourists, beach gadgets, in the shops in town. One of the men I built for, the middle one down there—"

"He has a tennis court lit up."

"No, that's his pool. A big one. His name's Clyde; he's a retired insurance executive." Glazer glanced at Mrs. Warne, wondering if the error about the pool meant that she was a little nearsighted. "He's a man of about sixty, never married, no near relatives. I wondered at the time why he wanted such a house. Well, it turns out that he has a hobby. He brings underprivileged kids down from the city."

"Do you think that is wise?"

Glazer looked at her sharply. "What do you mean?"

"When you have so little—it isn't always pleasant to see someone else with so much."

He had never thought of this side of it. "You don't think he's doing the kids such a favor?"

"He may, in the end, be making them most unhappy."

Her point of view made Glazer uncomfortable; he suspected in it somewhere, as he did in almost everything, an oblique reference to himself. He turned her words over and over in his mind, examining them. But in the end he was forced to admit there was no subterfuge in what she had said. Perhaps Clyde was, as she had said, merely adding to the discontent of children who might otherwise not have had much basis for unhappiness. He was displaying to their hitherto uncritical eyes a luxury they could not hope to possess. And a week in a mansion with a swimming pool was poor preparation for fifty-one weeks in a slum.

He had never thought until now that Clyde could have any but the noblest of motives. It struck him suddenly that Clyde might be an insufferable snob, showing off his treasures to those who could never compete in ownership. And kids to boot. Kids who would never suspect the truth about their host, who would suffer in silence and go away full of angry frustration.

He studied Mrs. Warne's cool, plain profile. She had possibilities, he decided, of being a surprising woman.

Two

Glazer always rose early, at around six o'clock, dressed in old clothes, and spent about an hour in the yard. A good deal of the time he spent in adding special ingredients to the soil in which his flowers grew. Each rose, camellia, vine, and poppy was systematically examined, and doctored as one would attend sickly children. Though the display was profuse, Glazer was never satisfied; he was sure that with a small addition of this or that element the bloom would startle the countryside.

He went in at about seven, showered, shaved, and dressed in a business suit, and went to the breakfast nook off the kitchen, where Mrs. Concannon served an unvarying menu of fried salt pork, scrambled eggs, coffee, and corn bread. Her complaints about the sameness of his food in the morning had no effect. He had taught her to boil the salt out of the pork before she fried it, and he had forced her to shorten the corn bread with bacon grease, and he had explained that this breakfast was one he had loved as a child and intended to have for the rest of his life if he could.

What he had not explained was that as a child this had been Sunday breakfast, a treat to be looked forward to and yearned for all week, a relief from the usual fare of soggy pancakes for which there had never been any butter or syrup. To this day Glazer hated pancakes.

While he ate he looked out of a small window at the garden. The early sun gave everything a fresh brilliance. All the poppies had opened, pouring down the terraces like spilled doubloons, stopping at the sheer overhang where the cliff ended. He remembered his chore of taking Mrs. Warne to show her the path to the beach. He wondered if she would be up before he left.

He had not long to wonder. She came in within the next five minutes. She looked neat and cool in a rose-colored dress of some soft material. The black hair curled behind her ears. "Good morning! How wonderful the coffee smells!"

He rose and lifted out a chair for her. Mrs. Concannon sat down after pouring coffee for herself and Mrs. Warne. Mrs. Warne had explained that she took nothing but coffee for breakfast.

Jamie would be up later. It was a good time to take Mrs. Warne out into the garden and explain the route to the beach.

She followed him down among the roses to the spilling border of poppies. He touched her arm, pointed below. "There's the old path. You see, I've put a marker, that row of stones. Painted them white—you can even see them at twilight, or later. Don't ever go close or let Jamie take you there or go there himself."

"May I look over, just once?"

"Certainly."

They went to the edge, the poppies crushing under their shoes, and Mrs. Warne put her head over. "It's a long way down. I don't see any path."

"Some of the outer rim fell away. I was glad it did. Jamie won't be tempted to try again."

"Is that your private beach down there?"

Glazer put a foot on one of the rocks and leaned over as she had. "It's almost the same as one. Rocks cut us off from the beach between here and town." He indicated the great flat outcropping of greenish slate which was pitted with potholes and over which the tide crawled sluggishly. "Sometimes fishermen work their way across the stone there. But not often."

She had turned a little to the right. Here was another outcropping of rock, not greenish but gray, not flat but tilted, standing out from the cliff like a flying buttress, a wall that shut in a second tinier strip of sand. "It seems you have two beaches."

"The second one is even more private, since there is no way at all to get to it. Not even for us. You couldn't climb that wall of stone. You can't swim in—I tried it once, and the rip tides drove me back. A boat would have its bottom stove in on those stray boulders. In the other direction, from the tip of the headland, there is even a stronger and more dangerous current with a swirling movement like a whirlpool."

She looked down as if drawn to the tiny, secluded beach. The cliff overhung it; it was almost like the floor of a cave. From it a wet salt smell rose as if from the depths of a sea grotto; Glazer had often noticed this effect. The water rippled among the broken stones which had fallen at some time out of the overhanging cliff; and the tide looked dark, green, and to Glazer somehow wicked.

"I should like to go there sometime," said Mrs. Warne.

"Take my advice. Don't try it." He was a trifle short with her. There must be no nonsense about the water. Jamie was too frolicsome and too irresponsible in his swimming as it was. "If you want a good swim, go out straight to the big rocks." He indicated three huge stones well out from shore whose tips showed black above the water. "They're under at high tide. Come this way and I'll show you the new path I had constructed."

At the edge of the cliff below the house was a shelter built of lath. It marked the head of the pathway, and in it Glazer kept camellias and rows of potted begonias, a fine show of which he was proud. Mrs. Warne passed them without comment to examine the way to the beach. As Glazer had said, it was a well-engineered affair, with a stone balustrade, steps built into the steepest sections, drained by tiles to preserve the graveled surface.

"Jamie is crazy about the beach," Glazer explained. "I had to see that there was a safe way up and down. Mrs. Concannon brought him down here every day. I rather think the climb was hard on her."

A touch of color had come into Mrs. Warne's face. "I'll bring him down today."

To Glazer's surprise—he had only meant to point out the proper way to the beach, then return to the house—she stepped out of the lath shelter and walked down the path. She turned and glanced back at him. He felt impelled to follow. But when he caught up with her at the foot of the path, he thought her color turned pale. She leaned against the stone balustrade and panted.

"Pretty steep," he commented uneasily, thinking inwardly that going down wasn't the difficult part.

In that strange husky voice of hers she said, "Do you like the sea?"

"Yes, very much," he agreed.

The water washed in toward them, very green and clear in the morning sunlight, the froth on the little white waves spinning off on the wind as the surf turned over. In the moment of silence Glazer heard the creaky noise made by the gulls; some of them had settled on the big rocks offshore and were waiting there for some unwary fish to swim by. Just then he thought of Mrs. Concannon. She would wonder where they had gone, and why.

"We'd better be getting back. Jamie expects his new routine to start off with a bang." He smiled, half apologetic; she mustn't think him a slave driver anxious to get a full day's labor. "When you bring him down this afternoon, see that he doesn't go out far. He thinks he can swim much better than he does."

"I'll remember."

She turned and, leaning against the balustrade, she looked up at the face of the cliff. In an early optimism Glazer had tried to drop seeds into the pockets and little clefts, and a few ragged poppies peeped out here and there. He had imagined a cascade of bloom all the way to the edge of the sand, but the landscape contractor had dissuaded him; there was no way to fasten soil to the sheer rock. "It's not so high as I had thought," she said. "But it's bare. It's ... ugly. And ominous."

Under her words, under everything she had said since they had come outside, lay something else—something Glazer couldn't put his finger on but which nevertheless made him faintly uneasy. He had long ago admitted to himself that he was not a subtle or overly discerning man. He liked to be told things simply and flatly. Even emotions, wild ones, could be made simple and flat if they were spread out into words of few syllables. He remembered some of the quarrels he'd had with Rheba before her death. And Mrs. Warne, though she seemed to be saying quite simple things, had other meanings in her head. The thing she wasn't saying peeped through the tones of her queer, breathless voice and looked from her eyes. Her eyes—which now, as last night under the light in Jamie's room, looked green as the sea.

He didn't like it. He didn't want anything complicated or obscure or containing any emotion of any sort. What he wanted of Mrs. Warne, though he had not phrased it exactly to himself, was a robot-like efficiency and stamina, and an unrobotlike warmth toward his son. Just that.

As he desired her, she would have been like a paper doll cut loose from the page in which she had lived, to be pasted briefly into Jamie's life, removed when the need was over.

He wondered briefly, standing there near her, watching the black hair glitter in the sun, if the thing that was the matter with her could be fear.

Suddenly she put her hands together, looked down at them, rubbed them as if they were cold. "Yes, let's go back."

Glazer took her back to the house and left her with Jamie, who was having breakfast. Then he took his car from the garage and went off to the job. The job was good, solid stuff—he examined the new foundation of the doctor's house and looked over the deliveries of lumber, pipe, and sheet-metal materials and talked to the subcontractor who was doing the cement work, and all the time under the satisfaction he felt the clinging cobwebs left by the woman. Dammit, she was disturbing. He had decided sometime before, he discovered, that he didn't like her. The dislike was impersonal and didn't obscure the fact that she had seemed the ideal person to help Jamie over the hard spot he was in. The fundamental thing was, he thought, that she didn't appeal to him as a woman. He didn't stop to consider that no one had since Rheba's death—a footnote not to loss but to the long torment of their marriage.

There was utter peace in the house for a week. Jamie began on the shelf of schoolbooks, reading from the primers, practicing writing, doing numbers. Mrs. Warne showed the results of an efficient training, and her attitude toward the child seemed a happy combination of good sense and realistic understanding. If there was a jarring note anywhere, Glazer thought, it was in the behavior of Mrs. Concannon. The big Irishwoman became increasingly quiet and self-contained. Such reserve was strange to her, and Glazer was inclined to put it down to jealousy. Mrs. Concannon had been fond of Jamie, almost a second mother to him, and now that post was filled by Mrs. Warne.

It was a week to the day that Mrs. Warne had arrived, a sunny morning, and from the excavation high on the hill where the new house was being built Glazer could look down the slope with its scattered big homes, its gardens and eucalyptus clumps, across the highway, to the headland where his own home stood. Far in the distance, out against the sea, it had the small perfection and the impermanence of a toy; Glazer felt that he could pick it up between thumb and forefinger like one of Jamie's blocks. Why he should have been looking at it at ten minutes past eleven, he was never to know.

He became aware that there was a bit of fluttering stuff, rose color that had somehow no resemblance to the color of a flower, out at the edge of the headland; he thought of Mrs. Warne's dress. Another scrap, bright pink, ran through the garden like a bug. From here it looked like the slow progress of a pink-shelled beetle, but Glazer's work in the Navy during the war had taught him something of perspective, of movement at a distance, and he realized all at once that Mrs. Concannon was progressing at a speed which, for her, he would have thought impossible. A prickle ran up the back of his neck.

The rose scrap at the edge of the bluff flickered and disappeared; the pink beetle froze in its tracks. He could imagine Mrs. Concannon there in the path, halfway from the house, stopped and staring. It struck him that she was undecided what to do: whether to go on to the edge of the headland or to return to the house. A pulse began to beat in Glazer's head. Mrs. Concannon didn't know whether to go on and do what had to be done or to go back to the phone. He couldn't say why this conviction possessed him with such fierceness, such clarity; it must have sprung from his long association with and observance of the housekeeper.

He held his breath and waited, and the pink beetle far below stood still to think. Then she turned back toward the house, and Glazer on his high bare eminence turned also—toward the construction shack which was his temporary headquarters. He walked toward the unpainted small structure, seeing and yet not seeing its bright pine boards naked under the sun, its telephone wire spun like the farthest reach of a spider's net to a pole beside its door. In his head the phone was already ringing.

He opened the door, and the subcontractor, Jenkins, looked up from the blueprints he had spread out on the small table. Glazer went over to the phone in somewhat the manner of a sleepwalker and put out his hand.

It was going to ring.

It would ring and say that through some mad perversity Mrs. Warne had gone down by the old track to the beach and that she had fallen and broken her neck and would he please come home and see what should be done. At the same moment, like the withdrawing of a veil, he sensed that the inexplicable factor in Mrs. Warne's manner had been the expectation of disaster.

She had looked up at that cliff and called it ominous, and he had been too stupid to see that she had known somehow that she was going to tumble down it. And now he knew, and it was too late.

The telephone rang, and he picked it up and a voice said, "Mr. Jenkins? I have your party for you."

Glazer turned around and handed Jenkins the phone and then hurried out and across the flat area which had been gouged into the hill. In the garden of his house—so far away, so full of mysterious happenings it might have been on another planet—the pink beetle was running again.

Mrs. Concannon was progressing with that same amazing speed back to the edge of the bluff. All the way. It was too far to see if she carried anything, though Glazer sensed that she did. At the same moment he thought of Jamie, and a shudder ran through him. He walked stiff-legged to his car, got in, started the motor, turned on the barren gravelly scar that would someday be Dr. Barton's private drive, and headed downhill.

He stopped abruptly on the garage ramp with a little squeak of brakes ordinarily too polite to protest bad treatment. He got out of the car and became aware of a noise. It came from the house, a high-pitched screaming wail. Jamie. Glazer ran, stumbling in his hurry, his legs suddenly leaden and awkward. He ran through the house to Jamie's room, and there was Jamie sitting up in bed—of course, his mind told him, Jamie always lay down for an hour before lunch; the doctor had ordered it—in pajamas, and obviously too vocally loud to be injured.

He shook Jamie's shoulder, but the sobs and the screams went on, not accompanied by words that made sense, though Glazer caught the dog's name, Jericho, several times.

Glazer went out through the front door again, slower now, not liking what he must do. He feared he was going to be buffeted by feminine hysterics, much more shrill than the boy's.

He walked out to the spot where Mrs. Concannon must be. She was hidden down among the flowers, he saw as he came close, lying on her stomach, the ends of a rope in her hands, fishing. At least it looked like fishing. She dangled the rope now here, now there, with muttered commands, over the edge of the bluff where the old path had begun.

He said, "What's happened?"

She looked back at him. Her face was red, covered with sweat. "Can you help, Mr. Glazer? She's down here. The dog fell and she tried to get him."

It was the last thing he would have thought of.

He knelt where Mrs. Concannon lay and took the rope from her hands and leaned over to fish. Right below, so close that it startled him, was Mrs. Warne's uplifted face. She was in under the bank, on a tiny ledge that remained of the old path; she was trembling and dirty. There was a funny impact in seeing the dirt all over her, in her hair, on her face and lashes, on her clothes. It was a little indecent. As though she were naked.

He couldn't think why the idea had occurred to him like that, a crazy notion out of nowhere, preposterous, foolish.

He held the rope so that she could reach it. "No, don't try to climb up by it. Tie it around your waist, and I'll pull you."

She tied the rope around her waist, her hands shaking, fumbling with the knots so that Glazer had to caution her, to remind her that the rope must be tied right or it wouldn't be safe. Then he braced himself, and her weight came on the line. There was the sound of loose dirt and small stones rattling down. She crawled over the edge of the bank; he thought for an instant that she would fall and lie there among the poppies. But she got to her feet.

For once her voice hadn't the elusive, husky note; it was just flat and tired, almost an old woman's voice, no resonance in it. "The dog's dead," she said. "He fell all the way to the bottom, and he doesn't move, and you can see—" Suddenly she retched. "His head's broken," she added at last.

Mrs. Concannon was brushing at her clothes. "The poor little mutt! But you shouldn't have tried to save him. After all, just a dog—even Jamie's dog. You might have fallen yourself."

Mrs. Warne shook her head in answer; she began to untie the rope about her waist, the rope whose end Glazer realized he still held. He dropped it, stepped over to the row of stones so carefully painted white, the line of stones that hadn't done any good so far as Jericho was concerned. He looked down at the crushed small body far below, like a plush toy forgotten on the beach, and the memory of Jamie's screams rang in his ears. He guessed with sudden insight how Jamie knew what had happened to the dog; he had heard Mrs. Concannon come in with a pounding rush for the rope, he'd hopped out of bed and demanded to know what was going on, and in her fear and frantic haste she'd driven him back to bed with the truth.

Glazer was aware of a pang of keen regret, even sorrow, for the little dog. Jericho had been a fine pet, a steadying comfort during the long days of illness, a playful companion on the beach, a watchful guardian in the night. Jamie would be inconsolable.

He turned to ask Mrs. Warne what on earth might have brought the dog here, to fall to his death—and also, perhaps, why she had happened to be near him. But when he met her eyes he had again the disturbing feeling that she was somehow vulnerable, terribly exposed—as he had felt when he had first looked down and seen all that dirt on her. A sense of heat came over him, ran through his veins; he thought to himself that he had been out too long in the sun. He muttered a comment that they should go to the house, and turned to lead the way.

Three

He awoke sometime in the night, and instantly the events of the day crowded his mind, preventing further sleep. He could feel on his palms the tenderness left by the friction of the spade handle; he had buried the dog at the farthest end of the garden, in a spot Jamie had chosen. Jamie had insisted on wrapping the dog in an old sweater—*so he'll remember me*. The hole in the earth had been deep and cool and lonely—and hard to dig, since the expensive topsoil extended only a couple of feet there. After the grave was filled, Jamie had simply gone to pieces. Finally Glazer had called the doctor, and the doctor had administered a sedative to the howling child. Before sleep had claimed him, however, he'd accused Mrs. Warne, an incident Glazer was embarrassed to remember.

She'd turned quite white, standing at the foot of the bed, her hands tugging each other helplessly.

"Be quiet, Jamie!"

"She did, she did! Jericho never went near the edge. Not by himself.

He wouldn't!"

"If you say anything more, Jamie, I'll have to whip you!"

"I don't care."

"'You'd better be careful, Son. I'm not fooling."

Jamie had hiccuped, covered his head with his pillow, and his silence had dismissed them, unforgiven.

Glazer and Mrs. Warne had gone into the living room. The windows were open; the warm air was full of the smell of the sea and the blossoming roses. There was no sign of Mrs. Concannon, though it was past time for lunch. She must be in her room, changing her uniform. Mrs. Warne said, "If you'd rather I went away, Mr. Glazer, I will. I don't want to stay if Jamie blames me."

"No, no," Glazer had answered; he had felt a touch of anger at her for the silly suggestion. "He's upset now. He wants to blame someone for this thing he can't understand. You'll see—when he wakes he'll feel entirely different about it."

"I hope so." She had glanced down at the dusty dress. "I'll go and change before lunch. Excuse me."

He had sat down and picked up a newspaper, not to read; he was determined to make a display of calm and relaxation in the midst of the overcharged emotions all around him. Presently Mrs. Concannon had come in to set the table for lunch. She had changed to a new pink uniform. The reddened skin around her eyes had been thickly powdered.

Lunch had been a very quiet meal.

Glazer turned over restlessly in bed. Perhaps if he got up, walked out to the kitchen, took a drink of water, even stepped outside for a moment and had a breath of sea wind, it would clear his head and let him get back to sleep. He reached for the lamp. The clock said twelve minutes past three.

He put on a robe, slid his feet into slippers. There was a night light in the hail, a small blue globe on the baseboard. He padded on. The great living room was like a cave, the windows giving a view of the sky, paler than the interior of the house. The room smelled warm, tainted faintly with the roses Mrs. Concannon had brought in. For all his absorption with the garden, Glazer was not fond of cut flowers; he always thought of them as dying. Or it may have been that far back in his mind was the memory of his father's funeral when he was eleven, the flowers lying limp and expiring on the coffin.

He did not turn on the light in the kitchen. There was a gray reflection from the sky outside, the last of the moonlight perhaps, and by its glow he went over to the cupboard, took down a glass, went to the sink, and filled it with water. Probably he had not made any noticeable noise.

As he set the glass down, he caught some other sound besides the one of the glass clicking the tile. It was a sort of metallic snap. Glazer thought at once of a door latch.

He went back to the living room and stood listening, but the house was quiet. No footsteps. No water running in a bathroom. He decided that his ears had played him a trick. He started to cross the room. Something outside, some pale blotch against the night, drew his eye to the window.

As he looked in that direction, the thing—whatever it was—wavered as if on the wind, then vanished in the dark.

Anger congealed in him like a stone.

As much as he hated excessive emotion and sentimentality, even more did he hate evasion and concealment, a hinting of things left unsaid; and he had associated such attitudes with Mrs. Warne ever since that morning on the beach. This business of slipping out, making a mystery ... In the dark he made a wry, disgusted face. His conviction that she was out in the garden was as certain as if he'd seen her there by daylight. Perhaps, drawn by some impulse, she'd gone to look at the spot where the dog had fallen. Or perhaps she had other motives. What ailed the woman, anyway?

This was the time to put a stop to such nonsense.

He went to the front door, opened it, stepped out, walked briskly to the point where the pale blotch like a blowing robe had disappeared. It was at the edge of the bluff near the entrance to the lath shelter at the top of the path. She'd gone down to the beach, then. Grieving over the dog? I think not, he told himself grimly. And the odd detail of Jericho's poor broken skull flickered through his memory. The dog had fallen into sand. What had crushed his head?

Glazer dismissed the minor puzzle and stepped into the lath shelter, walked on to the opening at the other end, where the stone balustrade of the path joined the shelter wall. He stood there and said loudly, "Mrs. Warne?"

There was no answer. He could hear the surf on the beach below, and in the sleeping town down the coast a siren whined. A motorcycle cop making a pinch, Glazer told himself. The only lights visible were the highway markers that burned all night, guiding traffic through town and on south to San Diego. He went out to the flat spot at the head of his path and looked down.

It was dark, but not so dark that he wouldn't have seen her down there. The pale robe (of course it had been a robe, a woman's garment) had stood out almost brightly against the dark in the moment before it had vanished.

He returned to the yard. He stood in front of his door, clenching and unclenching his hands, full of anger. In his mind he had a distinct image of her hiding from him, a small smile on her face while she waited for him to go away.

It occurred to him then to wonder at how little he knew of her. So far as he could remember, she had let drop no facts about herself since her arrival here. All he had was what Emily Graham had told him: that Francesca Warne was a widow, not quite thirty, that she had taught school, that she had had trouble with her husband before his death. What kind of trouble?

Emily's tone had made it seem impolite to ask.

His anger drove him into the house, down the hall, and there he rapped sharply on Mrs. Warne's door. He had a story—he'd heard Jamie whimpering. Would she take the boy's temperature in case something was really wrong? Only of course he wouldn't need that story. Mrs. Warne wasn't here.

She was out in the garden, being sly and elusive, amused at him because he couldn't find her.

Rage mounted in him. He gripped the knob and threw the door open and touched the light switch. Let her come in and know that he'd been looking for her, honestly looking, not sneaking after her in the dark, outwitted like a bumbling idiot....

He saw the black hair spread out on the pillow, the lashes like smudges on her cheeks, the hand curled against her throat, the thin lace of her gown on her shoulders. Then her eyes were open, clouded with sleep at first but growing aware. She pushed herself up on an elbow. She looked at the room with an unfamiliar air, as though surprised to find herself in it.

She hadn't seen him yet, and Glazer had an almost irresistible impulse to switch off the light and run. Five seconds later he was wishing with all his soul that he'd done just that.

For when Mrs. Warne turned in the bed and saw him in the doorway, her reaction was instantaneous. And unfortunate—embarrassing in a way that made Glazer cringe.

She screamed.

He stepped back out into the hall, and they looked at each other. She had drawn her knees up; she looked small and huddled, the black hair like the mane of a witch. There was no doubt that she was speechless with fright.

He said awkwardly, "I'm sorry to have startled you. I tried to rouse you by rapping. Jamie's—well, never mind." The lie was too weak; it would be like apologizing to a chicken after you'd cut off its head. He'd scared her almost to death. The decent thing was to leave. He reached for the doorknob.

"Wait. I—I didn't recognize you. Look the other way. I'll get into a robe." She slid toward the edge of the bed. He stepped into the shadowy part of the hall to wait. A minute later she came out of her room, tying the belt of a gray silk negligee. "What is it? Is Jamie sick?"

"I heard him whimpering, perhaps in his sleep. I—" Again Glazer felt the dead weight of the silly lie and knew that it was going to fall into her expectant silence like a stone through the roof of a greenhouse. "I've made a fool of myself." He said it earnestly and truthfully.

"No, I understand. You're worried about him. I am too." She began to walk down the hall.

Two things happened. Mrs. Concannon opened her door and stuck her head out. And Jamie skipped out of Glazer's door and stopped in the middle of the hall. Mrs. Warne, seeing the boy, slowed, hesitated, then came to a stop. She looked over her shoulder at Glazer. Glazer's throat was dry, his palms clammy. It must seem to her that he had tried to fob off the baldest lie.

He was remembering the mysterious click he'd heard from the kitchen. It had been Jamie, opening his door—Jamie, lonely because the dog was gone, needing company. He'd gone to slip into his father's bed. Only his father hadn't been there.

Glazer said lamely, "I was out in the kitchen for a while, getting a glass of water. He must have wakened while I was gone."

She didn't believe him. The touch of her glance drifting over him had the feel of ice. "He doesn't seem to need me."

The hall was a patchwork of light and shadow; the opened door of Glazer's room let out a broad beam in which Jamie stood, twisting from one foot to the other, and behind Mrs. Concannon another lamp glowed, throwing her silhouette on the opposite wall. She was roused suddenly to action. Perhaps she sensed Mrs. Warne's cold contempt, Glazer's embarrassment. She said to Jamie, "Into bed with you! No arguments! At four in the morning, mind—"

"It's lonesome without Jericho!" he protested, but she hurried him along.

Mrs. Warne turned back to her door. "Is that all you wished, Mr. Glazer?"

He was defeated; there wasn't any way he could explain.

She looked into her room; her face was white inside its frame of black hair. "Will you rap a little harder next time, please? I will wake up if you give me a minute or two." She went inside and shut the door.

"What the devil do you mean?" He said it to the closed door; not aloud, though his mind shouted the words. "Do you have some crazy idea that

I—that I—" And there his mind balked him. He felt the hard pulse inside his temples pounding in fury. But words wouldn't come. There weren't any words for the meaning he had read in Mrs. Warne's freezing glance.

He went into the living room. All desire for sleep had vanished. He turned on a lamp and sat down, tamped tobacco into a pipe, let the pipe hang unlit in his hands. Under the rage he felt because of the humiliation was a growing dumfoundedness that this plain and unappealing— he stressed the words in his mind—this plain and unappealing woman had somehow gotten so far under his skin. She affected him far out of all proportion to her importance in his life or in this household—both practically nil, he told himself. He tried to reason it out, but his thoughts balked. All he could remember clearly was that moment of heat when she had turned from him and gone into her room.

After a while he walked out into the kitchen, took a flashlight from a cupboard, came back through the living room to the front entry, and then out into the night. There was one thing he *could* do; he could find the damned elusive blowing thing that had led him out here to make a fool of himself in the first place.

He found it. Caught in the last branches of a rosebush that overhung the bluff was a sheet of newspaper, blown over his fence from God knew where, plastered to the damp shrubbery by the wind.

He stood there with the paper spotlighted by the flash. Sounds drifted up, the chuckle of the surf among the stones on the little beach where no one could ever go, the wind against the great granite buttress that knifed outward into the sea, the softer whisper of the small waves flattening just below where the sand was smooth. It struck him then, forcefully, that in leaving the bluff unfenced he had done an incredibly foolish thing.

It was a wonder that Jamie, running carelessly as he did, hadn't gone over it long ago.

When he had first come into possession of the place there had been nothing here but the house. The two bachelors who had built it had apparently not been interested in landscaping. The splendid windows had given a feeling of overlooking a great expanse of sea, and he had had some foolish notion that a fence at the cliff's edge might interfere with that lofty impression.... He had put steel link around the rest of the garden. Tomorrow he'd order steel link for the bluff too.

Too late for the little dog, too late to save Jamie his bitter loss. Glazer stubbornly risked his neck, going out far enough to kick the paper off the rosebush and over the rim of the bluff. It floated off, twisting as if alive. He let his light follow it as long as he could. He recognized the silliness of feeling bitter. It was an inanimate object, a piece of trash. But in some obscure way it seemed to have marked a milepost, some corner turned which he could not recover.

In the morning, in his office that was by itself at the rear of the house, he telephoned Emily Graham in Los Angeles. "I thought you'd like to know how we're getting along."

Emily was a plump little woman who always sounded full of life and cheerfulness over the telephone. "Of course. How's Francesca?"

"She thinks I tried to enter her room last night with ulterior purposes."

"Oh no!" Emily laughed, a sound like a small hen cackling over a strange egg in her nest. "She's much too sensible. Or—or did you?"

"That is a joke," he told her firmly.

"Yes, I guess it had better be. Is she happy with you?"

Glazer thought, Isn't the logical question whether we are happy having the woman? "I had thought so. Everything has gone smoothly until last night. Oh, of course Jamie's little dog was killed."

There was abrupt silence on the other end of the wire, a moment or two that implied Emily had put the brakes on suddenly to think. Then: "How?"

"Over the edge of the bluff. I haven't all the details straight as yet." His mind reminded—he'd never been offered any details. Jamie had insisted in hysterical grief that Mrs. Warne had in some way been to blame for the accident. Mrs. Warne had not, come to think of it, denied this charge; she had simply offered to leave. And Mrs. Concannon hadn't said a word, unusual for the talkative Irishwoman. He jerked himself up quickly—what sort of mountain was he constructing from this molehill?

Laid out before him on the desk were the plans for a home. He looked at them and wrinkled his forehead in distaste. Too, too modern. But Emily's voice, prattling on, fell upon his ear with strange emphasis.

"... I had made up my mind long ago that she ought to go to your house."

"You mean, that she'd be suitable?"

"I was thinking of Francesca."

Other details floated through Glazer's thoughts. "Tell me, did you ever happen to call here with her while I was away?"

"No." It was sharp and quick. "Of course I didn't. Why d'you ask?"

"I thought when she first came—" Glazer was remembering how Mrs. Warne had turned toward the windows on that first entrance, and then afterward how she had walked with him toward her room. "I thought she might have been here previously."

"She used to live in Seaview, you know." There was a funny caution under the words; Emily seemed to be speaking to him across a table, attracting his attention while she wiped something up carefully into a napkin. "Why don't you ask her?"

"I suppose I shall."

"You aren't working too hard, are you? And Jamie's getting better?"

"Quite okay."

"You ought to fence that bluff."

"I'm going to." Funny that she should bring up his idea of last night.

"I'm a lonely old woman. Bring Jamie to see me."

"Yes, we'll try to catch you between bridge sessions."

"You're impudent as ever." She giggled again, and then the giggle died down and Glazer realized that the conversation was over. What had he hoped to know, to discover? He couldn't say, even to himself.

He said good-by and hung up and sat there thinking of Emily. Her husband had befriended him when he was quite young, when he had first come out to California, raw and ignorant. Emily had tried to polish him with manners. Much too late. He grimaced at the sunny window, remembering her careful coaching, her hopes that he'd "catch on" socially and marry a society bud among the friends she had. But Ralph Graham, much more practical, had taken Glazer under his wing and taught him the contracting business. What on earth, in his raw youth and tough behavior, had attracted these two good people? He never had decided.

He owed them both all that he had and was, and since Ralph was dead, he owed it to Emily. His affection and gratitude made it hard to be objective in his view of her—it was too much like being objective about a mother—but he was impressed and a little frightened now and then by Emily's passion for do-goodery.

He wondered if she were practicing some of her Machiavellian art upon Francesca Warne.

There was a purpose behind her sending Mrs. Warne here—the feeling that this was true was like the slow growing of a fever, uneasy but immutable. And distinctly the impression was forced on him that the benefit, if any, was meant for Mrs. Warne.

Without his willing it or wanting it, the memory returned to Mrs. Warne lying asleep with her fingers curled against her throat; and then that other image that had some sort of shock in it—her looking up at him from under the bluff with all that dirt on her.

Glazer took out a freshly sharpened pencil and a sheet of paper and began to try to make estimates on the new house from the blueprints. He worked hurriedly and carelessly. He could not understand what was happening in his own mind.

Then he checked the runaway emotion that was disturbingly like panic and with a slow, deliberate hand, the pencil line heavy and dark, he wrote that woman's name. The first name.

Francesca.

The sound of it rolled over and over inside his head.

Four

Three days later, at two o'clock in the afternoon, Mrs. Warne and Jamie went down to the beach. It was a hot, sultry afternoon. The wind was blowing down from the warm interior, bringing dust and desert smells, drying the air and filling it with electricity.

Mrs. Warne wore a swim suit, dark blue, tight-fitting. She had no cap. On the beach, she paused to run her fingers through her hair to push it back, and it crackled at her touch.

"Your hair snapped," said Jamie with interest.

"It's so dry. What do you want to do first? Build something with sand?"

"I'm going right in the water," the little boy decided seriously.

He had, as Glazer had prophesied, forgotten his anger at her when the dog had died. He was as before, sober, anxious for approval, trusting, and eager. She looked down at him and her eyes softened, and she reached out to touch his tousled mop.

"I'm going to swim away, 'way out," he said, emboldened by her friendliness.

She squinted against the sun. "There are rocks out there, big ones, but much too far for you." She shivered as if some stray breath of cold had touched her. "Someday I might—might try it."

"You never *do* go in, not any further than up to here!" He bent over and sliced his hand against the leg between knee and ankle. "Can you swim?"

She pulled her eyes away from the sea and looked at him for a long moment; the softness had left her gaze and it was speculative and thoughtful. "Yes."

"Then why don't you?" He was jumping around her. "And I could hang on! Please! Please go in! Go out to the rocks!"

"It wouldn't— Your father wouldn't like it."

Jamie's eyes lit up slyly. "He isn't here. He won't know!"

She appeared to think it over with much deliberation. The wind lifted the black hair and trailed it across her throat, and the large eyes seemed to hold a flickering echo of sea color. Jamie thought she was a very pretty lady. He waited, wriggling his toes in the sand, staring up at her hopefully.

"Please!"

"All right," she said suddenly. "First, though, I'm going in alone. I want to—to get used to the water. I might have forgotten how to swim."

"I'll bet you haven't!"

"We'll see." She walked down to the edge of the surf and stood there looking into the crawling water. Hesitantly she went out to a deeper spot, paused a moment, looked back at Jamie—her face seemed too white all at once, the eyes big; big as a ghost's, thought Jamie—and then she plunged in. The green water rolled over her, and her hair swam on it like seaweed. Then she rose, swimming strongly.

She went out perhaps halfway to the large rocks and there disappeared under the water. After a moment Jamie was frightened for fear she might be drowning; he thought of running to call Mrs. Concannon. As the seconds ticked away the sea seemed suddenly unfriendly, dangerous. Jamie retreated to the shelter of the bluff. He shivered there. Was she dead? Was she dead like Jericho?

Then she stood up in the rolling surf, much closer in than where she had gone under. She waved at him. His fright was gone. He ran forward and waved back. "Come get me! I want to go to the rocks!"

She staggered in, buffeted by the surf. "Jamie, we wouldn't dare!"

"Yes, yes, I want to! *He* won't know."

Jamie caught her hand in his. In a child's way he sensed that he might get his way because her thoughts were taken up elsewhere. She did look ghostly, he saw, as if something had scared her. Not the sea, nor the swim. Something in her mind, like the boogies he imagined in the dark at night.

"All right," she said at last. "You hang onto my halter strap, here, behind my neck. Don't get scared and try to choke me. Promise?"

"Of course I won't get scared."

They waded out together through the froth of the running water. She stooped a little; Jamie boosted himself. She began to swim. The next minutes were delightful for the child. Mrs. Warne was strong, sure, and expert; her movement in the water had the effortless precision of a fish. Then, though they were not yet near the rocks, she stopped, circled, and began to paddle aimlessly. "We must go back, Jamie."

"No, no!" Jamie tried to remember that he mustn't panic, but her paddling seemed to have no power or smoothness and she kept sinking to her chin, letting him go lower than he liked. Water splashed into his nose, and under him he could suddenly sense the deeps, the dark currents, the washy miles of ocean floor.

"I'm not supposed to swim." The paddling became weaker. Under the sun her skin was too white, all its tan washed away. Her legs in the green water hung almost motionless. "Don't cry, Jamie. You promised you wouldn't be scared."

He choked. "I want to get *out!*"

"We'll go back." Still she didn't resume swimming. A half paralysis seemed to have overtaken her, or an indecision that kept her here between the rocks and the shore, not knowing which to choose.

Jamie blinked back tears. He could see the whole panorama of the coast, the sharp bluff that hid his house, the hills that rose behind, even the raw scar on the hill where is father was building a house. His father was up there now. The thought of Glazer's disapproval quieted Jamie.

She must have sensed his frightened stillness. She looked at him. "We'll go on to the rocks. It isn't far."

She stretched herself in the water, and the smooth, precise swimming began again. Jamie felt as if he were being pulled along by a friendly porpoise. There was so much power and skill in her progress that his fright left him. He made a sputtering sound, imitating a motor, fancying himself a little boat.

They came to the rocks. These were like the humped backs of dark monsters, crusted with sea growth and barnacles. Their widening bases could be seen for a little way going down into the sea, covered with fern-like weeds in which a swimming fish would momentarily flicker. Mrs. Warne circled the first rock, found a shelf that made a foothold, grasped Jamie, and boosted him. "Look out for barnacles. They'll cut you." He crawled up, panting, and she lifted herself beside him.

The sun was unexpectedly warm after the coolness of the water. Jamie rubbed the goose pimples off his arms, stood up, looked around. "We're a long way out. A *long* way. I'll bet nobody could see us. I'll bet Mrs. Concannon couldn't see us even if she was looking."

Now that they were away from the bluff, the house was visible, set in its patterned gardens like a big square jewel on green-and-gold plush. The great windows that gave the house its view glittered in the reflected light. Jamie stuck out his tongue in friendly impudence toward Mrs. Concannon. It was safe to do at this distance. "We can't ever do this again," Mrs. Warne muttered, her eyes on the house.

"Sure we can. Lots. When I learn to swim good enough, I'll come out by myself." He crouched down, and as a swell went by he rippled the water with his hand. Then he began picking at the barnacles.

"You wait here," said Mrs. Warne suddenly. "I'm going over to that other one." She pointed to another dark hump perhaps a hundred feet away.

Jamie watched interestedly as she plunged off, came up, cut the water cleanly with precise, powerful strokes, finally reaching the other rock and pulling herself up there. She threw the hair out of her face, looked across, and waved to him.

This was exciting. It was like being lost on a little island. Jamie let himself be scared a little, clinging to a craggy place and looking down into the depths. Something big and dark passed under the water. A shark, he thought, ignoring what his father had told him. Of course sharks came here. One was waiting down there, waiting for him to fall off his precious island.

He looked over at Mrs. Warne. She was standing again. As he watched, she seemed to fold over slowly, to fold herself down into the water, cutting it with scarcely a ripple, vanishing under the sea. When she came up again, she was nearer the third rock, the one farthest out.

He yelled and waved, but she didn't hear, or didn't pay any attention. She circled the third rock as if looking for a stepping place, but this third was also the most worn; it was carved away to little more than a pinnacle. Jamie saw a change in her progress and he sensed that she was paddling again in that strangely aimless and powerless fashion, as if she had forgotten how to swim. He yelled again.

She looked over her shoulder at him, and though it was too far to see her features distinctly, it seemed to Jamie that she looked almost a stranger. It was as if a mask had turned his way, a mask fashioned in Mrs. Warne's image but which actually hid a person he did not know.

She had gone away and now she was strange. And he was lost on his island. He looked back at his house, and the memory of his room there was unexpectedly vivid, all the stuff his father had bought and wanted him to use, and the blocks which Jamie liked and which had always annoyed Glazer.

Mrs. Warne had found a clinging place. She could not draw herself entirely out of the water because it was such a little place in which to cling, and so she lay half propped like a piece of flotsam cast there by the waves.

Jamie called, but she made no reply. He thought she had a sleepy, far-away look about her. She was thinking about something, he decided, that had nothing to do with him or this place. Between them lay a glittering expanse of water which threw up a glow that hurt his eyes. He turned back, facing the house. The breeze was suddenly colder. Jamie felt alone.

He let a leg hang over the edge of the stone rim. When the swells passed, his foot swam in water. It was fun to imagine the shark down there watching his toes, even though Jamie didn't really believe in the shark. It was better to think about the imaginary shark than about Mrs.

Warne. In a dim way Jamie realized that there was, in Mrs. Warne's behavior somewhere, a real danger.

Some minutes later he turned to look for her again, but she was out of sight. He could not see the black shining head anywhere. He rose on tiptoe and peered all around, his eyes stinging at the glare.

She had gone.

She had gone down into the sea, and perhaps the shark was really there and had got her. A queer hollowness came into Jamie's chest, and it was hard to breathe.

A swell passed, and it was higher than the others had been. It rippled at the stone rim, and when it had passed, a tangle of froth lay drying in the sun.

Jamie crept away to the highest hump of the rock and squatted there. He looked at the bluff and at the house. He had turned his back on the sea. Mrs. Warne would come by and by and take him back to the beach, and it would be fun again, a safe but exciting game; but until that time he didn't want to look for her. It was frightening to search the sea and find nothing.

More fearful yet to look at the long swells marching and marching, and each a little higher than the ones before.

Mrs. Concannon, timing her cookies by the electric clock on the range, became aware of the time, and a faint uneasiness stirred in her. Jamie and Mrs. Warne should have been back from the beach by now. Yes, long since. Jamie knew she was making cookies, liked to raid the racks set out to cool, and Mrs. Warne always complained that she felt a chill if she spent more than an hour down beside the sea.

Mrs. Concannon took the last batch off the cookie sheet, lifted them one by one with a spatula, settled them on the bars of the rack, then brushed her hands on her pink skirt and took a long look at the clock.

She went to the breakfast-room window, which overlooked the bluff, and waited for some sign of their arrival. But the sea remained glittering and placid, the flowers quiet, no human figures in view. Again she made the nervous gesture, rubbing her palms on her pink cotton skirt. Then she went back to the kitchen, out the kitchen entry to the garden. She walked down to the edge of the bluff and looked over. She could see a narrow strip of sand, but not much—if they were down there sunning themselves, they'd be nearer the bluff. She went on, down a path to the lath shelter that made an entrance to the way to the beach.

The camellias and potted begonias under the lath gave out a smell of greenery and wetness. Mrs. Concannon was careful not to brush against these pampered blooms. Someone had told Mr. Glazer that camellias and begonias could not do well so close to salt air, and he was very proud of having proved the news an error.

She peered down the slanting way with its turns and patches of stairs, and she saw Mrs. Warne stretched on the sand, face-down, but no sign of Jamie. But of course he was close, somewhere. She started to turn back.

Then she took a second look at Mrs. Warne. There was something oddly flattened and disjointed in the way she lay. As if she had been dropped there, Mrs. Concannon thought, flung face-down and then stepped on. She must be asleep to lie so motionless, so inert. Mrs. Concannon took a couple of steps on the slanting downward way. "Mrs. Warne!"

The woman didn't move. Mrs. Concannon braced herself—her weight was awkward on the slope—and began the descent. Meanwhile, she looked about for Jamie. When it became evident as she neared the bottom that he was not on the beach nor in the shallow water of the surf, a panic began to thud inside Mrs. Concannon's brain. And under the panic a kind of inevitability, a feeling that this had been meant to happen from the day that woman first set foot in Glazer's garden.

She ran over to Mrs. Warne, her feet big and clumsy in the clinging sand, and reached down to shake the bare shoulder. "Wake up! Where's Jamie?"

A kind of groan escaped Mrs. Warne's lips. Mrs. Concannon fell to her knees, pushed on the shoulder so that Mrs. Warne's face came up from the sand and she could see it. Grains glittered on the black brows and in the edge of Mrs. Warne's hair. Her eyes came open foggily.

"What's wrong with you?" cried Mrs. Concannon.

Mrs. Warne looked up at her without any sign of recognition.

"Tell me, where's Jamie?" And quite savagely this time Mrs. Concannon dug her fingers into Mrs. Warne's flesh to shake her.

Mrs. Warne flinched at the pain. She seemed to wake up a little from the half-mesmerized state, the sort of trance, which had held her. She looked at Mrs. Concannon, and recognition flickered in her eyes. Then she struggled to a sitting position and examined the beach. "What did you say?"

"I said, where's Jamie? He's not—" Then Mrs. Concannon was struck dumb; her gaze was on the sea. Something she didn't believe, a nightmare too stark for the mind to hold, rooted her and kept her voiceless. Far out, on a tip of stone that looked no bigger than a pinprick, stood a hopping form. Small, grasshoppery, silhouetted in the glare. And even as Mrs. Concannon watched with her breath stopped, a swell came, blotted the tiny form to its knees, swept it off its pinnacle. A cry escaped Mrs.

Concannon, a wordless but begging screech. She crossed herself mechanically. Then the swell had passed and the grasshopper was seen clinging lower down and then painfully making his way back to the topmost perch.

Mrs. Warne was looking at her in that foggy, uncomprehending way. "What is it? What do you see?"

"He's out *there!*" Mrs. Concannon raised an arm that felt like wood and pointed. "He's swum, or made a raft, or been swept away...." Suddenly she turned on Mrs. Warne like a fury. "Why weren't you watching as you're supposed to do? Why did you let him go so far?"

Mrs. Warne pushed to her feet and stood swaying. She was too white to have been so long in the sun; there were punched blue places under her eyes, and her hands were shaking. "Who?"

"You know who!" Mrs. Concannon slapped her, a resounding clap. Then she turned and ran; it was in her mind to telephone Glazer, even though she knew he couldn't get here in time. The tide was running in now with express-train speed; behind her she seemed to feel the great waves gaining, and she sobbed as she ran. "Help him, Saint—Saint—" Mrs. Concannon, never at a loss for a saint to whom to appeal among those she felt took an interest in her little world, let the plea die. A little boy, and all that great sea—God must know about *that!*

She reached the bottom of the path, breathless, her legs dead from pulling through the sand, her head pounding from the strain. There was no help for it, she must stop and wait. The angling way that hung above seemed endless as she looked up at it, a hurdle too steep to pass, and beyond it the telephone that might bring help. The telephone, so far away ...

Behind her she heard a light splash. She looked back. Mrs. Warne was in the water.

Mrs. Concannon remembered Jamie's chatter—that Mrs. Warne never went into the water except to wade a little. She had taken it for granted that Mrs. Warne could not swim.

The white arms flashed in the sun as Mrs. Warne knifed her way toward the rock on which Jamie was perched. To Mrs. Concannon, fallen like a dead woman against the cement bulwark of the steps, it seemed an eternity before Mrs. Warne even got out past the breakers. At least three times during that interval Jamie was half swept away and regained his foothold with difficulty. As Mrs. Warne approached the tip of rock, there was a sudden lifting of the tide and Jamie wobbled and teetered, knee-deep in water. Another minute and he'd be gone.

She saw Mrs. Warne reach the rock and climb out of the water to stand beside the child, as if to rest. A pang of new fear shot through Mrs. Concannon. No swimmer herself, she realized nevertheless the toll the tremendous effort must have taken of Mrs. Warne's strength. Now she had to return and at once, with a burden. Mrs. Concannon fell to her knees and began to pray. The sea's roar took on an echo of disaster; she shut her eyes.

Long, long later, it seemed, she heard a squeaky voice, and then wet arms were thrown around her. Jamie nuzzled her and whimpered. She stood up.

Mrs. Warne floated in the edge of the surf, face under, her black hair spread like seaweed in the froth.

Five

Glazer stood in the garden under the evening sky, smoking his after-dinner pipe, filled with uneasy thought. He had a distasteful duty to perform; there was no way out of it. He had to dismiss Mrs. Warne from her job here and send her away. His argument with Mrs. Concannon had not moved him.

The Irishwoman, heretofore no partisan of Mrs. Warne, had been indignant. "If you discharge her, you're doing a wrong. She all but gave her life for your boy. If I hadn't pulled her out of the water just when I did …"

In his mind his own voice, calm but inexorable, had answered, "She took Jamie out there. You just can't get around that."

"Talk to her when she's feeling better. There must be a reason."

"There can be no reason."

And still, his mind pricked at him, there was something under the surface that he did not know and perhaps now—and better so—would never discover. She was a woman who, though she did not appeal to him (he was still reassuring himself on this point), nevertheless had some disturbing quality about her. An aura, a miasma, of disaster. The black hair was too black, the eyes unpleasantly large, the face stark in its plain configuration. It had been a foolish move to keep her here where he saw her every day, where they faced each other at meals, conferred of necessity over Jamie's work, and where the hint of her perfume in a room told him she had passed through.

He looked down at his hands. One held the pipe and the other was clenched, and both were shaking.

It seemed to him in that instant, an instant that passed—thank God—quickly, that the garden was a lonely place and that the wide pale sky held an emptiness that was agonizing, and that the bleak solitariness of himself as he stood there had a kind of death in it. The feeling was almost one of panic. As if he were losing something, an irreplaceable thing; as if he must say good-by to something he could not endure to have taken from him. Glazer broke out in a sweat, then roused himself and began to walk back toward the house. The feeling was one that everybody experienced now and then, he told himself, when business pressure or personal worries became pressing. He refused to connect it with Mrs. Warne. It had to do with tiredness, mental fatigue, and nervous imbalance. Probably he should be taking some sort of vitamin.

He went in through the front entry and on to the kitchen. Mrs. Concannon was stacking dishes in the cupboard. She looked round at him.

"Will you see if Mrs. Warne is able to talk to me now?"

A coldness came into the bright Irish eyes. "She can see you. She's up. I took a cup of tea to her not five minutes ago."

He left the kitchen, crossed the big room, went down the hall to Mrs. Warne's bedroom, and rapped on the door.

"Come in," she said from within.

He opened the door. The lights were on and the room's bright luxury seemed to leap at him. Mrs. Warne sat on the side of the bed. She held a cup and saucer; the cup was empty, and as Glazer entered she leaned forward and set the cup and saucer on the night stand. Then she stood up. Glazer felt a sudden pang. She looked so thin and forlorn. The gray silk negligee hung slackly, as if she were a child too small to fill it out. She brushed at a black wing of hair. "I can guess what you have come to say."

Glazer's eyes swept the room. He saw that the small trunk had been dragged from the closet, that the two suitcases which she had carried when she had arrived were propped open on chairs. Some underthings were folded on the dressing table.

He tried to think of something to say. The pipe lay in his hand, a silly prop; he suddenly despised it. He dropped it into his jacket pocket. He then brushed a stray fleck of tobacco ash from his hand.

She came toward him a little. "You have been patient. I know it can't have been pleasant, having me here. I—I've tried to do the best I could with Jamie, to repay you." She stopped, as if expecting an answer.

He was aware of the familiar bafflement—with a difference. No anger rose in response to the enigmatic remark. He felt instead a certain pity. He said calmly, "What do you mean?"

Her eyes flickered. "Knowing who *I* am—"

"Yes?"

"It was—strange"—she stumbled over the words—"strange that you should hire me. Was it not?"

"I didn't think so," he said kindly.

She withdrew again to the bed, not to sit down but to stand irresolutely. She didn't look at Glazer. "I shouldn't have gone to the beach. You understand, when Emily urged that I apply to you, I didn't know what it would be like going down there." She wrung her hands bitterly.

He remembered the first time he had taken her down the slanting path, and now his curiosity was suddenly piqued. There must be something more here than he had supposed, some feminine vagary. He asked, "Why shouldn't you have gone to the beach?"

There was almost anguish in the look she gave him; Glazer was surprised. "But you know! Of course you know!"

He was at a loss. "You are afraid of the sea for some reason?" he hazarded wildly.

Her face grew still. There was a moment of complete silence. "Don't— make fun of me."

"I assure you I'm not." It sounded stuffy even to Glazer. What was wrong with the woman? Again he felt a kind of surprise that he wasn't angry with her. "Won't you explain? I can't imagine what you mean."

"My husband died on your beach."

Her words hung in the air, and the silence that followed was the sort that would follow an obscene remark shouted in church. A quiver ran up the side of Glazer's neck and he felt his cheek twitch. "What did you say?" But all at once he was tired of being patient, of sparring; all the hardness in him came to the fore. "No, wait—I heard what you said. What kind of nonsense is this? What are you trying to do?"

She looked frightened. Her face seemed to grow starker, narrower, and the cheekbones stood out under the haunted eyes. She didn't answer. She sat down slowly, tightening her arms across her bosom, exactly as if Glazer intended to strike her. The satin coverlet rustled under her light weight, and then the room grew still again. She didn't even appear to breathe.

He forced himself to be calm. He went over and sat down beside her. "I didn't mean to sound rough. Tell me what you mean."

She got her vocal cords working finally. "My husband, Adam Warne, died on your beach two years ago. I—I thought you must know. The police talked to everyone. They must have come here. You see, he was shot to death. He was shot from—from above, from the bluff perhaps, and the police were very curious about who had done it."

Glazer was aware of a sensation like a dream; he was going to wake up in a minute, in the dark, in bed. And even as this conviction ran through his thoughts a second rose to dispute it; there was no denying that Mrs. Warne had stated distinctly that her husband had been murdered. Here. Fantastic, dreamlike, or anything else, there was a core of truth in the way she spoke. The husky voice carried an impact he couldn't ignore. "I have never heard of your husband or his death. Believe me, Mrs. Warne. It's the truth. As for the police seeing me, it would have been impossible. We weren't living here two years ago."

She blinked slowly. "You weren't?" Her voice was doubtful now.

He felt an urge to touch her. In fact, to assure himself of her reality, he reached for her hand. It lay small and cold inside his own, and the bones felt sharp under the skin. "I bought this house in October—about a year and eight months ago. The owners were a couple of men, bachelors, who had apparently had some sort of dispute and were splitting up. Conway and Shelton. I didn't get to know them very well. Conway owned a bar in Seaview and Shelton was some sort of marine scientist. They left Seaview. We moved in. My wife decorated and I put in the gardens. My wife died." He seemed to have reached some sort of balking place. He could not talk about Rheba to this strange, quiet girl. He realized that, for some reason, if he could he would have kept her from knowing anything at all about his wife. Even that she had existed.

Mrs. Warne seemed unaware of much that he had said; she had seized on one item. "You aren't the one, then."

"No. I wasn't here."

She brushed at the hair again, a tired, mechanical motion. "I shouldn't have come."

"Was it Emily's idea?"

"She said you needed someone and that I should apply. She said I was going to be—neurotic, or something, if I didn't come and get it out of my system."

Glazer nodded to himself. "That always was Emily. She's the original girl for seizing bulls by the horns." Something was nagging in the depths of Glazer's mind, but he forbade himself to think of it. "Tell me about this afternoon, won't you?"

She seemed suddenly eager to talk. "I took Jamie down about two. He begged me to try to swim out to the rocks. I didn't think I could, so I dived in and experimented. I hadn't swum for a long time and I was rusty. But he begged—" Her hand clenched inside Glazer's. "I took him out to the rocks, towed him, left him where I thought he'd be safe. Then I thought I'd dive a little off one of the other rocks, only I began to remember—" She tried to pull her hand away, but Glazer gripped it. He was not aware that he did; it was just that he was at last about to get the truth out of this woman. She was being revealed finally as a three-dimensional human being, and he was determined not to be denied.

"Go on."

She made a choked sound. "You're hurting my hand!"

"What did you think of? Your husband?"

"No. Yes. I mean, I—" She began to shiver as if in fright. Glazer released his grip, feeling a little foolish. She rubbed one hand with the other. "I grew confused. It all seemed terrifying and unendurable, that I should be here where he died, that I should have set foot on that beach. It brought back things I thought I had forgotten. You see, I went through a very bad time then, when my husband was killed. I was sick; I was in the hospital. I had—I had lost our child."

Glazer got up abruptly from the bed.

She leaned forward, looking up at him. The husky voice was no more than a whisper. "Lately I have been feeling so much better. Jamie is a darling, and Mrs. Concannon has been kind, and I began to think the old mood wouldn't come back anymore."

She didn't mention Glazer's behavior, and he felt a cold disgust with himself.

"I'm so sorry I endangered Jamie. You don't have to tell me to go. I know I must." She huddled back, folding her arms again.

"No." Glazer himself was rather surprised at the firmness of the word. "I didn't come to ask you to leave. I came for your explanation. I knew that there must be one." This wasn't quite a lie; Glazer admitted to himself that the sight of the open suitcases had changed everything.

"I am not fit to care for the little boy."

Glazer sat down again. "Jamie needed you. He still needs you."

"I'm not reliable," she said wretchedly.

"You have made one mistake. Just one." Even to himself Glazer's voice seemed so calm, reasonable, and judicial that it carried conviction. "I'm sure that nothing of the sort will happen again. Of course it would have been better had I known of this other—affair." He intended to minimize what she had told him; there was no need to dwell on the dead husband, no matter how he had died. "But now that I understand, there will be less friction and less chance of mishap."

She looked at him with vague fear in her eyes. "I'm afraid it isn't that easy. I do have to know the truth. It's what I came for."

"The truth?" he echoed blankly.

"How Adam was killed."

Her words revealed to Glazer all too clearly what his real motive was in keeping her here. They were like a slap, a sting with a quirt, an affront. He sat in silence while she watched him. The husband, dead all this time—why should his presence intrude, come between them now? Glazer's mind filled with bitterness.

She moved close to him, put a hand on his arm. The slim lines of her legs were carved in the soft gray silk. "Since you weren't here, I'll have to find those other men, the ones who were. Somebody knows the truth."

Her closeness held him in suffocating immobility. "But the police— surely they told you all that was to be known."

"I had to take their word—*then*. I was sick and alone."

"But—all this while since— Two years." He felt that she was edging him in a direction he didn't want to go.

"When I got out of the hospital friends in Los Angeles took me in. I wasn't able to work for a long time. When finally I did get a job it was as a practical nurse, really little better than maid's work, and then the family moved to Santa Barbara. I began to think I'd never have a chance to come back here."

"Perhaps it would have been better," Glazer forced himself to say, "if you had not."

She took her hand off his arm. "I know you've never liked me."

"I didn't mean that at all. I was thinking of your own welfare. You will only open old wounds, probing into your husband's death."

She looked utterly forlorn, dejected, lost. "When you came in here a few minutes ago and were so kind and showed so much understanding, I hoped—I hoped you might help me."

She had come out with it, the bald appeal that Glazer had sensed under all she had said. He was suddenly on the verge of revolt. If she had done any obvious thing at that moment, if she had clung to him or showed tears or threatened hysterics, he would have cut her off quite shortly. But she did nothing. She continued to sit as if lost in despair. She didn't even look at the open suitcases or the little trunk; even that small a move to urge him would have caused Glazer's rebellion. As for Glazer, all he could see were the neatly folded garments ready to be lifted and laid down in one of the pieces of luggage.

He turned toward her abruptly and gripped her shoulders and pulled her against him. She was caught unawares. She reacted as if he had made a move to hit her. "What are you afraid of?"

Her face grew still. "Nothing."

"What's in this for me?"

She didn't pretend not to understand. She colored a little. "I like you very much. I did—from the beginning."

"How much?" From somewhere in Glazer's brawling past this ugly thing had come, this uncivilized creature that now occupied his mind. Or perhaps, as at their first meeting, he felt that he had already made the revealing mistake and that she knew at once he was not the gentleman his clothes, his too careful manners, and his house proclaimed him. Let her see then just what he was. The roughneck who had come practically barefooted out of the raw Texas hills, the kid who had been drinking whiskey and chewing tobacco at twelve, the hobo who had razored off an ear in a freight-car brawl in El Paso—he was all of these. And the refinement Emily had carefully painted on him was as thin and crackling as eggshell.

He kissed her. Not in the way he had had to kiss Rheba, but with a deliberate brutality that was more of a release than he had felt in years. The black hair slipped under his hands and he felt the shape of her skull, small and round. The smell of her skin was flowerlike. Her hands fluttered against him; he expected her resistance. But the hands fell away.

When their lips parted, she let him hold her. The black head lay against his shirt; he wondered if she could hear the pounding of his heart.

The real estate office was right on the highway, and inside, fat as a toad, Eddie Rayburn sat digesting breakfast and watching the traffic. When Glazer parked his car and came up the walk, a gleam settled in Eddie's eye. He half stood as Glazer came inside. "Hello there. Got a house you want sold? Or looking for another lot?" He smiled widely and then took in the expression on Glazer's face and let the smile slip a little.

Glazer ignored the chair indicated by Eddie's outstretched hand. "Why didn't you tell me there'd been a murder right below my place?"

Eddie blinked, and yet his lack of reaction was a betrayal; he had expected this question sooner or later. "So what? A guy gets bumped off. You going to hold that against the *house?* You expect haunts or something?" He made a bewildered motion with his hands.

"I just wondered why you hadn't had the decency to put me wise to something everybody else in town must know."

"Who've you been talking to? Nobody remembers that case anymore. It was a nine-day wonder and it died. Period."

Glazer sat on the edge of the desk, picked up a pencil, examined it as if something written on it was important. "Tell me about it."

"Ain't anything much to tell. They found this guy Warne—and a real stinker *he* was—laying dead under your bluff. Shot, I believe. It's been so long, I've forgotten a lot."

"Why did you say that about Warne?"

"Oh, he was a character. A real bum. Drank like a fish. I used to let him hit me up for a drink just to hear him yap. He had a line, all right. I even used to think I might make a real estate salesman out of him, but nah, he was always on the sauce." Eddie scratched his temple where the thin hair was growing gray. "That guy. Who should get excited over him?"

"I want information. How was the case settled?"

"Nothin'." Eddie shrugged, his face blank. "Personally, I think he committed suicide in some weird way and the gun got washed off with the tide. He must have known where he was headed—Camarillo or the mortuary. Even Warne would have seen that. He was cracking up."

"What about his wife?"

Eddie's fat face widened—not a smile, exactly, this time. Something more wolfish and more smug. "I hear Mrs. Warne is up at your place looking after your boy. That surprised me, Glazer. It sure did."

"It's none of your goddamned business."

Eddie was insult-proof, at least in regard to a contractor who might have houses for him to sell. "Don't get your bowels in an uproar. If you want information, go talk to old Billy Holt at the newspaper office. He knows as much as anybody."

"Thanks." Glazer walked out without another word.

Six

Billy Holt was a small man with a gray withered face, a nervous cough, and a twitch under one eye which gave the impression that a jumping bug had somehow gotten in under the skin and was struggling to break away. He was the editor of the weekly local paper, a small power in local politics, a rich man's son who had never had the nerve to sow wild oats nor the constitution to be a sport. He worked at an enormous untidy desk in the best country-newspaper tradition. He looked up as Glazer came into the office. Glazer had never paid much attention to him before, but now he thought to himself that Holt was exactly the kind of man who would know all about a local murder.

Holt shook hands and asked Glazer to sit down. "Going to advertise one of your homes? Thought you'd already sold that one on the hill; heard you'd sold it before it was even started to Dr. Barton." The spot under his eye jumped and he rubbed it automatically.

"Yes, it's not on the market. I didn't come to talk advertising. I came for information. I want to know about the man who was killed on my stretch of beach."

Holt's eyes grew brighter. "Well ... I presumed, somehow, that you'd heard all about that long ago."

"Not a word," said Glazer. "Very tactful people in this town."

"I don't think anyone was trying deliberately to keep it a secret. Oh, the real estate man might, the one who sold it to you—"

"I've already jumped him. He was expecting it, eventually. He's the one suggested I come here."

"Hmmm." Holt swung back in his chair, and the swivel squeaked. "It's been two years. Lots of water over the dam since then. I wouldn't remember it so clearly, except that it was really the only important local crime we've had here in the last ten years or so—you can't count those Mexicans off the fishing boat, the two sailors who knifed each other on the pier."

Well, Glazer thought, you might not count them if you were the editor of a snobby little sheet catering to the inhabitants of California's gold coast.

"I guess you know that Mrs. Warne is at my house, caring for my boy."

Holt didn't look up. "Yes, I'd heard something of the sort. It provided a final piquancy, I thought, relieving the grimness. Am I to understand that it was from Mrs. Warne that you learned of her husband's murder?"

"Yes, and that the case was never solved. She asked me to make inquiries about it."

"Rather late." Holt was toying with a pen.

"Circumstances have kept her away from Seaview."

"She was sick when he died, I remember. In the hospital, completely off her trolley, according to rumor." Holt rubbed the spot under his eye. "Warne was a queer fellow. He had a lot of charm—and then again, he didn't. I guess he appealed to just a certain type of person, those who saw through his disreputable exterior to the tormented human being within. If he was only mildly liquored up, you couldn't ask for better company. He was witty, perceptive; he could talk the birds out of the trees." Holt smiled faintly as if in reminiscence. "When he got too bad, we'd call one of his cronies and they'd come get him and take him off to quiet down. One of his chums was a man named Fowler. He went off the deep end, completely cracked up, and is in a sanitarium now, a strait-jacket case. The other man was Orville Tremaine. After Warne was killed and Fowler broke up, Tremaine went on the wagon. He still lives here, has a small house back in the canyon, does part-time gardening, straightened himself out and stuck with it. It's too bad it couldn't have happened that way with Warne. I'm sure he had brilliant possibilities."

Glazer wanted to hear about Warne's death, something definite that he could take back to Francesca and say, "Look, this is all there is. Now let's forget it." At the same time, he was aware that Holt intended to lead up to the main part of the story in his own way and that it wouldn't do any good to try to rush him. And then finally, under the impatience and the irritation, there was something new. Curiosity. He hadn't wanted Warne to come alive; he hadn't wanted to learn enough about the man so that he could visualize him, characterize him. But it was happening. And as the man grew and took on human attributes, an interest in his fate followed willy-nilly.

"I liked Warne. I couldn't help it," Holt went on after a moment of thought. "I knew how rotten he was. I knew how he treated his wife. But I always thought some inner devils tormented him and drove him back to drink. And it was drink that turned him into a beast. When he was cold sober, he was a quiet and gentle person."

"Well, that's an old story," said Glazer. "What about his murder?"

"I'm coming to it. There's no use my saying, 'Here's the way he died and here's what the cops did afterwards.' You don't get anything out of that. You've got to know the man a little first." The faint smile came back to Holt's thin lips. "Or perhaps Mrs. Warne has described him fully."

"She hasn't said anything about him except that he was killed below my house, that somebody shot him from the top of the bluff."

Holt shook his head. "Well, no, that really wasn't proved. He was shot in the top of the head, and the general theory was booted around that someone stood on the bluff to do it. But he could have been lying down. He'd been drinking. It was late twilight, almost night; he could have lain down to go to sleep. It wouldn't have been the first time he'd lain out all night."

"When did they find him? Right away?"

"Pretty quick. A fisherman down the beach heard the shot and went to have a look."

"It would have taken a little time to get across that expanse of flat rock—it's full of potholes."

"Yes, I guess it did take some minutes. Amazingly, Warne wasn't quite dead when he reached him. This fellow knew Warne, recognized him at once. He had a pocket lighter, and he bent over Warne and put the light to his face. He said Warne's eyes flickered and that Warne tried to tell him something. The police, I believe, took this account with a large grain of salt. Their doctor didn't think Warne could have lived that long with that kind of hole in his head. Now Dr. Barton, the one you're building the house for—he's said in my presence that he thinks the fisherman might have been telling the truth. Brain injuries are peculiar things. But because the police doctor didn't like that part of the story, the cops rather discredited all of it; they didn't believe he could have seen anyone on that slanting path or trail— I understand you've replaced it with something better."

"The fisherman saw someone on the trail to the top of the bluff?"

"Well, he said he thought there was *movement* there."

"What about the two men in my house? Conway? Shelton?"

"They were at home. Their housekeeper came by the day and had left early that evening, so there was just the two of them in the house. Conway was getting ready to go down to his bar and check the evening trade, and Shelton had spent the afternoon in the den mounting some kind of new sea animal he'd discovered. He was an expert on clams and such, had been a professor, I believe. The police did work on those two. You see, Conway had had trouble with Warne. Some hassle in his cocktail bar, though Conway depreciated the affair after Warne's death. Personally, I felt there was more than met the eye about Mr. Conway."

"Don't be mysterious," Glazer said, irritated. "What do you mean?"

"Conway didn't stay here long after Warne's death. He and Shelton sold their house as soon as possible. You got a bargain, and you must know it. Then Conway cleared out. Shelton's still around, moved down the coast a bit and bought himself a place on the beach. Encinitas, I think it is. But Conway moved entirely away. San Francisco, the last I heard."

"I should think the police would have been interested in this."

"No doubt they were." Holt took out a pack of cigarettes, offered them to Glazer, took one himself, then struck a match and lit both. "But you see, the thing that hampered them, that stuck them at the end, was the disappearance of the weapon. The only gun in your place was a small revolver Conway carried. He had a permit—his business, that was logical. He carried cash with him, and a bar or a bar owner are of course prime targets for holdups. But Warne's wound was made by a rifle."

"And they never found the rifle," Glazer surmised.

"Never."

Glazer was silent for a little while; he was trying to account to himself for Francesca's ignorance of all this. Ill as she must have been—almost dying, according to Holt—she'd have seen no newspapers. Her convalescence must have been difficult and slow for her to have missed even the end of the case. But of course when a murder case remains unsolved, interest dies quickly. Probably the papers hadn't played it up much more than a week or two. Then other news had crowded it out. She hadn't known anything of Conway and Shelton. Sometime later, through acquaintance with Emily perhaps, she had learned that he, Glazer, occupied the house above the beach where Warne had died. She had taken it for granted that he had been there at the time of the murder.

Well, he told himself, it was odd that she had made such a mistake, but not impossible. She was not a woman of whom you would expect logic and precise reasoning. She still showed signs of timidity and confusion; probably she had been much worse in the past, when the effects of her illness and Warne's death had been new. He remembered her acquiescence of last night, and a sense of heat ran across his skin. Had she been afraid of him? Had he taken advantage of her in a way that was entirely inexcusable?

He was aware that he had gritted his teeth. Probably some strain showed on his face, for Holt glanced at him curiously. Then Holt said, "How is Mrs. Warne?"

"I think there are times when she's upset. Probably it wasn't wise, her coming to my place. I didn't know, of course." Glazer was surprised at his own hypocrisy. He would have torn apart anyone who might have tried to remove Francesca Warne from his home.

"Warne led her a horrible life. She was a teacher here when she met him. I haven't told you Warne's business—he was a writer. I mean, he could make money writing, but what he really wanted to be, what he spent most of his time at, was painting. Of course our town is full of artists. Was full, before the Midwestern retired lumberyard owners and sewer contractors crowded in on us." Holt was definitely snobby now, his nose tilted in his gray face. The spot on his face jumped as though the bug inside was angry at all those stupid Midwestern tradesmen who had squeezed out the artists. "He had been butting his head on that stone wall for years. When he got hungry—or more likely, thirsty—he wrote something and sent it off and got a check back. It was amazing. He certainly had the commercial knack. No art to it; he knew he was a hack. I think that's why he had turned to art, to painting. There was something inside him that rebelled at the commercialism. So he took up something he'd be sure to starve at."

"She supported him?" Glazer hated himself, hated asking this. It was something he had no right to know, would be better off not knowing. What did he care if she'd made their living? It wouldn't happen this time.

"No. She quit teaching when they married. She was sick a lot. I wouldn't be surprised if she went hungry most of the time."

Glazer averted his thoughts from this direction. "Getting back to the crime itself, was the bullet recovered?"

Holt nodded. "Yes, I think they got that. I believe it went clear through him and was recovered from the beach sand. Actually, I'm not too strong on the scientific end of the affair. My interest lay in the human equation. If you've got a few minutes to spare, why don't you stop in at the police station? Of course our small local force only sports a couple of what you might call detectives. Most of the work, since we're astraddle of this damned highway, is traffic control. If you want me to, I'll go with you. I know Byronson, the man who worked on the Warne murder."

Glazer felt that Holt was pushing him along, deeper into this thing, and the fact that his own curiosity was drawing him in the same direction didn't allay his distaste. He wanted—and yet he didn't want—to know about Warne. He had made a bargain with Warne's widow; and though it hadn't been put into words, each knew the expectations of the other. He had no wish to upset the arrangement. He stood up and nodded to Holt. "Would you?"

Holt closed his desk, said good-by to his stenographer, got his hat, and they went out. The street was quiet, shadowed with eucalyptus, the roar from the through traffic on the highway only a distant hum. Holt looked with appreciation at the sunny morning. "Good to be outside. You're lucky, Glazer, that your work doesn't keep you tied up in an office."

"My job is no cinch," Glazer muttered.

"No trouble with old Dr. Barton, surely?"

"No, no."

"And now that all controls are off—"

"They can build them bigger and better than ever," Glazer agreed. "They can build anything they damned please." He thought all at once of Clyde and his immense swimming pool, built before the war—and of what Francesca Warne had said about it. Well, there'd be many more now, larger even than Clyde's, which Francesca had taken for a tennis court.

Holt shot him a curious glance. "You know—you'll have to forgive me for getting personal—but you look as if you might be working too hard. Of course we only met a few times, but as I remember, you used to be the happy-go-lucky sort. Relaxed. There's a kind of—of strain about you now."

Glazer grunted wordlessly. He felt silly with this small man examining him. He thought to himself that Holt was no picture of health and had little business talking to anyone else on the subject.

"I shouldn't have said anything," Holt went on in self-reproach. "Of course you've just found out about Warne's murder on your property. Well, the beach is actually public, but nobody ever went to your beach from town. Too rough. All that stone to cross. And since you've just discovered—"

"I'm not upset about the murder of a man I never saw," Glazer said in a hard tone, and again Holt gave him the quick, examining stare. Glazer wondered then if Holt thought he was on the trail of a story. Was he going to write up some silly guff about the murder, about the new owner of the house living there above the scene of the crime, unknowing, all this time?

The police station was at the end of the block, a small new white concrete structure. The architect had tried to disguise it as something else. It could have been a small medical building, or a telephone office, or a woman's club. The front of the building was shaded by palms and bougainvillea vines. There was no hint of grimness to affront the tourists. A small brass plaque set in the wall beside the door said *Police Headquarters*, but you had to walk in off the sidewalk to read it. Around in the rear, Glazer knew, it was another story; the private courtyard wasn't bashful about barred windows and floodlights. But the tourists never saw that courtyard unless they'd been behaving in unlawful ways.

He and Holt went into the reception hall, and Holt asked if Byronson was around. The uniformed clerk sent them down the hall to Byronson's office. It was a very neat, plain, rather chilly room. Byronson looked up, recognized Holt, and rose in welcome. "Hello, Mr. Holt."

"Hello, Ted. This is Mr. Glazer. One of our contractors here in town. He bought the house Conway and Shelton owned."

Byronson was young. He had crisp blond hair cut very short, big shoulders, a trim waist. There was something a trifle Prussian in his manner, Glazer thought. Or perhaps it was merely the effect of the uniform, which on Byronson seemed to have an unusual sharpness and fit. His eyes held Glazer's for a moment while he put out his hand. They were very pale eyes and had a flat sheen like steel.

"I am pleased to meet you," Byronson said. "What can I do for you gentlemen?"

"Do you have a little time to chat?" Holt asked, looking for a chair.

"Yes, of course." Byronson arranged a couple of chairs for them.

Holt sat down, dropped his hat on his knee, looked at the young officer. "Mr. Glazer has just found out about the murder of Adam Warne. He's looking for information."

"I see." It seemed to Glazer that there was the faintest hint of disappointment in the gray steel eyes. Perhaps Byronson had expected them to be bringing information, not asking it. And then Glazer remembered something else—he had seen Byronson before. He had seen him on his beach in a bathing suit. Months ago. And the detective hadn't given any hint of being an officer. He had chatted for a little while about the beach and the water. Then he had swum out into the bay, far past the three big rocks.

Byronson said carefully, "Do you remember meeting me on that beach, Mr. Glazer?" He spoke with extreme caution; he spoke as if he were at the same time putting eggs into a basket and a loud word might break some of them.

"Yes, I was just thinking of it."

"I thought you had recognized me."

Very sharp, this Prussian eaglet. Glazer decided that he didn't like Byronson much. Behind the steel-colored eyes was a quick, observing intelligence.

"It took me a minute. You weren't in uniform that day."

"I'd been swimming. I took a sudden notion to look at the scene of my defeat." He had seated himself. He looked at Glazer. "I don't wear the uniform all the time. When it seems advisable, I put on civilian clothes. I hadn't intended the swimming trunks as a disguise, however." He smiled. The smile changed him a little, but not much. It was not a warm, experienced smile. Probably he did not smile often enough to quite get the hang of it, Glazer decided. All at once Glazer had a queer feeling that he would have been better off not getting acquainted with this cop.

"You want to know about Warne? I hardly know where to begin, since I don't know what you have found out from Mr. Holt and others."

"I was wondering about the bullet. What sort of gun the murderer used, the angle of the wound, and so on."

"Warne was shot with a high-powered .22. The shot entered the top of the skull on the right side and came out under the left ear."

"He was shot from above?"

Byronson shrugged. "If he had been standing, yes."

"He died instantly?"

The gray eyes flickered. "We believed so, though one of the witnesses, the man who found Warne on the beach, said not. I think Mr. Holt must have told you about it."

"Who were the suspects?"

Byronson shook his head. "I'm sorry, Mr. Glazer. This case is still on the books. That information is police business."

Seven

Holt laughed. "Oh, come on, Ted. You know I'm not going to sneak back to the office and get out an extra on it. And Mr. Glazer is merely an innocent bystander."

Byronson's mouth was tight. "Sorry, Mr. Holt."

Glazer put in at random, "Well, can you tell me this—was suspicion directed especially at one person? Did you have one you were pretty sure of?"

Byronson licked his lips. The sunlight from the window turned his stubble of hair to a metallic color a little paler than gold. Finally he said, "Well, since it's to be in confidence, yes. I did have my conviction as to one person above the rest."

"You see," said Holt genially, as if Byronson was a child he had been coaxing to say something cute. "I knew he had an idea he wasn't giving out. I've always known it."

"Of course I can't tell you who that person is," Byronson added hurriedly.

"We didn't expect that. By the way, do you know what became of those two who were living in the house above the beach? Conway, especially—the one who owned the Fiddling Crab."

Byronson folded his hands before him on the desk. He looked like a judge, Glazer thought—a young and not too merciful judge. "I have followed Conway's movements. He's in San Diego; he owns the same kind of place there as he had here. High-class and dirty, if you know what I mean."

"Any narcotic connections?"

"Nothing like that was ever proved."

"I thought he went to San Francisco for a while," said Holt.

"Yes, he did. He spent about a year there, no occupation; he must have been living on his capital. Then he settled in San Diego."

Glazer remembered Conway vividly. He was a big, dark, loose-jointed man whose easy air covered a subtle watchfulness. "Do you think Conway has been back here?"

"I think he has," Byronson answered, and added nothing.

"What about Shelton?" Holt put in.

The flash of interest in the steel-colored eyes could not be concealed. Holt's question had struck a spark. "Shelton?" Byronson parried, gaining time to frame an answer. "Why—I thought you knew. He's in Encinitas, still monkeying with sea urchins and stuff. Getting a book ready to publish, in fact."

"I didn't get acquainted with them," Glazer said, "since our only contact was during the purchase of the house. But it struck me then, and strikes me even more now that I know the differences in their background and occupation, that they were a funny pair to be pals. To live together, build a house in joint ownership, occupy it together."

"I'll tell you what I thought about it," Holt replied. "I think Conway made a deliberate effort to hang onto Shelton. Shelton's education, his prestige as a teacher and scientist, was what attracted Conway. He thought a little of that respectability and high-minded culture might wear off, might make a kind of mask for himself. He always cultivated

Shelton's friends. He never brought home any of his bar-fly patrons."

Byronson was staring straight ahead, making no comment. It seemed to Glazer that he was guarding something.

Holt went on: "Now that Shelton is married and Conway isn't too far away, I'll bet he tries to horn in on that relationship."

"In what way?" said Byronson, scarcely moving his lips.

"Just hanging around," Holt answered. He did not seem to sense Byronson's rapt attention where Shelton was concerned. "Staying for dinner, crashing their parties, inviting himself for overnight visits— That girl Shelton married is young and timid. She wouldn't stand up to Conway. And Shelton apparently never could."

Byronson's face remained rigid, but his throat moved; he had swallowed, hard. A patch of color flamed briefly in each lean cheek. Glazer was watching him curiously. There was definite interest on Byronson's part in connection with Shelton. To egg matters on, Glazer remarked, "I didn't know Shelton married."

"Married the little Parico girl. Pretty thing. Used to clerk in the drugstore. Shelton must be more than twice her age—he's over fifty if he's a day."

"He must have married her after he sold me the house," Glazer said, "since I don't remember any wife."

"They were married in Mexico the day Shelton moved away," said Byronson suddenly.

"Funny," mused Holt. "We were talking about Warne's murder and now we're off on Shelton's marriage. Could there possibly be a connection?" He pulled at his lower lip with his fingers. The spot under his eye jumped with an independent life of its own. The question had seemed to be an idle one, but it was followed by a curious stillness.

"What connection could there be?" Glazer asked, trying to watch Byronson without staring directly at him. "I thought it was Conway that Warne had his trouble with, a fight in the bar."

Byronson came to life. "That affair was much worse than anyone let on. Warne wouldn't prosecute, but Conway gave him a bad beating. He didn't offer much of an excuse—said that Warne had insulted his patrons and he wanted to get rid of him permanently. I always thought the quarrel went deeper than that. There was some element neither man would discuss."

He's leading us away from Shelton, Glazer told himself.

But as if feeling that he had said enough, Byronson suddenly rose. He was younger than either Glazer or Holt by some years, but there was no doubt as to his mastery of the situation. His hardness, his bulk, and the imperishably crisp uniform gave him an authority that could not be overlooked. Holt and Glazer rose too, sensing dismissal. Glazer wondered if Holt was as annoyed at this officious young punk as he was. He thought he would like to see Byronson rolled in the dirt, his uniform torn and draggled.

They accepted Byronson's excuse of having work to do, made their good-bys, and went outside. Holt seemed pleased with the interview. He paused under the shade of the bougainvillea vine to light a cigarette. "Well, we learned a thing or two. Conway's back down south. San Diego. Only sixty-odd miles down the coast. And Ted thinks he paid a visit to town. Didn't give us any details. You know, Ted's so damned young and so cockeyed sure of himself; you've got to make allowances. He got under your skin, didn't he?" In the narrow gray face the eyes were laughing, and Glazer answered with an embarrassed smile. "Yeah, I saw that he did. Well, it occurred to me that if Conway came back to town he might have visited that old pal of Warne's out in the canyon. I'll admit to you now, Glazer, that I've been on a trail of my own for a long time. This Tremaine, the fellow I said went on the wagon and bought a place up the canyon—he's had a source of income that didn't meet the eye. As I said, he does gardening. He might make a living at it; he does put on a show of working now and then. But I just have a hunch he lives a little better than that part-time gardening would allow."

Glazer glanced at his wrist watch. Again he was aware that he disliked this prying into Warne's death and into Warne's affairs. His curiosity was aroused, but some stubborn part of his mind wanted to pursue the thing in his own way, not under Holt's direction. Furthermore, he didn't want Holt along if he uncovered something conclusive.

"We could run out to Tremaine's place in less than twenty minutes," Holt urged.

"No, I'm sorry—I've got to get on the job. I won't be free until late this afternoon. Would that do?"

To his relief, Holt said that he had another engagement late in the day. They agreed tentatively to meet again tomorrow and to pursue the idea of going to the house in the canyon. Glazer walked back to the newspaper office with Holt, got into his car, and drove away. He took the highway north, passing the entrance to his own drive and then swinging into the curving street that led up the hill, past new homes, to the raw excavation on the flank of the hill where Dr. Barton's home would someday stand.

He checked with the cement contractor, conferred with the building foreman, and looked at the lumber that had been delivered. Dr. Barton came by on his way home from the hospital for lunch. They discussed the house, and the doctor pointed out some minor changes he wished made.

At a little after noon Glazer arrived at his own front door. Jamie met him there. The little boy was hopping with excitement.

"Mrs. Warne went to town. To buy something. A man came for her!" He grabbed his father's hand, and Glazer had to suppress the impulse to shake him.

"Who was it? What was his name?"

"I don't know. He was tall and big and old. He had on a cowboy's hat!"

Glazer went into the house, turned toward the kitchen. Mrs. Concannon was there as he had expected her to be, making preparations for lunch. She looked up as he entered. "Mrs. Warne had to run an errand. She said to tell you she'd be back very shortly."

"I see." He went away to wash, to comb his hair and change to a clean shirt after the dust of the hillside. While he was in his bathroom he heard the sound of a car outside. He forced himself to be slow, deliberate, in reaching for the towel, in running the comb through his hair, and in donning the new shirt. And under the slowness, anger burned. He felt now as if he owned this woman. She had no right to go away with another man, no matter who.

He went and sat on the side of the bed and brushed his dusty shoes. And he tried, while performing this simple and mechanical task, to analyze his own motives and behavior. He had the feeling of being on uncertain ground.

As for motive, face it; he wanted the woman. There was no longer any use to pretend that he was not drawn to her or that she did not represent an irresistible magnet. Plain, slim, almost haggard she might be; she had an effect on him that he could remember no other woman having. What he had felt for Rheba compared with his feeling for Francesca Warne as a candle flame to a blast furnace.

He had not until now tried to figure out the failure of his marriage. It had seemed to start out well enough, a wartime romance that had a more solid foundation than most. He had known Rheba a year in Los Angeles, had been much with her before their marriage. She had been, he remembered, an immaculate and rather critical woman. Talented, too, a fine interior decorator. When Jamie was born they had still been in love. Or had they? Had they ever? It was certain he had felt in no way for her as he did for Mrs. Warne. This black-haired woman was an obsession. She was something he wanted to conquer, to tear down, to humble. She made him feel like a tiger.

Rheba had kept him on his good behavior because she had always trusted him to act like a gentleman. There was no such trust in Francesca Warne. She was afraid of him. Was that what roused him? It could—it would—be changed, he told himself. After their marriage she would see that he could be thoroughly domesticated. A tame tiger.

He knotted his tie, put on his jacket, and went out into the living room. Francesca Warne stood in the middle of the floor, Jamie beside her, her hand on the child's shoulder. When she heard Glazer's steps, she turned. She smiled somewhat uncertainly. "Did you wait lunch for me? You shouldn't have."

"No, I just got in," Glazer said. He saw that she carried a small package. She unwrapped it as he watched; inside were a drawing pad and crayons.

Jamie looked at his father briefly, watching his reaction. Then he took the drawing pad and the crayons and hugged them to his bosom. Glazer hid his impatience, though to himself he thought the stuff much too childish for the boy. He would rather she had bought something more difficult to use—water colors, for instance. Then he looked at her and forgot his irritation. Her skin had a frosty clearness, and the eyes were like those of a statue, too big and too placid to be alive. "I'd like to talk to you for a minute before lunch. Come into the den."

The den was in a small wing by itself, behind the part of the house that held the kitchen and service areas. They went down a short hall and Glazer opened the door, ushered her in. He remembered all at once that Shelton was supposed to have been here when Warne was killed, working with some of his sea life.

She went to the big desk, then turned to face him.

"I made some inquiries this morning," he said. "I talked to the newspaper editor, Holt, and to a police officer."

She wasn't looking at him, Glazer noted. She was gazing at the window, the view of the gardens and the humpy headland; but he sensed she wasn't really seeing that either. He wondered if she had conjured up some memory of her husband.

"The cop admitted that he has a definite suspect, someone he's pretty sure of. I sort of think it's Shelton, the marine scientist who lived here with the night-club fellow, Conway."

"What motive?" she said huskily.

"I don't know. I think the cop has some idea, but he didn't let it out. There's another angle. You must remember a friend of your husband's, a man named Tremaine."

She began to take off her white kidskin gloves. "Yes, I know him."

"Holt thinks he's being paid off for silence."

"That's ridiculous."

Glazer was surprised by her firmness, her defense of the man. "You know Tremaine well?"

"He was Adam's friend. He took me to town today."

"Holt seems to think Conway might have brought him money recently."

"It doesn't sound probable. Tremaine doesn't show any signs of wealth." She dropped the gloves on the desk. "Don't let this man Holt guide you or keep you from making an independent inquiry. You should keep after the police, get the name of their principal suspect." She sounded as if this was very important to her, and for a moment Glazer was repelled by the implied criticism of his methods.

"Well, it's just a beginning. I had to start somewhere. Holt did fill in the picture, generally." He took her hand in his and tried to pull her against him. "If you want me to, I'll hire a private detective."

She shook her head. "Don't do that. You can't—control—such people."

He stroked her hair; it was silky, slippery, under his palm. "I'll do all that I can." Even as their lips met, it occurred to Glazer that though he had examined, faced, and defined his own motives in the affair he had not made himself consider hers. Holt had left the impression Warne had treated her harshly. And still her determination to discover Warne's murderer had some vital basis. Uncomfortably he wondered, Did she love Warne so much, willy-nilly, that she must solve his death?

Deliberately he forced the question out of his mind and gave himself over to the feelings of the moment.

Byronson came out into the sun. The light lit a blaze in his hair until he covered his head with the dark blue cap. He walked to the police car at the end of the courtyard, got in, started the motor, and drove away. He took a side street that turned into the canyon boulevard that left the coast here and angled through the hills toward Santa Ana.

As he drove he took a stick of gum from his tunic pocket, stripped off the paper by holding it against the wheel, put the gum into his mouth, and began to chew. His jaws bulged and his teeth made grinding noises. On his face was an expression of peaceful contempt.

The town dropped behind and the road climbed a little and entered a narrow canyon. To the left was the bare embankment of the road, but to the right lay the bed of a tiny stream, dry in all but exceptionally rainy weather, and on its other side, tiny houses and bright patches of gardens.

Byronson turned in at a gate, crossed the gravelly patch that was the stream bed, and drew up under a portico. The house was a little better than its neighbors; it would not have been out of place in a nice neighborhood in town. The front yard was brilliant with masses of yellow flowers. Byronson parked the car and went up to the door and rang the bell.

An old dog came up from the yard and sniffed at Byronson's leg, and he kicked it with impersonal savagery. The dog made a noise between a whine and a grunt and slunk away. Byronson punched the bell a second time. When there was no answer, he took the gum out of his mouth and thumbed it into the little crater around the button so that the bell kept on shrilling. Then he went around the house to the back. A man with a wide-brimmed hat in his hand stood on the rear steps as if just about to enter. "Never mind," said Byronson. "It's me."

"My bell keeps ringing," the other man said.

"Let it ring. Come here. I want to talk to you."

The other man was tall, old, with rough hands, and hair that was speckled with gray. Reluctantly he set down a paper sack he was carrying and came over closer to Byronson.

"When did you see Conway?" Byronson asked.

"Honestly, Mr. Byronson, I've told you the truth. Conway didn't come to see me. I haven't seen him since he moved away from here."

Byronson took out another strip of gum and began to peel off its wrapper. "What I'm asking now, Tremaine, is what did Conway say about his partner?"

"You mean Mr. Shelton? But they weren't—"

"Of course they were. Warne knew it, he must have told you. Shelton owned a half interest in the Fiddling Crab. The most profitable business in California is selling liquor by the drink. You know that, don't you? And it wouldn't look nice, maybe, if a professor like Shelton came right out and admitted that he was in the drunk-making business." Byronson's tone held a gentle reasonableness, like a teacher's to a stubborn pupil.

The old man's seamed face was full of doubt and worry. "What do you want me to say?"

"Tell me the news Conway brought about Shelton. Are they still partners? Does Shelton own a piece of Conway's place in San Diego?"

Tremaine took out a dust-colored handkerchief and mopped at his face. He rubbed hard at the deep seams from nose to mouth where sweat and dust had settled. He coughed nervously and spat. "I'm just guessing, Mr. Byronson, but I'd say—no. I don't think those two wanted much to do with each other after Adam Warne's murder."

Byronson inspected the paper his gum had been packed in. "Well, that's interesting. Why do you think that?"

"Just a conviction that one of them killed Adam Warne and the other knew it."

"Sometimes that kind of thing makes people chummier than ever."

Tremaine waited, as if to let Byronson know that he would not argue the point. Then he said, "My doorbell's going to wear out if I don't go and fix it."

Byronson's steel-colored eyes went on studying the scrap of paper.

"Who was with Warne on that beach the night he died?"

The knob in Tremaine's weathered throat jumped up and down. "A fisherman found him."

"That isn't what I mean."

Tremaine's knotted hands clenched into fists. "You've had me all over it before, Mr. Byronson, and you tried to make me say what you wanted, and all I can add now is that my conviction is clearer than ever. I won't say the little Parico girl was with Adam Warne. Because I don't know."

"You saw them together earlier in the day."

"That doesn't mean she went to that deserted beach with him, nor that she was doing what you think she was doing."

The red patches gleamed suddenly on Byronson's face. In the steel-colored eyes hatred lay naked as a sword.

Eight

It was an accident that Glazer interviewed Shelton first among those on his mental list. An errand connected with business, contacting a possible new client, took him down the coast, and in coming back he passed through Encinitas and recalled that Shelton lived there. He found the address by looking into the telephone book and then getting street directions at a service station.

The house was close to the beach, quite removed from the highway. Glazer somehow had had the idea that when Shelton split up with Conway he had probably purchased a much cheaper home. But this place was as big as the house Glazer had bought. Its yard had an unkempt wildness which was familiar, and Glazer was reminded of the untouched yard at home which he had had to cover with topsoil and nursery stock. Evidently Shelton liked his surroundings as nature left them. The only flowers were a few wild straggling ones, lupine and buttercups and, lower, toward the beach, sand verbena. No grass, no pretense at a lawn; where the wind had scoured down to rock, the rock lay bare.

Glazer went from the street down some stone steps, along a walk, and into an enclosed patio. A swing sat there, turned so that its canvas cover made a shelter from the warm afternoon sun, and on the swing sat a woman. Glazer was startled by her appearance. She had vivid red-brown hair and large dark eyes, and though she was small, her figure was voluptuous. When she saw Glazer she rose quickly from the swing. She wore a peach-colored linen sport dress and white sandals. Her brown legs were bare. "Hello," she said.

Glazer was at a loss for a moment. Then something prompted: "Are you Mrs. Shelton?"

"Yes, I'm Mary Shelton."

"I wondered if I might see your husband for a minute."

"He just left for the store. Won't you sit down and wait? He won't be away long."

While Glazer hesitated, she moved a canvas chair so that it was shaded by an overhead trellis. He got the impression that she was glad of company.

"He's only gone as far as the highway, the grocery there," she told him. "And there wasn't much to buy. So you won't have long to wait."

Glazer sat down, dropped his hat on a redwood coffee table.

"Can I get you something cold to drink?" she wondered.

"It sounds inviting."

She hurried off into the house, came back quickly with a pitcher of lemon-colored drink and two glasses on a tray. She poured a glassful for Glazer, one for herself. Over the rim of the glass she looked at him. "Are you an ichthyologist too?" she asked.

"A *what?*" cried Glazer.

"No, you aren't, or you would have known the term. Actually, though, my husband defines himself as a molluscologist." She laughed a little, softly and breathlessly. "I was trying to find out what your business was."

"I'm a building contractor," said Glazer, taking her literally. "I should have introduced myself. Glazer's the name. Your husband sold me my house."

"That sounds odd," she commented. "How did it happen you didn't build one of your own?"

"I liked the location out on the bluff. And there wasn't any comparable piece of bare land on the market. You remember the house," he added idly, forgetting that his conversation with Holt and Byronson had been supposedly confidential.

"Yes, I remember it. But how did you know?"

He saw that he had made a small slip. "I can't remember where I heard it—but someone told me you and your husband met in that town."

She nodded. "Yes, that's right. I was in your house several times before my husband and Mr. Conway sold it."

"It's a beautiful house," Glazer said to keep the conversation rolling. But the remark roused no agreement in Mrs. Shelton. He plowed on: "I had the grounds completed. Or probably, if you've driven north recently, you saw that. It turned out very well after I had topsoil brought in."

"That's splendid," she said in an odd, flat voice.

They sipped the drinks for some moments in silence. Then Mrs. Shelton, in a somewhat different tone, with a gingerly hesitation, asked, "I suppose you are well acquainted in town by now?"

"Mostly clients, people I've built houses for," he answered.

"Is the town expanding?"

She talked as if she had never been back for all those months, Glazer thought. "Northward, mostly. I'm putting up some big homes in the hills behind the highway. Dr. Barton is having a place built now; it's going to be pretty nice."

"I remember him," she said. "He's an awfully nice man."

They were sparring, Glazer sensed; and on his part, he was doing it in the dark. All at once his usual mood under such circumstances seized him; he got tired of the thing. "Did you know a man named Adam Warne?" he asked.

She had been lifting the glass of lemonade toward her mouth. Her hand paused. Then she tried to get the glass back on the table. Glazer was at once appalled and fascinated by the slow-motion debacle. She struggled with the glass, and it tipped first one way and then another, slopping the drink, and her wrist shook so that she reached with the other hand to steady it. Too late. The glass went on the cement-block floor of the patio and shattered there, spattering lemonade on them both. It had taken only a moment, probably, but Glazer felt as if he had been watching that slipping glass for hours.

"How awkward of me!" Her voice was shrill; she jumped up. "I'll get something to wipe up with. Excuse me." She slipped into the house; the door closed after her.

She didn't come back. The spilled lemonade dried in the sun, and pretty soon a couple of ants were scouting the sticky remains. Glazer took out his pipe and packed it with tobacco. Well, he had done a stupid thing. He had alarmed the little bird, and it had flown. But its flight, too, was revealing. Mrs. Shelton was very sensitive on the subject of Francesca's dead husband.

He heard footsteps and rose from the chair and picked up his hat. Maybe Shelton, too, would be extremely sensitive and ask him to leave once his errand was stated. Glazer was ready.

Shelton came in from the bright sun and paused under the shade of the trellis and peered at Glazer. He was unexpectedly older than Glazer recalled. He was a short little man with a funny tufted gray beard, a bald spot that left him only a tonsure, and big glasses that made his pale eyes swim. "Oh," he said uncertainly. "Dear, dear—I know you. Glazer. You bought the house in ..." His voice died out huskily. Then he remembered to be the host and he tried to smile. He shifted the brown paper bag in his arms and held out his right hand.

His hand was hot and sticky, like a baby's. Glazer said, "I've been talking to your wife, waiting for you. She's inside, getting a mop or something." He pointed to the broken glass.

Shelton examined the glass, and a frightened expression crossed his face. "Yes, I see. Do you want to sit out here, Mr. Glazer, or indoors? We'll have an early dinner if you can join us. I've a crab here, really a good-looking fellow, and Mary can fix it thermidor. She likes that."

"I should think you'd have enough samples of your own without buying one at the store."

"Ha, ha, ha," said Shelton at the weak joke. "Well, they're not too tasty after they've been pickled a year or so. Excuse me, I'll go dump these groceries." He pattered off on his short legs.

Glazer sat down again and got the pipe started. He was smoking peaceably when Shelton returned. Shelton looked hot and dismayed. "Forgive Mary, Mr. Glazer—she's taken suddenly with a headache. It isn't important about the spilled lemonade." He stepped on the scouting ants before he sat down in a canvas chair. "Mary isn't feeling well, poor girl."

"I'm sorry to hear that."

"Uh ... well ... Is there anything especially that I can do for you, or is this a social call and can we enjoy ourselves?" He laughed self-consciously. The words had all come out in a rush. Glazer decided that Mary Shelton had put a bug in her husband's ear.

"I hope I'm not dragging up something that has unhappy memories for you," Glazer began, trying to sound tactful, "but I'm poking around into the death of this fellow Warne, the one who died on my beach. Your beach, then. My curiosity has been roused. I hoped perhaps to hear your version of the affair, and perhaps if you had some information the cops didn't— I mean, something they refused to accept. Byronson seems to have some rather firm ideas." He threw in the last at random, and it had a remarkable effect on Shelton.

The little man turned pale and looked as if he might be sick. "A—a thoroughly detestable man, Byronson. The worst sort to become a police officer. A martinet."

The Prussian eaglet, Glazer thought, throwing his weight around.

"Well," Glazer said soothingly, "do you mind talking about it?"

Shelton debated. There was a film of sweat on his face and over the bald spot on his scalp. "I don't know anything that's secret, Mr. Glazer." He put an unnecessary emphasis on the words. "It was an unhappy experience. Byronson hounded Conway and me until we thought we'd go crazy. Actually, it had a good deal to do with our decision to leave Seaview. I don't know if he actually suspected either of us of the murder. I used to think not. He is the type of man who likes to raise hell with people who can't fight back."

"I thought I caught a hint of the bully in him," Glazer agreed.

"Conway had had a fight with Warne, it's true. But he was always having to settle brawls, stop them quickly, in that bar of his. He hadn't any personal animosity after the affairs were over. But he had to act fast and hit hard. Warne was a particularly objectionable fellow. He couldn't hold his liquor. Many is the time early in the day, in town, I saw him staggering in the main street. What he must have been like later on—"

"It was late in the day when he was killed," Glazer reminded.

"Yes, practically dark. That summer two years ago was hot. The day had been a scorcher. We even had a bit of something that's rare out here on the coast—heat lightning. It played along the horizon, out over the sea, as dark came on."

The den gave no view of the sea, Glazer thought with surprise. The two windows looked at the hump of the headland and the gardens. But he made no comment.

"I was working in a room at the back of the house," Shelton continued, "a room I used as a study. Perhaps you have made it into an extra bedroom. There is a hall behind the kitchen—"

"I use it for an office," Glazer said.

"Yes. Well, the day was so hot I'd taken off my clothes and put on an old pair of swimming trunks. When the police came—the first I knew about Warne's death—they seemed very suspicious of my attire. It wasn't any use to tell them the truth, but I tried. They seemed to think no one could work up a sweat looking into a microscope."

"What about Conway?"

"He was getting ready to go down to his bar—he'd just showered, was just getting into fresh clothes. That, too, seemed to excite the police. They were almost ready to say eeny-meeny-miney-mo and take the loser away, we were both such matchless suspects."

"But there had to be motive as well as opportunity."

An uncomfortable light flickered in Shelton's eyes. "Uh—I guess that's what stopped them, then." There was more that he wasn't saying, and these unsaid things brought perspiration dripping down his face.

He hadn't been bashful about discussing Conway's possible motive, arguing it away, so the difficulty lay with some motive of his own. Glazer wished he knew some way to unlock the small man's lips. The silence lay between them, heavy with Shelton's fright and guilt.

"Did they search your house?" Glazer wondered.

Shelton started. "Not right away. Why do you ask?"

"I understand the weapon was missing, has never been found. I thought perhaps they looked for it there."

Relief flowed out of Shelton like a tangible thing. "I guess they didn't think of that."

Nothing to do with the hidden gun, Glazer noted. But the question about searching the house had probed an old fear, a guilty scar.

Glazer said, "I guess you heard that the fisherman who found Warne said that he thought there was something, some movement—that of a person, perhaps—on that trail to the top of the bluff."

"I don't recall particularly." There was no reaction; Shelton was on sure ground. He had answered this question before. "We had no fence about the grounds—no grounds to fence, actually. Someone could have been on the beach trail, have come to the top and run away."

"Did the police ask you about it?"

"I don't remember." Shelton reached out with a toe and mashed an ant, a newcomer to the sticky remains of lemonade. "It's so long ago. The thing has been finished for so long. I'm afraid your curiosity won't have much to be satisfied with."

"Perhaps I'd better explain; it's a little more than that. I've made the acquaintance of Mrs. Warne. She asked me to make inquiries."

The eyes behind the heavy lenses goggled and blinked. "That poor woman? I should think she'd let Warne rest in peace, and good riddance. She was sick, almost dead, in the hospital. Warne had beaten her up and she'd had a miscarriage."

Glazer flinched. His throat grew dry. Heat ran through his brain.

"As I said," Shelton murmured, "he was an objectionable fellow." He let a little while drift by in silence. A hummingbird came into the patio, looking for flowers, and found only the bare cement and the painted trellis and went back out to the lupine and buttercups. "By the way, I drove up the coast a few weeks ago on my way to see another man in my field at the university. I noticed what you had done with the gardens. They're beautiful."

He'd seen the disappointment of the little bird then. Glazer said, "I am rather proud of the way it all turned out."

"I have the opposite of a green thumb, whatever that is," Shelton said wearily. "Nothing will grow for me. Long ago I just gave up."

"It is a challenge," Glazer answered, and was surprised at his own insight. Making the flowers grow was a kind of battle. The stubborn greenery wanted to dawdle, to hold back bloom, to die out quickly; and he fought it and made it get big, lush, bountiful with blossom. And the conquering was what he liked, not the beauty.

Shelton was murmuring in a small voice, "I'll be glad to talk some other day. As a matter of fact, I expect to be in your vicinity tomorrow, looking for specimens. I can stop by and we can finish our conversation. Right now, when Mary's feeling so badly—"

"I shouldn't have kept you this long," Glazer agreed.

They shook hands. Shelton's relief at his going was obvious. As Glazer left, Shelton began to pick up the pieces of the broken glass.

Glazer got into his car and drove back to the highway. Except for the bad moments there when Shelton had mentioned Francesca, he had almost enjoyed himself. Of one thing he was convinced: Byronson was right in suspecting the little scientist. It stuck out all over Shelton that he was concealing something.

Glazer wondered what it could be.

Shelton took the broken glass into the kitchen, dumped it into a box under the sink. From a cupboard he got a cleaning rag and wet it under the faucet, then went back to the patio and scrubbed at the lemonade stain. Afterward he sprayed Flit about to discourage the omnivorous ants.

Back in the kitchen, he put the groceries away neatly on the shelves, the bread in the breadbox, a small cake on a covered plate. He was adroit and precise in his movements, and yet there was a certain air of deliberation and caution, as if much of the time he worked with extremely delicate things. When the kitchen was quite tidy he went to his own room, removed his coat, went into the bathroom, and splashed his face with water. He dried himself, looking into the mirror.

He thought about Glazer. A big man; ruthless, probably. There was a hard core under the smooth exterior, the businesslike politeness. How old? Thirty-four? Thirty-five? Shelton thought wistfully of the fifteen years' difference, and then even more wistfully of the twenty-seven that separated him from his wife.

When he had finished combing his hair and beard, when he thought to himself that he looked quite cool and calm, he went into Mary's bedroom. The shades were drawn. She lay on her face on the big low bed.

Her voice was muffled. "What did he say?"

"Nothing much. He's made the acquaintance of Warne's wife, and she has set him asking questions."

Mary's head lifted quickly. "Francesca Warne? What's she doing here? I thought she had gone away long ago."

"He didn't say how or where he made her acquaintance." Shelton sat down gingerly on the edge of the bed. He looked at his wife's bare ankles. "I wonder how well he knows her. There was a little incident there that puzzled me. I mentioned how Warne had beaten her and how she lost the child. And he looked rather heated up."

"Maybe she hadn't told him."

Shelton's eyes swam foggily behind the lenses. "You didn't know it either."

She put her head down again, resting her forehead on her hands. "I didn't know it—then." There was a space of silence. "If he showed some emotion, maybe it means he's interested in her."

"I thought of that. Of course he's nothing like Warne."

"Nothing at all."

Shelton sat still, looking at the closed curtains high on the wall. It seemed that in the air a figure floated, a ghost. A thin man with a shock of black hair and a handsome though weak and introspective face, eyes that seemed full of dreams, a mouth that twisted slightly as if over some inner humor. Shabby clothes. Beach-sleeping clothes. You felt, even seeing that ghost, that here was a man lost and burned out who yet could make you feel by comparison a clod. Shabby; and you were sleek, and yet you would have traded with him any day. A knot of sickness clutched the pit of Shelton's stomach. He fought it down.

Carefully he put his hand down close to Mary's bare leg so that on his skin he could feel the warmth of hers. She permitted this; she didn't draw away. She even spoke to him. "Maybe you ought to look up Mrs. Warne."

"I thought I might find out from Glazer where she is."

"She was a beautiful woman," said Mary in a muffled voice.

"But not so beautiful as you—" He almost bit his tongue in anger. He shouldn't make such a comparison, not just after talking about Adam Warne. Mary was his wife now. How beautiful she was in relation to other women was his business alone. The knot gripped his stomach again.

If he were to avoid a bad upset, he had better go and take one of the pills the doctor had recommended.

The doctor had warned him, too, about emotional effects on the digestive tract. Bad. Disastrous. It could irritate itself into cancer, perhaps. And then Adam Warne would have the last laugh after all.

The ghost by the windows smiled. Will Shelton closed his eyes.

Nine

Glazer was in the den, figuring on the new job he expected to start next week. He had blueprints spread out on the desk. It was past dark; through the open window a cool sea breeze was blowing.

He heard running steps, pounding, stumbling. He lifted his head. Bess had been there that day, helped Mrs. Concannon with the washing and ironing. He knew that this was Bess coming back in a hurry. Running, in fact, as if the devil were after her. Then he heard a cry: "Mr. Glazer!"

He ran to the window, but she had just flashed past and was fumbling with the kitchen door. He heard Mrs. Concannon's voice, sharp with surprise.

He hurried down the hall and to the right, into the kitchen. Bess was clinging to Mrs. Concannon. She was dirt- and grass-stained. The bandanna on her head had fallen back, and the wind had blown her hair. Blood dripped from one hand.

"... followed me, sneaking-like. I ran, and he ran. Then I fell down and I screamed. He kicked me as he went past." Her voice rose to a scream, as if she had suffered some ultimate, inconceivable outrage. *"He k-kicked me!"*

Glazer went over and caught her hand and looked at it. The bleeding came from a superficial cut, but there was dirt around it. An extra bathroom and shower adjoined the kitchen entry for the use of bathers; Glazer led her in there. He washed the cut and put iodine on it, swathed it carefully in bandages. "Who was it?"

"I don't know. It's dark out there."

"He was near the house when he started following you?"

"He must have been," she cried. "He must have been hanging around close, maybe even peeking in. A sex fiend." She hiccuped over her sobs, and Mrs. Concannon held her. "He was waiting to *r-r-r-rape* somebody!"

Jamie and Mrs. Warne had come and stood in the doorway. Glazer said, "Take him back to his room, please, Francesca." He was unaware that he had used her first name, nor did he note the glance Mrs. Concannon gave him. "I'm going to telephone the police. Give her a shot of whiskey in water, will you?"

After he had reported the presence of the prowler to the police, he came back to Bess, led her into the living room, made her sit down. "Do you think I could catch him if I went out there?"

"He's gone by now. He was running hard. Going toward the highway. He'll be down the road or hidden in the eucalyptus somewhere by now."

"You don't have any idea what he looked like?"

Bess rubbed her face, pulled off the bandanna, inspected the bandage Glazer had made. "He ran like a young man. He wasn't panting; he didn't have any trouble catching up with me. The kick hurt." She touched her ribs, then doubled over.

Glazer said to Mrs. Concannon, "Call Dr. Barton. Tell him I'm bringing her."

In the car he plied Bess with more questions. "Did he say anything? Call to you?"

"He hissed at me. That's what started me running. You know, the busstop corner is dark—the light's down the block. I wasn't quite in sight of the bench where the bus stops, and it isn't too plain to see, of course, when I heard this sharp noise in the shadows, and I sensed a man there."

Bess's worst expectations had come true, Glazer thought. She had always been firmly convinced that a rapist would get after her someday, what with the dark and the isolation.

"Then I tripped." She sobbed again. Hysterics were just under the surface. A police car went past on its way out of town, probably to look for the prowler. Bess calmed somewhat as the siren went by. "They won't get him. He knew his way. He ran down that road as if he'd done it a million times."

Glazer said, "I'll never let you go home on the bus again, Bess. I know this sounds like shutting the barn door after the horse is gone, but we like your work and we need you. If you'll keep coming, I'll take you home nights."

"Th-thank you. That's kind of you."

They reached the doctor's home on the outskirts of town, a plain house in a plain street. Dr. Barton had saved for a long time for that big house on the hill. They went inside, and the doctor took Bess into his examining room.

The verdict wasn't serious. Mild shock, bruises, a skinned knee, and the light cut which Glazer had already treated. Cut by a stone as she fell, Bess thought. The doctor's sedative had made her sleepy even before Glazer dropped her off at her home.

Glazer went home and in the quiet of the den he tried to settle himself again to work, but he was much more disturbed by the thing that had happened to Bess than he liked to admit. In spite of Bess's constant worry over rapists and robbers, there had been nothing like that in the neighborhood, nothing that touched them here to make them aware of danger. Now there was a man, a real man, and he had been prowling the dark in the immediate vicinity, almost as if his attention had been fixed for the purpose of tracking down a woman from Glazer's house. In the back of his mind, though he refused to face it, Glazer's curiosity was directed toward Francesca Warne. Was this ugly though minor attack related in some way to the mystery in which she had forced him to meddle?

He laid out the new blueprints and tried to work up estimates from them, but his thoughts backtracked and he found himself reviewing what he had done, the people he had contacted in regard to the murder of Adam Warne.

There was the real estate man, then Holt at the newspaper office, then the cop he hadn't liked, Byronson. From these three he'd gotten information about Warne, the kind of man he was and how he'd treated his wife, but no hint to solve the riddle of Warne's dying. The Sheltons had something to hide, but it might not be guilt of Warne's murder. There was something odd under the surface relationship between the beautiful young wife and the fiftyish scientist; in Shelton he had sensed a ponderous though repressed despair, and the girl seemed ready to fly to pieces at a touch, though her calm curiosity had at first fooled him.

Glazer went out into the garden with his pipe. The night was still, cool, and filled with flower odors. The lights down the coast made Glazer think of a sparkling necklace laid against black plush, or a lot of diamonds tossed to fall in a wavering arc; they faded into the faraway, almost invisible pale glow that was San Diego. Glazer walked down to the edge of the bluff, and the sound of the sea came up to him. There was something eternal and comforting in the never-ending watery rustle. When it was very calm and still like this, and when he felt himself a part of the earth, the night, and the sea, when he seemed a creature put down here to belong rightfully with the rest of it, he found it hard to comprehend the fever that seized him in his contacts with Francesca.

She was something unnatural to him, like an illness, he thought. She distorted his feeling of reality. When he possessed her finally, completely, he promised himself, there would be relief. The fever didn't endure through the commonplaces of marriage. Then he would see her truly, perhaps appreciate her more reasonably, an intriguing but not too beautiful woman whose scars were those of a bad marriage, whose wounds had left her with this strange urge to poke into the murder of her husband, a man who from her point of view should have been better off dead.

He remembered, out of any context, that today he and Holt had been going to call on Tremaine, Warne's old crony. Instead, he had made the trip down the coast and had called at Shelton's place.

Glazer glanced at his wrist, at the radiant numerals on his watch. It was not yet ten o'clock. There was a chance that Tremaine would still be up.

He went back inside for a jacket, then took the car to the canyon, to the address he'd looked up in the telephone book in his den. His headlights brought up a blaze of yellow flowers in the front yard, and he was aware of a subtle jealousy. They didn't look too well tended; the excess of bloom hardly seemed fair. And when he stepped from the car, the path was hard and dry underfoot. Probably Tremaine didn't even water his yard faithfully.

There was a light inside. Glazer felt for the bell, pressed it. A man with gray hair and a seamed face came to the door. He might be fifty, Glazer thought, or he might be younger than his appearance suggested because the drinking had left its mark. He'd been Adam Warne's crony; it didn't suggest temperance.

"Yes, sir," said the gray-haired man. "What can I do for you, sir?"

"My name is Glazer. Mrs. Warne is at my home, employed there, and she wanted me to make inquiries about her husband's death. I understand you knew him."

He opened the screen door and stepped back. An elderly mongrel of an indefinite worn-out brown color stood behind Tremaine; he looked at Glazer with what seemed apprehension.

"I saw Mrs. Warne yesterday," Tremaine said.

They were still standing by the door. Tremaine turned, indicated a chair for Glazer, sat down in a shabby rocker. The room was clean, but the furniture in it was musty, forlorn with age.

"She said you took her to town," Glazer said.

"Yes, I did." Tremaine didn't add anything further; he seemed to expect Glazer to go on. There was something defensive about his attitude.

Glazer tried to think of something to ask him. Finally he plunged into the heart of the matter. "What is your theory about Adam Warne's death?"

"I think it's possible that Conway and Shelton know more than they've told," Tremaine said quickly. "If the police ever get the truth from them, they might solve it. Without that source—and neither man has ever shown any sign of breaking—they won't."

"But what do *you* think?" Glazer persisted.

"I've told the police my opinion. One of the two had something to do with the murder."

His vagueness seemed deliberate, defensive. "Did Warne discuss with you the enmity that seemed to exist between him and Conway?"

"He despised Conway."

"Did he fear him?"

"I doubt it. Adam Warne had his own problems, bigger ones than his scrap with Conway." Tremaine hesitated before going on. "My real conviction about the murder is that it shouldn't be reopened. It will stir up cruelty and evil. Take this officer, Byronson; he was here yesterday. I hadn't been home but a few minutes after dropping Francesca at your house. He was ugly. He will hurt innocent people if he is goaded. It would be wiser if you could talk Francesca into forgetting the matter."

"She seems determined to have the truth."

"She has been ill. Her judgment isn't to be relied upon." The old dog came to lay his head on Tremaine's knee; the dog's eyes were questioning, uneasy. Either Glazer's presence disturbed him, or something in his master's manner was strange. Tremaine had spoken in a strained, didactic manner. His hands were nervous.

"One thing I did find out," Glazer said, wondering at the propriety of passing it on to Tremaine. "Shelton made a slip. He told me that he was in the den of my house at the time the murder was happening on the beach below. He described what he saw, the sea, the lightning out along the horizon. But from the den where he was supposed to be working you don't even get a glimpse of the ocean."

Tremaine nodded. "It does seem like a mistake on his part."

"I don't think he was in the den, as he claimed. I think he went out and then had reason to deny doing so."

Tremaine seemed lost in sudden, absent-minded thought. The old dog sneezed and rubbed at his nose with his paw, and Tremaine patted his head as if to reassure him of his presence.

Glazer said, "Maybe I ought to mention this to Byronson."

Tremaine's eyes seemed to catch fire; his whole face was transformed. He looked younger, angry, hardened. "Don't ever tell Byronson anything. Don't, especially, ever tell him anything that could bring him into contact with Francesca. He hates her."

Glazer was immensely surprised. "I didn't dream that. She's never said anything. And he seemed a plodding, hidebound type." Even as he spoke, his mind corrected the statement; on the surface Byronson was the correct and routine-conscious policeman, but under the rigid solemnity lay something more, a thing Glazer couldn't quite analyze, a thing that made Byronson dangerous. The thought of the young cop being Francesca's enemy was disturbing.

"I don't think she realizes how Byronson feels about the case," Tremaine said. "You see, for one thing, it was the only major crime we've had here for years, the lone sensation, the one spot in which Byronson might have shone. And he didn't crack it."

"But he shouldn't feel enmity for the wife—God knows she was innocent enough."

Tremaine's eyes were on his dog. "Byronson tried to say not. At first, that is, before he settled on someone else. He upbraided the doctor for keeping him out of her hospital room. He grilled her nurse."

Glazer felt the hot color that had come into his own face, the thudding anger in his brain. "How asinine can you get? The only hospital in town—if she was there, as I presume"—he saw Tremaine's nod of agreement—"is on a headland entirely across the bay from my stretch of beach. What did he pretend to think? That she walked through the town in a hospital nightdress?"

Tremaine didn't look up. "That must have stumped him, finally, and started him looking for someone else."

"And who did he choose?"

"Shelton."

Glazer frowned. "In spite of the slip Shelton made to me, I can't quite see him in the role of murderer. My idea was he'd covered up something for Conway. It was Conway that Adam Warne had had trouble with."

Tremaine said cautiously, "Byronson had a personal reason for wanting to pin it on Shelton. Not right then, I mean, but later. After the Parico girl married Shelton. You see, Byronson liked that girl."

Glazer didn't reply; this surprising information was sinking in, and he saw that the case was taking on a complexity he hadn't dreamed of.

"That's why you mustn't tell him about the slip Shelton made in his conversation with you," Tremaine went on. "It would make Byronson very happy. And I wouldn't want to see him pleased in that way."

The old dog began to sniffle and choke. Tremaine took him off into the kitchen, presumably to get him a drink. Glazer heard water running into a receptacle, heard something put down upon the floor. Tremaine came back in a moment, wiping his worn hands on a bandanna handkerchief.

"My dog has asthma. He gets so at night he can hardly breathe. I guess he hasn't a real long time to live anymore." Tremaine put the handkerchief away. "When your best friend and your dog are gone," he added reflectively, "then it seems as if maybe your own days are numbered."

Glazer said awkwardly, "You mustn't let yourself be depressed."

"You never knew Adam Warne," said Tremaine, looking directly at him. "If you've been talking to people here in town, you've got an impression he was lower than dirt."

The direct stare made Glazer uncomfortable. There seemed an accusation in it.

"But you can't add up a man that way," Tremaine went on. "You can't just say he was like this and he was rotten, because none of us are just one thing or even one kind of human being. We're a lot of creatures rolled into a skin and penned up, imprisoned, for the time we have to live. And Adam Warne was a man who never did find out which creature he was meant to be. He experimented. He tried to discover himself."

Under the bald overhead light Tremaine's seamed face was full of memory and worry.

Glazer, feeling that Tremaine wished him to say something, stammered: "I did hear that he could write well when he wanted to but that somehow he preferred to try to become an artist."

"That was on the surface," Tremaine said. "I meant something much deeper than that. The writing was a job. The painting was something he dabbled with to fill the time. Look, I'll show you." He went off into an inner room; Glazer heard the opening of a door—a closet door, perhaps. Then Tremaine came back with a couple of canvases. He set them on the shabby couch, facing Glazer.

Glazer looked at them incredulously. Living in this art-conscious community where Holt's retired lumberyard owners and sewer contractors took lessons avidly so as to imitate the genuine artists they were crowding out, Glazer was familiar with the various schools and the arguments among them. He knew there were factions who deliberately imitated the unschooled, the primitive. The pictures he now saw did not surprise him by their amateur appearance, but because he sensed the amateurishness was not intended. They were meant to be good. And they were terrible.

"You see what I mean," Tremaine commented in a husky, rather tired tone. "Adam was too sensitive a man to be deluded about this work. He knew that he would never be any good as an artist. This was not a part of that search he made for himself. The drinking was. He uncovered something within himself when he drank. I don't think anyone understood that except me. It was as if he had to reveal and to look at a thing he couldn't quite believe was a part of him; a monster, if you like."

Glazer said stiffly, "There wasn't any excuse for what he did to his wife."

Tremaine's eyes widened a little. "Oh, I'm not excusing him. I'm explaining him, the Adam Warne I knew, the tormented man who was my friend."

Glazer remembered Holt's comment, that he could not hope to understand the crime without knowing a little of the victim, but to Tremaine he said, "There are things no man can do and remain a part of the civilized community. And beating your wife is one of them. Warne even indirectly destroyed his own child."

Tremaine's shoulders sagged. "So he did. He knew it too. I think, if he had any warning that death was near, he was glad to meet it. He must have wanted to die."

The words seemed a sort of defense for Warne. Glazer was aware, as before, of a great distaste for learning the intimate facts about the man. Warne had been a husband to the woman who now engrossed him. He wished to handle the murder with a pair of mental tongs, not coming too close, not getting a sharp view of the victim.

"If I were you," Tremaine said, "I would get Francesca to leave this place. If I were in love with her, as I guess you to be, I'd take her. I'd take her whether she wanted to go or not."

"I promised her to investigate Warne's death."

Tremaine shook his head sadly; he didn't seem to have anything else to say. The old dog coughed and sniffled in the kitchen.

Outside a gust of wind ran up the canyon. Tree branches swept against a window. Glazer stood up, preparing to leave. He was aware of Tremaine's steady regard as he walked toward the door. Tremaine's eyes seemed to hold both a plea and a warning, one and the same: Leave Adam Warne's murder alone. Let it be. Just be glad, as Warne may have been, that he was dead.

Ten

In the early morning, working in his garden, Glazer was aware of an echo of uneasiness in his mind, something left from his interview with Tremaine the night before. As he turned the imported loam with his trowel, added fertilizer, watered with a fine spray, inspected the blooms for signs of an invasion of bugs, he kept remembering Tremaine's advice to take Mrs. Warne away.

He stood up from a new planting of yellow asters and looked at the sky. The wide blue heaven seemed to invite him with an opportunity of escape. There was nothing he couldn't leave for a month if he had to. He might miss getting bids in on a couple of houses, but he could spare the highly taxable additional income. Dr. Barton's house would be delayed, but the doctor would understand. He could take Francesca south, to Mexico. To Guaymas, Acapulco ... In his mind he saw a rim of azure sea, a lot of little boats, a beach yellow with sunlight. There would be long lazy days and the sudden dark of tropic nights. They could be married on the way, in Mexicali, for instance. She'd forget her obsession with Warne's murder. And he could forget the bits and pieces he had dug up about the man.

He glanced in the direction of the house. Francesca would be stirring in her room now, preparing for a day with Jamie. He might talk to her right away, without waiting, while the idea was fresh. Surely she'd see that what he wanted was the right and sensible thing.

He put down the trowel and dusted his hands on his denim pants. He scraped his shoes thoroughly at the front door, a habit he had acquired since he'd been living on carpets. Then he went inside; he was almost at the hall entry when the telephone rang.

It was Dr. Barton with a new idea for one of his bathrooms. Glazer listened patiently and without comment; he had discovered some time past that it was useless to point out that each change in this stage of house-building meant greatly increased expense, that the fads and fancies should have been incorporated into the original plans drawn by the architect and covered by Glazer's bid.

He had a hunch that Dr. Barton was a little afraid of his architect, a competent but somewhat opinionated young man named Hickok, and that he had deliberately withheld some of the more freakish items until he could deal directly with Glazer, with whom he was more familiar.

When the idea had been explained—a hot-air dryer built into the wall—and Glazer had said that he'd see about finding one, the doctor rang off; but Glazer was still not free to head for Mrs. Warne's room. Mrs. Concannon stepped out of the dining room to ask when he would be ready for breakfast. And in another moment the phone rang again.

He picked up the receiver impatiently; it took him a moment to recognize Holt's voice. The newspaper owner said with a touch of hesitation, "Hello? Glazer? Hope I didn't wake you."

"I've been in the garden for an hour."

"Good lord! You mean working?" Without waiting for Glazer to say yes and to explain how much one could get done in the time between six and seven, he rushed on: "Look, I came into La Niña's for breakfast just now, and who do you think's sitting at the counter?"

"Who?" said Glazer, feeling annoyed and stupid too; how could he be expected to know whom Holt had run into?

"Conway."

The little editor announced the name with a twitch of victory, as if he'd produced some miracle.

"I see," said Glazer cautiously.

"You'll want to talk to him," Holt rushed on, "and so I'm going to keep him here. Shall I tell him you're looking into Warne's murder? No, perhaps not; he might be sensitive on the subject because of the way the police treated him. I'll think of some excuse. You hurry down."

All of the things he intended to say to Francesca Warne about going with him to Mexico rushed through Glazer's mind. He said abruptly, "What have I to do with Conway?" and slammed down the phone.

He sensed her presence before he turned and saw her. She looked slim and straight as usual, but the big eyes held unexpected anger. "Who was that?"

"Holt, the newspaper editor. He said that Conway is in a café with him, having breakfast."

She looked Glazer over as if suddenly recognizing some aspect of his appearance. "Aren't you going down?"

"There's something I've got to say to you. An idea I got from Tremaine. I went to his house last night. He thinks you should leave this town, that being here is bad for you. I thought we might make a trip to Mexico— a month or so. We could stay on the coast. It's cool there."

Her body was motionless, the face without expression, the eyes looking at, or through, him with that strange placidity that always made him think of a painted statue. "I think you have made a mistake."

He went closer to her. "You don't understand; I've been clumsy in saying what I meant. I want you to marry me. Besides, from what Tremaine told me, your husband was ready to die; perhaps even glad to escape the kind of life he was leading." He knew there were doors open between them and the kitchen and that Mrs. Concannon must be listening. Well, let her hear. "I love you. I don't want you to go on tormenting yourself about a dead man."

He caught her arms and pulled her against him, and he was aware again of the urge to crush and subdue. The remoteness that had seemed a barrier, separating them, some crazy obstinacy on her part, as he considered it, suddenly shifted, so quickly that he was confused. It was as if from solid stone she had turned warm and melting between his hands; or as if, touching a frieze of figures carved in a wall, he found one shivering with life. He almost took his hands off her, almost stepped back.

"You mustn't listen to Tremaine." The words had no relation to her looks or actions. They were a command. They struck Glazer coldly even as he stood mesmerized by the change in her, the melting submission, the promise of conquest.

"His idea sounded sensible to me." The thought of taking her to Mexico was suddenly more exciting; his throat thickened.

"I'll go when you have done your part."

The moment was passing; she was regaining her solitary poise. In desperation, wanting to hold the woman he had glimpsed behind the mask, Glazer cried: "I can go on with the thing when we get back."

"You must do it now." She freed herself gently from his grip and walked away, over to the windows that faced the sea.

Glazer's instincts told him his own defeat. He foresaw the empty days of search, of questioning, prying into the death of a man he hated. He said weakly, "Perhaps I won't succeed in finding out anything important."

"Do what you can."

She was dismissing him, he realized uneasily. In my own house, where he was presumed master, she was telling him to get on with it and to leave her alone while he did it.

He stuck his head into the kitchen. "I have a hurry-up call to come downtown. I won't eat breakfast here."

Mrs. Concannon nodded, her glance quick to slide off his face.

La Niña's was on a side street. It was small and clean and not much patronized by tourists since it was a distance from the through highway to San Diego. As it had to depend on local trade and repeat business, the food was much better than average. At the entrance there was a mirrored door, and here Glazer looked at himself bitterly in the glass, wondering where under the tough, competent exterior there lay the core of weakness that Francesca Warne had uncovered. He went inside, hung up his hat, approached the counter. As he slid upon a stool he glanced around.

Holt and Conway were in a booth facing each other. As Glazer's eyes met Holt's the editor gave an almost imperceptible shake of his head, warning Glazer not to make an approach. The waiter came; Glazer ordered coffee and a doughnut.

After about three or four minutes Holt got up from the booth and came over. He said, "Well, I wonder if you remember me, Mr. Glazer." His voice must have carried to Conway.

Conway hadn't looked up when Glazer entered. He did so now. Glazer noticed that Conway had taken on weight in the months since he had bought the house from him. The dark hair on his head had pencilings of gray over the temples. The eyes were as usual: under an expressionless calm lay a watchfulness like a cat's.

"Of course I remember you," Glazer said, carefully hearty.

"Come on over to the booth," Holt urged. "I think you know Mr. Conway. We ran into each other here this morning. I haven't seen him since he left town."

Glazer indicated to the waiter that he could bring the coffee and doughnuts to Holt's table. Holt slid in upon the bench, and Glazer sat down next the aisle. "Hello," he said to Conway.

"How in hell did you grow all those flowers?" Conway asked without preamble.

"I brought in soil, made terraces, put in sprinklers. It was quite a job, of course."

"Everything yellow," Conway mused, looking at Glazer over his cup.

"I like yellow flowers," Glazer answered.

"When did you find out about Warne's murder?" Conway asked, again without any lead-in.

"A week or so ago."

"Mrs. Warne told you?"

"Yes."

Conway smiled slightly. He had a large mouth, deep lines running from his nose on either side. "I had a telephone call from Shelton. He said you came to see him."

Conway was no fool, Glazer thought; surely it must seem suspicious to him, this accident of running into the newspaper editor and Glazer, so apt from the point of view of extracting information. "I'm afraid I upset his wife," Glazer said.

"You couldn't be expected to know about the Parico girl and Adam Warne," Conway explained.

Glazer was astonished. Last night Tremaine had hinted that the police officer, Byronson, had been the Parico girl's close friend.

Holt said uneasily. "That was a dirty piece of gossip that had no basis in any provable fact. She was sorry for Warne. He had the ability to rouse pity in some people. If you could stand him at all, I think you began to realize the shape he was in mentally. Or spiritually—if there is a spirit."

Conway looked at the little editor with the flat, observing stare, and the spot on Holt's face jumped with a nervous twitch. "Warne was a foul mess. Only a fool could have felt anything for him but nausea."

Glazer butted in, impatient to get at the meat of the matter. "Where was Shelton during the time the murder took place?"

Conway stirred his coffee. "He was in the den, working at the microscope. Looking at some embryo shellfish or other." He waited a moment, then added: "I was under the shower when the police came. I'd spent part of the afternoon on the beach, grew sleepy down there, came up and fell into bed, and slept for almost two hours—time I shouldn't have used that way. I should have been in the Fiddling Crab attending to business."

Holt nodded slowly, as if agreeing. Glazer found Conway's flat stare disconcerting. Conway seemed to be looking inside his skull, he thought, and weighing the ideas he found there.

"The official theory, as applied to me," Conway went on dryly, "appeared to be that I had stripped naked, rushed down the goat path to the beach far enough to shoot Warne accurately with a .22, then ran back to wash off all signs of being outdoors or of having handled a gun. I admit, the theory had its points. Something the cops never thought of occurred to me—any light, bright stuff like summer clothing should have been visible to the fisherman as he looked over in the direction of the shot. It shouldn't have been the vague impression of movement he complained about, but the definite sight of a figure."

Holt's eyes grew bright. "You've hit on something."

"He's also led us away from Shelton," Glazer pointed out. "A naked figure, unless tanned to the near black of a lifeguard's, is about as visible as pale clothing."

"Hmmmm." Holt obviously didn't want to give up Conway's theory, perhaps sensing a story in it.

"Shelton was quite tanned that summer," Conway added evenly, looking at Glazer. "I think he had some weird idea of impressing the Parico girl, of trying to stack up against some of her pals. Byronson, for instance. God knows Warne was never any color except that of the underside of a shark."

Conway sipped at his coffee. Holt looked uncertainly at his wrist watch. Glazer, remembering some of his talk with Shelton, asked: "Did the police search your house?"

"When they had a warrant to do it," Conway snapped.

"That was later?"

"It held them up a little while," Conway said, with a glint of amusement, Glazer thought.

"What could have been in your house that they wanted?"

Holt coughed behind his hand in a stammering way. Glazer got the idea that his methods were somewhat direct for Holt; the man must want to handle Conway as he'd done with the cop, a slow teasing out of bits and scraps, the attitude of not wishing to offend with bluntness. Glazer thought, To hell with that. He pressed Conway: "Was it the gun they wanted—or something else?"

Conway's fingers turned his coffee cup this way, then the other. "I wasn't in Byronson's confidence about what he wanted to find. He liked me for a suspect—I saw that. Later, when Shelton married the Parico girl and took her away, he shifted his attention. He's not making it public, I'm sure, but he'd like to railroad Shelton and get the girl back."

Holt looked nervously about, as if fearing they might be overheard.

Conway went on: "I told Shelton he was a fool to stay in this part of the country. He ought to go East. Florida, for instance, since he likes to dabble in the ocean without freezing himself to death."

Holt said, "Surely you aren't implying that Byronson would cook up evidence and frame your friend."

"I'm just saying he'd better not. You can tell him that." Conway's eyes took in Holt's nervous air with dry amusement.

Glazer saw that Conway was his own type—direct, blunt, without subterfuge. He was threatening the young cop, ordering him indirectly to leave the little scientist alone. With the feeling that Conway's reaction to the information should be interesting, he said, "Shelton's statement to me contained something that didn't jibe. He said he'd been in the den when Warne was killed. But he described the look of the sea at that hour, twilight coming on and lightning playing out around the horizon."

Conway's face seemed to freeze into an expression of caution which betrayed nothing. Holt pulled at his collar, his eyelids fluttering.

Glazer said, "You can't see the ocean at all from the windows of the den. You can see the slope of the hill, the gardens—since I've put them in."

Holt said quickly, "Perhaps he'd gone into some other part of the house on some errand."

"He didn't say so. He says he was in the den at work all that late afternoon."

"The bathroom," Holt suggested.

"The den has one of its own."

Conway hadn't moved, hadn't taken part in the discussion. Now he suddenly spread his hands on the table, leaned toward Glazer and Holt; the stare he bent on them was cold, reptilian. "This is my advice, Glazer. Keep your mouth shut about it."

Glazer could scarcely believe his ears. Heat spread over his skin. "Are you ordering me around?"

"You heard me."

Holt gulped in audible misery.

"And if I decide not to obey?" Glazer asked through his teeth.

"You'll stay healthier keeping your nose clean," Conway told him.

Holt's breakfast had included a ham slice and with it had been a steak knife; this lay at the top of his plate. It was a sharp, businesslike-looking blade with a serrated edge at the tip. Glazer was hardly aware of having noticed it; but as Conway made a move as if to rise, Glazer found the knife in his hand.

Conway stopped where he was, in the process of getting up. Holt made a slight, whimpering noise; he looked sick. All three of them were looking at the knife in Glazer's fist, Glazer with a sense of incredulity. So soon had the polite veneer cracked away, and so quickly had the hoodlum come out. In that flickering moment Glazer seemed to be back in the boxcar on the siding in El Paso; a man lay screaming on the floor, two others huddled away in a corner, and in Glazer's hands hung a bloody razor.

"Well, well," said Conway on a note of surprise.

For an instant Glazer almost dropped the knife back upon Holt's plate, almost cracked his stiff lips in a smile, trying to pass it off casually. But it was too late. There was no way he could fool Conway. Conway had recognized him—knowing his own kind, perhaps; though the bar owner, like Glazer, had a patina of manners, good grammar, and well-tailored clothes.

He sensed Conway's quick, studying glance.

He flipped the knife in his fingers so that the blade jutted forward. He leaned across the table and put the point of the knife at the base of Conway's throat, where the sport collar lay open, showing the tanned skin. Holt opened his mouth as if he meant to scream, though no sound came.

There was no further conversation between Glazer and Conway, nor was there need of any. Violence trembled at the point of the knife, and Conway stood unmoving. His face purpled. He wet his lips with his tongue after a moment. His eyes hadn't changed; they were not eyes you could read.

It could have been no more than ten seconds that Glazer stood with the bright blade creasing Conway's skin. It must have seemed much longer to the really frightened one in the booth, Holt. Then Glazer lowered his arm slowly. Conway straightened from his half-stooped position, reached for his hat, left the table. Holt's breath made a whistling sound.

Glazer returned the knife carefully to the spot where Holt had placed it. At the restaurant door, Conway paused, his hat lifted toward his head, and looked back. He seemed to be making a note of something, an item of interest or the notice of an engagement, in his mind.

"Any time," said Glazer under his breath.

Eleven

Glazer sat down, feeling Holt's astounded stare on him. "My God," Holt stuttered. "That business with the knife ... You're *crazy!*"

Glazer turned to face him. "I had a tough bringing-up."

The spot under Holt's eye was jerking as if the cricket there had gone mad. "That's no excuse. I thought you were going to kill him for a minute. One little slip—"

"I don't slip with a knife," Glazer said. The little editor's gabbling fright amused and disgusted him; it was about the stage he'd been in when he was five. No, come to think of it, he'd been fighting well at five—kids up to eight, nine. In guts, Holt was about at the threeand-a-half level. A baby. A scared baby who had had a rich dad, whose timidity could hide behind money, who could dabble at writing and newspaper work because he had cash to buy a paper. "In the world I came from that business with Conway was nothing. A handshake. You can tell a lot about a man by shaking his hand. You can tell whether his circulation is up to par and how much he uses tools in his job and whether he'd be any good at something like mountain climbing, for instance."

Puzzlement spread in Holt's face, relieving the pallor. "Mountain climbing? What do you mean?"

"Would you want to climb mountains with a man who had no strength to his grip?" Glazer offered.

"I don't climb at all."

Glazer shrugged. "Well, Conway knows a few things about me now, just from that handshake. I think what he knows will do him good."

Holt drank the remains of his cold coffee. "Where *were* you raised?"

"Until the time I was fifteen," Glazer said, "I lived in the raggedest West Texas shantytown you can imagine. No, that's wrong—you couldn't imagine a place like that. You'd dress the houses up with paint and put curtains inside. I never saw a curtain until I left home. My mother died, and I cleared out. I didn't even wait to see her buried. I'd been there when my dad was put away when I was eleven, and that was sort of grim. You don't really know what those old words mean, that 'dust to dust' business, until you see your father put down into a raw hole in a coffin made of such rotten wood you know it won't bear the weight of the earth."

Holt was penned into the booth; otherwise, Glazer thought, he'd have bolted.

"My God, that's—that's sad," Holt managed to get out. "I'm terribly sorry."

"Oh hell," Glazer growled. "Do you think I'm asking your pity?"

"No, no."

"I thought you might be interested in why I pulled the knife on Conway."

"You had a reason," Holt said earnestly, and obviously without any conviction that he was speaking the truth. "He was getting ugly."

"He doesn't even know how to get ugly," Glazer informed the editor. "Not in my league." He saw Holt's glance flicker back to the knife and jerk away as if the sight scared him. "Here's what I want you to do. Tell the cop, Byronson, that Shelton made a slip when he talked to me. Tell

Byronson I'm too tenderhearted to go to him with it, you're just passing it along under the counter, so to speak, and maybe he can do something with it."

Holt licked his lips nervously. "You're taking your anger out on Shelton. It's not fair. I mean, after all, it's Conway who made you mad."

"He's funny about his pal," Glazer said. "I want to test just how funny he can get. Maybe he thinks Shelton will crack if the pressure goes on. And maybe when Shelton cracks, Conway's on a spot. It's an interesting idea. You stir Byronson up about it."

Some frantic thoughts were mirrored in Holt's eyes. "Are you sure this is what Mrs. Warne would want?"

"I'm running things for her," Glazer told him. He looked at his cooling coffee, the doughnut, and decided he didn't want them.

Holt said hopefully, "Well, maybe Shelton will have a perfectly logical explanation of that seeming slip he made."

"Yeah." Glazer pulled a bill from his wallet and laid it down for the waiter. "We'll see how he comes out with Byronson."

Holt reached for Glazer's arm, clutched his sleeve. He must have had some idea of making a last plea for Shelton; but when Glazer looked at him, no words came.

"You can revive the Warne murder in your paper," Glazer pointed out in a quiet way. "It's a local property; you can do wonders with it. None of the big L.A. dailies have any idea there's a chance it might be solved."

"I don't think it can be solved either," Holt stammered.

"I didn't, at first. But now the people involved are starting to throw rocks at each other. And in my country, after a rock fight, you knew the men from the boys. I think when the dust settles we'll know who murdered Adam Warne."

Holt had withdrawn his hand from Glazer's sleeve. He was far back in the corner. "You must be very fond of her."

"That's none of your damned business," said Glazer, leaving the booth.

He went home again and told Mrs. Concannon he'd have breakfast after all. He felt better about poking into the Warne murder all at once; and though he didn't put the knowledge into words, under the sense of fitness and pleasure was the realization that it was the promise of violence that he enjoyed. He had found an enemy worthy of his time and skill. Tremaine, Shelton, the girl Shelton had married, even Byronson, were people with whom he would have scorned to come to grips. True, there was danger of a sort in Byronson; Glazer had sensed the miasma given off by an unpredictable temper. But Byronson was not a man who would fight according to the rules of the jungle Glazer had known. If you threatened or annoyed him sufficiently, he'd just beat you over the head with his gun butt, reminding you meanwhile that he was a cop and so allowed to pulp you legally, and then throw you in the can.

Glazer settled himself at the table in the breakfast nook and gave himself over to the enjoyment of his fried salt pork, scrambled eggs, and corn bread. It all had an exceptional relish. Outside, the yellow bloom spilled down the slope of the hill, and the sea sparkled.

He thought about Conway. The thing that had struck him most was that Conway and the little scientist, Shelton, made an oddly assorted pair. He wondered when the relationship had begun, and where, and why. Who might know? Someone Conway had known in a business way, perhaps. A liquor wholesaler. When he finished eating, Glazer went into the den and looked at the business listings in the telephone book. Of course Conway might have been tied up with some wholesaler in Santa Ana or even L.A. But this was worth a try. He called the three local firms; they were little outfits, he knew. He hadn't expected much in the way of results, but on the third try, to a firm named Butler's, Distributors, he found Conway's former source of supply.

He waited while a clerk called Mr. Butler to the telephone. When he came, Butler had a gravelly voice. "Yes, sir?"

"My name is Glazer. I'm a contractor."

"Sure. Sure, I know your name, Mr. Glazer."

Glazer came right to the point. "I want some information about a man named Conway, used to run a bar called the Fiddling Crab—"

Mr. Butler exploded into profanity. He called Conway some vivid names having to do with his ancestry and personal attributes.

Glazer, surprised, said: "I thought you did business with him?"

"I did, I did. I'm just getting over Mr. Conway's business." He went on into details which Glazer found uninteresting. It seemed that Conway had cheated him with sharp practices.

"He has a pal named Shelton," Glazer managed to put in.

"Yeah, a little guy with whiskers," Butler agreed.

"Well, perhaps you can't help me. I wanted to find out where Shelton and Conway met up with each other and why they were such friends."

Butler waited a moment or so, perhaps weighing what he intended to say. "You don't know Conway very well if you weren't wise that Shelton was his partner. Shelton had the dough. Conway was a tramp. I think Shelton must have found him homeless on a beach somewhere."

"Conway ran the bar."

"It *looked* like Conway ran the bar. You understand, I don't want you telling anybody I spilled this. But when they first came here and began to look the town over, you could tell that Conway had been a long time on the rocks. He was shaky. His face had that burned-out look—God knows I ought to recognize his kind when I see it. They come here to me sometimes when the bars won't give them any more credit."

"Did Warne?"

"Who?"

"Adam Warne, the man who was killed two years ago. Did he come to you?"

"No, he never did," said Butler slowly, as if wondering where their talk was heading.

"Conway beat him up. Why would Conway beat a stumble-bum when he'd been one?"

"You don't know them when they reform," said Butler. "Conway had to stay in the bar and not drink. He'd get a little on edge now and then. I didn't know Warne at all, but I heard after his death that he was a grog hound if there ever was one. And maybe that would make Conway irritable. Seeing a guy weaving drunk, while he had to keep control."

"Were your dealings with Conway or with Shelton?"

"It was strictly on the quiet about Shelton's being a partner," Butler cautioned. "I never had a word with him, except once at the house, and that wasn't until after they'd sold the Fiddling Crab."

"I see."

"I guess that's about all I can tell you, Mr. Glazer. I've seen some of those houses you've built and I like them. I might want to talk to you about a new place next spring. My wife's getting the building fever."

"Sure. You do that."

Butler said good-by and hung up. Glazer put on a leather jacket and went out to the garages with the idea of going up to the doctor's house. But he was brought up short by the sight of a woman there. She seemed to be trying to observe the house and yet stay out of sight. Hearing Glazer's steps, she swung around. It was Mrs. Shelton.

The red-brown hair had been tied back with a pink ribbon; it gave her an unexpectedly childish appearance. The color was insipid against the reddish blaze of her hair, but it was the sort of ribbon a little girl would save off a candy box and use to decorate herself. She had on a purple linen dress, cut quite low, so that her tanned arms and shoulders were bare. No hose. Her bare feet were encased in sandals that were no more than a couple of strips of beige kid and cork soles. She'd painted her toenails an unexpected shade, a silver gray, and Glazer sensed all at once that she played with and experimented with her appearance, eager for any change, and that under this preoccupation must lie a desperate boredom.

He touched his hat. "How do you do, Mrs. Shelton?"

Fright at his sudden arrival struggled in her with an obvious desire to be casual. She managed, "I'd just dropped by, hoping to see you. I—I want to talk to you."

"Will you come in the house?"

"No, it's— I can't stay long." She smiled at him, and though he would have given her an A for effort, the smile was not a success. "I happened to be driving through, and since I wasn't very hospitable when you came to see my husband, I wanted to—to tell you how sorry I was."

"Think nothing of it." He looked for her car, but it wasn't anywhere near. He wondered if she might have left it on the highway and walked down the road, some half mile.

"You're very kind." She was carrying a large fuchsia-colored kidskin handbag, and she now fiddled with its catch, then took out a handkerchief as if on an afterthought and brushed at her nose. She was, Glazer sensed, at a loss as to how to get at the real purpose of her errand with him.

"Is your car far?" Glazer asked. "Could I give you a lift?"

"Yes." She seized on the idea gratefully. Glazer ran out the car and she hopped in and shut the door before he could get out and go through the formalities. "I left my car by the bus stop. I just felt I needed a little hike. It's such a beautiful morning."

"You must have left home rather early," Glazer offered.

The chatter came to an abrupt stop. Glazer's idle remark seemed to have reminded her of troublesome things. She sat nibbling her full underlip as the car slid out of the drive and into the road to the highway.

Her car was in among some shrubs, hidden, Glazer realized, from the passing traffic. He braked to a stop and looked at her expectantly. She had something to say—all that had gone before was uneasy prelude—but as he sat waiting, he thought her intention had changed. She touched the door handle. Above the strapless bodice of the linen dress her brown skin was as smooth as silk. She looked at him; her eyes were dark, almost echoing the purple of the dress, and the lashes were thick. She was exactly the kind of girl, Glazer thought, to set a futile type like Shelton spinning. He must be pinching himself.

With her hand still on the door handle she said, "Mr. Glazer, I didn't really come here to apologize about the way I treated you. It's about something else—a proposition I have."

He merely nodded, not wanting to scare her again with an ill-timed remark.

She touched her lips with her tongue. "You're looking into the murder of Adam Warne, aren't you? Is it because of Francesca Warne? Are you fond of her?"

Her eyes were shy, hopeful; and Glazer somehow did not feel the resentment Holt had roused with his surmise. "Yes," he said frankly, "I am quite fond of Francesca."

"I want to make a trade," she went on quickly. "I need money. I need five thousand dollars, Mr. Glazer."

He shrugged. "No information about Adam Warne is worth that much to me."

"It isn't about Adam Warne." Her voice had grown uneven; he thought her glance at him had a touch of nervous fear. "It's about—*her*."

He controlled his temper. "I can't dicker on anything that vague. What have you got?"

She sat motionless for a minute, the big bag on her knees, her hands spread on the leather. Her nails were painted a silver gray to match her toes, he noted. He felt a sudden misgiving about her. She was easily upset. She was shallow. Perhaps what she had to say was some fantastic lie.

She folded her hands together, lacing the fingers. "Will you believe this? I was with Adam Warne on that beach below your house."

Glazer forgot his distrust of her. He reached for the key, killed the motor. "When he was murdered?"

"Yes." She started to look at him, then changed her mind. A shiver ran over the smooth brown skin. "No one knows this except my husband. If you tell anyone, I'll say it is a lie."

"Of course I'm not going to tell," he said impatiently. "If you were with Warne then, you must have seen who shot him. Or do you mean that you—" His look turned speculative.

"I didn't kill Adam," she flung out. "I wouldn't have done that!"

"What was Warne to you?" Glazer's tone held contempt, not much disguised. "A lover? He seems to have had a way with women."

Color crept into her face; the thick lashes fluttered. "I don't know what he might have been to me if he had lived. It's a problem that no longer concerns anyone but my husband. And if he'd let it alone, it needn't even bother him."

"You knew Warne had beaten his wife, that she'd had a miscarriage because of it?"

"At the time of his death, no. I thought she had left him because of his drinking. He was drunk most of the time." Though she was still flushed, her glance was defiant. She was daring Glazer to discover what she had seen in Adam Warne, a drunken bum.

"You and he were on the beach together. Do you want to tell me about it? Or is this the story that five thousand dollars can buy?"

"I need the money!" The words were a bleat, a cry. Her fingers twisted the strap of the fuchsia-colored bag. "But I—I can't force you to pay any-thing, of course, and so I'll tell you what I know and then you can de-cide what you think it is worth. Adam and I were on the beach below your place. Shelton and Conway's place, then. It was growing twilight. The sea had that shining surface, that metallic appearance that comes sometimes under a gray sky. I noticed the surf fisherman down the beach, on the other side of those great flat stones. We had come that way, I remember thinking; he must have followed shortly after. Out about as far as those big rocks that stick up like islands from the water, a small boat was drifting. It must have been a dinghy from a yacht."

"It was empty?"

"Yes. I remember that Adam pointed to it and commented that some-body was stuck ashore. At that time there were several small yachts and power boats in the basin on the other side of the bay; they were on their way from Los Angeles to La Paz, some hunting expedition to Baja Cal-ifornia. And Adam laughed and said the Baja California lizards would be a little safer for the time being."

"How long was this before he was shot?"

"Just a minute or so."

"What about the top of the bluff? Anything up there?"

"I don't know." She shifted her bare legs; the lacquered toenails glit-tered under the weird paint. "We were facing the sea. He was lying stretched out on his stomach, his chin on his fists. I was sitting beside him. It was cool for that time of year, and all I had on was a dress like this one"—she indicated the strapless bodice—"over a swim suit."

The picture was plain to Glazer: the seedy and liquor-saturated writer, the naïve young girl smitten by something—pity, perhaps—who had gone with him to an out-of-the-way spot and into a situation which could only be thought of as compromising. He forced himself to remain detached, not to turn his thoughts to Warne's unprincipled behavior. "And what else happened?"

"He asked me if I intended to spend the night with him."

Glazer studied her bent face. "And had you?"

"I—I don't know." Her fingers twisted the strap of the bag into loops, figure eights, zigzags, then jerked it straight to start over. "I began to shiver. I guess it was the cold, and the strange lights out along the hori-zon, little flickerings of electricity."

"Lightning," Glazer supplied.

"Yes. I couldn't remember seeing any before. Adam told me what it was."

The California child, Glazer told himself, ignorant of ninety per cent of nature's possibilities.

"He crawled to his knees and put his arms around me," she went on, "and all at once I was struck by how thin he was. He was just bones, and with the growth of beard and the smell of liquor—" Her nails dug into the smooth fuchsia-colored leather. "He said not to be afraid, not of anything. The things you have to be scared of are inside of you. The inward devils ..."

In the car, in spite of the hot bright morning, Glazer seemed to feel the cold breath of that twilight of two years ago. He saw the gray metallic sea, the lowering sky, the figure of the fisherman like a toy, the bobbing boat out among the rocks.

"... but not lightning. And I said to him, crying, 'Adam, you're just throwing your life away.' And he answered, 'My life will go on to its intended disintegration, unless my wife kills me.'" Her glance touched Glazer swiftly, then dropped away. "*Unless my wife kills me.*' That's what he said!"

Twelve

They sat silent, she waiting perhaps for some comment from Glazer and he looking fixedly ahead through the windshield. A bee flew in through the open left-hand window and began to buzz along the glass. Glazer reached over to the glove compartment, opened it, took out a folded map, swatted the bee expertly, and dropped the body outside, then returned the map to its place. "Tell me about the shot."

"It happened the instant after Adam said that about his wife," she replied quickly. "I didn't think of it as a sound made by a gun, not just at first. In fact, I hardly noticed it at all. I felt him begin to sag against me, hard, and when I tried to prop him up, thinking he was sick from the liquor he'd been drinking, he fell down flat. That's when I saw the blood."

"You screamed?"

"No. I—I ran."

He smiled slightly, as if coming at last to some answer he had anticipated. "Up the bluff?"

"It was a tiny trail, rocky, full of weeds. At the top I looked back. The fisherman must have seen me. He was running my way."

"You think he knew you?"

"No. When the account came out in the paper next day—the L.A. paper; ours is just a weekly and it didn't print an extra until the second day—when I read his name there, it wasn't anybody I knew."

"What did you do next?"

"I—" She stopped to brush a hand over the red-brown hair, a nervous gesture. "I ran to the highway and hiked home."

"No, you didn't," Glazer corrected. "You ran and pounded on the rear door of that house I bought, and Shelton let you in and hid you. That's why he boggled over his answer when I talked to him about whether the cops had searched his house. He'd been making a play for you, according to Conway. He's sort of old for you, and kind of funny-looking because of the whiskers. Not to mention the bald spot. I've wondered ever since I took that trip down to your place how you came to marry him. Now I think I know."

She tightened all over, like a horse when you touch it with a whip. He saw the tension in the brown shoulders, the jumping muscles in her bare legs. Her throat worked as if she were choking over something too big to swallow.

"And now you need money. Five thousand dollars. Who's it for? Byronson? To keep him from hounding Shelton and finding out that you were with Warne and probably killed him?"

Her hands had begun to shake. She tried to control them by clenching the bag, but it didn't work. The trembling crept into her wrists.

Glazer watched her distress with impersonal detachment. "Tell me, Mrs. Shelton—just how were you dressed when you ran up that bluff? This morning I had an interesting idea presented to me—that the murderer might have trotted up that trail naked. And though there was no speculation at the time about *you*—"

She made a strangled sound.

"—there was some reason you had to get out of sight in a hell of a hurry. Something more important than staying to see if Adam Warne could be kept from dying of his wound. Something you couldn't manage with the eyes of that fisherman on you. Like putting on your clothes."

"Just—just my dress," she whispered.

"Just the dress. I guess you had it over your arm when Shelton met you at the door. And now you wonder why Shelton can't get over the idea of Warne and you on that beach together. He's made your life miserable, of course. What does he call you when you're alone together and he gets excited?"

She flinched, as if she heard some remembered phrase in Shelton's voice.

"Tell me," said Glazer, "and think hard before you answer. How much of a look outside did Shelton get through that kitchen door?"

"I—don't understand."

"Just answer it."

"He opened the door a crack, just enough to see me. I said I needed help. He opened the door a little bit more and I slid in. He took me right to the den."

"Then I've got news for you. You don't have to worry about his opinion of your behavior that late twilight. You can start giving him as good as he's given you. Because Shelton was outdoors before you got up there."

Her eyes, heavy with misery and incomprehension, moved over the interior of the car.

"Do you understand what I'm saying?" Glazer demanded.

"What does it mean?"

"It could mean that Shelton was spying on you and Warne and that when things got to the boiling point, his temper along with Warne's lovemaking, he put his eye to a gun sight and his finger to a trigger."

She drew a deep breath. "No, he wouldn't have done that."

"Think about it," Glazer advised, almost kindly.

"There wasn't any reason," she said stubbornly. "I'd had my dress off because I went for a short swim. If he was spying on us—" She came to an abrupt stop.

"Adam Warne had just put his arms around you," Glazer reminded. "To keep you from being frightened of the lightning. His wife was almost dead from his manhandling in the hospital, but he was worried because you shivered a little. He was comforting you, hugging you. But to a man on the edge of the bluff it could have looked like something else."

"You make it sound—beastly," she cried.

"Warne didn't know how to be beastly," Glazer said, "except to someone weak like his wife. I'd like to have shown him what beastly can be like. You say you need five thousand dollars. My advice, Mrs. Shelton, is to go home and demand it from your husband. Tell him you think he killed Adam Warne and if he doesn't fork over you'll go to the cops. To your own special cop, Byronson, who'll be only too glad for a little action."

With an air of courtesy which was more of a mockery than any attitude he could have assumed, Glazer got out of the car, walked around to the other door, and opened it for Mrs. Shelton. She got out. She looked wobbly, he thought, and for an instant a feeling of pity mingled with the scorn he had for her.

She put out a hand, not quite touching him. "Please!"

He shook his head. "I'm sorry. I'll tell you what—call me tomorrow if everything else fails you. I'll help out to the tune of a few hundred."

There was sweat on her temples. "I have to go away. I can't stay with him any longer. Not another day."

"If that's your problem—what about Byronson?"

Her face got whiter than ever. In the hollow spot at the base of her throat a pulse beat rapidly. "You have no idea what you are saying," she said in a choked tone. Then she walked away quickly on the cork-soled sandals. She pushed aside the branches of oleander and palm to get into her car. When she backed out, the tires spun in the gravel, the car lurched, and the springs complained.

Glazer waited until she had swung out on the highway, turned south, and disappeared. Then he got behind his own wheel again and drove up the flank of the hill to the job. He was starting a new house in a few days and he had to be sure things were moving smoothly here. Dr. Barton was a good man, a sturdy friend; he deserved the best and Glazer intended to see that he got it. While he examined the framing and the sub-floors now going in, he remembered the hot-air dryer Dr. Barton wanted in the bath next to the master bedroom. Since the electrical sub-contractor was also at the site, Glazer went over to the construction shack and took it up with him.

His mind returned once or twice to the things Mrs. Shelton had told him. When he thought of Warne, he had difficulty in keeping his rage under control. The man couldn't even die decently without trying to leave the smear on his wife.

He would never tell Francesca what her husband had said about her. Not even to destroy any silly illusions she still held. Better to let her think, as some others seemed to, that he was a tormented and bewildered man. The idea that she would have murdered Warne was too ridiculous to repeat.

Mrs. Shelton ran the car into the driveway, turned off the switch, set the brakes, and got out. She looked tired, dull, and dusty. She stood beside the car for a moment as if considering her next move. In the quiet the faint squeak of the canvas-covered swing in the patio could be heard. Her eyes flickered in that direction.

"Mary?"

She swallowed. "Yes?"

"Just wondering if it was you," Shelton called.

She looked back at the car as if it represented some refuge or escape. Her tongue came out, circled the lips from which lipstick had worn off. She remembered that she had had nothing to eat that day. She rubbed a hand hard over her stomach. "It's me," she said.

Shelton appeared in the archway to the patio. He had on a T-shirt of thin knitted cotton and a wrinkled pair of khaki shorts. His legs and arms were quite hairy. The beard with its untidy tufts, the swimming lenses made him look strange and grotesque. Mrs. Shelton glanced at him and shivered.

"You left at an ungodly hour," Shelton said. "I woke up when you drove the car out. Where have you been?"

"Seaview," she said unwillingly. She opened the bag and took out a lipstick and a compact and examined her mouth.

"Who did you see there?"

She shrugged. "Oh, I just drove around. I hadn't been there for ages." She applied lip rouge hastily and unevenly. "I was restless."

He was studying her with curious interest. She dropped the compact and lipstick into the bag and began to walk briskly to the house. Shelton looked at the car, then stepped over and glanced in through the driver's window, as if seeking some sign of a trespasser. He reached in through the spokes of the wheel and pulled down the small ash tray in the dash. It was clean, empty. He pushed it into place.

He followed her, his rope sandals making a slapping sound on the patio tiles. She had gone to the kitchen.

At the sink she took down a glass and ran water into it from the faucet. She was lifting it to her mouth when Shelton spoke. "Conway's coming over."

She drank the water slowly. When she set down the glass she wiped her mouth on the back of her hand. Lipstick came off in a long smear, and she stared at it in surprise, as if forgetting what she had just done outside by the car. "I don't want to see him. Tell him I'm sick."

"He wants to talk to both of us."

She looked over her shoulder at her husband. "I can't stand him."

"Just this once," Shelton suggested. "He won't stay long. He has to be back in San Diego this afternoon. It's just business with him."

She took a cleansing tissue from her bag and began to scrub at her stained hand. "It's like being married to two men."

Shelton frowned, giving him an unexpectedly severe appearance. "That's rather a disgusting thing to say."

"Take it any way you like." She had dropped the handbag on the tiled sink. Now she went over to the big refrigerator, opened its door, and examined the contents. She took out two eggs and a package of bacon. Shelton watched in surprise.

"Haven't you eaten anything?"

"No."

She opened a cupboard to get a frying pan, dropped several slices of bacon in, put the unbroken eggs close to the skillet on top of the stove. "Watch it, will you? I'm going to change my dress."

"Mary."

She paused by the door.

Shelton cleared his throat. "You aren't doing anything foolish, are you?

You didn't—for instance—go to this man Glazer?"

She looked down at her right foot, turning the cork-soled shoe side-wise as if testing its fit. "Why do you mention him? I mean, more than anyone else. More than Byronson, for instance. Is Glazer more dangerous than Byronson?"

The bacon began to sputter a little. Shelton took a fork out of a drawer and approached the stove, but his eyes were on his wife. "I don't think there is any danger to anyone. Few cases are solved after so long a time. The evidence the police might have found is long gone."

"All but the gun."

"We don't know where the gun is," he pointed out. His tone was precise and calm. "The police never did find the weapon." He began to stir the bacon. "I don't think they ever will."

"I thought you were going to try to see Mrs. Warne."

"She's living at Glazer's house," Shelton said, as if that closed the subject.

When Conway arrived about twenty minutes later, both the Sheltons were in the kitchen nook, facing each other across the plastic-topped table. Mary had finished the bacon and eggs and was sipping a second cup of coffee. Her husband had a book open before him. It was a book on marine zoology.

Conway had not knocked. He appeared in the kitchen doorway and nodded at them. Shelton said, "Hello. Bring that stool over here and sit down."

"I don't need the stool. I'll sit by Mary." Conway ignored the glance she gave him and pushed in beside her. She made a point of getting as far into the corner as she could, but he seemed not to notice. He said to Shelton, "You pulled one hell of a boner."

Shelton's gaze jumped. "What do you mean?"

Conway put his left elbow on the table, leaned his head into his palm, rubbed the skin at the hairline. He seemed deliberately to prolong the moment of silence, of Shelton's anxiety. Finally he added, "It's going to get to the police. Already has. Holt took it. I watched him, and he went right from the café to the damned police headquarters."

Mary Shelton had paled a little. Shelton picked at the pages of his book with his fingernails. "You still haven't explained."

Conway looked at a spot on the wall over Shelton's head. "I'm going to have to do something about Glazer."

Shelton's eyes looked big and scared through the lenses of his glasses. "Who is Holt? What do you mean—he took *it* to the police? What was *it*?"

"Your little mistake," Conway grunted.

Shelton must have seen how the other man was playing with him, almost teasing him. "I haven't made any mistake. And you leave Glazer alone. If you beat up any more men—I mean, after all, you almost killed Warne, and if he'd have wanted to—"

Conway slammed a fist on the table; Shelton stopped talking.

"Glazer's got ants in his pants. I don't know why. You should have told him to get the hell out when he came snooping."

"I didn't really say much," Shelton defended. "I don't know anything to tell."

Conway's mouth twisted. "You told him about the weather on that late afternoon when Warne was killed. You said there was lightning out along the horizon, something I hadn't known before. But you were supposed to be in the den working under artificial lights. How did you know what the ocean looked like?"

Shelton looked dazedly down at his book, as if some answer awaited him there. "It doesn't seem much of a slip to me."

A cruel light came into Conway's eyes. "Haven't you any conception of what a smart cop could do with that? Are you so damned wrapped up in your sea beetles that you've forgotten about your own safety?"

Shelton plucked at his lower lip. In spite of the odd tufty beard, the glasses, the bald spot, he seemed a child who was being scolded.

Mary Shelton had said nothing; she was, if possible, farther from Conway than ever. Now he turned to her. "What did Glazer say to *you*?" He saw the panic building up in her and sneered. "You were here that day Glazer came by, weren't you? What do you think he wanted?"

She had thought in that frantic moment that he had seen her on her errand in Seaview that morning. Some of the edge-of-disaster fright left her face. "He said that Mrs. Warne wanted him to inquire into her husband's murder. I—I was so surprised I sort of lost my head."

"That figures," he snapped.

"You haven't any right to come here and talk to us like this," she got out. "You owe everything you have to Will. You ought to be ashamed of yourself."

"I've paid Will back in some pretty fancy coin," Conway growled. "You don't hear him reminding me what I owe him, do you? He must be remembering that if I hadn't fronted for him as a bar owner he'd be spending his winters in Minnesota in a jerk-water college at thirty-eight hundred a year."

Her chin rose. "He saved his bank roll out of that salary."

"How do you think he lived while he saved it?" Conway's glittering eyes bored into hers; she flushed uncomfortably. "I'll tell you how. He lived in a cold flea trap. He ate canned soup heated on an alcohol burner. He took in a second-rate movie maybe twice a month. He patched his own shoes with that guck they sell in the dime stores. He bought his landlady's paper for a penny when she'd finished with it."

"Please," said Shelton miserably in an almost inaudible voice.

"He couldn't afford any friends except the little laundress who lived in the room over his head," Conway ground on. "Sometimes on Sunday he took her for a walk through the zoo—that was free—and sometimes they talked about getting married. But he was saving his dough for the Big Break. And professors, even professors with self-pasted shoe soles, don't marry girls who work in laundries. He slept with her once in a while. Guiltily."

"Let me out of here!" Mary cried.

"Shut up. She didn't look much like you, Mary. He showed me her picture once. She had a washed-out tiredness from working in all that steam. No tan. You don't turn brown in a basement laundry ironing shirts from dawn till dark. You do get t.b. if you aren't careful. She died in 1937. I wonder if he ever thinks that some of the dough might have saved her life." Conway glanced at the other man. Shelton was perspiring, his head hanging, his nervous hands plucking at the book. "Probably not. He has you, and you're tanned all over from lying in the sun on a private beach. You're pretty plump, too." Conway took Mary's twisting arm and stroked the smooth skin from shoulder to wrist. "I helped him buy you, Mary. The dirty dough that came out of the Fiddling Crab—"

She jerked away and slapped him, then bent and disappeared from the corner by crawling under the table. She was sobbing as she ran toward the door. Shelton licked his lips. "I wish you hadn't said any of that."

"To hell with it," Conway said. "Let's get back to business. What are we going to do about Glazer?"

"Nothing." Shelton's neck was bent, as if his head was too heavy to hold erect.

"Do you think he might be stuck on the Warne woman?"

Shelton didn't look up. "I don't know. I don't care. I'm not going to fight. I'm through fighting."

Conway leaned on the table, spoke confidentially. "What is it, Will? Something disappointed you? Mary? Isn't she as good as you thought she'd be?"

"I'm tired," Shelton said tonelessly. "Leave Mary alone. Stay away from Glazer."

"Man, he's on your tail!"

"I'm here when they want me." Shelton stood up and tucked the book under his arm. He gave Conway a single piercing look. "Don't ever touch Mary again. Don't put your hands on her as you did a minute ago. That's the only thing I won't take. You leave her be."

Thirteen

Mary Shelton examined her reddened eyes in the vast round mirror of her dressing table, then powdered carefully. I never really was pretty, she told herself. I'm a peasant, like those women in Dad's family, the crazy pictures he'd saved from the old country. I'm blocky. My lashes, hair, lips are too thick, too noticeable. It would take a man like Will, somebody older and a little anxious, to fall for my kind of looks. Or Conway. Conway would like a touch of coarseness in a woman; he'd take the surface for all of her. A man like Glazer wouldn't touch me. Glazer's tough and hard under the shell of manners, but he'd like his women delicate and ladylike.

It was Adam alone who ever looked for anything under the surface, who thought I had feelings, hopes, fears. He was so beaten, most of the time almost blanked out. And yet he took time to try to find out what I really was. Who I was. Not Mary Parico, a fountain waitress, one of ten kids who left home because there was never quite enough to eat. But Mary Parico, a woman.

She picked up the lipstick slowly, repaired her rouge. Beyond the windows she knew a blaze of sun lay on the beach, though the windows, being high under the eaves, gave no view here. It might be nice to get out of the house, to lie on the sand; to get the taste of Conway out of her mouth by tasting the sea wind.

She listened for any sound from her husband, decided he was in his study. She thought, I won't tell him I'm going. He might want to follow.

She slipped from the purple dress, the underthings, dropped the cork-soled sandals in the closet. The swim suit she chose was of elasticized tile-red shantung, extremely brief. The pants hugged her hips; the upper part was a boned brassiere without straps, laced at the front. As a final inspiration she put manicure things into a beach bag. She looked at the bottle of silver-gray nail paint, changed it for one of pansy-blue. She let herself out at a side door and walked away from the house.

The sand was hot under her bare feet, but the breeze as usual had an unexpected briskness. She drew in deep breaths of the sea air. The sun on the water had a golden sparkle, dazzling the eye, but out beyond the shore the color changed, took on an azure softness. It would be very cool there, she thought. You could sink down into that cool water and forget you ever had a care.

She stopped on a sandy hummock and dropped the bag. Then she heard movement behind her and caught a glimpse of someone there from the corner of her eye. She turned. Byronson was not ten feet away. He looked much bigger in swimming trunks than he did in the blue uniform. He had a towel over one arm, under it some denim pants. The sun made his hair look very yellow, very much alive.

Mary Shelton looked briefly at the house; she seemed to be measuring the distance for a sprint.

"I want to talk to you," said Byronson.

"Go away." She glanced at the beach bag as if weighing its abandonment. "You leave me alone. I'm not—"

"I've got news for you." He came closer. "About your husband."

"I know all about that," she said, backing a little. "It wasn't anything important. A little slip. Somebody told him what it was like outside. I might have."

His arms jumped from his side. The towel and the trousers slid off and fell across her bag. He gripped her, pulled her hard against himself. She thought, looking into his face, that the pale eyes had an inhuman brilliance; and at the same moment she wondered why, among the men she had thought of as being attracted to her, she hadn't included Byronson, who had always been smitten harder than anyone else. I just forgot him, she thought. I forgot him because even living with Will would be better than having somebody like this cop get hold of you. He's a cop all the way through, all the time. Everything he does, he does like a cop. Everything he sees, he sees from a viewpoint of merciless authority. Her muddled mind corrected itself. There must be decent men who are cops, kind men, sensitive men; it's just Byronson who twists the fact of being a policeman into something that makes you want to vomit.

He shifted one hand to her throat, to the underside of her chin, and began to pull her mouth up toward his.

"My husband will see us."

"Yeah." He crushed her face suddenly against his. It's a kiss in name only, Mary thought; he couldn't feel it even if I did respond. It hurts. He drew back finally. "As I say, I've got to talk to you. Come on, my car's on the road over there."

"I'm not going to your car." She writhed out of his grip, rubbing her mouth.

He smiled a little, then grabbed her around the waist, lifted her as effortlessly as a doll; she twisted, trying to kick him in the groin. He bent her over his knee until the reddish hair fell across her face; then he brought the side of his hand down on her neck in a chopping, expert, though seemingly careless blow. His eyes glowed as he waited.

Pain clawed down through her, a hideous paralysis of sheet-fire. Breath seemed packed into her lungs so that she must explode. Her stomach contracted. She stiffened into an agonized backward arch while her hands fluttered in search of succor. The beach whirled under a bursting sky. "Teach you," he said. He carried her clumsily, heedless of the fact that the jolting grip could all but tear the flesh.

After a while the world began to come back to her. She was in his car, the hateful Seaview police car, and the radio was grumbling messages in code. He leaned toward her from behind the wheel. The towel lay across his shoulders. The folded pants and the beach bag lay on the seat between them. She crowded down a surging nausea. She wouldn't be sick; it would please him. But as he continued to look at her, she became aware of what she wore, the silly suit, the tight pants, the brassiere that slyly didn't quite meet in front. The lacing left an open space, showing the skin between her breasts. She put a hand there.

"Look at me," he said.

She brought her eyes up defiantly. "You'd better let me go."

"I'll tell you what I'm going to do with you. We're going to the beach where Warne died. You're going to show me just what happened there, what you were doing with him when he was shot."

"Glazer told you," she whispered.

"Glazer? He's nothing. I knew a long time ago that you were with Warne. I couldn't get it out of you. I didn't have anything to pry it out with."

A fright more horrible than any she had known, much worse even than the feeling when Warne had toppled against her, dying, beat in her brain. Breath and pulse seemed frozen. She tried to control the paralysis in her throat. "Let me tell you here."

He reached for the key in the switch. "Nope. We'll go to the scene of the crime. We'll re-enact it, as the movies say."

"My husband will kill you!"

"Don't kid me, honey," said Byronson. "I've got the two of you over a barrel."

Over a barrel ... The phrase returned to taunt her as she lay huddled against the car window. They were in Seaview now; the familiar streets flew past. Now and then a curious face was turned toward the police car from the sidewalk, and one of these she thought she recognized as Adam's old friend, Tremaine. She averted her head quickly.

There had been patches of fog on the road as they drove north. The sky had taken on a gray overcast. She thought the town looked stark and a little impermanent, the way beach towns always looked when the sun wasn't at its brightest. The damp air crept into the car. She shivered.

Byronson paused for a red light at the main intersection. The street swam before her eyes. I could jump out and run, she thought, but everyone out there would join to help him catch me. My feet would fly—until someone stuck out a leg and I tripped. She thought of falling on the pavement, the tearing impact, and nausea rushed through her in hysteric pulses. The car began to climb the grade northward toward Glazer's place, circling the small bay, past narrow headlands.

"Straighten up and turn your head from the window," Byronson said. "You're in a police car—look funny and people will be saying you're drunk."

She obeyed numbly. Her thoughts turned to their destination, to Glazer. Why hadn't Glazer been willing to give her the money? Was he so in love with Mrs. Warne that no hint of suspicion could reach him? She should have pointed out carefully that Adam's fear of his wife, his feeling that she would kill him if she could, was an important secret. At the time, on the beach, she had felt only sympathy for him; she hadn't known of his mistreatment of his wife, his guilt. As the months had passed since, the remark had taken on more significance. Had Adam felt a premonition just before being shot? I wish I'd asked for only a thousand, she thought confusedly. I could have managed for a time on that. Or I could have tried to resign myself to living with Will. Forever. She licked her dry lips.

They were turning from the highway. She saw that Byronson intended to park in the same spot she had used that morning, in the oleanders and palms. His handling of the car was familiar and exact. He's parked here before, she thought. She wondered then if he had ever spied on the occupants of Glazer's house.

He pulled the brake and silence dropped over them. She suffered from a crazy desire to yawn, but her face seemed frozen. She put her hand on the door handle.

"Don't try anything funny," he warned. "Get out of the car, shut the door, and walk to the back."

She crawled from the seat. As she pushed the door to she caught a glimpse of the gun rack in the rear compartment, two shotguns and a rifle in brackets attached to the back of the front seat. She thought, There must be all kinds of things there—tear gas, for instance—that I might have used on Byronson and got away. And then her thoughts added that Byronson wouldn't have hesitated to shoot her. He had the right. No one would question it.

The fog had lowered; the end of the headland swam in a misty gulf. She wrapped her arms about her and said to Byronson, "I can't go down there like this. I'm cold."

He threw the towel at her. "Come on."

She took a hesitant step. "Are you going to use Glazer's path?"

"No. There's a trail here the fishermen use." He led the way through a tangle of palms and overgrown lantana. They came out above the beach. It was not so high here; much lower, in fact, than at Glazer's place. The path down the face of the embankment showed signs of use. It was pitted, rocky; she flinched at the pain in her feet.

He stopped. "Do you want me to carry you?"

"No. I'm all right."

"Whatever you want." He shrugged and went on. She stared at his broad back. Under the tanned skin the muscles moved smoothly; he gave off an aura of animal-like strength and grace. And the increasing cold seemed not to affect him. She shivered under the towel, hating and fearing him.

He stopped at the foot of the path and looked back at her. "No hurry. We've got all afternoon. No one's around, either. Probably the fog drove them off the beach." He put out a hand, but she stopped abruptly. She was a few feet above him. She leaned against the earth cliff. "What's the matter with you?" he asked. "You act like I'm going to eat you. We had dates once, remember? I took you to shows. I kissed you good night." His glance had turned brooding, angry. She tried to swallow her fear, to force her features to show a composure she didn't own. He laughed slightly. "Was I pretty slow, Mary? Was I?"

"I thought you were all right." Some of the dirt fell away under her nervous fingers; the little rocks stung her ankles.

"Come here."

She tugged at the towel, hugging it across her chest. "Please let me go."

He took a long step, a sort of leap, and she realized that her holding back had enraged him. It had been a mistake. "I said, come here." He dragged her down the last few feet of the incline. "You're going to tell me. Why did you marry Shelton? Why did you take him when you knew I wanted you?"

She tried to think of an answer. He knew she hadn't loved the funny little man with the beard, the bald head, the glasses. "I was afraid," she said finally.

It surprised him. The blond head with its short Prussian haircut turned aside as if Byronson doubted what he had heard. "Of what?"

"Of being involved in Adam's murder."

"Who would involve you?"

"I thought—Mrs. Warne."

His face twisted, and he pushed her away, so hard that she went off balance and almost fell. "She had reason. Is that it?"

Mary tried to think of something to say that wouldn't be a lie, wouldn't make Byronson madder than he was. She should have remembered his jealousy of Adam Warne. "He's dead now," she said lamely. "You don't have to keep on thinking about him."

His jaw worked; she sensed that he was gritting his teeth. "I want information. Getting facts is my job. Come on." He turned and stalked off in the direction of the great expanse of flat, sea-worn rock which obtruded from the sand and was now laid bare by the low tide. Beyond lay Glazer's beach, at its far end the buttress of stone, gauzy now with fog.

Mary went after him reluctantly. If she could have endured to handle Byronson differently, distract him ... There at the foot of the embankment she might have hidden her revulsion; if she had pretended a sudden liking, even let him have a hint of how she really felt about Will Shelton, his temper wouldn't have flared. Then, of course, he would have made love to her. A cold sweat came out on her skin; she wanted to retch.

He's going to grind at you, she promised herself, until you spill every detail of that day with Warne. Considering what Glazer had thought, Glazer who had no motive of jealousy and hatred, you might as well be prepared for the worst, the ultimate indignity. It would be better to run out into the sea. She looked at the green water lapping at the edge of the stone shelf and saw how the fog had come down. It was closing in around the big rocks offshore. If she could swim well enough, get out there somehow, cling down out of sight ... Desperate, mocking fancies flitted through her mind. Not looking where she was going, she stepped into a pothole worn by the tide. She fell heavily, crushingly.

He came back, looked at her thinly, put down a hand. She shook her head. "No, never mind." She stood up. All at once there was a terrible pain in her left side, under her ribs. When she drew a quick breath, a stabbing fire pierced her flesh. She had torn the suit, too—on her right thigh the seam had split; on the skin was a blood-red line.

She put the towel down quickly to cover it.

"I can't waste time." He jerked her, tossed her across his shoulders. The fire danced under her ribs and she tried to draw a breath to scream. He must have heard the great gasp she made. "Shut up. One yell and I'll knock you silly."

She bit her lip, and the salt flavor of blood ran through her mouth. A stumbling prayer, more a wordless beseeching, flickered in her thoughts. *Save me* ... It was addressed to no one; there was no one to come to her aid. She realized dimly that Byronson had shifted her weight, was putting her down on the sand. Above was the cliff, the little pockets of yellow flowers, misty in the fog, and the rock balustrade of Glazer's path. If she could have leaped up and run … But she was tired. There was blood in her mouth again, too much to be from the bitten spot in her lip.

Byronson was kneeling, pulling her upright. "Talk. Tell me about Warne." The fog seemed to have congealed in his flat gray eyes.

"I'm—choking."

"You cut your lip when you fell. Spit it out." He pushed her head forward. His hand was hard on her skull, his fingers tangling in her hair. She gave a wailing cry; he shook her.

In her paralysis of fright it seemed that she and Warne were there together. The damp cold, the darkening light were the same. Hands gripped her, ungentle hands—though Adam had meant no unkindness, when he had talked about his wife he had become agitated and his fingers had turned to talons. Mary turned her head to look upward, almost sure in that instant of confusion and terror that she would find Adam Warne bent above her.

What she saw was a flash of fire from the top of the cliff.

The echo was sharp, pocketed by the fog and the earth embankment. She looked at Byronson to see if he had heard and seen it too. There was a look of shock on his face. A corner of his mouth twitched. Then he began to fold against her. His flesh was warm, dampened by the fog, but under the skin she sensed an unnatural slackness.

She tried to push him off, but his weight slipped through her defenses. She fell back and he pinned her. There was a sudden spatter of gunfire, and little geysers of sand leaped around them. Then she caught sight of something she thought was a bird, a dark shape flying through the mist. It was a gun, a rifle. It turned end over end, sluggishly, as if the fog impeded its fall.

She tried to scream, but the fire under her ribs snatched up her breath and tore it from her throat. She lay still, and by and by she tried to listen. There were footsteps on the path.

She had a feeling of being lost and that a great deal of time had gone by while she lay blacked out. With an effort she crawled from under Byronson's inert body. There were droplets of fog in his yellow hair. His cheek had sand on it. Behind his left ear a gush of blood had left a long bright stain.

She staggered to her feet and waited. It was Glazer on the path. He had on work clothes, denim slacks and a leather jacket. His face was cold and composed.

She clung to the bottom of the stone balustrade. Glazer went and looked at Byronson and the gun, touching neither, then came back to her. "I don't doubt that he deserved it. Or Warne, either. But aren't you overdoing your activities on my beach, Mrs. Shelton?"

Her hands strayed over her face, her hair; she plucked at the torn place in her suit, trying to urge the two edges of elastic cloth together—all this was absent-minded, meaningless. She was struggling to understand what Glazer had just said. "Did you shoot him?" she asked.

Glazer said patiently, "You don't have to pretend, Mrs. Shelton. It's rather obvious what you've been through. No one's going to blame you for defending yourself."

It was the first note of kindness she'd heard in a long time. She leaned against the stone wall and began to cry.

Fourteen

Glazer waited until she began to dry her eyes with the backs of her hands. Her motions were childlike, confused; she had the air of a little girl who was lost. He said, trying to be patient: "We'd better go up to the telephone. I can get you a wrap, too." He avoided looking at the expanse of flesh left bare by the skimpy suit. She reminded him unpleasantly of girls he had known in his youth, before he began to make money; and he suspected that she had come originally from a large poor family.

"Did you hear the shots?"

Glazer nodded. "I wasn't sure at first what they were. I waited awhile before deciding to have a look down here."

"If you had come sooner, you might have caught him." He raised his heavy brows inquiringly.

"The murderer."

Irritation surged in him. She was stupid as well as lacking in taste. He saw that she was looking up at the face of the cliff as if expecting his gaze to follow hers. Stubbornly he kept his eyes on her. "Shall we go up?"

She glanced at him quickly and with, he thought, a touch of fright. "Did you see anyone up there? Is—is Mrs. Warne there?"

"I do not know where Mrs. Warne is at the moment. Let me give you some advice. Do not try to put Byronson's killing off on her."

She shrank. "No, I hadn't meant that." She went stumbling up the incline ahead of him, but at the shelter where the potted plants spread their green jungle she half collapsed and began to cough. She turned her head from him.

"What's wrong?"

"It's—when I breathe. It stabs here." She pointed briefly to her side. "Then— Please, I've got to spit." She coughed again and a rush of blood seeped through her fingers; above her hands, her eyes were enormous and afraid. Glazer was astonished; he had thought, on seeing her scratched and disheveled appearance, of some scuffle between the girl and Byronson.

"He hurt you!"

"I fell down. I didn't want to go to your beach. Please, Mr. Glazer, let me go to your bathroom. I'm going to be sick."

"Do you want me to help you?"

She shook her head. Glazer went on quickly to the house; she followed. Mrs. Concannon had the afternoon off; Jamie should be in his room for a period of quiet study. Glazer looked briefly into the kitchen and into Francesca's bedroom; she didn't seem to be about. Then he decided that she might be with Jamie, after all, though the boy customarily spent about an hour in the afternoon in silent reading. He wouldn't disturb her just now. He took Mrs. Shelton into the den and showed her the adjoining bath. Then he went to the telephone. He decided to call Dr. Barton. She should have medical attention before the cops had a go at her.

Fifteen minutes later he went down the hall to Jamie's room and rapped, then opened the door. Jamie was sitting at a desk and Francesca Warne was on the bed, propped with pillows; both were reading. As she looked up and he took in again the fine skin, the delicate planes of her face, he was aware of a rush of gratitude for the foolish girl in the study with Dr. Barton. There was safety now; there was an end to the nonsense and the mystery. Mary Shelton had killed Byronson, and it would be brought out that she had killed Adam Warne. And the woman who had been Adam Warne's wife could forget him and start being really interested in a man who loved her.

"I have something to tell you. Let's see ... Jamie." He frowned, trying to decide. "No, you might as well hear this. You'll get the gossip later anyway from other kids." He went in and sat down on a chair near the foot of the bed. "The cop, Byronson, has been shot on the beach. Mary Shelton was with him. I gather he gave her a bad time before his death. I called Dr. Barton and, when he got here, the cops."

All the color had left Francesca's face; she was sitting straight, the book fallen to the bed beside her. "What are you saying?"

He repeated the details carefully. "Dr. Barton says she must go to the hospital. He thinks she has some broken ribs."

"Do you mean you didn't notify the police until the doctor had seen her? Was that wise?"

"I felt sorry for her," Glazer defended.

"She killed him, of course."

"I don't see any other explanation. Byronson is dead on the beach and the gun is lying near him." Glazer frowned over it, remembering that the weapon had been a rifle, that both Byronson and Mary Shelton had been dressed in swimming outfits, that Byronson would logically have chosen a less conspicuous weapon to force the girl to come with him. "It will come out that she killed your husband."

Jamie said shakily, "I heard the noise of the gun. I tried to find somebody. I was scared."

Francesca frowned slightly. "I met Jamie in the hall and brought him here to calm him," she said. "I hadn't heard anything. I thought he must be imagining things."

"You met him right away?" Glazer asked.

"Why should you ask that?" Her eyes were level; even, he thought, unfriendly.

"No reason." Glazer went over to his son and stroked the tousled top. "You mustn't worry about this affair, Jamie. It's all a very unhappy mess. A grown-up sort of mess." He saw the boy's frailty, his nervous fear, and he remembered with annoyance that at Jamie's age he had seen a neighbor horsewhipping an errant daughter and had been little affected by the girl's screams except to wonder how she could keep them up so long so loudly. Well, that had been a different world, another boy. You were tough when your environment was tough; it's what Emily had said, making excuses for him. He said, "If you have any questions, save them and we'll talk about it later. The police may want to ask you about the noise you heard. Do you remember the time?"

Jamie shook his head. His cotton shirt shook with the strain of his uneven breathing. "Were you home then?"

"I drove in with some extra groceries for Mrs. Concannon. I heard the shots when I got out of the car. But I took the box into the kitchen before I decided to go and have a look."

"It's foggy out there," Jamie said.

"Yes, you can't see far." Glazer gripped his shoulder, patted his thin back. He had heard a siren from the direction of the highway. He turned to the woman on the bed. "I'll have to talk to the police now. Probably they'll blow their tops over the fact I got medical attention first for Mrs. Shelton."

"They'll want to talk to Jamie and me," she said thoughtfully.

"Yes, I guess they will."

"We'll be ready for them." There was not much nervousness in her manner, though she was still pale.

Glazer went over to the door. It struck him that the room was chilly, that the air felt as if Jamie had had the windows open, letting in the smell of the fog. "You should set the thermostat up for a little while. The day turns cold as soon as the fog comes in."

"Probably Jamie dashed in and out a couple of times," she pointed out. "I'll fix the heat."

She was at the wall, examining the thermostat, as he went out.

Glazer had seen the chief of police in the town, but they had not met, and now on meeting James Marsh he was aware of an almost instant dislike. The chief was a replica of officers he'd run into during his wanderings as a hobo kid; he epitomized a sort of pattern so many of them followed: big, slow, and graying, with heavy shoulders and the suggestion of a paunch, the air of authority ingrained, a face without expression except for sharp, knowing eyes. He had brought two officers with him; they waited in the living room while Marsh went to the den and talked to Dr. Barton. Glazer could hear the doctor's voice raised in anger. He had called an ambulance for Mrs. Shelton and had every intention of taking her to the hospital. If the police interfered, he'd be a witness in any suit Mrs. Shelton chose to bring later. She must have attention or she might die.

The door shut. Glazer imagined the doctor standing there like a dragon, the girl lying on the armless couch, covered by a blanket, and Marsh trying to put a few questions to her. Very shortly Marsh came out again.

He looked at his two young officers and said, "Get down to the beach. Don't touch anything, just wait." As they went out, he turned to Glazer. "Let's have your story."

"I came home from town with a load of groceries for my housekeeper—"

Marsh shook his head. "Before that."

"I was on the job this morning. I'm building Dr. Barton a house and starting excavation for another, higher on the hill. I didn't come home for lunch; I'd lost some time earlier in the day, an errand in town." He remembered the breakfast scene in the little café, Holt's fright, his own satisfaction with Conway's implied promise of excitement. "Anyway, my housekeeper has part of the day off. I called the house and told her to leave at noon, that Jamie and Mrs. Warne could have a cold snack and I'd eat when I could get away."

The chief's face didn't move a muscle at the mention of Francesca, and Glazer surmised he had known of her presence here.

"I went into town around two, I guess. I bought the groceries Mrs. Concannon wanted and drove out here. As I got out of the car I heard a series of snapping noises. I thought of firecrackers at the time and wondered if Jamie by any means had gotten hold of some. I took the box of food into the kitchen and put some of the things—the things that needed to be cold—in the refrigerator. Then all at once I had the feeling I'd better investigate."

"Pretty late," Marsh said.

"Yes, I guess I was sort of slow about it."

"You went right down to the beach?"

"No, I looked about over the yard, even up the slope beyond my fence. I was still trying to convince myself it had been firecrackers and I'd find some kids shooting them off in the bushes. You know, they're illegal here in California, but people bring them from Mexico."

"Yeah, I know that. When did you go to the beach?"

"Afterward. I found Mrs. Shelton down there, Byronson dead, the gun lying almost buried in the sand nearby. Mrs. Shelton looked beat up."

Marsh's knowing eyes searched Glazer's face. "You make any statements to her? Any accusations?"

Glazer sensed that Mrs. Shelton might have said as much to Marsh in the den. "Yes, I'm afraid so. It wasn't my place to draw conclusions, of course, but I said something about her having the right to defend herself, that no one would blame her for it."

Marsh's mouth tightened in an odd way across his teeth, as if he were about to whistle. "You tell that to anybody else?"

"I think I mentioned something of it to Dr. Barton."

"Did you see Byronson doing anything to her?"

"No. He was dead, she was crawling to her feet, as I came down."

"How do you know he did anything to her?"

Glazer paused to think. "I guess I took it for granted that's what made her look the way she did—Byronson picking on her, I mean."

"Byronson was a police officer working in the line of duty," Marsh said, looking out the broad windows at the view, blowing fog now, cutting off the sea. "A police officer has the right to request cooperation of a witness and to restrain the escape of a suspect."

"A suspect in what? The Warne murder?" Glazer made no attempt to hide his disgust. "Frankly, I don't care for cops who make investigations out of uniform, on my beach, abusing a woman. Why didn't he take Mrs. Shelton to headquarters? Why wasn't she wearing more clothes? If you want to know what I think, I think he kidnaped her from her home and brought her here against her will. And if that's working in the line of duty—"

"Mr. Glazer," said the chief in a heavy, authoritative tone, "you are the man who supplied the information which brought Mrs. Shelton into the Warne investigation."

Astounded, Glazer quit talking and listened.

Marsh went on: "You sent Mr. Holt, our newspaper editor, to Byronson this morning with certain facts which indicated the Sheltons should be interviewed again in regard to Adam Warne's death. Byronson came to me for permission to contact either of the Sheltons. I gave that permission."

He hadn't put it into words, but what he was saying was: *You are the cause of Byronson lying dead on your beach. You started the wheels moving and you shouldn't complain if he came to your doorstep to die.*

Marsh gave Glazer time to figure it out to the logical conclusion. Then he motioned toward the door. "Will you come down with me to the beach and show us just where Mrs. Shelton was standing when you saw her, and so forth? I won't keep you long. In fact, I'm going to ask you to come back here and see that everyone in the house stays put until I can talk to them."

"There isn't anyone but my son and his governess."

Marsh nodded. "I'll see them after a while." He walked out and Glazer fell into step. They went down the path through the flowers and into the lath shelter where the potted plants grew profusely. Glazer looked at them idly in passing, inclined to wonder why he had worked so hard to make them grow. Someone had prophesied, he remembered, that the sea air would stunt them. An unimportant matter. It had been after Rheba's death, and after he had begun to feel some disappointment about Jamie, that he had begun to put so much effort into the garden. And he had conquered here, he thought with a kind of shock, though his wife had escaped him by dying and Jamie evaded his guidance in a way he couldn't analyze.

He gave up thinking about himself once the brief instant of insight had passed. Below lay the beach and the running surf. It was not inviting. The gray light made the scene too cold, took the sparkle and color from the sea. Byronson's body looked ridiculous, Glazer thought. He looked as if he had fallen down while drunk. Marsh went over and examined Byronson without touching him, then looked at the gun. The two young officers stood by, as watchful as cats.

Marsh looked at one of them. "Tell that doctor to come down here before he leaves with Mrs. Shelton." Then, looking at Glazer: "All right. You did what, and where?"

Glazer, feeling foolish, acted out his part in coming down, meeting Mrs. Shelton, taking her to the foot of the path. Then he remembered a further detail, Mrs. Shelton looking up at the bluff. He showed Marsh where he had stood. "She stared up at the top of the bluff as if she expected to see somebody there. She kept asking if I'd seen the murderer."

Marsh sucked at his teeth. "What'd you tell her?"

"I hadn't seen anyone, and that's what I answered."

"Do you recognize the gun there?"

"No. Why should I?"

Marsh shrugged. "Dunno. It's one of ours. We found Byronson's car as we came in off the highway. The rifle's missing." His sharp eyes roved Glazer from head to foot; Glazer felt his hackles rise under that stare. It combined all the surveys he'd suffered in station houses, sheriffs' offices, and railroad dicks' shacks during the years of his wandering. "I figure somebody just took the gun 'cause it was handy," Marsh went on. "Handy—and they needed it at the moment. I don't figure Byronson would take it along; it appears more likely he'd want a smaller gun. The police revolver, for instance, in the bracket under the dash." The chief sucked his teeth again and then flinched as if he might have a cavity. "Provided he needed a gun to get the Parico girl to go with him."

"She's Mrs. Shelton now."

"Yeah."

"You mean that you've accepted her story, that somebody stood at the top of the bluff to shoot Byronson?" Glazer tried to read the slack-jowled expressionless face and failed. "I guess I can see one point—if somebody else, a third party, took the gun and killed him, you won't have to explain too much about why Mrs. Shelton has those cracked ribs and the bruises. If you get to dwelling on the idea she killed him, you'd have to look around a little for a motive—maybe just a little, but some—and it might be embarrassing to the Police Department. The papers are undependable and just might print something of Mrs. Shelton's experiences in getting to my beach. I gather it might make an interesting tale."

You had to hand it to Marsh, Glazer thought—the old cop was tough. He didn't seem bothered about what Byronson had had done to her, though Glazer suspected that the girl and the doctor would have told him.

Marsh shifted his weight, took out a pocket watch, and examined it. "I judge that somewhere along the line, Mr. Glazer, you had some experience in making cops mad. You're pretty good at it. Only I'm busy now. Here comes Dr. Barton, and I want to talk to him, because the medical examiner is going to take a little time getting here from Santa Ana. Will you go up now and do like I asked? See that the folks in your house stay put?"

Glazer stalked off, climbed the ramp, passing the doctor, who nodded to him. At the house he glanced into Jamie's room, found the boy alone.

Jamie said, "Mrs. Warne went out, maybe to her own room to lie down. She didn't seem to feel good. Have they taken the dead man away?"

"Not yet. Why don't you lie down too, Son?" He went down the hall and rapped at Francesca's door, but there was no answer. He had a look at the kitchen, thinking she might be making coffee, even mixing herself a drink after the shock of hearing of Byronson's death. But the place was as empty and immaculate as Mrs. Concannon had left it.

He opened the door to the den, expecting it to be vacated now, the girl gone with the ambulance. But apparently there had been a delay, and Dr. Barton had gone to see what Marsh wanted. Mrs. Shelton lay on the studio couch, wrapped in the blanket Glazer had provided; she had her eyes shut and looked gray and shrunken enough to be dead.

He had not realized there was another person in the room until he shifted his gaze to the spot behind his desk. Francesca Warne was there. She had reached one hand to the venetian blind at the window behind her, the white cord twisted in her fingers. Before her on the desk lay the big scissors Glazer used sometimes to alter and to experiment with house plans.

The tableau had a horrible impact on Glazer; he felt that he had jolted up the curtain on a nightmare. The face she turned to him seemed the face of a stranger, its beauty drained away, the mouth bitter, the eyes ravaged and vacant. The cord twisted in her fingers had the significance of some poisonous snake.

He tried to speak and could not, and waned without words for what she meant to do next.

Fifteen

"Why do you look at me like that?" Her voice was as usual, soft and breathy and faintly dragging, but it struck Glazer with a new meaning. He had thought of it until now as subtle and seductive, but it was neither. It was tired, perhaps a little querulous. It was the voice of a woman who had grieved for a long time. It was like the worn-out voice of his mother after his father had died.

She pulled the cord of the blind, softening the gray gloom of the room, then moved away from the window. She had not glanced at the scissors on the desk. "I thought I might find you here."

"I had supposed Mrs. Shelton would have been taken away by now."

"She looks very ill." Francesca stood a little distance from the couch and regarded Mary Shelton thoughtfully. "What is wrong with her?"

"I thought I told you. Dr. Barton says she has a couple of ribs broken, that they've punctured her lung." They were speaking in whispers now. As they looked at the sick girl on the couch, there was a rap at the door. Glazer opened it, found the young officer there with two white-coated attendants bearing a stretcher.

The attendants put the stretcher on the floor beside the couch. It was a big chrome-trimmed affair with wheels; the sheets and blankets looked very white. As they prepared to move Mrs. Shelton onto it, Francesca went out of the room. Glazer followed her, still aware of confusion and of the impact of that instant when he had thought she meant to cut the venetian-blind cord and use it on Mary Shelton.

She stopped by a couch that faced the big windows in the living room. "I don't hate her anymore." The fact seemed to be a new discovery to her.

He didn't know what to say. He didn't feel like trying to make love to her. He thought that perhaps he had never really seen her as she was, and the thought was disturbing. There was much more here than the simple, stubborn curiosity about Warne's death that he had supposed.

"I always knew she was on that beach with him when he died."

"How did you know?"

The foggy light made a frame for her. She brushed at the black hair, pulling it from her collar. "I—knew."

"The hospital is all the way across the bay from here," Glazer pointed out. "But if you'd had a powerful pair of glasses, you might have seen them."

She moved restlessly. "What do you mean? It was nearly dark."

"You were pretty sick then," he said slowly. "I'm surprised that you remember."

"Some things you never forget."

The words sank through his mind. They seemed ominous; his thoughts washed away from them, as if on a tide, and then surged back. He couldn't leave it alone. "How can you think of him when he treated you as he did?"

She turned from the window to face him, so that the gray light lay in her hair and on the shoulders of the pale silk dress. "Why do you consider yourself in love with me? Because of my admirable qualities? Because I've been kind to you? You know better."

His thoughts stumbled here and there, bewildered by what seemed an attack from her. "You're the—the sort of woman I've always wanted, that's all."

"Why? Why should you want my sort?"

He tried to answer; he wanted to say that because she had at first seemed distant, because some of her actions had been inexplicable, his curiosity had been aroused. This was true. But then he found himself at an impasse. When had he crossed over from half dislike to infatuation? Where had been the sill between one room and the other, the passing place, the change?

She said, "You don't know. There isn't any answer; there never will be. Some psychologists have tried to explain that the roots of desire go back into our childhood, our infancy, to people who no longer resemble those early images, or even to people who may be dead; but they're as lost as we. Nobody knows. I wanted Adam Warne, and when he asked me, I married him."

Glazer's fists clenched; a directionless rage floated to the top of the confusion in his mind.

"He wasn't handsome. He lived like a tramp. Alcohol had sapped his ambition and strength long before. But I—" Her hands flattened against her thighs, pulling the silk tight across her body. Glazer looked away. "I would have lived with him anywhere, without marriage even, in rags, in dirt. I used to think I could never get enough of looking at him."

Glazer sat down on the couch. The attendants came through, wheeling the stretcher. The wheels made a faint clicking noise. Mary Shelton, wrapped from head to foot in white blankets, was motionless as a mummy. The officer went ahead to the front entry and opened the door, stood aside, then closed the door behind all of them.

She knelt on the floor beside Glazer. "You are not a merciful man. Look at the way you treat your son. And so I shall not ask mercy of you. But I have told you the truth because I knew you had blinded yourself to it. You wanted to think of my life with Adam Warne as a myth, a mistaken dream, something without reality. That wasn't the way it was. Adam was a very real man. He was weak and he had a vicious streak that seemed to fascinate him, as some people keep looking at a sore, a birthmark, or a crooked part of their body."

Glazer moved away from her. He put his hands on his knees and studied them. They were tough-looking hands, and the short fingers had scars on them from the life he had led. Inwardly he writhed.

"You see, I am not the sort of woman you want at all," she went on. "I lived with a man who beat me; I accepted the life he dealt me. There is nothing fine or aristocratic about me, though this, I think, is what you want. I am, when you come right down to it, I guess—a slut."

All Glazer could think of was that she was reneging on their bargain. She was backing out, weaseling, by telling him he didn't really want her. He said slowly, "Did you kill him?"

She remained motionless for a few moments, then put down a hand, pushed herself half erect, stumbled a little before she reached the couch beside him. He made no move to help her.

"Maybe you don't even know. Maybe that's what you're trying to find out," he went on as if speaking to himself. "You were out of your mind, dying. Almost dying, anyway. There were some boats in the harbor, according to Mary Shelton, little yachts and power boats on the way down the peninsula to Baja California. La Paz, I think she said. To hunt. Now I realize that those boats would have had guns aboard, and if one gun turned up missing when they got to the tip of Baja California, who would think it might have been stolen at anchor here in Seaview? And who would connect a drifting dinghy ashore on the beach under the hospital with the murder of Adam Warne?"

She wrung her hands. "What are you saying?"

He shrugged. "I don't know. What did you mean about the way I treat my son?"

Her face was averted. "Forget that. What are you going to do? Will you send me away now?"

"Do you want to go?"

Her hands twisted together, the fingers interlocked as if in agony. "I haven't anywhere to go."

"Are you asking me now to feel sorry for you?"

"You—you said you felt sorry for Mary Parico."

He remembered the moment in the lath shelter, Mary Shelton's eyes big and scared above her dripping hands. "I guess I did, yes."

"But not—me?"

"I guess I had you confused with two other people," Glazer said with no intention of flippancy. He got up from the couch and walked across the space by the windows. There was a vase on a table there, full of fading flowers; Glazer knotted his fist and dashed it to the floor. There was a crackle of china, a splash. He looked at Francesca Warne. She was sitting hunched, her face in her hands. The black hair looked suddenly untidy, the bent throat too thin. He thought, She looks exactly the way she did that first late evening when she came to the fence, and I decided I didn't like her much.

He tried to recapture in his memory the time between, when he had thought only of this woman, when she had obsessed him day and night; it was like trying to capture a feather on the wind.

He walked out through the front entry to the garden. The fog had thinned near the horizon, and now that the sun was lowering, there was a slanting brightness from the west. He filled his pipe and lit it. He tried to imagine that he felt inwardly peaceful, but it was a lie; he felt as if some inner part of him had died.

At the head of the ramp beyond the lath house he studied the beach.

More officers had arrived. Dr. Barton was gone; another man who might be the medical examiner from Santa Ana was looking at Byronson's body. When he stood up, two cops came forward with a stretcher. It was not like the stretcher in which Mary Shelton had been carried away; it was plain khaki canvas looped at the sides over plain wood poles, a khaki blanket folded down the center. One cop removed the blanket; when Byronson's body was on the stretcher, he covered it neatly. They started up the ramp.

Glazer waited for Marsh. When he came Marsh said, "I'm leaving an officer down there. Don't want visitors until we can sift that sand. Found two more bullets. Either the first shot was a miss, or someone took a few extra for good measure. Or maybe they weren't shooting at Byronson at all." He took out the pocket watch again and looked at the time. "Mr. Glazer, I'll tell you what I'd like you to do. Go downtown and make your statement to the police stenographer at headquarters. I'll come along later and read it over with you, and you can sign it. Meanwhile, I'll talk to your boy and Mrs. Warne."

"What's the idea?"

"I'm not going to browbeat either of them, if that's what's worrying you. I do like to talk to possible witnesses alone, and private."

Glazer shrugged. "Oh, I don't care."

"You can drive your car," Marsh suggested. "Then we won't have to bring you back."

"Whatever you want." Glazer went to his car and got in, started the motor. He backed from the drive, then swung onto the meandering road that led up the headland to the highway. Ahead he saw Byronson's police car, still parked among the oleanders and little palm trees. A damned funny and sneaking way for a cop to behave, Glazer thought; of course he hadn't been so much investigating the Warne murder as taking out some delayed rage on Mrs. Shelton. Women could drive you nuts. They could get you killed if you monkeyed around with them under the wrong circumstances. Glazer thought about it as he waited for a traffic light to change. He seized the opportunity to refill his pipe.

A few blocks farther on he should have turned left from the beach, up the street to the police station. But he made no turn. He sent the car surging down the road toward Encinitas. It would be a little while before the cops missed him. Let them do the worrying.

He drove and smoked, and some of the dead feeling went away as he began to sense the possibility of excitement.

He parked his car in Shelton's driveway and walked into the patio. It was barred with shadow from the overhead trellis. The canvas swing was empty. Some dead leaves, last winter's leavings from the trees out by the road, had blown into a corner by the wall of the house and rustled there under an air current; the sound reminded Glazer of the stirring of a snake. He went over to the door and pressed the button. He heard chimes ring inside the house.

There was no answer and no movement except that of the dry leaves by the wall. Glazer reached out, turned the knob. The door swung open. He saw a hall paneled in light wood, a big slant-ceilinged living room beyond, windows that showed the surf. He listened. The house was hollow with silence.

He went back to his car, stood beside it to look around. A side road led off, paralleling the beach. He got into the car and drove a little way down the road and turned the car facing the sand, as if bathers had parked it there. Then he went back to Shelton's house. The door still swung open and the big room had no one in it.

He closed the front door and went through the place room by room. His experienced eyes took in builder's details: this was not as good nor as solid a house as his own, Shelton's former dwelling, but it had newer ideas in it. An architect with imagination, Glazer thought, and not afraid of experimenting at his client's expense. In ten years, he reflected, his own house would be just what it was now, a conservative and useful home; but this house might seem outdated because its gimmicks possibly would have been improved upon or bypassed. He hated slab walls; they needed thick protection from the coast weather or they turned shabby. And the freakish windows, high under the eaves in all directions except the west, made the rooms seem to him like cells in a jail. His eyes were busy with other details as well. He found Shelton's study, a madhouse smelling of disinfectant and sea life. Mrs. Shelton's bedroom was furnished lavishly, but it needed dusting. The clothes were in heaps, some of them, on the bed and on chairs, so Glazer judged that if the Sheltons had household help it was someone who came in only occasionally and coped with just the worst.

The kitchen table still held remains of breakfast for one, coffee for another. Glazer studied it and decided that Mrs. Shelton had rushed off early to request the five thousand of him, had eaten when she came home. Her husband had had coffee with her. What had he known of that crazy request?

Glazer looked into a couple of cupboards before he found a bottle of whiskey. He was a cautious drinker, coldly aware of the mistakes bred in the bottle. He made a small drink and went back to the living room and sat down on Shelton's twelve-foot foam-rubber cerise satin couch.

How had Byronson accomplished Mrs. Shelton's abduction? Had he come here, confronted the two of them, bullied Shelton into submission, walked off with the wife? Glazer considered it, then discarded the idea. Shelton was a meek and spooky sort on the surface, but he was not the man Glazer would have tried to steal a woman from. He would not tell himself that women were like streetcars and that another one would be along presently in place of the one the cop had taken away. He would get extremely upset and excited over the removal of a girl like Mary Parico, who was tanned, and plump in the right spots, and whose red-brown hair didn't show her Italian blood, though the fine full lips and the straight heavy brows did.

If the cop had grabbed Mary Shelton on the beach—and judging by the skimpy suit she could scarcely have intended being anywhere else—and the husband had caught a glimpse of it, Glazer thought, you could come up with a very interesting theory indeed.

Shelton had a car and there was nothing to prevent his following Byronson and his wife, and watching in desperation as the girl was dragged to the spot where she had shared Warne's last moments. The husband could be maddened with rage at the treatment of the girl and kill Byronson for it, or he could be worried for fear Byronson was going to get to the bottom of Warne's murder and kill him before he succeeded. Or both. You could stack Shelton up against any other suspect, and he came out ahead hands down, perfect, in spades or any way you wanted it. Of course Marsh had thought of this.

Glazer sipped at the drink. It was a poor grade of scotch, with the imitation smoky flavor, probably chemical, that poor scotch always had. If Shelton was in partners on the bars, he was getting the dregs of the stock. Probably he didn't know the difference. If you stayed very long in a study like his, among specimens pickled in formaldehyde, the taste of things wouldn't be too distinct.

A really funny old duck, Glazer thought. A professor who set up a broken-down tough in the bar trade so that he could share the profits and go on looking at the insides of shellfish. The dough might have come hard; he and Conway, according to the liquor wholesaler, Butler, had just met up with each other when they went into business in Seaview. Easy or hard, Glazer sensed, Shelton had here a paradise he'd always wanted: the shore, the crawling things in its surf, a battery of microscopes, beakers, and photographic equipment, plus the final reward of a beautiful young wife.

Another stray detail occurred to Glazer, a remark made by Holt. Holt had asked Byronson if there had been narcotic connections in Conway's bar business, and Byronson had said it had never been proved. He had distinctly not said the narcotic connections had never existed. Add marijuana and heroin to Conway's whiskey business and you might have something really fancy in the way of profits.

Glazer put down the glass and went back to Shelton's den. The middle of the room was taken up with a long littered table full of Shelton's scientific paraphernalia. In one corner, under a load of books, was a desk. Glazer explored the drawers of the desk.

After a few minutes he began to have a pretty clear idea about Shelton's financial sense. Shelton was the squirrel type. He put money into savings accounts here and there, tucking it away into limbo. It must represent sums left over from living expenses. Totaling five of the accounts, Glazer whistled soundlessly.

Shelton kept his savings books in with old bills, scientific notes, and back-issue shopping lists. The drawers were in about the order a stiff wind would have left them. Digging further into the mess, Shelton found some old receipts from Butler's firm, proving that Butler was right in his surmise that Shelton was in on Conway's Fiddling Crab.

One thing Glazer made especial note of: the money was all in Shelton's name. No account was held jointly with Mary.

He could be afraid that his young wife had no budget ability. Or he could have forgotten to put her name on accounts started before his marriage. Or he could have suspected she'd need five thousand to run off, and help herself. Lots of possibilities. Mary Shelton wanted five thousand now, or had wanted it this morning. Her husband's money wasn't available.

She had had one thing to sell, the words spoken on the beach by Adam Warne just before he died. And Glazer was her market.

He wondered what would have happened if he'd given her some cash, enough to start on, with the promise of more to come. Byronson could be alive now, perhaps, Shelton waiting bewilderedly at home, Mary Shelton flying before some unendurable thing on the verge of catching up with her. Or escaping from Shelton's devotion. He would, Glazer thought dryly, be a most devoted husband to a girl like Mary.

Glazer was shutting the top desk drawer when he heard a sound from the living room.

Sixteen

Glazer and Will Shelton looked at each other wordlessly across the expanse of yellow carpet, over the long cerise couch and the lime-colored modernistic chairs. Glazer thought that Shelton was sick or on the edge of tears. The face above the tufty beard was pinched, squinting. All at once then Shelton found his voice, a croak. "What are you doing here?"

"Waiting for you," Glazer said. "I think we ought to have a talk."

Shelton looked all around, as if examining the room for fire exits. He was perspiring visibly, though the place was not warm. The untidy beard hid his mouth, but his eyes were frantic. "There isn't any time."

"Are you abandoning your wife? Skipping out?"

The little professor seemed to get hold of himself with a jerk. "I don't know what you're talking about, Mr. Glazer. I resent your intrusion here. I would prefer that you go."

"Yes, I guess you would. You didn't ask any questions about Mrs. Shelton's predicament, so I guess you know what it is. She's in the jug for murder."

Shelton took out a handkerchief and mopped at his neck under the beard. Glazer noted that he had on a pair of pants without a belt and a knitted T-shirt. Above the edge of the trousers at the waist some other garment peeped, soiled cotton in a brownish gray—beach trunks, Glazer thought, and it must mean that Shelton had donned the pants in a hurry.

Shelton finished mopping his neck. "You speak in riddles, Mr. Glazer."

"I'm just damned well passing along something you already know," Glazer told him. "I figured you might have trailed Byronson and your wife and shot him for what he was doing to her. I didn't follow on, to your leaving her to face the rap. You didn't seem the type."

"Of course I don't intend to abandon my wife."

"You know where she is?"

Shelton nodded jerkily. "She's in the hospital in Seaview. They're giving her transfusions."

"You're quick, all right," Glazer commented. "How did you find out?"

"I asked." Shelton was recovering from the fright he'd had over Glazer's unexpected appearance in his house; and Glazer wondered if he might have been dreading the presence here of someone else, someone who represented more of a danger than himself. "I'm to pack some of her things and take them to the hospital. She has nothing with her, nothing at all."

"I know. I saw her. How did Byronson take her away?"

Shelton shook his head. "I have no idea."

The primness irritated Glazer. "Come on now, Shelton. You know you have no intention of showing up at the hospital. If you called up and got information about your wife, you did it under a phony name. You said you were her father, perhaps. The cops must be looking high and low for you. You're just the fellow they want to meet."

Shelton sidled over to the couch, looked down wistfully at the cerise satin, changed his mind about sitting down. His feet might hurt him, Glazer decided. The rope-soled sandals were poor affairs. "I don't know why you are persecuting me, Mr. Glazer. Mr. Conway came here this morning to warn me. He said you supplied the police with information about some slip or other I'm supposed to have made. If that is true, then Mary's predicament might be the outcome of something you have started." His eyes came up; behind the lenses they were unexpectedly clear and searching.

"Your friend Mr. Conway interests me very much," Glazer answered, refusing to be embarrassed.

"Is it Conway you're after?"

"Yes."

Shelton rubbed the beard, tried to smooth it, an impossible job. "Why?"

Glazer sauntered over closer to the other man. The back of the long couch, sticking out from the wall so that it faced the view, was the only thing separating them. Close this way, Shelton's haggard expression, the lines in his face were much clearer. Something had hit him hard: his wife's trouble, perhaps. Glazer said, "I'm doing just what I told you I was—looking into the murder of Adam Warne."

Shelton swallowed nervously. "On account of Mrs. Warne?"

"Yes." The answer came automatically, but it was yesterday's answer. The last interview with Francesca had changed everything. Glazer turned his mind from her.

"And why have you chosen Conway?"

"He strikes me as the right sort of guy for it."

"I see what you mean," Shelton said. "You think that because murder represents the ultimate violence it must be the deed of a violent person." He smiled faintly, uneasily, and shook his head. "I don't agree. Someone like Conway isn't afraid of using his fists or a handy tool and getting in close enough to his quarry to risk getting hurt himself. He has confidence in his own toughness and endurance. He thinks he can deal out more than he will absorb. And so usually he stops short of killing. He hurts, injures, and is hurt in turn, and it satisfies the part of him that craves action or vengeance. But—consider somebody like me. I'm tired, I feel horribly old most of the time, I hate the thought of pain or punishment for myself. I'm the one who would stand on the cliff and use a gun to get my man."

"That's very neat," Glazer said, "though I've no doubt you could twist it back to Conway if you wished. If you thought the police believed all that for instance. I'll think it over. Meanwhile, tell me this: why don't you give your wife some money?"

Shelton looked puzzled. "She has money."

"A few dollars, maybe. She wants five thousand. She came to me this morning and asked for that. She had something to trade, information about Warne."

Shelton licked his lips. His tongue looked pink and wet among the whiskers; it made Glazer think of a cat's. "Well, that was—unwise."

"She's too desperate to be wise. I guess she always did think you killed Warne because he was making love to her. And, following your own line of thought, maybe you're the guy could do it, and I was wrong in suspecting her and wrong about Conway."

"You're wrong about all of us." Shelton retreated a little way. He seemed unable to make up his mind what to do about Glazer. "Mary shouldn't have gone to you. I can't imagine why she did."

"She thought I had five thousand dollars," Glazer said reasonably.

"If she thought you'd hand over that much, the information must have concerned something other than just Warne's murder." Shelton paused as if to think, but his eyes were busy. "It may have concerned Mrs. Warne."

"It did, and it was ridiculous."

"Perhaps you don't know the full details concerning Warne's wife. The police, Byronson especially, were very suspicious of her. She would have been indicted, I believe, but for three items." He ticked them off on his spread fingers. "There was no way of finding out what ability she had as a swimmer." If he saw the start Glazer gave, he seemed not to. "They could never get the nurse to admit that Mrs. Warne wasn't being watched enough to keep her from leaving the hospital. The nurse swore over and over that she'd had an eye on the patient, though the nurse's reputation wasn't too good, and not too long afterwards she was kicked off the job for shenanigans on duty with an orderly. The third point was, they never found the gun."

When he finished speaking he went on looking at Glazer, and Glazer, too deep in his own thoughts to sense Shelton's intention, was unprepared when Shelton moved.

Shelton leaped to a small bookcase, jerked out a book, and threw it. His aim was good, but Glazer's lessons had been learned early and thoroughly. He ducked automatically; even so, the book hit his shoulder. It was heavy. He swung half around. His fingers caught at the satin-covered couch and slid off. He went down to a knee. Shelton fired three more books.

Glazer got out of range by ducking below the level of the couch. He cursed himself for his inattention. Then he listened and heard Shelton running; there was the *slap-slap* of the rope-soled sandals, then a door slammed. Glazer jumped to his feet and leaped for the door in the opposite wall. He found himself looking down a white-painted passageway into the kitchen. Shelton had stopped; he was standing oddly. Even as Glazer watched, he lifted hands that seemed heavy as lead and clutched his stomach.

Then Conway stepped into view. He landed another blow on Shelton's midriff, knocking him up against the sink. Shelton kept trying to grab his stomach and bend over, while Conway stepped in closer to slap him this way and that. Glazer took a brief look backward. A fieldstone fireplace stood at his left; there were solid hearth tools in a bronze rack. Glazer went over silently and lifted the poker and hefted it. It felt good; it felt like the kind of thing he liked.

He slid back into the passageway. Shelton, backed against the sink, could see him, but Conway had his back turned. He had a handful of Shelton's beard; the little scientist's face was up, pulled up to look at Conway.

"You've bitched it for the last time," Conway ground out. "I told you—I do the hard work. There's a time and a place. You interrupt deliveries and you get cops in our hair and we're sitting in San Quentin. For that—that—"

Shelton's voice was a whistling squeak, a mouse-voice. "You leave Mary out of this!"

Conway dragged cruelly on the beard. "I've had it. For the last time. You won't forget it. No matter how good she is and how long you waited for her, when I'm carrying cargo you keep still. The cops skin her alive, and you keep your mouth shut. I'm telling you." He fended off Shelton's weak flapping blows, brought a knee up, hard. Shelton gave a muffled scream.

They were talking about dope, narcotics. Conway obviously was the runner, getting supplies; he was mad now because he thought the excitement in Seaview might bring cops looking at him, looking into his car. But Glazer saw that some sense of danger was bringing Conway's head around to search behind him. It was too late to step away, to set an ambush beside the door. Glazer stood still, and Conway's stare settled on him.

A fire flared in Conway's eyes as he realized that Glazer had heard him. Then the color went out of his face. Not from fear; he wasn't a man who would be afraid in a spot like this. He edged around, pulling Shelton with him like a dummy. His movements were sidling and cautious. Shelton looked so sick that Glazer doubted he knew what was happening.

Shelton made a shield for Conway, one arm twisted behind him. He wasn't as tall as Conway, but Conway crouched slightly. He reached with a slow hand and opened a drawer, took a quick glance to select what he wanted. He came out with a knife, long and slender, sharp-looking.

Shelton sagged at the knees, and Conway jerked on the bent arm and brought him up again. "Stay put, Will. We've got company."

"Please ..." Shelton's head bobbled like a pumpkin on a stick. "I don't want— I told you—"

Conway ignored the stammering words. "Our friend here has a taste for steel. We might accommodate him." He licked his lips. All of the easy, good-natured looseness had dropped off him. He was a machine for dealing out punishment. He was Death, if you got close enough.

Glazer let the poker hang still in his hand, the weight of it in his arm, solid, reassuring. Conway looked at it measuringly. The last of the sunlight was dying outside; the kitchen was gray with dusk. Against the stark white wall, Conway and Shelton had the immobility of statues.

Shelton said gaspingly, "I'm going away. I'm going to take Mary, just Mary; none of this other stuff matters. It isn't important. My work doesn't amount to anything. I can't solve the simplest problems, I can't even dissect and dye and mount specimens decently, I'm just deluding myself. The house can sit here till it falls down...." He shuddered as Conway took a hitch on the arm behind him.

They were motionless again. But Glazer began to move. He came down the white-painted passage with quick soft steps and paused at the kitchen doorway. He put a hand to the light switch, clicked it. Shelton blinked at the sudden glow. There was no change in Conway.

The big white range was at Glazer's right, beyond it a steel-topped worktable with cabinets below, then the refrigerator. All of the drawers that might have knives or tools in them were over by the sink, by Conway. Glazer let his fingers curl on the handle of the poker, experimenting with his grip.

Shelton whined, "I never wanted the narcotics. Alcohol—well, that's everywhere; they can sleep that off, they'll get it one place or another and there's no permanent damage, no craving. It's the dope, the heroin—" He choked over what he wanted to say. Glazer didn't think that Shelton had been speaking to him or to Conway. He'd been apologizing to God, perhaps.

Conway had plans behind his eyes. He was waiting for Glazer to make the right move or get into the right spot. Still holding Shelton by his twisted arm, he slid sidewise until he covered the drawer from which the knife had come. The refrigerator clicked on a moment later; the soft hum of the motor sounded above Shelton's husky breathing, the quiet step of Glazer's shoe.

Glazer said, "Let him go, Conway."

Conway smiled. "You amuse me. You're like a goddamn goat running around and butting its head on a lot of stone walls. You don't have any inkling of what this frolic is all about. You're stupid. Take Francesca Warne, for instance. You're gone on her, but good. You think she's pretty nice. Did she ever tell you she knew me, that I took her more than once to that house you bought? Did you know why I beat up Warne—the real reason I wanted to kill him?" The smile died on his lips, but its reflection stayed on in his eyes.

Glazer remembered in that flashing moment how, when he and Francesca had first gone into the house, she had known her way around in it. She had known the way to the hall, to the bedrooms. A chilling frenzy beat through his brain, shame for himself for being a dullard. She'd been in love with Warne and he had been unfaithful; and she wasn't the first to pay a man back in his own coin. In this case, with a big loose-jointed man who wasn't too bad-looking, who was probably, in fact, a lot more attractive than her husband.

"You're getting a little white around the gills," Conway jeered, his gaze searching, "so I judge you hadn't known about us."

But it now occurred to Glazer on second thought that this was much the same trick Shelton had pulled before he began firing those books. Conway was telling his yarn for its effect, to throw Glazer off, to distract him.

Glazer said, "It's a lie. She may have been in your house. But she wasn't any friend of yours." Conviction grew in him even as he said the words. Whatever else she had been, she had not been Conway's woman. "Maybe she went to your place to demand that you leave her husband alone. And maybe you beat Warne up because you thought he knew something about your business you didn't want known. The narcotic angle."

Conway must have decided that Glazer's mental processes were tied up in figuring this all out. He moved. He thrust Shelton forward, propelling him with his knee. There must have been a last excruciating twist on Shelton's arm, for he gave a squawk like a chicken's. For a moment or two Conway must have thought the maneuver a complete success; Shelton sprawled against Glazer as he was meant to do, and Glazer went off balance against the doorframe. Conway leaped forward, the knife in his fist. Glazer looked at the knife even as he hit the wall behind him. Conway held it with the handle toward his thumb, the blade sticking out of the heel of his hand; he lifted it as if to stab. Glazer's mouth twitched as if he wanted to smile.

He waited until the point of the knife was headed his way across Shelton's collapsing shoulder. Then he threw Shelton back, low, against Conway's knees. At the same moment the heavy poker came up like a whip across Conway's face.

Conway drew back. Shelton's glasses had fallen off; the lenses crunched under Conway's heel. Conway said thickly, "You bastard. You—bastard."

"You're repeating yourself."

There was no fear as yet in Conway's eyes, but there was caution. The thick welt left by the poker had first paled under his skin, now was filling with blood; it crossed Conway's face just below his mouth. He put up his left hand, touching the mark gingerly.

On the floor, Shelton was whimpering and crawling, his hands outspread, hunting his glasses.

"Let's get him out of here first," Glazer said. Conway lifted his head sharply, as if sensing the appetite for violence that lay under the words. "He can't see. He'll get hurt if we keep on using him for a buffer."

Buffer ... A word Emily Graham had taught him among all those others she was sure would make him sound like an educated man, would bring the debs flocking. Sometimes when you learned a word you had no idea when you'd use it, and sometimes when you used it you wanted to laugh at the circumstances of learning it. Glazer didn't laugh, but he allowed himself to smile.

"He's all right," Conway decided. He moved to the right, away from Shelton's blindly searching hands, and then he leaped again.

In that moment of waiting, Glazer told him in his mind, silently: *When you jump with a knife, holding it the way you're holding it now, you've got to bring it down before it does any good. But you hold it pointing forward at waist level, and when you get there, the knife's there. It's in somebody if you're lucky at all.*

Glazer couldn't remember when or where he had learned the technique of the knife. From the Alvarez brothers, perhaps, the skinny Mexican kids who'd been his most faithful companions. He waited, full of cold attention, as Conway came at him. The knife shone. Conway jerked it higher; his whole body was tightened in that spasm of slashing downward. He slashed downward, and Glazer simply moved away.

Glazer did not hit him in passing. When Conway turned, Glazer was already across the kitchen by the sink, and the drawer was sliding open under the touch of his left hand. The poker was ready—not lifted, just balanced nicely in his hand. Conway could see the fine control in the muscles of Glazer's wrist.

Glazer glanced briefly into the drawer, a flick of the eyes, and saw the knives in a row. He thought Shelton must have put them there in that arrangement; it was much neater than the desk, but he was a man who would be neat with tools and sloppy with records. With his left hand Glazer began to take the knives out one by one. He put each knife on the sink and tested its keenness with his thumb. He did this slowly and carefully, and with his eyes on Conway.

Conway wanted to jump again; the desire flickered over his face, lighting and then darkening; he couldn't quite make up his mind. He was interested, too, after a minute, in seeing which knife Glazer was going to choose. On the floor, Shelton was scrabbling and crying.

At the sixth knife, Glazer paused. He ran his thumb along the blade again, then brought the knife around slowly where he could see it without looking away from Conway. It was a somewhat short-bladed knife, wide, with a brown plastic handle. It didn't look as if it had been meant to be what it was now; it looked like a cheese slicer which Shelton had for some reason decided to rehone into something resembling a razor.

Glazer laid the poker on the tile sink and shifted the knife to his right hand. He felt cold and light, his body weightless, his mind composed. It was then that he saw the change beginning to come over Conway, a look familiar to him; it was like the spreading of a sickness, an ague. A funny color bloomed in Conway's face, as if his heart had given a tremendous surge and yielded up all its blood to his skin. He glanced down uncertainly at his own weapon, then back to the knife Glazer held.

"Make up your mind," Glazer said.

Conway hesitated. His eyes settled on the poker, bright brass against the white tile. He licked his lips. "You—you'd rather—"

"Much rather," Glazer agreed. "It's no fun beating a man with a poker."

There was a last rush of hatred filling and dying in Conway's eyes. Then he dropped his knife and kicked it away toward Glazer.

Seventeen

Through the open wire Chief Marsh said irritably, "All right, all right, get on with it. I've got a squad car on the way and I'm going to telephone the police in Encinitas. But if you've got to do it this way, do it. *But do it.*"

Conway sat by the telephone on Shelton's desk. He was hunched forward. Glazer stood behind him. The short, wide-bladed knife was thrust through Glazer's belt, but Conway was uneasy about it; he kept trying to look over his shoulder.

"Talk," Glazer said.

"I want to confess to the murder of Adam Warne and the police officer, Byronson," Conway began in a strange choked tone.

"Your own free will? No coercion?" Marsh asked.

"My own free will." Conway all but gagged over the words. "I killed Warne because he—he found out I was selling narcotics, marijuana and heroin, at the Fiddling Crab."

"And Byronson?"

"I saw him take Mary Shelton away. I thought he might get something out of her, something she'd seen that would connect me with Warne's murder."

"How'd you do it?" Marsh asked, sounding suspicious.

Conway took a look at Glazer. Glazer said, too quietly for the phone to catch, "What's he want?"

Conway covered the receiver. "Details. How I did Byronson in."

"You remember how," Glazer reminded. He had jogged Conway's memory before the call, not being sure that Conway's recollections would be clear.

Conway took his hand off the receiver. "I found a gun in the police car."

"You used to carry your own," said Marsh.

"Using that would have been a fool's trick," Conway protested.

"Okay. You took the police rifle. Then what?"

"I went to the top of the bluff, waited until I could get a clear sight through the fog, and fired."

"By God, you might be telling the truth," Marsh said. "We got a weather report, and the fog didn't get down as far as you are now."

"I threw the gun over the cliff, hoping Mary Shelton might handle it and so put her fingerprints on it."

"You stay put, brother," Marsh warned. "We're coming for you." Glazer jerked the phone from Conway's hands and rapped it several times sharply on the side of the desk. He could hear Marsh squawking through the receiver. Then he jammed it into its cradle. He looked coldly at the man crouched in the chair.

"What now?" Conway whispered.

"Run," Glazer said.

Glazer went into the kitchen. Shelton was still there; he'd gotten into the breakfast nook and was sitting with his arms propped on the table before him. His blind, staring eyes bugged out as Glazer came in.

"Me," said Glazer. He slid in on the other bench. "Your friend Conway is gone. He confessed to the Seaview cops to the murders of Warne and Byronson. Then he pushed me aside with a wild leap and got away. I'm going to phone Chief Marsh as soon as my head quits ringing."

Shelton laughed, or rather he made a noise to indicate that he thought Glazer was a pretty humorous fellow.

"Did you ever like him?" Glazer wondered.

"I sort of pitied him in the beginning," Shelton said, "but that was before I revised my estimate of him. He hadn't needed any pity—ever."

Glazer studied the older man's efforts to see him. "How well can you see without glasses?"

"Scarcely at all. I have something like less than one per cent of normal vision. Even glasses only bring me up to about halfway."

"I guess you couldn't have shot Warne or Byronson from that cliff without a lot of luck."

"Luck is something I never had," Shelton answered. "It was decent of Conway to take me off the hook on the murder charge."

"Oh, he turned out to be a swell fellow."

Shelton laughed again, this time on an uneasy note, as if wondering what Glazer might be up to.

"Do you have any extra glasses? I'll get them for you if you do."

"No, there aren't any. I'll have to get new ones."

"Just before you tossed those books my way," Glazer said, "you were telling me about the police interest in Mrs. Warne."

Shelton rubbed his hands back and forth on the surface of the table. "I don't want to make you mad, Glazer."

"I'm not mad. I feel good. I want you to finish the story, that's all."

"She was dropped as a suspect long ago."

Glazer nodded. "Yes, I guess so. Are you telling me to leave it alone?"

"One thing I can tell you," Shelton offered. "She wouldn't have had anything to do with my partner. She might have come to the house— a lot of people did. He gave parties, big ones. She could have been a guest."

"Forget it. I knew he was lying."

Shelton leaned toward Glazer as if trying to improve his view of him. "Look at it this way—suppose she *did* kill Warne. Hadn't she a right?"

Glazer didn't answer.

Shelton waited uneasily. Then he said, "What did you do to him to scare him like that?"

"You mean Conway? I'm damned if I know. I was picking a knife; it was a smaller one than he'd got. I don't know why he went chicken all of a sudden."

"I don't know either, because I couldn't see what you were doing."

Glazer shifted his body, settling lower in the booth, relaxing. "Getting back to Francesca Warne, I'll admit her husband had the works coming to him. It doesn't answer the question."

"You don't need an answer. Conway's running now; he'll keep on running because he's got the dope rap facing him, and he's on borrowed time—he broke parole in the East."

Glazer said patiently, "It's come around to this. Believe it or not, she asked me to start looking for the murderer of her husband. And full circle, it's back to her, as round as a hoop. Did she do it? And why ask me to catch her for her crime?"

"I don't know." Shelton gave it some silent thought. "It could be that she isn't sure. Or it might be punishment she's seeking."

Glazer thought of the things never explained: the death of Jamie's dog, the business of Francesca taking the boy out to the rocks and apparently abandoning him there. Once he had believed—or tried not to believe, it amounted to the same—that Francesca had thought him the possible murderer of her husband and that she had been nerving herself to killing him in return by first practicing on the dog and the child. But if she had been in the house during Conway's occupancy and known of Conway's treatment of her husband and that some fear or grudge must lie behind it, she could not possibly have been deluded that Glazer, a total stranger to them all, had committed the crime. Even though she might not have known the date of the sale, when the house had changed owners; even if she had taken for granted that Glazer was in the place when Warne was killed, still she must have seen that he had no motive for the murder of Warne.

He turned to another point, explaining it to Shelton. "You talk as if she has wings like a bird's. If she left the hospital, somehow, and stole a dinghy and rowed part way to my beach and swam the rest—what then? How did she get to the top of the cliff? Warne and the girl would have seen her if she had come out of the surf there. The other beach, the little one beyond that outstanding wall of rock, is inaccessible."

"Not quite, I think," Shelton said. "I wanted some specimens from it. I climbed down that rock buttress. It was hard and dangerous, but I did it."

Glazer frowned. "You're saying she landed down there from the surf and climbed the rock?"

"The shot that killed Warne came from the rock," Shelton said almost inaudibly.

"*You* think."

"I know." Shelton's face was gray, wretched. The roots of the tufty beard were dark with sweat, though the room was cool. "You've kept saying I must have been outside the house that afternoon—and I was. I was afraid to say so when the cops came and wanted to search the house, and I was afraid they'd find Mary hidden in the den." His voice, rough, weak, took on sudden strength. "I did it—I told the lie—to protect her."

"Besides, you didn't want her to know you'd been spying on her," Glazer said cynically.

"Well—yes. I'd found out that late afternoons, when the beach was deserted, Warne was meeting her below our place. I think the meetings were innocent—at least the intention behind them was innocent, from Mary's point of view. I don't know what Warne had in his mind. He was a horrible man. Everyone expected his wife to die from the beating, the loss of their child. The thought of Mary becoming entangled with someone like him, her life ruined, her reputation gone—" Shelton broke off; his mouth was working as if with rage.

"Maybe you did have a bit of luck," Glazer said. "You could see a man's head outlined against beach sand without twenty-twenty vision." He remembered idly in this connection that Conway had been accusing Shelton of committing the cop's murder when he had interrupted the scene between the two in the kitchen. The thought had little impact; the conversation was directionless. Glazer felt almost lethargic after his victory over Conway. Besides, some inner part of his mind added, you convicted Francesca Warne in your opinion when you found her with that venetian-blind cord in her hand. He shifted irritably, dismissing the memory of the scene in his den.

"I did see the murderer," Shelton said. "But it was too far to identify anyone. I was hidden out in the direction of the highway, in some shrubbery, almost at the opposite end of our beach from that stone tower. It must make a wall about ten feet wide at the top, allowing for the rough surface; thirty or more at the bottom where it disappears into the sand. I used to think, if it could be blasted away, the beach would be improved. You could use that other section."

"After the shot—what?" Glazer asked.

"I don't know where the murderer went. If it had been Mrs. Warne, of course, she'd have climbed back down and gone into the sea."

"Anybody else would have climbed up and run."

"I went immediately to the house," Shelton said. "I was very nervous. I decided I'd better say that I had been inside all during the afternoon."

"Then Mary came."

"Yes, she did. There were reasons—appearances—that would have made it seem bad for her to have remained down there."

"Like having her clothes off."

"Just a dress, the bare-shoulder sort of thing girls wear sometimes over swim suits."

"At that, she was better off than when Byronson grabbed her today." Shelton nodded absently.

"You followed them, of course."

Shelton's blind eyes moved uneasily around the little nook. "No. No, I didn't."

"Come on," Glazer urged. "You can tell me now. Conway's the boy with the cops on his tail. You're home free." He smiled at the bewildered little man, though it was doubtful Shelton could see this. "Besides, I've been honest with you, discussing the case against Mrs. Warne."

Shelton cleared his throat huskily. "There's something different in the way you talk about her. I can't explain what it is. You sound as if she were a stranger."

Glazer's smile went away. "You didn't see who killed Byronson?"

"No."

Shelton's fingers plucked and scratched at the table's edge. The kitchen was quite bright, the glow from the big fixtures in the ceiling reflected on the stark white walls. Glazer got up. "I'm thirsty." He went over to the sink and began to run water into a glass.

"There's whiskey," Shelton told him.

Glazer remembered the whiskey, the chemical-tasting scotch. He took down the bottle, poured recklessly into the glass from which he had dumped the water. What did you want out of life? he jeered at himself.

It doesn't matter. This is what you've got.

He opened the door of Jamie's room. Mrs. Concannon was there in a chair beside the bed, a book open; she'd obviously been reading to the little boy, who was in pajamas, sitting on top of the spread. The lamp had a parchment shade, decorated with a pattern of horseshoes and branding marks.

"Mr. Glazer!" She half rose from the chair, the fright and indignation over this scandal and violence almost bursting in sparks from her eyes. "I've been waiting hours! If I'd known where to phone you—"

"I'm sorry."

"The police came here not long ago. Looking for you. The chief said you'd captured the murderer, forced him to confess; he didn't say who—"

"Conway. Where is Mrs. Warne?"

She settled down into the chair. The pink uniform had stains on its bosom, as if Jamie had wept there. "We don't know. She isn't here."

Glazer looked at his son. "When did she leave?"

Jamie sat as if struck dumb, his big eyes fluttering. Glazer went over and took his hand and rubbed the small cool palm. "Don't be scared. Were you lonely? Did she leave you alone for a long time?"

"No," said Jamie. "She said it was time for Mrs. Concannon to come, and it was."

"I might have passed her on the road to the highway," Mrs. Concannon said worriedly.

"What about her clothes?"

"Nothing's gone. I looked at her closet, just in case."

Glazer patted Jamie's shaking arm. "What was she wearing? Do you know?"

"Like when she came," Jamie stammered.

"The black coat? The scarf on her hair?"

"She kissed me good-by." Jamie began to sob; no tears came, but he shuddered with his grief. It was as if the grief lay a long way inside him, where his father must not see it. "She asked me if I'd remember her sometimes. She said maybe soon you'd get a new dog and I must name him Jericho and that my old Jericho was a brave good dog because he tried to keep her from climbing down the rock, and that's how he fell, wanting to save somebody." The boy's face was tight, knotted with the effort of control.

Mrs. Concannon smoothed the pajama-clad knee. "Now, now, Jamie!"

The small, lost hiccuping voice went on: "She said to remember that when I grow up I can be anything I want. I can be me." The child's face crumpled; he hid it in his hands. "I can be me," he repeated in a whisper.

Mrs. Concannon looked uneasily at Glazer. Glazer sat down on the side of the bed. He waited several moments and then said, "Lean on me, Son."

Without taking his hands from his face, crawling on his knees, Jamie put his head against Glazer's shoulder. His spine was sharp under Glazer's hand. His breath sounded wet and shaky. Glazer suddenly sensed Jamie's grief as if it were his own, the desolate lostness, the absence of the one who had understood. Holding his son, he examined the room beyond, the sun porch where all the elaborate things had been installed to interest the boy; and then his glance settled on those nearer at hand, on the table by the bed, the blocks and the coloring book and the simple crayons. After a little while the bleakness went out of Glazer's expression; his face softened, and he smiled.

"You can leave him with me," Mrs. Concannon offered. "He'll be all right."

"Sure he will." Glazer rubbed the narrow back.

"Maybe he'd like some cocoa."

"Yes, what about it, Jamie?"

"Okay," said Jamie, muffled.

"He puts the cocoa in himself," said Mrs. Concannon proudly.

"My gosh," Glazer exclaimed, "I didn't know he could do that!"

"The sugar too," Jamie said.

"Do you ever try it with a marshmallow on top?" Glazer asked. "Or for a change, cinnamon, the way the Mexicans like it?"

Jamie's head lifted. "Do they?"

"Try it. Don't use much. Mrs. Concannon will know how much."

"Can I?" said Jamie to the big Irishwoman.

"Sure." She held out her hand, and he took it and hopped off the bed.

Glazer went to the den, dialed Dr. Barton's number. When the doctor came on he said, "I was wondering about Mary Shelton."

"All information about Mrs. Shelton has to go through the police."

"Oh, come on. I found her; I called you. How is she?"

"About as well as can be expected," said Dr. Barton in a tone as if he were handing over a clutch of rubies.

Glazer smiled at the receiver. "That's just the usual run-around you doctors give out."

"It's the truth," the doctor defended.

"Well, then, here's another question. About Jamie. Could Jamie's long sick spell, all that virus and pneumonia and so forth, have been a"—he searched for a word, not one of Emily's words; a short, basic word—"a jab at me for trying to push him too hard?"

"It could have been a refuge, an escape."

You came back to Emily's words anyway, Glazer thought. "Did the notion occur to you?"

"Yes, it did. I didn't have enough evidence to speak up about, though." Dr. Barton paused, as if thinking about Jamie, the meek patient who acquired something new as soon as you cured him of what he had. "How is Mrs. Warne getting along? Doing a good job?"

"She did fine," said Glazer. He was suddenly weary.

"I thought I saw her on the canyon bus about a half hour ago."

Glazer's hand tightened on the phone. "Are you sure?"

"No. It was just a glimpse I had."

"Thank you very much," Glazer said, the receiver on its way to the cradle.

"How's my house?" Dr. Barton demanded just before the connection was cut.

Eighteen

There was a sharp rap on the door of the den; then the opening space showed Marsh, the chief of police.

"You ever hear of ringing doorbells?" Glazer asked.

"Your housekeeper let me in and told me where to find you," said Marsh evenly. He looked all around the den as if expecting somebody.

"I wanted to ask you where Mrs. Warne is."

"She's not here just now." Glazer began to fill his pipe from a humidor of tobacco on the desk. The air was filled with the rich sweet smell from the contents of the jar. "Why? What business do you have with her?"

"I want to question her again." Marsh came into the den, looked the desk over, the couch, all the furnishings, as if Dr. Barton had chased him out too soon when Mary Shelton was here. "I talked to her briefly as soon as Byronson's body was taken away. She hadn't seen anything, she said."

"Probably not." Glazer coaxed flame from a match into the bowl, turning the pipe carefully in his fingers.

"Just this once," said Marsh, still evenly, "you'd better level with me."

"When didn't I?" Glazer pretended to be wounded.

"We got Conway." Marsh sat down on the couch and stretched his legs. "He says he didn't kill Byronson. He says you had a knife at his neck while he talked to me."

Glazer shrugged. "Of course he has to say something like that. Ask Shelton. He was there."

"It seems he was there without his glasses," Marsh put in, "which is about the same as being blindfolded. He won't speak up for Conway, though; I guess he's afraid we'll charge him with being Conway's partner in the narcotics trade."

Glazer didn't answer. He still seemed to be having difficulty with the pipe.

"How long did you know Conway was shipping and selling heroin?" Marsh demanded.

"Never did *know* it. The day Holt and I talked to Byronson some word was dropped, and Byronson put a lot of emphasis on the fact that the dope traffic at the Fiddling Crab wasn't officially on record. You cops always know a lot you can't prove. Or maybe could prove if only they'd just turn you loose with your rubber hoses and your gun butts, which they don't do often."

Marsh's flinty eyes lit up with a moment's anger. He leaned toward Glazer, propping an elbow on a knee. His paunch got in the way of his breathing a little. "Why would Byronson take Mary Shelton to the beach to prove something against Conway?"

"Always attack the weakest member," said Glazer. "Did you find anything in Conway's car, or did he have time to get rid of it?"

"It represented his bank roll, so he'd kept it." Marsh exuded some satisfaction. "So he's in on a narcotics charge. I don't think he murdered my officer." His eyes searched the room again.

"Look under the rug if you want to," Glazer offered.

Marsh's mouth got tight. "Very funny, Mr. Glazer."

Glazer turned, leaning against the desk. Marsh thought he looked mean and tough. "I didn't used to be a prominent citizen, Chief. I was a kid on the run. I traveled in boxcars and on couplings and underneath on the rods. I stole out of garbage cans. I got to hate cops pretty quick, all cops."

Marsh argued, "Yeah, I've heard it before. You take some stray thieving kid come through here now, scaling your fence, prowling around, you'd howl like an alderman if he wasn't picked up by those same cops you want to kick in the tail."

"I might. Only the prowler we had out here wasn't any stray kid. He was somebody who had a hell of a lot of confidence in himself and what he could get away with. He knocked down my housemaid, and when she tried to yell he kicked her. A man who won't hesitate to kick a woman is a little bit rare except among two classes of people. Real criminals. And wrong cops."

For the first time Marsh showed traces of discomfort. "Well, we got down to it, anyway. That's what I came about. Another officer who knew Byronson pretty well thought that Byronson was watching your place on the side when he was off duty. Somehow that makes me think he was watching Mrs. Warne."

"Somehow it makes me think he was a goddamn fool," said Glazer, the heat under his voice threatening to explode. "I wish I had him here now, alive."

Marsh looked interested. "You feel pretty strongly about Mrs. Warne?"

"I feel pretty sick about a rotten cop spying on me."

"Byronson wasn't perfect," Marsh admitted, "but we need men like him sometimes. I don't know why I bother to argue with you, Mr. Glazer." He took out a cigar and bit at it. "Well, yes, I do—it's because you know a lot of our big brass here in town, and I'm the chief of police. We ought to be seeing things in the same light, and we would, but you've got a chip on your shoulder because you got a rough start." He got the cigar going; its fumes had no resemblance to the rich aroma of Glazer's tobacco, but the chief smoked it happily. It seemed to relax him. Or maybe he was trying to fool Glazer. "Please tell me where I can find Mrs. Warne."

Now Glazer went over behind the desk and sat down and pretended to be utterly relaxed too. He smoked quietly in silence. Then he said, "Figure it for me. You're positive Byronson's murder was a follow-up on Warne's?"

"No, I'm not," said Marsh promptly. "I guess you've got a right to know. She's employed here, taking care of your son." He looked admiringly at the ill-smelling cigar. "I think Byronson's murder was a mistake."

"Oh?" said Glazer wonderingly.

"I think Mary Shelton was the target," Marsh went on. "Byronson got in the way. Mary Shelton says that he got it the first shot, and I'm beginning to believe her. The sand was peppered with bullets from Byronson's rifle."

"Her husband doesn't see very well," Glazer offered softly.

"So—I don't think he'd have tried anything for fear of hitting her."

"Okay," said Glazer, as if resigned. "Francesca Warne hated the Parico girl—I mean Mary Shelton—for trying to take her husband away from her. Why wait so long?"

"Opportunity," Marsh suggested.

"That beach house in Encinitas doesn't have a moat around it."

"It wasn't advertised that they lived there, either."

Glazer sought coldly but hurriedly for something to disprove all that Marsh had said, the final inconsistency that would overturn the applecart. "You got these theories from Mrs. Shelton? Isn't that source suspect itself?"

"We've never closed the file on Warne's murder," said Marsh. "And his wife's name and what we could find out about her were there with the rest. She was in the hospital across the bay, true. Supposedly she was almost dead; she had lost her baby because of a fight she'd had with Warne. Over Mary Parico, I might add. You say that Mary Parico should be suspect, and you're right. But not the way you mean it. She might have a hate on Mrs. Warne, some feeling of rivalry left over from her affair with Warne. So we can discount her statement in some directions. As for instance when she says Warne told her his wife might kill him. I think that's a lot of baloney."

Glazer's thought was shot through with surprise. He realized that this item had been one on which Mary Shelton had convinced him. It didn't mean that Warne's fears had come to pass. But he had somehow been convinced, when Mary Shelton had spoken to him in the car, that what she said was true. She had wanted five thousand dollars for it; she was too naïve to expect to sell a lie.

"You look kind of surprised," said Marsh quietly.

"What does she want out of it? Revenge? Can't she leave Mrs. Warne alone?"

"You get this straight," Marsh said with some force. "I'm not running an errand for Mrs. Shelton. I'm not persecuting Mrs. Warne on just anybody's say-so. I would like to ask her some questions." He stood up, and the pose of relaxation dropped off him like lethargy off a hunting hound at a whistle from the hunter. "I've got a job to do and I'm doing it. Not Byronson's way, my way. I just want the truth."

"About Warne?"

"About who murdered my young cop," said Marsh.

"When she comes in I'll tell her you want to see her," Glazer promised.

"Yeah, do that."

Glazer sat in the den, deep in thought. He wondered how quickly the police would act if they knew, in addition to what they had, all that he had found out. Had anybody ever made inquiry about missing guns among that hunting flotilla to La Paz? Had anybody thought to ask questions about a stray dinghy? Suppose some gossip reached them someday about Mrs. Warne's swim out to the rocks with Jamie, the rescue that came later? According to what Jamie had dropped, she was like a fish in the water.

Glazer got up from the desk and went over to the window and slatted the blinds. It was dark outside, no sign of lights. He had no thought of the view; it was a way of turning his back on the room, the quiet, bright safe house where he could stay, from which she had had to run.

She was on the bus to the canyon a short time past, according to Dr. Barton. A glimpse; it could have been another woman. But Glazer remembered Tremaine. Tremaine had been Warne's friend; he seemed to have gained Francesca's trust. She'd go to him for help. She thought that Glazer had abandoned her.

I did, he admitted, for a little while. There were things I had to get used to. I had to look it in the face about Warne, about how she'd loved him and what he had meant to her. I had to let the picture I'd made of her fall into ashes, another to take its place. I know now just what she is. Even if I don't want her, for Jamie's sake I have to help her.

He went out of the den, down the hall, crossed the living room, where all the lamps glowed, out into the dark. He could hear the sea at the foot of the cliff. The air still smelled of fog, though the fog was thinning and here and there in the night sky he could see patches of stars.

He drove into the downtown district, parked on a side street, walked to the corner, and entered a drugstore. He took some time there, looking at magazines, finally buying a man's book with the picture of a couple of prize fighters on the front of it. The fighters looked equally bloody and exhausted, and Glazer thought idly that you seldom saw it in life; one would get the worst of it and quit, one would be almost unscathed— in any fight, even street brawls. He went back to the car and got behind the wheel and waited. He had thought that Marsh might have put a tail on him; now his precautions seemed to be a little silly. No one was near him, nor watching him.

He turned the car in the middle of the dark block and headed back for the canyon road. The fog had settled here, escaping from the sea wind that tore it to shreds higher across the hills. He drove slowly, meeting no other cars.

At Tremaine's drive he hesitated, then drove past, parked the car at a vacant spot beyond the next house. Overhead the eucalyptus dripped with moisture; the sound of the drops on the earth and dead leaves had an eerie aliveness, as if something stirred there. Glazer walked back. There was a porch light burning in the house this side of Tremaine's. By its beam, through the fog he found his way across the dry creek bed and through Tremaine's flowers to his front porch.

He could hear voices inside. He could not be sure if one of them belonged to Francesca Warne. Instead of mounting the steps to the porch, he walked softly along the side of the house, looking for a window. He had no business with Tremaine unless the woman was with him.

He came to a window with a drawn blind, the blind worn and splintered with cracks, but giving no view of the room. He continued. Then he caught the smell of a kitchen. He sensed that he was by a back porch, that an inner door was open. He reached out and found a screen door.

He stepped in without noise and waited. The conversation in the front part of the house had come to a stop. He wondered if he could have made some sound, unheard by him, which had startled them, warned them. He breathed lightly through his mouth, listened; there seemed an emptiness beyond the porch, as if the occupants had suddenly vacated.

Walking on the balls of his feet, sliding one foot ahead of the other, testing for squeaky boards in Tremaine's floor, he crossed the screened porch and entered the kitchen. He smelled strong soap, ham grease, fried onions. Onions fried tonight, Glazer judged, the pan set to soak, the strong soap rubbed on a rag and added to the water to loosen the stubborn crust of food. He knew that combination so well, he thought wryly. When his mother had been sick in the years following his father's death, he'd done the dishes in the lean-to kitchen, and he had set pans to soak so that he could run out sooner with the Alvarez kids and look for someone to fight or something to steal.

Standing still in the smelly dark of Tremaine's kitchen, he felt the breath of those faraway years blow over him, touch him with nostalgia. There had been a flavor, since lost; an appetite, a zest. All gone now, hustled along with the luckless parents, the Alvarez brothers, the rickety shack, a time that lived again only when he thought of it, when memories bloomed as now against the dark. It was nothing he could really share with another human being. It was a memory to think of once in a while, then to put away.

He put it away, and someone spoke in the next room. Tremaine said,

"I expected you to have more sense."

There was a pause. Francesca's voice was a kind of shock to Glazer, though he knew as well as his own her breathy manner of speech. "I'm not trying to trouble or annoy you. All this time I've only been looking for the truth."

"I warned your friend Mr. Glazer that a stirring up was the last thing should be done."

"You were Adam's friend." She seemed to be pleading with Tremaine.

"What can I do? Rile the cops, they'll have me in the can. Go poking my nose into Conway's ruck, I get my head shot off."

"I thought, if we talked— If you and I put all we knew together—"

"You don't think Glazer's going on with it?"

"No."

The moment of silence stretched out after her word, a soundless comment on Glazer's rejection. Finally Tremaine said, "I sort of thought he was fond of you. Real fond."

She hesitated over her reply. "Not me. An image he had. Something he thought I was. A mistake."

Tremaine seemed incredulous. "You mean he's dropped you?"

"I made him see," she answered almost inaudibly, "that I wasn't that person he thought I was. There wasn't any use letting him love me, when all he was loving was a creature in his mind."

"I don't get it," Tremaine said, sounding mystified.

"I was that way with Adam," she went on, her voice a little stronger. "I had delusions about him. It's terrible when you fasten all your life to a mirage. I wouldn't let Glazer do it." There was silence again; perhaps the two of them exchanged a glance. "The worst of all is when you begin to see the truth—not the truth as the other might have revealed it, but finding it scrap by scrap, little by little. All the time you're clinging to what you thought was there, and the change, the corruption, is eating it away, and finally there is nothing at all and you think it would be better to die."

"Adam didn't do right by you," Tremaine said, "but most of all, he didn't do right by himself. I was a friend, I knew him before you did, I saw him times and places you wouldn't of spit on him."

"You could have warned me," she said softly.

"Almost, I did. It was summer—it must of been a day shortly before you two were married. You were married a year; summer would be right. You had on a yellow dress; you were in Mrs. Bandy's place, the sandwich shop. He was there. You told me he'd proposed to you and you might accept and you might not, and because you were having such fun over it I couldn't throw cold water and say please to leave Adam alone, he'd hurt you." Tremaine's voice took on a wondering note. "It always seemed sort of impossible to me that he'd done what he did, just in a year."

"Just a year," she echoed.

"There wasn't any way I could save you."

"Maybe—maybe I saved myself," she said slowly. Glazer, familiar with her voice, was puzzled by a change in it, a tightening, a sort of anger.

"What do you mean?" Tremaine asked. "You wouldn't—not that you killed him. You didn't kill him."

"I don't know," she answered.

Nineteen

"I don't know," she repeated slowly. Glazer wanted to shout at her, to rush into the other room with a warning to keep still; he couldn't imagine what reckless nonsense possessed her. Was she trying to put a noose around her neck? Was she eaten up by some perverse yearning for punishment? He moved uneasily nearer the partially opened door. Still he could see neither Francesca nor Tremaine, though light now lay on his own body in a broad band. He could hear Tremaine's quick unsteady answer, something about being sure she hadn't done the murder, that the very thought was impossible, that he'd rather not listen. But she went on. There was determination in her tone.

"A time comes when you must search out the truth about yourself," she said, "and this is it—for me. I came to you because there wasn't anybody else."

And not to me, Glazer thought. She knew I'd failed her.

"I'm your friend," Tremaine answered earnestly, "and that's why I'm telling you, don't talk this way."

"When I leave Seaview this time, I'll never come back. I have to know. I can't bear the thought of guilt any longer. You have to listen."

"You were too sick, too confused in your mind, to remember," he insisted.

"Then perhaps it was all a dream and you can reassure me—"

"Please don't try to accuse yourself," Tremaine begged. "Not even to me. I might get drunk someday—"

"You don't drink anymore."

There was another of the sharp, strange silences. Glazer put a hand on the doorframe, leaned there. He felt empty, almost weak, as if the words Francesca had said had drained away energy and will.

She began to talk again. "As you say, I was mentally confused, I'd been very ill. But I've thought so many times since that mentally disturbed people often have unusual strength, endurance, and agility."

"And they imagine things," he put in firmly.

"I'm not sure. My memory of that day is patchy, a series of flashes, vivid as the disconnected fragments of a nightmare. But how can I know it was all a dream? You must help me."

Tremaine now held a protesting silence, and Glazer imagined his seamed face set in stony unwillingness.

"At times I awoke to notice the muggy heat, the oppressive stillness," Francesca said. "The hours seemed endless, and at times I wondered hazily if I had somehow telescoped the impressions of several days, woven them together in delirium. The day nurse was a conscientious woman; she woke me twice to sponge me, insisted I take a salt tablet, put an ice bag on my head. When she went off duty, I must have drowsed for some time."

There was again no word from Tremaine; the lack of response was meant to remind Francesca of his disapproval.

"All at once I sat up in the hospital bed," she went on, "and my mind seemed swept clear of any weariness or haziness. I noticed that the day was turning to twilight, that the air felt cooler, and through the open window I could see lightning flashes out along the horizon. I suppose it was the lightning that woke me."

She paused as if to collect again her impressions of that day two years gone. Against the door Glazer was motionless as a rock.

"There was a conversation in the hall. I recognized the young doctor's voice and that of the nurse who came on duty in the evening. The nurse wanted to know what he thought my chances were. I recall his answer distinctly; physically, he said, I was in pretty good condition. The nurse then asked, 'What about—the other?' And he wouldn't commit himself."

They never do, Glazer thought, remembering Dr. Barton.

"He wouldn't give a definite answer, but I sensed in his hesitation a lack of confidence in my recovery," she continued, "and then I told myself calmly, 'He means that I'm insane, that my mind is gone.' Trying to accept this, I was puzzled at the remarkable clarity of my thoughts, the brilliance of the impression made by my surroundings, everything so sharp, colorful, and distinct that just looking at the room made my eyes ache. If I were mad, why this unnatural awareness? I sat brooding, and then I heard the nurse ask something about restraint. I knew what restraint meant; it was putting the patient into a strait jacket."

This was the nurse, Glazer recalled, that Shelton had characterized as inefficient, later discharged for some indiscretion with a male member of the hospital staff.

"In this strange clear way that my mind worked I knew that the nurse wanted to dispose of me to relieve her of responsibility, give her freedom for some purpose of her own. I waited, trembling, until the doctor gave his verdict. I was not to be restrained, he said; if I were suddenly to regain my senses, the effect of finding myself under restraint might be adverse. She argued a little; he cut her off short."

Still Tremaine kept silent, a wordless invitation for Francesca to desist.

"The nurse didn't come into the room, and I began to experiment with movement. It seemed that the strength and precision of my thoughts had invaded all my body. I was like a machine; all the effects of illness had faded away. When I stepped to the floor there was no weakness, no faintness, as I might have expected. I just felt wondrously alive. The next incident has a touch of unreality, though. I thought I had my suitcase open on the bed, the lid up, and that in it I had found my swimming suit. I recall the color perfectly, the faded blue; and this was an old suit I'd worn two summers before and had discarded, so why should it have been packed in the things they sent to the hospital from the apartment? It has ooccurred to me that my landlady, who must have packed the bag, was elderly and absent-minded. And then there is another possibility."

Tremaine cleared his throat loudly. "You see? You're all mixed up."

"Perhaps. The other possibility is that my imagination fooled me. Some sense of modesty made it seem imperative that I go out dressed, so I imagined the suit. I don't know. I could have tucked the hospital gown up a bit and it wouldn't have looked too unlike some of the beach coats you see, a short white cotton garment, bare legs below."

"No, I guess not," Tremaine agreed, as if he couldn't think of anything else to say, no check to her flow of words.

"As I said, my memories of that day, though vivid, as if illumined by the lightning out along the edge of the sea, are disconnected. There is a space here where I've forgotten, lost the thread. I don't know how I came to be in the dinghy with the gun, where I found the boat, where the rifle came from. I suppose I stole them both from one of the small yachts in the harbor where people had gone ashore. I looked up at the sky and it seemed a vast starry bowl. This was the first time in this dream or adventure, or call it what you will, that I thought of Adam. I looked up at the sky and thought how it covered all of us, Adam and I and the Parico girl and even the people in the towns and cities where I would never go. The moment held a strange fatalism, a nostalgia for something—some place, some kind of life—I had never known."

She waited a moment as if caught up again in memory.

"The cross-bay current was pulling the dinghy toward the opposite headland; there was no need to row. I turned my face gratefully to the fresh breeze. And that's all—until I climbed the rock."

Tremaine's voice exploded in a crackling anger. "Of course you didn't! How could you have? It was all the fever, the long strain of your sickness, the torment of losing the child—"

"Losing the child was a relief. I didn't want Adam's child by then," she said candidly. "Please don't think me a monster. I knew that to be free of him, as I had to be, there must be no ties, no reminders."

"I didn't think you could feel that way," he reproved her.

"Neither did I."

"But anyway, whether you wanted the child or not, this climbing of the rock is something that never could have happened."

"I don't know. The rock was terribly real. And sometime past, since I came back to Seaview, I tested that impression by trying to climb down it. My experiment cost the life of a little dog, Jamie's pet. I can't forget that. He thought I was in danger, tried to pull me back, fell. But I do know that the texture of the rock, its tilt and curve, are the same—exactly the same—as they were in this memory. And I can't see how I would have known, unless I did climb there that other day."

"*Any* rock would feel like that," Tremaine pointed out. "That old solid core rock, that granite, it must be the same all over the world. You take up a piece in your hand, you know what it's like; that's what you did somewhere."

"I had the gun with me, tied to a strap of the suit. It was long, an awkward burden, and banged against me and against the stone buttress. It was protected from sea damp by a plastic covering."

"Ohhh," Tremaine cried impatiently, "you make it up, then try to explain it. Why should it have needed a cover? The owner didn't know you'd be in the water with it."

She hesitated, then repeated, "In the water?"

He said quickly, "Or do you mean you'd brought the boat all the way in, through those scattered rocks off the bluff? Is that it?"

She didn't reply immediately. Glazer wondered what look passed between them. "At the time, in my memory of this incident, there was no thought of the boat, no knowledge of where I'd left it. I was engrossed in climbing, in keeping the gun from entangling itself in my legs. All at once it seemed that I had reached the spot where I had meant to go, that I must open the plastic cover and take the gun out and use it. The memory of searching over the plastic surface for an opening, some kind of catch or zipper, is like the rest of my impressions of that day—vivid, so real that just thinking of it now brings back every sharp detail. There was moisture on the covering. I dripped. My hair dripped on my hands as I fumbled for the catch to uncover the gun. Too, I had the sense of being high in the air. My legs were trembling horribly, as if from long exertion. Would a dream have been so real?"

"I've had them that real," Tremaine told her. "When you shot him—was the sound loud and sharp? Were you scared by it?"

"In this dream I never fired the gun," she said, her voice still low. "I lay against the rock and wondered if I would fall. Ahead of me lay the beach, all the way into town, but as I watched it, it seemed the sea rushed in, a dreadful tide, and buried everything deep. I tried to scream even as I knew it hadn't happened, that this was a trick my mind played on me."

Tremaine coughed. "They say if you fall from a height in a dream, if you hit bottom falling, you'll die. I never believed it."

"I didn't fall. I shut my eyes to keep from seeing the nightmare tide and then I felt someone take the gun out of my hands. I heard the shot. It was not so loud as I had thought it would be; it seemed far away. In my ears was the tide, roaring, tearing the face of the cliff."

"Our minds play strange tricks on us," said Tremaine, thoughtfully now, and he moved, shuffling his feet. A moment later Glazer heard the dog whine, then the pad of his feet approaching the door. He paused, his shadow reaching to Glazer's feet, sensing the presence of the stranger. He came on slowly; his brown eyes lifted, studying the intruder. Glazer waited, wondering if the dog might remember and accept him.

There was an instant of doubt between them. Glazer expected an attack, at least a fit of barking, and then exposure. But with a deep breath like a sigh the dog went over to the pan beside the sink and drank from it.

Glazer's attention returned to the two people in the other room. "Who did it?" Francesca asked. "Who took the gun and fired it and then put it back into my hands?" She began to speak more quickly. "I haven't any desire for vengeance. What's done is done. But I must know the truth. I must know if my memory has played me false."

"Suppose you did do it? Suppose you decide that you are guilty? Then what? Do you mean you'd give yourself up? You'd have courage for that?"

"I don't know."

Tremaine began to tear into her story. "It's all unbelievable. How'd you get back to the hospital? Where is the gun? Why didn't the nurse report you missing?"

"I think that when I climbed down I must have rested in the shelter of that smaller beach. No one could have seen me there. The last fragment I recall is the swim from the shore out to the dinghy—it floated among those three big rocks offshore where the current breaks. As I climbed into the dinghy the gun loosened from the strap of my suit and disappeared into the dark water. It was almost night then."

She moved in her chair; Glazer heard her steps. She walked into view, turned slowly, leaned against a table. Her glance skipped past the door behind which Glazer stood, then jerked back to it. Their eyes locked. She brushed at the black hair from which the scarf was removed; the hair clung to her hand; it looked damp, straightened by the fog.

"I can only suppose that I got back to the hospital in the same way I left, through an open window and the gardens that border the beach, and by using the stolen dinghy. There is no other way. You can argue that I was too weak from lying ill, that in the confusion of my mental processes a fairy tale was born; and all I can answer is that I was possessed of a strange vigor and endurance, an almost inhuman capacity for effort."

"You've got no proof!" Tremaine almost shouted.

Still she looked at Glazer. "I swam out one day not too long past and I saw the gun. Or rather, I should say—I'm almost sure that the gun is what I saw, lying on the sea floor between those three great rocks...." Her voice dwindled wretchedly; Glazer wondered if what he imagined to be in her face was true, a look that begged his understanding. "Seeing it there was such a terrible shock, confirming as it did the thing I've tried to tell myself was nightmare, that I—I almost caused another tragedy. So I abandoned the thought of going on with the investigation. I decided to ask help of someone else."

"Is that when you talked to Glazer?"

"Yes."

An edge came into Tremaine's voice. "You told him all of this?"

"No." She turned from Glazer to face the man across the room. "I don't think he has enough belief in me to understand; he'd say, as you do, that it's something I've made up."

"Well, look, you do get right up *to* it," Tremaine pointed out, "and then sort of switch the story to take the guilt off yourself. If you killed Adam—"

"I've said I didn't."

"But wait a minute—you admit the intention behind it all, escaping the hospital, stealing the dinghy and the rifle, climbing the rock tower there at the end of the beach—"

She interrupted: "I don't remember getting the gun. Nowhere in the memory of that day was there a plan, an intention, which would end in Adam's death. Perhaps, I think, I meant finally to kill myself."

"You knew where he took *her* every evening," Tremaine added patiently. "That's where you went."

She rubbed her temples, looking tired, defeated. "The current took me."

Tremaine was briefly silent, then he said, "I really think you must have killed him." His chair squeaked and there was the sound of walking. Thus warned, Glazer receded into the dark kitchen where the old dog, still standing beside the sink cupboards, watched with dull curiosity. Tremaine came into view in the lighted space, stopping in front of Francesca, looking at her thoughtfully.

"I thought lately that perhaps—*you* had," Francesca said.

"Me?" Tremaine cackled. His seamed face had a yellowish pallor under the bald overhead light. "Why'd you think that?"

"I came back to Seaview hoping that whoever lived in that house above the beach had killed Adam. Conway or Shelton—or if they'd sold out during the time I was sick, the new owner. But recently a strange fancy has taken possession of me—that Adam's murder might not have had a motive of cruelty or vengeance behind it."

Tremaine moved uneasily. "What then?"

"To deal death might not always be a crime. You might, in some cases, consider it a kindness."

"Oh, you know better than that!" Tremaine protested.

She touched his arm. "He was so near the end, so deep in agony, so lost. Drink wasn't a help, a release, any longer; it was a fire that burned steadily away at the last traces of decency. If you had been his friend, his real friend for so long, you couldn't have endured seeing him that way."

"Murder is a serious affair," Tremaine said, still looking down at her, still smiling and patient. It seemed to Glazer that Tremaine had at last been hypnotized by the long recital of Francesca's story, and Glazer wondered if she had planned it, rehearsed and perfected it, in order to get this result. Certainly her choice of words, her phrasing, had been much too stylized to be an impulsive confidence. She had moved carefully in building toward her climax, forcing Tremaine to listen, cutting in over and over on his protests, ignoring his disbelief, until finally the husky voice, persisting like the sound of the sea under Glazer's cliffs at home, had lulled Tremaine into quiescent acceptance. "A very serious affair," he repeated.

"That shot, if it occurred as I think it did, was a matter of impulse. No plan could have brought you there, no intention to murder, only an accident. If you climbed down the rock to where I hung against it, almost falling, it may have been to help me. At first. Then you would have seen the gun; perhaps what you thought I meant to do flashed through your mind and the urge to complete the act was overwhelming. It was all over so quickly."

His face had stilled. "You know what?" he said after a moment's silence. "If I admit killing Adam, you'll say: What about Byronson? And you couldn't find such a good excuse, a right noble reason, for that one."

She plucked at his sleeve. "Tell me. Let me know what really happened. Set me free. I've loathed myself so long, thought of myself as a murderess. I can't endure it anymore." When he remained aloof she said, "You always liked the little Parico girl. She was kind to you. She always felt sorry for the unfortunate ones. Ones like Adam. She slipped you food from the drugstore fountain when you were down on your luck, broke. Probably she's remembered you since, sent small gifts. You've been seeing Conway; he might have brought them."

"I won't be seeing Conway again," said Tremaine almost dreamily.

"Did he involve you in his business?" she urged.

In the kitchen Glazer drew swift conclusions. Conway would have needed a collection point, at times even a go-between, in his narcotics business. He had used Tremaine. Tremaine had been too weak, too needy, or too indifferent to danger to refuse.

"I did some jobs for him now and then," Tremaine said.

"Did he want you to kill Adam?"

Tremaine shrugged as if in a sudden giving up. "The idea to kill Adam was yours and mine," he whispered, leaning toward her. "You brought the gun. I found you with it on the rock tower, trying to open the plastic cover. I just pulled the trigger for you. I was Adam's friend and, as you said, I couldn't see him ruin himself and others anymore."

Glazer thought that Francesca was frightened now that she finally had forced Tremaine's admission. She backed from him a little, until the table caught her. "What about Byronson?"

"See?" he said regretfully. "You won't leave it alone. I've relieved your mind that you didn't kill Adam, but you won't stop with that."

"Byronson had taken Mary Parico—Mary Shelton—to the beach. The police car must have passed through town. Did you catch sight of her then? Did she somehow appeal to you for help?"

Tremaine swung his head from side to side like a tormented animal.

Francesca went on: "Of course—she was behind the murder of both Adam and Byronson. How blind everyone has been, thinking Shelton had the best motive, or Conway, or even Mary Parico herself. The truth is so simple. You were crazy about her, an old man in love with a fresh young girl. You killed to save her from the wrong kind of man. Both times." She tried to turn away, but Tremaine seized her. And again Glazer was surprised, for the average woman, feeling that grip and knowing the capabilities of the man, would have fought, struggled; but Francesca stood quiet and allowed Tremaine to pull her back to face him.

"You know more than you've told me," he growled.

Her voice was steady. "I saw you today. From the little boy's room. I opened the window when I heard the shots, leaned out. You were running from the cliff's edge."

Glazer remembered the clammy room, his own uneasy feeling that something had happened there. He'd taken for granted that Jamie had been in the room when Byronson had been shot, but this was a mistake; Francesca had been there alone, had gone out to find Jamie in the hall.

Tremaine said, "Who'd you tell?"

"No one. I had to find out the truth first about Adam's murder. If I had turned you in to the police for killing Byronson, I might never have known if I fired that shot that killed Adam—or not."

"You've wondered about it these two years?"

"Never a day went by that I didn't accuse myself."

"You can die happy then," he said in grim humor; his fingers bowed into talons and he collared her throat with them. She bent against the table, twisting, trying to push him away. Her slim back was turned to Glazer, the black coat pulled tight by the struggle; and all at once Glazer knew something clearly and without doubt: he still wanted this woman. A fury rushed through him such as he had never known; it had no relation to the cold calm he'd felt about Conway. It beat behind his eyes, red waves of hate. He came out of the kitchen in a single leap. Tremaine looked up. The flesh knotted about his eyes as he squinted at what he must have thought to be an apparition. His hands faltered, fell from the woman's throat, to hang at his sides.

"You've been there all the time!" he accused weakly.

Glazer took hold of Francesca, pulled her into the shelter of his arms. She clung to him, her face wet, her body trembling. "You're all through, Tremaine," Glazer said.

Tremaine took out the bandanna handkerchief, mopped his face, went on looking fixedly at Glazer. "I'm glad you came. You might not believe it, but I am. I didn't want to kill any more people. You think you'll do it once, that the one time is all you need, and then it all happens again—"

Glazer thought about Mary Parico, the girl with the earthy beauty; she had been kind to this lost soul and so brought murder on the men who sought her. "Why didn't you try to kill Shelton?"

Tremaine shook his head. "She needed somebody and he was good to her. He was good the way I'd have been." He swallowed hard. "I didn't have any crazy idea she'd look at me. I just wanted her safe, safe with a man who had good sense and plenty of money." The old dog came out of the kitchen, lumbering, his breath hoarse and tired, and found

Tremaine's hand hanging at his side and licked it lovingly. Tremaine knelt and rubbed the dog's head. Tears came into his eyes. "I'm too old to care what happens. I wish I could have scared that young cop; I didn't want to kill him. But he wouldn't be scared of me. Never was. I got rattled after I'd done it; I kept firing the gun, couldn't seem to stop. I almost—almost kind of blamed *her* too. It's a wonder I didn't kill her along with Byronson."

There was a space of silence.

Tremaine looked up. "What're you going to do?"

Glazer said, "I'm no cop, no judge. You figure it out for yourself." He took Francesca's arm in his and went out through the front door. Behind them the old dog whined and Tremaine said broken words to it. Ahead was the fog, the dark.

She pulled against his arm. "Please—I can't go to your house."

"You don't have to put up with me," Glazer told her. In the light from the next-door porch, the pale glow softened by the mist, he could see her head, a dark silhouette. "Will you stay with Jamie for the rest of the summer? It was our bargain. I'll leave you alone."

The dripping of the eucalyptus seemed loud and strange in the quiet.

"I love Jamie—he's a kind and sweet little boy—but I can't remake him as you want him. No one can. He's a little slow. He'll always be that way; he'll never catch up with the bright ones. It doesn't mean he can't be happy in a useful, contented life. I just won't stay and see your disappointment, the way you want pressure put on him, the pattern you mean him to follow." In her voice were anger and tears.

"I've been a damned fool," Glazer said softly. "You think I can't realize it?" He reached out to touch her; the coat was damp with the beading of the fog. "Come home with me. Please."

She didn't move. "There's so much else now. I led Tremaine along with the story I'd planned and rehearsed, made him admit killing Adam. But I'll still wonder—would I have fired the gun if he hadn't been there to do it?"

"I don't think you would have," Glazer told her. "There's a big difference between wanting and doing. And why convict yourself when no jury on earth would do it? You have a doctor's word that you were on the edge of a mental breakup, a nurse's opinion that you should have been in a strait jacket. Didn't that nurse know, by the way, that you'd been gone?"

"She must have. Of course it was to her own interest to keep still. Even under police pressure she couldn't admit such neglect of a patient."

"None of the story made any difference to me. Won't you come home?"

She turned suddenly. "Where is your car?"

He guided her to the place where the car sat in the deep dark under the trees. He opened the door and the light went on in the dome and he saw her face. It was set and tired. She'd forgotten the scarf, or lost it somewhere. The black hair clung to the line of her jaw. In that moment Glazer decided that she was beautiful. She was a woman you might look at for a long time before you caught all of her; and then perhaps you never could.

They were together in the front seat, the motor purring, only the lights in the dash to dim the gloom, when he said, "At the end of summer, when you think you have to leave, give me one more thought. I won't ever be a gentleman. I know that; it's as well I found it out. Maybe I can work around somehow to being human; maybe when I quit fooling myself I can find out what I am. Inside. The part I wanted to cover up. If you ever want to take a chance on that, let me know." He let the car creep forward. The black pavement, shining with wet, whispered under the touch of the tires.

The moment drew out in silence and she said nothing. There would perhaps be no answer until September, Glazer thought. And maybe not then.... But he could hope. He would never give up hoping.

He glanced at the clock mounted in the dash. It was a quarter of ten.

At ten o'clock, from the small tower of the Spanish-style city hall, the curfew bell rang with a musical tolling. It meant that all juveniles should be off the streets of Seaview, though little attention was paid to it; the custom of ringing the bell had been handed down from earlier days.

Glazer heard it. He was closing the garage. Francesca had gone on into the house. At the sound of the bell Glazer automatically checked the luminous dial of his watch. Then he walked briskly up the pathway between the rows of bloom. He looked out at the cliff, remembered his intention to fence it. He did not think of Adam Warne or of the officer, Byronson, who had died below at the edge of the sea. He was eager to get inside, to the light and comfort of the house, to the woman who had preceded him.

He felt sudden confidence in his chances of winning her over, in their future happiness.

In her hospital room Mary Shelton had been asleep. The bell woke her. She looked at the window, sensing the foggy dark beyond, the gardens that led down to the sea, the great expanse of black water. There was no light in the room, though a dim glow seeped from the hall around the rim of the door, left ajar. With a jerky motion she brought her hands together, folding them in an attitude of prayer on her bosom. "When I get

well again, O Lord, help me to be a good wife. Help me to be kind to Will."
She waited, but the words brought no release, no promise of hope. She
thought of the house in Encinitas, of her life there with her husband.
A kind of fright at the vistas of the future forced her to sit upright. She
began to cough.

It occurred to her that it would be possible not to get well, that in sitting erect she was injuring herself, undoing what Dr. Barton had
mended. She gathered the bedclothes and smothered her face in them,
muffling the cough, while phantoms raised by the pain floated before
her eyes. Byronson, Shelton, Conway ... Then Adam Warne, shabby in
his slept-in clothes; Adam, whose bewilderment had seemed an echo of
her own.

She went on coughing into the blankets, and in her mind she was on
the beach again, it was getting dark, and the man she had wholly loved
was leaning above her in the soft gray light.

The ten o'clock bell sounded hollow and far away in the reaches of the
canyon. Tremaine looked at his clock. It had lost three minutes during
the day. Tremaine left the old dog lying by the couch and went over and
fixed the hands at the correct time. He said to the dog, "It didn't matter, but I put it right. Time doesn't count. I haven't much of it left. What's
three minutes to a man like me?"

He went to the telephone on a small table near the door and looked
at it for a while before lifting the receiver and dialing the number of Police Headquarters.

A voice crackled inquiringly at him, and he said, "Marsh," and then
stood waiting, planning what he should say.

THE END

Dolores Hitchens Bibliography
(1907-1973)

Novels:

As by Dolores Hitchens

Jim Sader mysteries
Sleep with Strangers (1955)
Sleep with Slander (1960)

Standalone books:
Stairway to an Empty Room
  (1951)
Nets to Catch the Wind (1952;
  reprinted as Widows Won't
  Wait, 1954)
Terror Lurks in Darkness (1953)
Beat Back the Tide (1954;
  abridged as The Fatal Flirt,
  1954)
Fool's Gold (1958)
The Watcher (1959)
Footsteps in the Night (1961)
The Abductor (1962)
The Bank with the Bamboo Door
  (1965)
The Man Who Cried All the Way
  Home (1966)
Postscript to Nightmare (1967;
  UK as Cabin of Fear, 1968)
A Collection of Strangers (1969;
  UK as Collection of Strangers,
  1970)
The Baxter Letters (1971)
In a House Unknown (1973)

As by Bert and Dolores Hitchens

F.O.B. Murder (1955)
One-Way Ticket (1956)
End of the Line (1957)
The Man Who Followed Women
  (1959)
The Grudge (1963)

As by D. B. Olsen

Rachel Murdock mysteries
Cat Saw Murder (1939)
Alarm of Black Cat (1942)
Catspaw for Murder (1943;
  reprinted as Cat's Claw, 1943)
The Cat Wears a Noose (1944)
Cats Don't Smile (1945)
Cats Don't Need Coffins (1946)
Cats Have Tall Shadows (1948)
The Cat Wears a Mask (1949)
Death Wears Cat's Eyes (1950)
Cat and Capricorn (1951)
The Cat Walk (1953)
Death Walks on Cat Feet (1956)

Prof. A. Pennyfeather mysteries
Shroud for the Bride (1945;
  reprinted as Bring the Bride a
  Shroud, 1945)
Gallows for the Groom (1947)
Devious Design (1948)
Something About Midnight
  (1950)
Love Me in Death (1951)
Enrollment Cancelled (1952;
  reprinted as Dead Babes in the
  Wood, 1954)

Lt. Stephen Mayhew mysteries
The Clue in the Clay (1938)
Death Cuts a Silhouette (1939)

As by Dolan Birkley

Blue Geranium (1944)
The Unloved (1965)

As by Noel Burke

Shivering Bough (1942)

Short Stories/Magazine Novels:

Stairway to an Empty Room
(*Collier's*, Mar 31, Apr 7, Apr
14, Apr 21, Apr 28 1951)
Strip for Murder (*Mercury
Mystery Magazine*, Oct 1958)
The Watcher (*Cosmopolitan*,
May 1959)
Footsteps in the Dark
(*Cosmopolitan*, Feb 1961)

Abductor! Abductor! Abductor!
(*Cosmopolitan*, July 1961)
The Unloved (*Redbook,* Oct
1965)
If You See This Woman (*Ellery
Queen's Mystery Magazine,* Jan
1966)
Postscript to Nightmare
(*Cosmopolitan*, June 1967)
A Collection of Strangers
(*Redbook*, Sept 1969)
The Baxter Letters (*Star Weekly*,
June 26 1971)
Blueprint for Murder (*Ellery
Queen's Mystery Magazine*, Aug
1973)

Plays:

A Cookie for Henry: one-act play
for six women (1941, as Dolores
Birk Hitchens)

Suspense Classics from the Godmother of Noir...

Elisabeth Sanxay Holding

Lady Killer / Miasma
978-0-9667848-7-9 $19.95
Murder is suspected aboard a cruise ship to the Caribbean, and a young doctor falls into a miasma of doubt when he agrees to become medical assistant in a house of mystery.

The Death Wish / Net of Cobwebs
978-0-9667848-9-3 $19.95
Poor Mr. Delancey is pulled into a murderous affair when he comes to the aid of a friend, and a merchant seaman suffering from battle trauma becomes the first suspect when Aunt Evie is found murdered.

Strange Crime in Bermuda /
Too Many Bottles
978-0-9749438-5-5 $19.95
An intriguing tale of a sudden disappearance on a Caribbean island, and a mysterious death by pills, which could have been accidental—or murder.

The Old Battle Ax / Dark Power
978-1-933586-16-8 $19.95
Mrs. Herriott spins a web of deception when her sister is found dead on the sidewalk, and a woman's vision of a family reunion is quickly shattered by feelings of dread when she answers her uncle's invitation to visit.

The Unfinished Crime /
The Girl Who Had to Die
978-1-933586-41-0 $19.95
Branscombe tries to control everyone around him with such a web of deceit that he is the one finally caught up in its tangled skein. Jocelyn is convinced she is going to be murdered, so naturally everyone suspects young Killian when she is pushed off the cruise ship.

Speak of the Devil /
The Obstinate Murderer
978-1-933586-71-7 $17.95
Murder stalks the halls at a Caribbean resort hotel, and an aging alcoholic is called in to solve a murder that hasn't happened yet. "Strongly recommended."—*Baltimore Sun*.

Kill Joy / The Virgin Huntress
978-1-933586-97-7 $19.95
A young lady finds trouble when she follows her employer to a house where death seems to stalk its every visitor; and a young man tries to stay one step ahead of the huntress who tries to uncover his questionable past. "Unbearable suspense."—*St. Louis Post-Dispatch*

Widow's Mite / Who's Afraid?
978-1-944520-34-2 $19.95
Tilly finds herself under suspicion of murder when her rich cousin is found poisoned; and a new door-to-door job goes horribly wrong for a young woman when her first customer is found stabbed to death.
"One of the cleverest productions of the season."—*Baltimore Evening Sun*

The Unlit Lamp & Selected Stories
978-1-944520-69-4 $19.95
A classic 1920s social drama, paired with a collection of six stories from the same period. "Subtle, psychologically nuanced portraits of women making sense of troubled marriages [and] conflicted relationships."—Sarah Weinman, *Troubled Daughters, Twisted Wives*.

www.ingramcontent.com/pod-product-compliance
Lightning Source LLC
Chambersburg PA
CBHW071740190726
48292CB00003B/820